Jim Henry remembered nothing of what must have been repeated loading and firing, nothing of the past hour of war.

His company was surrounded, split in half and ill provisioned to make a stand. Major Pyron hadn't thought to engage the enemy here in the narrow canyon, hadn't thought Union soldiers were near the high-walled pass of La Glorieta. The army of Sibley's men wasn't used to an opposing force; they'd whipped the Irregulars at Valverde, they'd hauled through towns and called it a victory. They weren't supposed to be pinned down in this godforsaken canyon.

It made no matter to Jim Henry that the enemy weren't supposed to be in the tight brushed canyon. It mattered only that he was low on ammunition, that he could see into the murderous barrels of the rifles aimed at him, that something hard and clawing held his belly in a vise and swept weakness through his body.

FLAGS OVER TEXAS

William A. Luckey

BALLANTINE BOOKS • NEW YORK

Library of Congress Catalog Card Number: 91-91892

ISBN 0-345-36190-3

Manufactured in the United States of America

First Edition: August 1991

To Benjamin and William Andrews, and their descendants:
Otis Perry and his family, of Dover, New Hampshire

The land known today as the Big Bend in Texas was lacking in people and the basics of civilization until after the end of the Mexican War in 1848. Prior to that time, the Spanish had tried and failed to tame this land, which offered them only suffering and death. Comanche and Apache Indians roamed the grasslands at their will, able to survive where a "civilized" man would dry up and blow away. Today it is still a harsh and unforgiving section of Texas.

The end of the Mexican War brought a good number of Anglos into the area, which the Spanish had termed *despoblado*, or uninhabited. Supply trains began to search for shorter routes to California, and men came and stayed for any number of private reasons. Many of them were soldiers mustered out at the end of the war and unwilling to return home. They staked out homesteads, farming along the Rio Grande for their needs, never straying far from their loaded rifles, always expecting the enemy. It was a difficult life, and often a short one. But as more and more people moved into the area, it became possible to survive and to look into the future.

A few of the people in this book are real, taken from the history of the period: men who arrived with the end of the Mexican War, men with no recorded background and no desire to explain themselves. Ben Leaton and his fort are real, as are John Spencer and his rancho, although the site has been changed to provide a flow in the story. Spencer first attempted to raise horses along the river, then made a contract with the army at the newly built Fort Davis to supply beef cattle. These men were in the spotlight for a few years in the *despoblado*, then disappeared. There is little of record about John Spencer's end; Ben Leaton was killed in the early 1850s, but his family and his name were carried on by an assortment of sons.

The rest of the characters in the book are products of my imagination, except for the higher commanding officers in the actual Glorieta conflict. Historical facts support the events, and an abbreviated journal of one Texas boy who lived to return home from the New Mexico campaign was inspirational for the core of *Flags over Texas*. By and large, this book may be considered fiction loosely woven around fact.

I would like to thank Marshall Trimble for his encouragement, and Lew Llewellyn, Jeff Hengesbaugh, and Jeff Kask for their invaluable help. And a special thanks goes to Mary V. Osgood for the use of her family name of McCraw.

William A. Luckey
Santa Fe, New Mexico
April 1990

PROLOGUE

IT WENT WRONG the spring of his eleventh year, when his pa shoved him facedown in the dirt. It took only one of his pa's big hands to cover his back and flatten him in the sand.

"Jim Henry, you stay put. Mind me, boy, don't move."

He didn't know what frightened Pa, he couldn't see anything with his face buried in the dirt. He tried to lift his head, but the big hand kept him still. Then the pressure released, and the hand cuffed him on the ear. Pa never hit him, Pa never raised his hand to him or Benny. Jim Henry hugged the ground; his ear hurt where Pa had hit him.

Pa's voice barked at him again, the words coarse and wavering, and Jim Henry was finally afraid. "Boy, you mind me good. Quiet now, don't you move till I say so."

Then there was no hand to hold him down, but he heard Pa's words and stayed flat in the small protection of a thorny bush. He opened his eyes once, to see nothing but rock and sand and a thin yellow flower rising inches from its shallow roots. He closed his eyes again and squeezed them until silver dots danced behind his eyelids and the world turned flashing colors.

He tried to move, first one foot, then the other, then a hand that was stung by a nettle. He was too old to cry at eleven; he put the hurt finger in his mouth.

It seemed like a long time before he disobeyed Pa and raised his head and opened his eyes. What he saw terrified him, and he dropped back down, sobbing.

Indians . . . Indians racing around the yard. And there was fire and smoke coming from the cabin, and the Indians whooped and howled and kept galloping. Indians were sup-

1

posed to run from Mr. Spencer's men. And Mr. Spencer had left four vaqueros with Jim Henry's pa and then had ridden upriver to Presidio—and now there was no one to protect the burning cabin.

First it was Ramón, who had broken his leg trying to ride out a blowing sorrel. They'd left him in the stable with a bottle of mescal, and this morning Pa hadn't let Benny and Jim Henry in there to see him.

Jesús, Ramón's brother, had ridden out last night against Pa's orders. Jesús liked to laugh, and he told stories and carved small animals from bits of soft wood, but Jesús had left them alone last night—gone off to find help for his brother.

This morning Patricio had been found by the river, his throat slit, his eyes staring at the sky. Benny had cried out, and Jim Henry had held him when they'd found Patricio. The fourth man could not be found at all, so it was only Pa and Jim Henry, and baby Benny, to guard Mr. Spencer's horses.

Jim Henry rolled in the gravel without feeling the stinging cuts. It had all gone wrong this morning, after he and Benny had found Patricio near the river.

Horses galloped close to him, and Jim Henry curled up into a ball, tight inside himself. The thorns of the mesquite bush dug deep, and he wanted to cry. A series of flashing legs flew past, and one horse leaped the bush that shielded him. Suddenly a hoof came down on Jim Henry and rolled him from the thorny protection. A white-stockinged leg grazed his shoulder, a black leg hit his thigh and spun him into the stream of horses. Jim Henry laced his arms over his head and cried out fearful sobs that smeared his face with muddy streaks.

It was almost quiet when at last he raised his head. Instantly he was struck above his eye and flopped back into the churned dirt. Twice more he was hit by the galloping herd, along his ribs and across his back. The final blow knocked him unconscious and rolled him into the safety of the mesquite thorns.

He came back to voices talking a language he did not understand. But he knew the meaning of the words: Be still, be patient. Pa always said, If you didn't know it, wait it out, figure and think, but don't move. Jim Henry knew the thorns cut into him, he knew the pain in his head and back, and he knew Pa's words. He waited until the voices over him were silent.

At last he opened one eye; a chipped and shoeless hoof told him what he already knew: Indians. A black leg lifted and stamped at a pest, raising more dust to invade Jim Henry's mouth and choke him. He swallowed hard against the need to cough, felt his throat close, and risked everything to put a balled fist in his mouth. The black leg near him lifted and moved. Two more legs followed, then a fourth; then there was a forest of moving bone and hide until there was only dust and no more sound.

The coughing came in spasms, so that the boy did not see the last of the riders pull up and cock his head to look back. For a brief time the small paint horse and dark rider were the only life on the desert, then horse and rider disappeared.

It was a long time before Jim Henry tried to move again. Finally he raised a hand to his own face and fingered the dried blood on his forehead and down his cheek. He did not flinch when he found the open cut above his eye.

When he sat up and saw fresh blood on the tips of his fingers, he wanted to cry and could not. Instead, he peeled off crusted dirt from the cut, then picked the dried blood from his face. As he stood, he wobbled and had to grab an ocotillo whip for support. The fresh bite and sting of the thorny plant brought him to complete consciousness.

He could walk, but he would not go near the yard. He followed the path he and Benny had made, the path back of the house to the slow river. When he knelt on the familiar spot to draw water, a pressure built from behind his eyes— it was from the blow. He would not see his own tears ripple the clean, still water.

He lay down then and slept, and when he woke he drank again from the dark river and moved aside to relieve himself. It was a safe place; he did not have to go to the house. Not yet. He slept again, and again, then woke to a violent hunger and a lessening of the pain in his head.

Vultures rose from their work when he drifted into the yard. Smoke still spiraled from the shattered roof of the adobe house, and a presence walked beside Jim Henry as he headed for the low doorway. When he stepped inside, his eyes widened to see through the darkness.

He looked a long time at what he would not forget, then he backed out through the doorway into the bright sun. He burned his eyes looking at the light. He did not go to his father and Ramón at the stable. He did nothing but stare at the sun.

When the column of dust registered in his mind, he glanced at it, then ran, falling once to his knees in the loose sand. They would not catch him here; he would hide in an arroyo, he would wait until they went away again. If one of them did come near his hiding place, he would not give up without a fight. He would be like his father and die buried in the enemy's blood.

Hidden behind a balanced rock the boy settled in to wait. The enemy would come looking, and they would find the fierce rage of James Henry McCraw.

The thin plume of smoke told them all they needed to know long before they reached the house. The group of horsemen crested a hill and were silent as they gazed down at the scarred adobe house and stables. Their leader, an angular man on a fine sorrel, laced his hands on the head of his saddle and stared out to the ribbon of water beyond the house. He began to curse then, mouth working on the bitter words. Only a few sounds passed his lips. The men around him sat on their mounts and waited.

"Uh, Mr. Spencer, want us to go down and see? Might be someone alive down there. Might be. Them *indios* gone, fire's most burned out. Mr. Spencer? . . ."

The man on the fine sorrel spoke as if nothing had been said. "It's the McCraws, dammit. I left four good men with them. There was no Indian trouble, no sign. *Damn* them!"

John Spencer spoke to himself, not caring that the men around him heard. "McCraw knew when he hired to me this was no place for a family. Especially not his pretty wife and them two boys."

Spencer hawked and spat, then, as if he'd just remembered, gave his orders: "Limm, you track the horse herd, see if any escaped. Juan, Tag, Emilio, we ride down there, see what's left. Any of you got a head from last night, keep away. I don't want your guts all over me."

He jerked on the sorrel as the older man called Limm reined a stubborn dun off from the group and headed out. Spencer's sorrel whirled and reared, then settled. As a group, the horsemen picked their way carefully down the hill, through the loose rock and spiny cactus, around the height of a maguey clump.

The fine bureau and bed frame, which belonged to the McCraw woman were still smoking. And the vultures had almost finished their chores. Spencer spat to the side, and a man behind him gagged.

McCraw had died fighting. Spencer knew he would; it was why he'd hired the man against good sense. No Anglo with a family lived in the *despoblado*. McCraw was running, like most of the men John Spencer hired. Castoffs from the war in Mexico, running from the new Texas government. Whoever he was, Robert McCraw had gone down hard. Spencer looked at the tale laid out for him to read.

A dark crust divided what was left of the man. The vultures had gone right to the core, and by now McCraw was little more than a hollow shape. A leg lay by itself in the doorway of the stable, swollen black and bound with cactus whips and rotting cloth. That counted for two men—which meant one had been useless when *los indios* came.

Tag rode back from the river and told of finding Patricio's body. But there was no sign of Jesús or the other man. Spencer bet there never would be a counting, 'less a stray dog brought in a human bone or an indio brat showed up wearing a fancy plaited vest.

He didn't want to look inside the small adobe, but the others, up at Leaton's Fort, they would want to hear him tell all of what was there. Mrs. McCraw had come to mean something to these lonely men. A real lady, she was, with soft, dark eyes and fine blond hair, graceful even in her homespun dresses.

John Spencer sighed and slid off his sorrel horse. Smoke drifted out the door and spiraled up through the broken roof. Ducking down to avoid the smoldering wood, he stepped inside.

The woman was angled against the far wall, a small body twisted across her feet. One flayed hand was stretched out and down as if to caress the child; the other was held protectively across her breast. There wasn't even the blond hair to remind John Spencer of her beauty. The bones of her face were jelled, the flesh of her breast and legs clotted stripes.

His belly tightened, his bowels burned. Smoke teared his eyes and drove him outside, where the three men waited in silence.

Then Limm Tyler came down the hill and rode close, his dun horse blowing and heaving. Tyler spoke slowly, watching John Spencer's face: "Bad in there, huh? They got the woman?" When Spencer's face grimaced in mute response, Tyler continued. "Any sign of the boys? There was two of 'em, I 'member."

Spencer coughed and spat out black phlegm. He wished Tyler would stop his questions. He also wished for a bottle of wine, a chaw, anything to wipe out the bitter taste in his mouth. "Tag, put McCraw and what's left of the other, put them inside the house. Then all of you, tie on a rope and pull the place down. No one'll ever live here again, and trying to dig a grave in this ground makes no sense. They died defending their home; bury them in its remains."

But Limm Tyler didn't quit. "What about the boys? The one called Jim Henry, he would be with his pa. What about him?"

Spencer spun around, face flushed, eyes glittering with rage. "Tyler, you always talk too much. Little kid's in there, with his ma. Indios got the other one. You care so damned much, *you* go looking for him!" Air rushed in over his clenched teeth as he broke off. John Spencer could say no more.

But Tyler had heard enough. He spurred his dun horse, and jumped the trampled garden. The horse hit a run and rolled past the splintered corrals to the high ridge and desert plains.

* * *

The kid was dead, like Spencer said. If he were a believing man, Tyler would curse and bring down the wrath of God on Spencer's unfeeling soul. But there was no use in cursing, no God to hear it. Tyler knew that from the Mexican War; Tyler knew no God fought alongside the soldiers. And no God lived in this forsaken part of Texas.

Horse and rider had come to a narrow draw, and its rocky sides rose above their heads, mesquite and cactus embedded in the slanted earth. Tyler settled the tiring dun. He was restless; this was no place to be, chasing *los indios* and a missing kid. He gigged the dun and then jerked as the horse sidestepped in fright.

But he was too slow; a ball rammed his shoulders and knocked him from the dun. Tyler rolled quickly and dove forward as his attacker pounded his head and back. Tyler's skull bounced off the dun's legs, and the terrified horse struck out. He ducked in time, then managed to catch a hand and give it a cruel twist. The cry shocked him. By God, he'd found the McCraw kid.

He held the wrist as the boy sat on his chest and kicked him in the ribs. A fist struck Tyler in the mouth, and he cursed, then tried to catch hold of both arms. "Boy, stop!" he yelled, grabbing wildly. "It's a friend, boy. A friend."

Still the boy didn't quit; he kicked Limm again in the ribs and pounded on his chest with one fist. At last Limm caught the arm and drew the boy's face down close to his. "Hey, McCraw. It's Limm Tyler. I'm your *friend*, boy. I ain't the enemy, I ain't no Indian."

When the small body slumped on Tyler's chest and the feet stopped banging on his ribs, Tyler lifted the boy and set him on the ground. He didn't move an inch while Tyler struggled to untangle himself and dust off the worst of the cactus and rock snugged in his clothes. All the while he worked on himself, Tyler talked out loud, looking once or twice at the boy to see if he was listening. When the boy's face got back some of its color, he figured it was time to ask questions and quit fussing with his shirtfront.

"Boy, what we saw . . . well, we buried your ma and pa and your brother inside your house. Pulled the walls down on 'em, they's buried inside, in peace." Tyler let out a gulp of air. "They was all dead, boy. You understand?"

Limm Tyler wasn't much on education, but he knew a child gone through what this one had, there were tears in him, and anger and much grief. And it came out best in crying and screaming. It weren't good for Tyler to see the McCraw boy sitting still.

"Boy, you pay heed. You got kinfolk back where you come from? Here, boy, you got to talk to me. You sure as . . . sure can't live out here alone."

The McCraw boy stood up, and Tyler figured he'd got to him. But the boy took him off stride again. "Mr. Tyler, your horse is loose," he said solemnly. Nothing showed on the young face. That gave Tyler an edgy feeling in his gut. But he went and caught up his horse and brought him back to face Jim Henry square.

"I'll set up behind you, if you don't mind, Mr. Tyler."

Tyler shook his head; he didn't like the practicality of the conversation. "Boy, you got to hear me. It's your family buried back there, and it's you we got to do something with. Now you by God talk to me."

"Yessir, I know they's dead, Mr. Tyler. I'll ride in behind you, be no trouble. I thought you was Indians come back for me."

The boy shimmied up the dun's saddle, leaving Tyler standing flatfooted and shaking his head. He'd ridden a long time, seen some of the world outside. Lived through Indian attacks, massacres where men and women were skinned out, horses gutted and broken. But the boy perched behind the dun's crude saddle was new to him.

Tyler shivered from his thoughts and climbed on the dun. The boy's arms closed around his belly, and the horse half reared and pranced sideways. They came into Spencer's Rancho that way. A vaquero pulled back the heavy gate and let them in. The boy was down and at the dun's head before Tyler could dismount.

"I'll put him up, Mr. Tyler. Pa showed me where the gear goes, and I remember."

Tyler slid down and put his hands to the small of his back and stretched while he watched the boy. There had to be a cry breaking in there, yet all he got was a backward glance and a half salute as the boy led the dun away. It weren't natural, weren't right. That was what Limm Tyler knew. That was all he knew.

He ran his three-fingered hand through his sparse hair and remembered—a trap set by a greenhorn, a blind grab at the steel maw, the clash that cut the two fingers clean. The stubs still hurt; hell of a way to learn.

Tyler had a life on the rancho, like a lot of folk headed out from something small and shameful. Spencer gave clean work for a man to do, a bottle of mescal or wine at nights. Then there were the river women, who came across in the dark and stayed with a man. There was one woman, Rosa Ignacio, who pleased Tyler best. Maybe she would know what to do with the McCraw boy.

The gravel voice behind him startled Tyler, and he jumped sideways to see old John Spencer himself watching. "Well, so you got in. I see you found the McCraw boy. Tag found two of the mares up on Hight's Butte. Says it's the Vasco mare and her filly. You go get 'em come morning, I don't want nothing left for them indios. Ben Leaton may have made a pact with the devils, but I ain't done so, and I ain't planning on it. Tyler, you hear me?"

Tyler snorted; bad-mouthing dead Ben Leaton was sport out here. There'd been long speculation old Leaton traded with the Indians, swapped whiskey and weapons for them leaving him and his alone. With his widow married now to Ed Hall, there was still talk of the boys carrying on their pa's habits.

Spencer got talking again, and Limm Tyler held still for listening. "Boy, you come here, tell me what happened to your family, how you got loose. I need to know."

Tyler held his breath, wondering if this would be enough to break the boy.

But the kid was pure spook; a maverick kid no bigger than a gnat, standing straight and giving a report like a longtime scout. There weren't much emotion in the boy as he delivered his account, but the picture he drew up was horrible, and Tyler flinched and hated John Spencer as they both listened.

Finally, mercifully, the report was done, and John Spencer had no more questions. The three of them were silent, each waiting for an end. Then Spencer started up again, and Tyler's anger grew.

"Tyler, you get this child on a wagon train out of here. I don't want an orphan hanging 'round. Too much trouble."

Limm Tyler waited, certain of the boy's response.

"Mr. Spencer, my pa told me this was home. Our home. We got a place here and nothing to go back to in Tennessee. I figure to stay and earn my keep. Won't be a trouble to no one."

For a wonder, Spencer was silent. The boy walked off, headed toward a rough shed near a river ditch. A body could live in that shed given a mind; wash up in the ditch, fashion out a bed from corn shucks, take feedings where they were found. He admired the boy.

Spencer snorted hard. "Tyler, bring in all the loose horses you can find. I don't trust them Indians, horseflesh tastes too sweet to them. Me, I'm headed to Leaton's Fort. Got word the army's building. I'm going to sell that army their daily beef. Get me out of this horse business where I can make some money." Spencer waved a hand. "I guess the kid stays."

Word of the massacre spread quickly through the unofficial community, and one of the ladies who crossed the river at night quickly came to worry about the survivor. If the McCraw child were much like his papa, he would be in deep pain.

So Rosa Ignacio went to look for the boy in all the small places on the rancho. She found the old shed and saw the dusty tracks, and she stood at the door, peering cautiously into the darkness and listening in vain for the sounds of crying. She had to wait and be content in talking to herself until the McCraw child came to her. He would not let her hold him, but he did stand quietly while she wiped the dirt from his forehead and rubbed grease into the wound to protect it. When she touched his head, she could feel his small body tremble, and she herself began to cry, shedding the tears the young one would not cry for himself.

The child looked at her, with those hazel eyes like his papa's and the fine blond hair much like his mother's, and Rosa Ignacio could not help her grieving. The young one had lost so much. Rosa Ignacio had lost a child of her own, a child of barely three months. A child with dark features and straight black hair, not much like the pale skin and blondness of the McCraws. But a child of her own, a beloved *niño*.

So Rosa Ignacio wanted to take the yellow-haired child and draw him to her breast and comfort him as she herself had needed comfort. But she looked into the shaded golden eyes and saw there was nothing she could do for the brave *niño*—nothing she could do but clean the wound and spread the healing grease, and pray for his tortured soul. There would be a small line above his eye to mark his loss, yet inside, Rosa knew, there would be worse scarring. She trembled with her own thoughts; there would be a mark on this one that could never be erased.

The child thanked her and turned away, to go back into his burrow with his private sorrow. He did not want the comfort of Rosa Ignacio, but there were other men who would want her. Limm Tyler often took her to one of the small rooms and held her. The need for a man grew in Rosa Ignacio, the need to be close. Yet it was her empty hands that patted her plump shoulders and the swelling of her hips, as if to be certain the charms were intact. Trembling fingers combed through the black hair and reset a silver earring, tugged at the waist of her skirt.

At last the woman left the doorway of the rough shed and went to find Limm Tyler, or any man who would want her.

There was ice on the water early in the mornings now, and each breath a man took frosted gray in the thin sunlight. John Spencer slapped his sorrel on the neck and felt the coarseness of the winter hair. He looked closely at the red horse and noted the shiny coat, the mane picked clean of straw, the tail long and flowing.

It had been a hot summer, the hottest one Spencer remembered in the *despoblado*. Then again, he'd said that every summer he'd been here; hadn't picked the land to be kind, only profitable. It had been once, it would be again. He had the army contract for beef, and he was waiting for them to pick their site—Painted Comanche Camp on Limpia Creek, or across the Rio Grande from Presidio del Norte, or near Fort Leaton, God damn the old man even if he was dead. Or maybe the Chihuahua crossing. Didn't matter to Spencer, long as they picked and settled and he could make his money off the army's stomach. The cattle were bought and waiting to hit the trail.

Spencer slapped the sorrel's neck again; the horse whinnied and danced as the rancher mounted. Riders drifted in: Emilio and Limm Tyler, Tag and two new vaqueros. They formed a half circle around Spencer, and a shadow struggled with the big gate to let the riders out.

Jim Henry McCraw kept his hand on the monstrous iron latch and watched the procession of men. He saw John Spencer in the lead, saw the man's fingers stroke the shiny sorrel neck. The big horse whinnied and pranced sideways, from the unaccustomed cold and the heaviness of its rider's hand.

Jim Henry McCraw almost smiled. The shiny sorrel, the clean coat and flowing tail, they were his protection and his bribe. As long as the fine sorrel was kept clean, John Spencer would let him stay at Spencer's Rancho.

PART ONE

CHAPTER 1

THE BOY RODE silently beside him. It weren't fair to still call him a child—he was past eighteen now and tall like his pa, as much as Limm Tyler could remember. Had reddish hairs on his jaw and the lines and calluses of rough work on his face and hands. A hard worker and not much for talking, like his pa. Tyler took care of the talking for both of them.

Far as Tyler knew, the boy hadn't ever grieved in the seven years, hadn't said nothing about his family dying, hadn't been once to the rubble of the adobe house. Only thing left of the distant raid was the thin white line bleached through the constant burn of the boy's skin. It wasn't much of a memory.

Tyler glanced sideways, then checked the three men riding fanned out beside them. The McCraw boy lifted his darkening head and stared off at a ridge, paying no mind to Tyler. Manuel reined in his horse as the other two men circled and came close.

It was the boy who spoke out. "Mr. Tyler, cattle's bunched wrong up that ridge."

Manuel nodded eagerly, but Tyler told the kid to go see and held Manuel back with a flat hand. A lot more cattle needed to be choused out of the brush. Let the boy ride up, let him see what was wrong.

Tyler sat and watched the kid, and inspected the land. Low clumps of the wire grass that fattened Spencer's cattle were cropped short. Herd'd been here too long.

No getting 'round it, Mr. Spencer hit it right with his cattle and his army contract. The man was a ring-tailed lion to work for, but he paid out good wages, better than most in the *despoblado*. Even now, in the year of our Lord 1859, a man

15

rode for his brand and his *patrón*, and prayed to the same good Lord that *los indios* did not find him far from a rifle and all alone. Spencer knew; Spencer armed his men well.

Tyler yanked down the brim of his hat and drove the coyote bay deep into a thicket, scattering out three bawling steers. He circled them back toward the main herd. The two silent men rode nearby, each with a hand to his rifle. No one was safe. Tyler touched the butt of his long rifle for luck, knowing the others would do the same. Then he looked up to try and follow the kid's trail.

Jim Henry knew even before his pony crested the hill. His tongue tested the corners of his mouth and felt the dryness. Head down, his eyes easily followed signs: Indian, unshod horse ridden through the bunched steers. Outline of a single moccasin print. The steers didn't move; it was all wrong.

He swung wide around the dulled herd, eyes shifting from the broken ground to the thick bush and back to the cattle. The cream pony he rode stopped short and tossed its head. Jim Henry stiffened; an Indian could stay hidden easily up here until his prey came close enough.

As he spurred the cream closer to the herd, the pony dropped a shoulder and spun hard. Jim Henry caught the loose reins and hauled on the tender mouth until the cream stopped with its head resting on Jim Henry's knee. He patted the damp neck and felt the little horse tremble. They'd both caught the scent of trouble.

The cattle stood in pools of drying blood. A brindle steer tried to stamp at a pestering fly, then lowered its head and moaned. Jim Henry dropped his eyes and picked up a clear moccasin track, fresh enough that dark balls of moist dirt rolled in the shallow depression. He shuddered; the knife that cut those tendons and muscles was hidden and waiting. He drew his own knife, felt the coolness of the crude handle slip in his wet palm.

The figure rose out of the mesquite bush to meet him, black eyes fired with hate, mouth drawn in a silent warrior's scream. The ruby-tipped knife gleamed as the Indian went for the cream pony's neck.

Jim Henry pushed himself off the cream and hit his attacker chest high. The Indian's knife sliced through his shirt and skinned his ribs. Jim Henry twisted and stabbed at the greased body beneath him. He felt his knife hit rock as the red body bucked and plunged. Jim Henry rolled free, scrambled to his feet, and spun back to face the enemy. A line of blood stained his shirt and ran down the side of his leather pants.

The Indian was slow to come up and swayed on his feet, the lethal knife unsteady in his hand. Jim Henry saw blood smeared on a flat rock behind him and had time to raise his eyes, examine the face of his enemy. He drew in a deep breath and went too far back . . . to things he did not want to remember. The enemy was Itaya Sol. A face from seven years back, from the slaughter. When Jim Henry was a child and a coward and hid under a mesquite bush and heard his father's death, his mother's screams.

Itaya Sol. A child himself painted for death, riding a scrawny pinto. Who used to play with Jim Henry and little brother, Benny, who stopped and looked back at the sound of Jim Henry's crying.

Itaya Sol. There had to be the same memory in the savage's mind, for he hesitated too long, the knife in his hand held back from its kill. The black eyes watched . . . and waited.

Jim Henry lunged and jammed the knife deep into the red chest. The strength and force of the blow drew him close to the standing corpse, and he felt the slick muscle separate and spasm in death. There was no defense; dark red flowed suddenly from the opened mouth, and Jim Henry fell forward with the flesh and bone. Lying across the stained skin, he heard the heart pump quickly and then stop.

He stood up and set himself. The handle of his knife rose solid from the corpse, and he pulled it free with great effort, then jabbed the blade over and over in loose sand to draw it clean. He caught up the still-trembling cream pony and, without looking back, rode to the edge of the ridge and down to the cattle and Limm Tyler.

Manuel was the first to see him; the other two gathered in to listen. One man touched his own testicles, the other raised his head and slowly stroked his own neck. They were safe.

They had seen the mark of blood on the young rider and knew they were safe.

Tyler was busy with a calf. A dry cough from the boy made him look up.

"It were slaughter, Mr. Tyler. Indian half butchered them steers, left 'em alive and dying. No way to save 'em.'' The boy waited and watched Tyler watching him. Then: "I got the Indian did the work. I killed him.''

Tyler had to look at the kid again; he saw blood but no weakness, so it was the indio's blood staining him. But why were the hazel eyes half closed, and why was there sweat on the bare face? Boy's growing up, he thought, and it ain't been a pleasant trip.

The calf bound at Tyler's feet bawled hard. A festered cut had sickened it, but a good smearing of grease and turpentine would make the difference. Doctoring was cattle work Limm Tyler liked. He let the calf up, took a long time doing it.

"Got the son of a bitch, huh? You need any of this here grease? Keep out the flies, you got cut up some. Calf here ain't got no complaints.'' Tyler scratched his head. The boy was bruised and mauled good, and his shirt was most torn away, looked there was a cut along his ribs. Quite a fight. "Right proper, you kill the bastard,'' he said. "One less to worry over. Good work, Mr. Spencer'll be pleased.''

The boy's face twisted and Tyler wondered, but the kid turned away and Tyler quit worrying. There weren't no soft heart to this kid, not ever.

"What you want done with the steers?'' the boy asked.

"Ain't no way to save any. That . . . he got 'em good.''

"Slaughter and skin 'em. Pack in the meat. Tonight we'll eat our fill. A good steak, that sounds right. Won't please Spencer, but we're doing the best we can.''

The slaughter was brutal, stinking work. Tyler sent Manuel and a guard back to the rancho to tell Spencer and bring back a pack mule. Manuel came back with word that el Patrón wanted Tyler and the boy to ride to Fort Davis when they were done. Army wanted reports on all Indian activity. And they could stay a day extra to the town.

Tyler knew better, but he always hoped. When he told Jim Henry of the stay in town, he wanted more than the blank

face and uninterested nod. Bless the poor son of a bitch,
bless him. Something someday would take that blankness
and cut the boy wide open underneath, and the boy would
go down hard under the shock. Tyler knew he wouldn't be
around then, so he told Manuel and the others to get back to
their work.

In the late spring of '59, Fort Davis was a deteriorating collection of canvas and slab-wood huts commanded by Lieutenant Colonel Washington Seawall. The fort stood in a flat
meadow surrounded by high rock walls on three sides. A
mile above the fort was Painted Comanche Camp and the
clear running waters of Limpia Creek, the source of water
for the camp.

The town itself straggled away from the fort's protection.
A stage line came through now, bringing in a steady trickle
of people to the grasslands above the bitter Texas desert.
Travelers, drummers, soldiers, and storekeepers met in the
dusty streets of the raw new town.

Limm Tyler liked Fort Davis, liked its difference from the
isolated safety of Spencer's Rancho. It was a place to visit
and to howl, and then leave. He also liked watching the
scrubbed clean face of Jim Henry as their horses took them
toward the army post. Tyler's coyoto bay had been in the
confusion before, but Jim Henry's cream jigged and shied,
and they made a parade all their own. They were coming to
Fort Davis, the army post and the town and the hundred or
so people crowding it. Limm Tyler watched and laughed.

He kept to instructions and spoke his piece to one Colonel
Seawall. The kid stayed outside with the horses as Tyler
grinned and shuffled his feet and told the colonel a short yarn
about the Indian on the ridge and the boy's killing. He yawned
and shook his head when the colonel asked too many questions, and said he didn't know nothing more than what he'd
said already. If he talked too much, the colonel might take a
notion he knew something, and Tyler purely didn't want to
waste the time. He knew the colonel's reputation. And he
wanted to get to town.

He glanced outside once, kind of over his own shoulder,
and he saw the kid standing erect, staring hard out to some-

thing caught his attention. Tyler hoped it was better than what he had to look at behind the colonel's wooden desk.

Then he was done and dismissed in a military manner, and he came close to saluting the colonel before he remembered it weren't the Mexican War all over again. He worked for John Spencer, not the U.S. Army, God bless 'em.

He got up right behind Jim Henry before the kid knew he was there. Tyler craned his neck, but saw nothing more than a garden under a cottonwood that had the kid moon-eyed. Probably a spring there, too. He didn't figure the kid's fascination with a spring and a garden patch.

"We head to Spencer's pens now. Put up the horses there, we can bed down the night if we've a mind. Got a lot to see and only tonight and some of the morning. Get going, boy. You deaf?"

The boy mounted and followed, and Tyler gave up pointing out what might interest him. Instead, he looked around and grinned at the folks on the narrow street; this was his idea of a town.

When they hit Spencer's corrals, Tyler was down and tearing at the bay's rigging while the boy sat his cream. He slapped the boy's long leg, and the kid woke up and slid down, stripped the cream real fast. They turned out the horses and watched the pair dig in the stale cow dirt and lower down for a good roll. Then Tyler hauled on the boy's shoulder and got talking. "We got us women to see, Jim Henry. Lots of women. I seen the half tent back a ways, offering whiskey, and I bet that one's got women right there with the bottles. Now you come along peaceable, and we'll set this poor little town straight up on the truth and veracity of Limm Tyler and Jim Henry McCraw. Let's go, boy. We got a lot of celebrating to do."

Jim Henry'd grown used to Limm Tyler's ways. Had to, he'd lived with the old man and the river woman, Rosa Ignacio, for the past seven years. But they weren't his ma and pa. Usually he forgot that, but the face of Itaya Sol brought back the memory. So he shied away from the raw pictures and refused Tyler's offer. He had better things to do.

He ducked the wide span of Tyler's rough hand and walked

quickly until he was certain Tyler wasn't coming along. He knew the old man wanted his pleasure. But Jim Henry wasn't sure that kind of pleasure was worth having.

There had been a girl at the spring. By herself, sitting quietly under the cottonwood. He was going up there, to the spring, and he hoped she was still there.

The spring was deserted. He squatted and placed the flat of his hand at the base of the tree and imagined he could feel her warmth and presence here, with him.

"I saw you earlier. You were with that old man, you were holding two horses. That was you, holding those horses, wasn't it?"

His feet tangled, and he fell into the tree trunk and skinned his hand. His pants were too tight, and his belly ached, and his left ear itched, and he needed to wipe his nose.

She was beautiful, she was talking to him, and he was too dumb to do more than hold on to the tree and swallow hard. She was just like he imagined: light brown hair tied with a ribbon, a soft face filled with blue eyes, and a red mouth that kept spilling out sounds he couldn't understand.

Finally Jim Henry straightened up and saw that the girl was no more than fifteen and wearing men's pants and had a blue scarf tied around her neck. He had never seen anything so beautiful in his whole life. He grabbed his hat and rolled the brim through his hands; he remembered that much of his mother's manners. He had to look past the girl before he could talk. His voice stuttered and broke, and he blushed and tried to find the words.

"Yes'm. Yes, miss. I was to the colonel's with them horses. That was me, holding them horses."

He almost quit then. His ma taught him better, but he lived with Tyler and Rosa and the vaqueros, and he'd forgot what Ma said. "Yes, miss, that was me." That was better, but the girl didn't seem to notice the difference.

"My papa's Captain Stockbridge. I'm Phillipa Stock-bridge. What is your name, and why are you here? I've never seen you around here. Papa told me there was no one my age for miles, 'cepting ranch girls. You're my age, or close. And at least you aren't old and smelly like most of the soldiers and the people in town. You aren't twenty yet, are you?

I want to know someone who is my age. Why won't you tell me your name? You do know your name, don't you?''

She finally had to stop and take a breath, and Jim Henry fell in love. No one he'd ever met talked like this girl. Not even Tyler when he was explaining, or Rosa Ignacio when she wanted to comfort him. This girl was different.

''Well?''

It was as if she'd stamped her foot in high temper. Jim Henry couldn't stop staring at her; she wore men's trousers. Even the Indian women wore long fringed skirts for modesty, and the Mexican ladies favored bright cloth to their ankles. He could see the outline of her legs and thighs, the roundness of her hips. Jim Henry blushed brighter and turned away, shamed by his body's reaction.

''My name's . . . uh . . . Jim . . . James Henry, miss. James Henry McCraw.''

He'd barely finished before she started again. ''That's much too long a name. And I would guess they call you Jim Henry. You do not look like a Jimmy, and Hank is too crude, Mac much too old. So I shall call you James. Hello, James.''

She put out her hand and waited. Jim Henry felt the breath of her skin on his callused palm. She took his hand firmly and pumped it twice. Then she must have felt something, for she blushed, and her fingers slipped in his hand, and the tips stroked across the heel and the cupped palm and the fingers before she broke the grasp. Sweat beaded Jim Henry's forehead and the back of his neck; he shivered and wanted to cough up the lump in his throat.

They started to walk around the small garden, and her voice was softer, gentler, this time. Jim Henry had to keep his balance constantly to avoid touching her body as they walked.

It had to be that she could read his mind, for she looked at him and then blushed again. She wavered from the path, as if she did not want him too near, and Jim Henry stepped back a pace to give her room. It didn't work, for she wore men's trousers, and he could see the flex of her haunch as she walked. He licked his mouth and felt sweat on the palms of his hands.

''My papa lets me ride his cavalry charger, sometimes. In

the afternoon, when I have finished my schoolwork. Do you go to school? It's awful, isn't it? Papa has promised me a horse of my own when I can ride better. Maybe then I can ride out into the hills. Papa says the Indians might come after me. Papa says the Indians are terrible here.

"Weren't you afraid when you came to the fort today? Weren't you afraid of the Indians? I've heard they do terrible things to people. The sergeant told me they butchered a man and his family a few years ago. Rode right into their house and murdered them. That's terrible, don't you think, James?"

He didn't want to deal with the questions, he wanted to stand next to her and listen to her speak and smell the bright-ness of her ribboned hair. For once the memory of his family was buried under a different thought; for once he did not suffer a deadness from the questions of well-meaning strangers.

She didn't give him any time. "Won't you come with me to see the horses, especially the one Papa lets me ride? Please, walk with me."

He could not believe her; a family, a caring papa, a school, and all the men at the fort, and she wanted him to walk with her and see the horses.

They had circled the garden and stopped at the cottonwood where Jim Henry had first seen her. "Isn't it nice to have flowers? Aren't they the prettiest you ever saw? I never thought there would be flowers in the desert, but Fort Davis really isn't desert, not like the places Papa told me about, like Presidio and Mr. Leaton's fort and some of the ranches. What terrible places they must be to live, don't you think? James?"

She did it to him again. Still caught in his ignorance, Jim Henry tried to make it his best. "Yes'm, it is nice here to the fort. But living down to Presidio, on a ranch, it ain't . . . I sure would like to see that horse, miss."

Phillipa Stockbridge hated herself for what she must be doing to the young man. But she really didn't mean to hurt him. He must live near Presidio, she decided, he must have known the murdered family. How terrible of her to keep talking, but he confused her so, made her feel hot and cold at the same time. She couldn't stop the talking, and when she listened to herself, she hated her needless cruelty.

The poor boy; the leather pants he wore were greasy and spotted and torn and sewn together in too many places to be decent. And the pants smelled. The shirt was fairly clean, but it, too, was patched and repaired. And it had no proper collar. It would be hard not to laugh at his clothing, why his boots were not a matched pair, yet she found she did not care. There was a kindness to him, an air of good breeding and manners despite the poverty of his attire. She began to talk again, and the brittle sound of her own voice startled her. "Papa calls his horse Sultan, but I think that is a cruel name. The horse likes it when I give him treats, but the sergeant says I am spoiling him. I like the feeling of his lips on my hand: he is so gentle and his whiskers tickle. That's why I call him Jolly. Sultan is much too cruel."

Phillipa was amazed. She was telling a total stranger everything that came into her mind. But the talk kept him near, and she wanted him near. He was handsome in the sunlight; his hair glowed like bronze, and his eyes were lined with the longest black lashes, and she liked the strength in his hands and the shape of his body under the threadbare clothing.

He was much more intriguing than the polite, pale boys in New York who had been in her dancing classes and her church on Sundays. James was dangerous-looking, with his darkly burned face and the hard muscles of his forearms and neck. But when he looked at her and his golden eyes darkened and his wide mouth smiled, he was no longer frightening, and she wanted to touch his face and ask him about the faint white scar on his brow.

"Yes, miss. I think Jolly is a good name for a horse. Sultan is a ruler's name, not a friend's." He drew a deep breath. "I would much appreciate to see your horse, Miss Phillipa."

She wanted to kiss him. The delicious thought flooded her completely, so she did not see the figure approaching them from the side. She did not recognize the long strides of her father, Captain Murdoch Stockbridge.

Jim Henry did not hear the sound of the whip before it struck him across the shoulders. He lurched forward and put out a hand for balance; his hand slid down Miss Phillipa's shoulder and grazed her breast, and he jerked back. When the whip struck again, he drew his own knife and whirled around in defense.

He reached for Phillipa, to protect her, but she ran to the man and put a hand on his raised arm and began talking. "Why, Papa, he's a friend! He wouldn't hurt me. He likes horses, Papa, and I was going to show him Jolly."

Anger deafened Jim Henry; this man would kill him if he could. Then Phillipa's voice pleaded and begged, and the whip was lowered. She turned to him, and Jim Henry heard his name spoken as she talked, and he nodded and put his knife away. She wanted him to meet this man, and he would try to oblige her.

But the officer held Phillipa by the wrist and stared into Jim Henry's face. His words were harsh, threatening. Jim Henry was to leave the fort and not return. Ever. Jim Henry was to make no attempt to meet with Miss Phillipa.

Jim Henry was to stay away from the captain's daughter. That was an order, enforced by the pistol at the captain's side, the men gathering near the garden, and the fear in Miss Phillipa's eyes.

He walked until he came to a corral fence. He walked in the company of anger and humiliation. He stood at the rough wooden rails, and his senses returned when the cream pony came up to sniff at his fingers.

Then hunger rattled his belly, and he patted through his pockets for change, until he remembered Limm saying he would take care of the few pesos they had. The need to find Limm and ask for a handout fueled the anger, added to the humiliation. He worked a man's day, he deserved his own wage.

Anger stirred up too many painful thoughts, all of them swirling close to the surface. He shoved them back down in the need to find Limm Tyler. Then he would try to sleep. He slapped the fence rail, and the cream ducked and ran. At least he knew Limm hadn't ridden out; the cream settled next to the patient bay, and the two ponies watched for his next move.

Light showed under the crude door; maybe Limm was

inside with a pot of beans and some tortillas. Or a bowl of thick stew and biscuits. Jim Henry was hungry, and it was getting late. He lifted the rawhide latch.

One step inside and his foot hit an empty bottle. Limm Tyler was here all right. The man's pants were hooked to a whittled peg in the wall, a belt and knife sheath hung from another peg; a hat and a pair of ladies' high-topped boots sat at the end of the bed. A lone table held a candle burned down to the nub, and its thin flame trembled over the figures of Limm Tyler and a woman.

The powdered face peered at him over Tyler's back. The rope bedsprings groaned as Tyler's buttocks pumped into the flesh lying under him.

Jim Henry stood and watched until it was too much for him. He could not stop his cry; Tyler's head came up at the sounds, his eyes hot and unfocused. Jim Henry turned away, so he did not see the woman reach between her belly and Tyler's haunches and work her fingers until Tyler returned to her and renewed his assault on her body. The woman paid little attention to Tyler then; she smiled at Jim Henry with greedy eyes. He waited too long, took a long look at Tyler and the grinning female under him, and finally pushed himself back through the door to the clarity of the night sky.

The hunger bit hard as he walked back to the spring and sat under the big tree. It was late now, the fort was dark. He could sit and watch the shadows of the barracks, the shapes of the houses. No one would know he was there.

His belly growled, and he drank from the spring. Then he rolled on his back and watched the stars. When his thinking began to drift dangerously, he pounded his fists in the dirt and choked on the emerging memories.

He would not remember his own hand slipping across the girl's breast and the sight of Tyler's ugly buttocks slamming into the woman's body; he would not let what he felt for the girl mix with the impulse that had held him in the doorway much too long. He turned the anger on himself, and when he did sleep for brief periods of time, he woke quickly, drenched in his own sweat. Tyler had betrayed him as he had betrayed himself and the girl. At last he gave up and slept more than an hour, then woke at false dawn and watched the sky change.

He came down to the office and pounded on the door long before Limm Tyler was moving. He wanted to get out of Fort Davis, but Tyler wanted breakfast and a shot of hard liquor for his head before he left town. As usual, Tyler's logic won out.

It came to Jim Henry when they reached the compound gate that he could not look at Rosa Ignacio without seeing the pasty skin and leering eyes of the woman Tyler had covered. So he could not accept Rosa's greeting, or her touch, and he took the horses to the corrals, spent a long time grooming them before he went inside the hut. Supper was waiting, a plate of something steaming, a wooden spoon laid out on the table.

He couldn't stay in the hut after the stubborn silence of the meal. He heard the muffled grunts, the patterned squeal of the rope bed. It was too much to think on, the sounds carried too heavy a load of shame. He went back to the now roofless shed where he had spent his first months after the massacre. It was quiet and separate, and he lay on the hard ground, surrounded by the melting adobe walls of the shed, blanketed by the shifting stars, and he thought only of how to rework the roof and where he had seen a bed and how he could fill up the frame with straw.

In the morning, he went to John Spencer and asked for his wages. "Mr. Spencer, I figure you to start paying me. Been doing a man's work last few years. You pay, and I'll work. That's fair."

John Spencer pushed back from the table. The young cock; he'd wondered when it would come to this. Took him long enough—too long, Spencer thought. But then he'd missed the mark often on this one, right from the beginning.

He studied the young rooster for some time. And began to put it together. Tyler had told him this morning that the kid had moved out last night. Tyler had a big, leftover grin but said he didn't know what had got into the kid. Had himself a good time, so Tyler told Spencer.

Spencer stared at the kid. The boy'd grown well. Couldn't guess his age, but the height was easy. Almost to six feet and would finish out over the top. And tough, skinny, and hard-muscled. Spencer'd seen him wrestling a mule too stubborn for doctoring. The kid was a worker, worth every penny of a man's wage.

"All right with me, boy. Got to move cattle to the fort on a regular basis. They like their beef every day, God bless 'em. Tyler says you're a good hand with the stock, so you do your work, I'll pay. I ain't put in all this time to have you run out on me now. You owe me, *comprende*?"

That was all from John Spencer. He looked again at the kid and shook his head. The kid was tough, but he was still a kid.

Without thinking much, Jim Henry went looking for Limm. In the past, he would have sat on the top rail of the corral fence and traded an insult or two, then told him the good news about his wages. Limm would stop his work on a spooky horse and grin at him and hand back the same insult.

It was different today. Jim Henry sat on the fence and watched Limm and didn't say much. He didn't want to share his news. He didn't know why. It wasn't that Limm had changed. Jim Henry knew the man was a constant: the wide shoulders and bowed legs, the thick arms and stubby hands. The black hair had grayed some, but it was still unruly and clubbed at the base of Limm's neck with a strip of rawhide. Even with his back to him, Jim Henry could see the man's face—broad and ruddy, with the bright blue eyes embedded deep under heavy brows. The same man he'd always known. Even the same worn shirt and frayed pants. Limm Tyler had little vanity.

He was a good man. Robert McCraw had trusted him. And Ma, Jim Henry's fading mother, had sat and talked with him, even let him play with Benny. He remembered all that, but there was a new side to Limm that kept Jim Henry quiet.

He watched Limm work the bronc, and he thought about talking to him. No, there was nothing different in Limm; the change was in Jim Henry. He would not go to Limm again, he would not trust him, or Rosa Ignacio. What he did not fully understand was why.

* * *

Jim Henry spent his nights in a fever of reading. Spencer had brought in books from the town of Franklin, upriver. And Jim Henry himself had ridden up to Leaton's Fort, borrowed a children's primer and a book of numbers from Leaton's widow, Mrs. Hall. He spent his nights figuring and guessing and making the sounds out loud until he exhausted himself trying to understand. Then, if he still couldn't sleep, he walked through the compound.

When the compound was quiet, when his legs ached from walking and his eyes were blurred and sore, Jim Henry lay down on the hard straw bed. There were nights he lay outside on a folded blanket, staring blindly at the sky. It felt as if he never slept, but the dreams that rose with him from the damp bed in the morning told him there were times when his eyes shut and he rolled in restless slumber.

The dreams were constant: a faceless Indian with a blood-red heart open in his chest rode beside Jim Henry. Other faces turned to him when he rode through the deserted fort, faces that drifted in black air without a yielding body. Sometimes there was a girl who rode a dark cavalry charger and raced through him without recognition. Then there were other times, when the same girl lay under countless men and they pumped into her flesh for countless hours. Her hands held piled coin, her eyes held to Jim Henry's heart.

He faced sleep when it wore him down, and he welcomed the early light and the endless, mindless work.

CHAPTER 2

"**H**IE, EYYAH, GET that brockle son. Hie, he's quitting, bring in the pie-faced, get going, all you ball-less mothers' sons!"

The herd took shape slowly behind the lead steer, a mottled giant that dipped and swung its horns in a deliberate rhythm. Jim Henry rode drag, separate from the vaqueros, his nose and mouth covered with a dulled cotton square. Two strides to his right, clear of the hanging dust, was a new rider.

He gave his name as Thomas Hapgood Railsford, and when the pronunciation of his Christian name quickly became Tomás, he grinned and said to call him Hap like his pa did. He was dark-haired and dark-eyed and smiled easily. He could be another Mex from across the river, but his drawl was southern, and he carried a natural arrogance to his walk and his speech. He talked a lot, like old Limm Tyler.

Jim Henry patted the neck of the coyoto bay, Limm Tyler's best horse. Tyler was back at Spencer's Rancho, laid out and hurting from a shattered leg. Three days past his twentieth birthday, Jim Henry was taking Tyler's place.

There was little left of the frightened child of nine years ago for the buried parents to recognize. The white-blond hair and lively eyes had darkened in time. The hair was streaked by the Texas sun, the eyes lost in protective webbing. A hard child who was years past his age, distant from those around him. His parents would have mourned their lost child and not understood the man.

The new rider signed on to work for John Spencer had no previous experience, so he talked at Jim Henry and watched and kept talking: "I did hear you were an unfriendly sort,

30

but I didn't pay those boys no mind. Figured you was lonesome for your own kind.

"So how do, Mr. James McCraw, my name is Thomas Hapgood Railsford if you ain't been listening, and you can call me Hap like my pa done called me."

The string of words broke a long drought for Jim Henry. He couldn't rein in the grin or the lift of his spirit as the newcomer pushed his flea-bitten gray almost to Jim Henry's knee.

Hap Railsford took the grin for introduction and acceptance. "Well, by God, you *can* move that leather skin into a sort of human face! I would have took bets you couldn't, but no one would give odds. Nice to make your acquaintance, Jim Henry McCraw."

The words blew past, but the hand stuck across the saddle was an old gesture, a commitment Jim Henry wasn't comfortable with. He thought to knee Tyler's coyoto bay sideways, but something in the other man's eyes told him the speckled gray would follow and the hand would still be waiting.

"Yes."

Jim Henry nodded to the short word he spoke and pumped the hand once, then moved from the closeness of the gray to chouse a reluctant steer with its eye on a particular clump of sideways grass. Hap was there when the brindle thought to protest with a wide sweep of horns that backed both horses from the threat. Hap's reata flicked a puff of dust from the mottled rump, and the steer bellowed before loping back to the moving herd.

"Thanks, mister. I could've done that."

"Well, Jim Henry. There's lots you can do by yourself, but there ain't always a need or a reason to be alone. Why, that steer could've decided to up and eat your bay friend, and you two ain't no match for that fire-eating brindle when he gets mad. Good Lord, man, ain't you ever thought to ask for a bigger mount? Your legs are about to that one's knees, and at a run you must be playing catch-up with the ground. You hit a corner fast and you'll be coming up without a foot. I think ol' Spencer, he needs to take another look at you, my friend. Maybe you growed some the past year. It sure enough ain't safe to mount you so bad. He forgets you ain't a Mex, he forgets you got some leg to you, could walk down the devil if you had the mind. Yessir, Jim Henry, how do.''

Jim Henry felt his smile dim, and he tightened in the saddle. The restless bay he rode humped against his weight, and he thought of Limm Tyler. It was Limm's horse he rode, Limm's place he took. And a stranger now tried to draw him in to talking when he didn't want to. The coyoto bay's edginess got into Jim Henry, and he whirled the little horse, slapped the dusty neck hard, and wanted to choke the speaker of all those words into silence.

He was pulled back into the day's brightness by more of Railsford's mocking words, and this time he began to listen closely.

''Well now, Jim Henry McCraw. You come back and stand that bay quiet, and you listen. Esequiel told you some time back to ride up a draw we passed, check it through for strays. Now, I could let you ride on through them orders, but that Esequiel, he might get prickly about you not doing his word, and, well, we shook hands, so I would be obliged to take up your cause, and there could be harsh words and some worse come of your not listening.

'' 'Sides, I heard you was a good hand, and I wants to see what makes these hombres think such a thought. So it'd be best we was to ride back and check in that draw. Sure enough would please the big boss, and Esequiel himself.''

This time 'round Jim Henry listened to the man, and he swung Tyler's good bay horse back on his hocks in a quick turn. He thought he heard a whistle as the other man reined his own pony around and caught up to him at a fast lope.

The narrow draw showed fresh tracks, the wide-cleft print of range cattle. At least two steers had hustled themselves into hiding up a ways, and Jim Henry shook out his reata while he settled the bay to an edgy walk. Hap opened his mouth once to talk, but Jim Henry put up a cautioning finger, and the windy man had the sense to keep still.

The bay walked carefully, long ears flopping in concert with the four beats of his walk. Jim Henry tightened his butt and thighs, to raise himself from the pony's back; he was going to be prepared for almost anything that could be ahead.

The narrow draw, striated years back by a hard run of spring rain, had twisted mesquite and slow, stunted piñon woven through its sandy soil. The path of the steers was easy to read, marked by fresh-turned earth and broken branches.

As if he could smell the rank scent, Jim Henry knew what was ahead. He patted the bay's neck to steady him, then signaled for Hap to come up. The savvy horse's ears came almost to a point as the bay blew softly through wide nostrils. Jim Henry started to tell Hap what was coming, when the new man drove in his spurs and chased his gray forward, pushing past Jim Henry to tear up the draw.

A black-spotted steer charged from the darkness of a pin oak thicket as the gray flashed by. The steer headed down the wash, tipped horns wider than the small bay gelding. The bay leaped up the embankment to avoid the slashing head and lost purchase in the loose sand. He went to his knees, muzzle buried in the banking. Jim Henry leaned uphill, holding his mount with sheer will and a hard hand. He steadied the gelding with a touch on the rigid muscle in front of the saddle, then heard a raucous yell that sent another steer, a blue roan with one horn tipped down, out of the dense brush.

The bay shook violently as the blue steer raced past. Then there was another yell, a wilder, more strident sound that chilled the blood. Jim Henry wrenched the bay's head downhill and slammed in the spurs as the horse jumped into air and hit the floor of the dry wash at a full run. Horse and rider doubled around a bent oak, and Jim Henry's boot toe shoveled sand. The bay straightened out and ran.

Hap was down. The gray was mired hock deep in powdered clay, struggling to get free. Hap lay on his side, arms waving overhead, the rawhide reata twenty feet out of reach. A white steer lowered its head and dug one hoof into the light clay, covering itself with a soft cloud. The animal dropped its head and bellowed.

Jim Henry never let the bay slow; they ran straight at the steer. Inches from the horns, he kneed the horse hard right, and as they slipped past, Jim Henry spanked the wet black nose with the coiled reata. The bay reared against his rider's hand and spun as he came down, racing back past Hap and the still-struggling gray, down the narrow draw.

The white steer took the challenge. Jim Henry leaned over the bay's neck and prayed as the horse dodged grasping piñon limbs and jumped exposed humps of root and sharp rock. He could hear the white steer's bellowing and clamped his legs hard to the bay's sides, riding a mad gallop with his hands and seat. The trio burst out onto flat ground, scattering herd stragglers before them. The white steer lost his quarry in the confusion of cattle and wildly cheering vaqueros and, bewildered, found a place in the long line of cattle as it lumbered into a trot.

Jim Henry brought the coyoto bay to a stand. He dismounted slowly and walked around the small gelding, hands searching the soaked hide for damage. The horse blew wildly and dropped its head. Jim Henry did not listen to the catcalls that came from the milling riders. When his searching hand found a stickiness, he looked closely at the red line across the dirty rump. The white steer had been that close to catching them. He patted the wet neck and drew the pony's head to his hands, scratching under the animal's jaw as partial payment.

"Well now, James Henry McCraw. I was told you were good with the stock, but I swear I never seen a man herd a steer like you just done. By God, that's a surefire way to roust them cattle from where they got no right to be! You get them running after you, and they forget all about wanting to hide and save their own skins. That's a good idea, Jim Henry. Kind of hard on my heart, though. Leaves it sitting in my mouth."

At the fresh round of laughter and rapid sallies, Jim Henry felt the familiar flush start at his neck and cover his face. He fought to act calm, then looked up to the wide face of Hap Railsford, a smart comment sitting in his mouth, waiting for the man to speak and give him room.

"Jim Henry, I owe you. That ghost steer was heading for my lights."

The voice was out of character, gentle and low, carrying no mocking humor or sharp bite to it. Jim Henry took a long look at the man who came by the name of Hap and saw a genuine liking in the face, a real try at a thank-you. The anger building in him dissolved, and he turned away, mumbling words he was not much on using.

" 'S all right, Hap. You'd do the same for me."

He was relieved Hap didn't ask him to repeat the softly spoken words. A hand came down to rest briefly on his shoulder, and then Jim Henry heard the now pleasant nonsense begin again.

"Well, by God, we better get back to riding behind these critters. Don't want no more of them heading south when they got to trail north. I got to see this Fort Davis. Heard a lot about it down to Mexico, and it sounds like my kind of place. Yessir.

"You coming along, Jim Henry, or you planning to pat that pony all night?"

It wasn't until the outriders saw the tent structures of Fort Davis that they could relax their guard and resheathe their rifles. The cattle herded easily into the big pens, and the vaqueros no longer had to keep one eye on ridges and trees. The Indians would not attack this close to the army.

And it wasn't until the last of the steers was penned that Jim Henry thought about the fact of Fort Davis. He no longer had to hate and fear the fort's presence; a friend rode beside him. Twice in the past two years he had ridden to Fort Davis, both times alone, both times running from the Indians and desperate to see a glimpse of the girl. This time he would not have to ride to the small spring and wait with tired hope. This time he was spared his lonely vigil. He could see her face, smell the sweetness of her skin, feel her hand small and slender in his.

And he could still hear her father's words. He shuddered as the memory of the captain's whip rose above him.

This time he had a friend, this time he would not be alone.

Hap Railsford brought his flea-bitten gray up to Tyler's coyoto bay. He slapped a gloved hand on his own thigh and sighed mightily. "Jim Henry, you know we got time to see the sights of this here town. A lot to see, kid, and not much time. You follow me, we'll see it all."

CHAPTER 3

T HE SMALL COLLECTION of tents and buildings swirled with crowds. Voices raised, hands clenched around pistols, knives loosely sheathed in belts, eyes bright and angry, groups of people clustered in front of printed papers nailed to anything that would hold them. Posters could be seen all through the growing settlement, printed with florid headlines and proclaiming their theses in smaller-lettered lines. Hap drove his feisty gray into a gathering, and Jim Henry couldn't hear his voice above the excitement. Then Hap reappeared at his side, holding one of the long sheets of paper, a hole torn through the top.

"Well, look at this, Jim Henry. We got us some fussing in the government, I do believe. This gentleman says right here in black print that there ain't no way the government's going to deny a state's right to keep slaves. Why, I do believe there's folks all over worked up with such a declaration. We glad we ain't back east or up in them cold-hearted Northern states. They's trying to take away the right of each state to declare itself."

The cheerful voice turned sour, and Jim Henry looked sideways at Hap. The man had a dark look to him, and the gray gelding half reared from the force of the bit in angry hands.

"Well, Jim Henry. I didn't figure this particular crowd cared if they got to read the gentleman's words or not, so I brought 'em along for us to go over when we got time. But, now I know you some, I bet you ain't got a political thought in your head. You got a stake in all this, boy. You can damn well bet on it. You listen to me and learn.

"The army up here is a blue army, right out of federal

orders. And most of the men out here in this godforsaken town is Texas and Southern men, and spoiling for a fight. So it seems to me that Northern army will be moved out if this all comes to war.''

A sly look stole into the cheerful face, and Hap held his legs to the gray, readying to fly if his words struck anything touchy. ''Now, if I understand from the word around the compound, you got you a reason for wanting them blue-backed boys to stay on, most especially the pa of this one pretty girl. I don't know, Jim Henry. I think you might want to do some reading and come political real fast.''

Jim Henry was only half listening to the words, more interested in the movement of the crowd; it took him a beat of silence to understand what Hap was saying. Then his head came up fast, and a deep anger ran through him.

''Who the hell . . . what you trying to say, Hap?''

He was betrayed, by someone who talked too much and by the buried depth of his feelings. He pushed the tired bay closer to the gray, and Hap backed the horse to Jim Henry's advance.

''Now, boy, you got to understand. I bet you never did understand. There's folks back to the rancho worry about you even if you pulled away from them. Don't fool yourself to thinking you been living alone, boy. You been right in the middle of a family, Jim Henry, and there's some who still care. Don't know why myself, riding up here with you and talking at you for days, don't figure why they still care. But then again, you ain't a murderer so far as I know. Only got one Indian to your credit. And you ride a horse fine, got you a strange way of herding cattle, but you'll do, boy. You'll do.''

Hap had the sense finally to let the talking fall away as he watched the old hardness in Jim Henry's eyes relax for once into the look of a young man. Hap shook his head. The gray horse settled to a quiet walk, the bay willing to lay behind, its steps shortened by the long weight of its rider.

''Now, boy, I got me a mind to have a drink of whiskey. Seeing you is the way you is, I can let you keep an eye to my back. I'll have me a drink or two, and you can set with a

soda bottle and sip and watch. It could turn out to be kind
of fun, boy. What you say?"

There it was again, a knowledge about him and his habits
that couldn't come from the drive to Fort Davis. Hap Railsford knew too much, but the grinning offer of friendship that
was in the blocky face, and the constant cheer of the windy
talking soothed Jim Henry. It took him time to come to an
answer, and the two horses slowed to walk side by side.
Finally Jim Henry spoke his piece: "We best put the horses
up to the pens. They earned a rest. It'll give you a better
evening, Hap—knowing your horse is fed and your fancy rig
is out of temptation."

Hap appreciated Jim Henry's speech—it was a lot of thinking out loud for the boy. He watched Jim Henry rein the bay
abruptly down an alley, and he had something quick and
bright to say to the retreating back, but he thought better of
the smart words and followed Jim Henry in unaccustomed
silence.

True to Hap's prediction, Jim Henry found him a corner of
the rude tent that served as a saloon and general emporium.
There were crude stools if a man needed to sit, and Jim
Henry dragged one to a corner near the wood stove. Fort
Davis was high in the mountains, and come winter it could
be cold. But a cavernous tent holding drunken men created
its own source of heat, and tonight the stove was cold to the
touch. Jim Henry rested his soda on its surface and sat to
watch Hap and the evening performance.

The antics of the drinkers soon bored him, and he wasn't
ready for the two dry-mouthed soldiers who were angered by
Hap's rising volume of words, and cornered him with
clenched fists. They were whey-faced men, sullen-mannered,
low on the military ranking system. Northerners from their
unintelligible speech, soaked in the concept that there could
be no slaves in the glory of the United States.

Hap didn't agree with them and their sour talk, and he
gave them all the reasons. Why slaves were a necessity for
planting large crops, why white folk held a natural superiority over those brought here to do the work, and over the
Mexes and their mongrel blood. Heads came up at that one,

but the few dark-skinned men in the tent finished their drinks and left quickly.

Jim Henry listened to the fancy flow of words and was spellbound by his new friend's manner. Hap knew more than Jim Henry ever thought to figure out, all the reasons and philosophies and long-winded words that said the same thing over and over.

Hap got back to the Mexes soon enough and how they was inferior to the natural rulers of this new country. Then he went off again into states' rights and the sovereign power given to each state to protect its own destiny. But he forgot his audience and stayed with the Mexes a little too long. Men standing to the bar eyed him with a growing suspicion, and the two Northern boys had brought in reserves. There were four of them now, and still Hap kept talking.

When he'd first met Hap, Jim Henry had the same notion that was now circling the canvas room. Hap's coal-black, shiny hair, his dark eyes and sun-tanned color, his wide, stocky build . . . He talked too much of the Mex's inferiority, and he stood there looking like a chili eater himself.

The way Hap kept repeating his words got under Jim Henry's skin and stirred up uneasy feelings. Back in his mind was a sense of betrayal from Ramón and Patricio, and most of all Jesús—all mixed in with a dying mother and a raging pa, a small brother's lifeless body. Jim Henry hadn't ever consciously connected the feelings before, but something fitted in from the harsh words said to the gathering company. A fire was lit in him at the treachery shown his family by the men who were there to protect them.

But Hap weren't a Mex, Hap weren't a black nigger. He was a friend, come up on the trail with a herd, come for adventure in the desert lands. And now he was standing up to a room full of men and the Northern scum, telling folks how things ought to be in the great land of Texas.

The attack came with little warning, but Jim Henry was moving when the butt end of an army-issue pistol slammed into his friend. Hap went down without a sound, in a boneless sprawl at the foot of his attackers. There was a moment of stunned silence, then one of the Northern boys spoke his piece: "That's what loud-mouthed traitors deserve, that's what—"

The fool never finished; Jim Henry caught him from behind and wrapped his arms around the man's chest, and they crashed into the canvas wall. He pounded the man's head on the dirt-packed floor, then reared back like a bitted horse, came up from the floor, and swung around into the fist of the downed man's buddy.

Arms flailing, Jim Henry went stumbling backward, found his footing, and rushed forward to whoever was waiting. He reached his man with an arm-twisting hug, and they pounded on each other's backs, rolling and sliding in the churned footing. Jim Henry had rarely fought, but he had watched. He drew his knee up into the man's crotch, and the crushing arms around him let go instantly. Jim Henry stepped back and let the man sink to his knees and then curl up in a pained ball.

Too raw to stay alert, Jim Henry turned his head into the misjudged arc of a cut of firewood that grazed his temple and thumped him on the breastbone. Stunned, he fell on his attacker, who held him for a moment and then pushed him away. Jim Henry stumbled to his knees, then another blow from somewhere flattened him to the dirt floor.

When he opened his eyes, he found Hap's face inches from his line of sight. Before he could decide if Hap was dead, one eye opened, the lid fluttered briefly, closed again, then finally opened wide. The pupil shuttered to a narrow point, the bloodied lips pulled together. Hap stirred enough to spit out a mouthful of sawdust. "Well, Jim Henry, did we beat the sorry bastards?"

Jim Henry coughed and choked. Win? They hadn't come close enough to raise a dust cloud! He rolled his head away, found his legs under him. He could see past the forest of mule-hide boots to a group of blue legs with the yellow stripe down the outside. He counted carefully, adding blue legs and dividing by two. Lessons from Ma, useful lying on a dirt floor in the swill of spilled whiskey. Not what his ma would expect of him.

He found his knees under him, raised his chest on bent

elbows, and lifted himself enough to see the entire tent. A disinterested drover saw him, and as he stood slowly, the man grinned and raised a half-empty glass in mocking salute. As Jim Henry moved on unsteady legs, the drover went back to his drinking. The message was clear: There would be no interference, or help.

Three of them, backs to him, heads bent to the seriousness of whiskey. He needed an ally; the same stick of firewood that had brought him down. It had a knob at one end, rust-colored and sticky to the touch. Jim Henry hefted the wood and touched his own head. He looked at his stained fingertips and the darkened wood.

It was only three long strides, hand raised with the weapon, a hard downward swing on the unsuspecting head of the soldier. Jim Henry felt a deep satisfaction as the man went down, but he did not have time to admire his handiwork. The two soldiers came at him, heads tucked into raised shoulders, hands fisted, feet moving quickly. Jim Henry took the left soldier and ducked as the first came for him. He shifted the stick and drove it sharp-end into the man's belly. His answer was a deep grunt and a belch of whiskey-soured breath.

The stick moved by itself, carrying Jim Henry with it, and a ham-size fist caught him at the base of his neck and dropped him back to his knees. Jim Henry held to the knobbed stick and gasped.

A boot caught his ribs, and another blow to his shoulders drove him to the floor. Then he heard harsh words above him, and there was a moment with no attack. He rolled over, knuckles scoured on the graveled dirt as he clung to the stick. He came up to find a soldier shaking free of two grinning teamsters. He had time to nod his thanks, and one of the men nodded at him.

"You doing a good job on these boys, son," he said. "You just need more practice. Wanted to give you an even chance."

There was a lull as the soldier shook himself and settled his feet wide apart. Jim Henry could see a body stirring on the floor, rolling into a corner, where a thoughtful onlooker shoved it out of harm. The gut-bellied man was partially erect, face deadly pale, hands shaking. The odds were getting better.

Jim Henry doubled his fist around the stick and drove it again into the man's gut. He heard the grunt as the man went down, and he raised the stick to the third soldier and swung. The man ducked easily, and the stick broke on a tent pole. Jim Henry felt a rusty fear in his mouth as the crouched soldier drew a knife and wove a small circle with the blade. He went for his own knife and found nothing in the sheath. He spread his arms wide, palms up, to let the man know he was unarmed. The man grinned and took a step forward.

The gut-bellied soldier found his legs and stood carefully; the snap of leather as he pulled the pistol free sounded loud in the quiet tent. And the remaining soldier, eyes blurred, hefted a new piece of firewood and watched Jim Henry's face. He was ringed by the angry men, surrounded by their willingness to fight.

"That's it—all of you. Boy, you get your friend and make tracks out of here. Leave the rest of us to drink in peace. Soldier boys, you're setting up for trouble if you kill this here kid. He ain't nothing but a raw boy, and the three of you's armed for bear. Look around you, you ain't got a chance."

Jim Henry lifted his gaze from his attackers and looked to the man who spoke the quiet words. He stood behind the bar with a very efficient shotgun in his large hands. Each man in the room who had chosen earlier to stay out of the fight now had a hand resting on a weapon of sorts. The drinking tent was primed; Jim Henry felt like a newborn bear cub at a Sunday picnic.

Two men had Hap suspended between them. Hap's dark eyes were almost in focus and his head was raised, but the feet had no connection yet to the stocky body. When the men let him go, Hap would have fallen if Jim Henry had not been there.

But Hap's grin was in place. His right foot dragged as they crossed the dirt floor and left a trail, but he still had a wicked grin. Jim Henry had to stop and get a better hold on his friend. The third soldier was close, and while Jim Henry struggled, he caught the edge of the low-voiced threat.

"This ain't over yet, kid. Not for either of you. No one brings me down in front of my men. I'll get to you again, you count on it as a fact."

Jim Henry shook his head at the words. The face of the man disappeared as the immediate necessity of getting outside with his burden became the focus of his efforts. Threats didn't matter; getting free now was more important.

Outside, he took a deep breath of clean air. Towns weren't for him, not towns like this one. Towns with brawling soldiers and canvas saloons and aching heads. But he still had to do something with Hap. The man hung in Jim Henry's arms like a slaughtered calf, legs useless, eyes closed again, sour air pumping in and out of him too slowly, too raggedly. Jim Henry didn't like the feel of Hap's weight at all.

He half dragged the injured man to the small building that was part of John Spencer's cattle pens. There was a cot to the back of the room, its blankets rumpled and smelling of wet wool and old sweat. The unwanted picture of Limm Tyler and the woman underneath him came and went through Jim Henry's mind as he rolled Hap onto the traitorous bunk and pulled the rotted blanket over him.

There was a slat bucket in a corner. Jim Henry took it outside and pumped icy water into it for more than five minutes before he filled it half-full and brought it back inside. There was nothing to use for a cloth, so he pulled out the tail of Hap's ruined shirt and tore off a corner.

He used the cloth to wipe at the blood and dirt crusted on Hap's gray face. His stomach lurched when he exposed the serrated flesh and white bone, but finally it was done. He folded the cloth twice and soaked it in fresh water, then laid it on the wound, pressing gently to stop the oozing blood.

That done, he leaned back and closed his own eyes and let time slip away from him. He slept uncomfortably, until his head jerked and his eyes flew open. The damp cloth slid from Hap's face, and the gummed eyes opened in spasms. Hap watched him and then started to talk. His voice was soft, and Jim Henry had to lean down to hear him.

"We got them sons, didn't we, Jim Henry? We whipped them bastards all to hell. You tell me that, Jim Henry. You tell me we whipped them bastards all to hell."

Hap Railsford was a dreamer, but Jim Henry didn't want to disappoint him. "You be quiet, Hap. You stay still. Yeah, you could say we whipped them sons. We got out alive, and they's nursing some good bruises. We most likely whipped 'em, Hap.''

"That's good, boy. Won't feel right, lose to a bunch of Northern boys. We got to them, that's what counts.''

Hap's eyes closed, and this time his sleeping was more peaceful, his breathing close to regular. Jim Henry propped himself in a corner, laid his head back on the cool adobe wall, and slept in jerky, half-wild bouts of unconsciousness until morning.

CHAPTER 4

"**S**HE MUST BE pretty, Jim Henry, real pretty."

The soft words came to Jim Henry as he went to empty the wooden bucket of its smelly contents. He left the bucket outside the door and stood for a moment before going back in. He was careful as he headed to the cot; quick anger had to be ridden with a tight rein.

"What you saying, Hap?"

"Nothing else would keep you here this long but the chance of meeting her—the pretty girl, I mean. Tyler told me . . ."

The anger in him soured at the mention of Tyler's name; the wound opened deeper. The raging face of Phillipa's father had stayed with him day and night, the sense of her walking beside him never left. Tyler had no right.

"Ain't his business to talk of such. He don't know nothing. And what you mean, I stayed here only because of her?"

The betrayal stung him. He'd stayed the two days and nights because Hap couldn't ride, couldn't even get to the backhouse by himself. He'd sat awake most of the time, fearful that Hap would roll off the narrow cot in his restless, talky sleep, that he would reopen the head wound and do himself more damage. There had been no time to visit anyone, nor had anyone paid them the slightest notice. The vaqueros had ridden out yesterday morning, complaining of swollen heads, bragging of the whiskey drunk, the señoritas pleasured. No one had come to check on Hap or Jim Henry, no one had thought to bring food or medicine or a few pesos. The damned Mexes, the damned, unfeeling sons.

Jim Henry had stayed to take care of an injured friend and to let his own aches do some healing, not to catch a glimpse of a pretty girl on a dark cavalry charger. He had thought of going out early in the morning, before true dawn, to stand near the spring until reveille blew and shadows began to move around the horse corrals and the long buildings. But he hadn't gone; he couldn't leave Hap alone.

They'd both slept most of the first day, then Jim Henry woke to coming dusk and paid a small boy a hard-earned dollar to bring soup, a half loaf of bread, and a pot of coffee to the small cabin. The meager vittles had been enough to sustain him, and he'd managed to get some of the soup broth down Hap by soaking chunks of the coarse bread and holding them to Hap's mouth, letting him suck on its nourishment.

Now he was accused of staying for reasons other than Hap and his injury. The accusation bruised Jim Henry deeper than the knobbed stick of firewood. He fed the pain, stuck it in with a list of injustices, and the ache in him grew.

"Hap, you're wrong. . . ."

"Ah, to hell with it, boy. I feel well enough to perfect now. 'Course I ain't tried standing yet. But I'm willing to bet we can ride out today." He struggled up onto his elbows and grinned at his nurse. Then he made as if to swing his legs over the side, and it took only the beginning of that thought to roll a spasm through him he couldn't hide and a low gasp of pain to accompany it.

"Well now, goddammit, boy, maybe we best wait till tomorrow. You got any more of that soup? I'm tired to beat all hell. Jim Henry . . ." Hap laid his body back down very slowly, face paling, mouth a thin line. His words were barely recognizable, but Jim Henry had gotten used to their flow and could fill in the gaps. Then Hap was asleep, one hand hanging over the low side of the bed.

Jim Henry was gone only a short while, returning with a steaming bowl of thin stew and another half loaf of the bread. Hap was able to sit up enough to eat the dipped chunks. Color flushed to his face, and he tried for another grin.

"Guess it'll be tomorrow, Jim Henry. Tomorrow we'll ride out of this god-awful place. Tomorrow."

Hap was asleep then, and Jim Henry stood above him for a moment, listening to the regularity of his breathing. He was past the worst of the head wound; tomorrow sounded good. He felt for the wound at the base of his own skull, and there was little pain to the touch. Then he bent over, drew in a deep breath, and exhaled before he straightened up. The beatings had settled out; both he and Hap would survive.

He didn't know that Hap's careless words about a pretty girl were deep inside him. But thoughts rolled and churned in him, thoughts and feelings he knew would drive him crazy. He couldn't stop the dreaming, and he knew the dream was close by. So he tended to the multitude of necessary chores in the hut. He rolled up his meager bed, rinsed out the slop bucket and placed it near Hap, shook out the torn shirt and scrubbed the bloody stains, left it outside to dry. Quick chores done by practiced hands. Jim Henry was eager to leave the confines of the cabin.

The narrow path took him directly to the spring. The garden that had been raw earth when he first came to the fort was now a seasoned plot of turned ground. Obviously there were competent gardeners in the fort personnel. A compost heap was layered with waste and soil, thin irrigation ditches ran between each row, a crude dam widened the spring pool. The soil had been worked carefully, and Jim Henry could smell the turned richness. He sank to his haunches and leaned on the cottonwood. The restlessness that had driven him from the hut held him still now. He had no hope of seeing her, yet anticipation unnerved him. He half closed his eyes in memory.

He must have slept, for it was bare light from a half moon that woke him—a moon that glistened over the dusty army corrals and fluttered in the water of the spring pool. He stood slowly, aware of his stiffened muscles and of the heavy ache in his groin. He remembered now, he had been dreaming of the girl on the flying charger, the girl who had once spoken his name. He blushed at the effect of his dissolving dream; she had come to him at the spring, and they had lain on the soft grass and lived in each other's bodies.

Then Jim Henry turned back in shock: She was standing beside him. Phillipa Stockbridge had materialized from his dream, with her loose hair tangled around her head and her eyes shining in the placid light. He stepped back and shuddered, caught between his sleep and reality.

But this time she was real; he caught her scent, inhaled the sweetness of flowers and fresh herbs. His head ached violently, his body pounded with the pulse of his wrist and groin. She was real, she was standing in front of him. He knew better, but he wanted to reach out and touch her.

Instead, he spoke, and his words were harsh, designed to drive her away: "Miss, your pa'll strap you, he finds you here with me. I ain't forgot, and he ain't likely to, neither." As the words came from his mouth he cursed them for their stupidity. But there was no other way to make her leave. "Miss, you best leave, you be getting us both in trouble." It was for her protection, not for his.

"James, please. My name is Phillipa. Don't you remember my name? Please, tell me you remember."

Phillipa had seen him two days earlier, and she had been instantly certain it was him. So for those two nights she had come to the spring. She knew James would come to her. Two nights, alone and crying, frightened by the howls of the evening beasts; two nights of waiting alone until morning. Then she'd ventured out for one more night; she'd crawled through the bedroom window and hurried to the spring. She knew he would come, she ached to know that he was there.

He was her James for always. In her dreams, in her heart, each day and night, until she knew the world was different. A soldier touched her arm to help her mount a horse, and she thought of James. A man brushed near her in the street, and she remembered James. Nights and vivid dreams were part of James. The ache in her body was for him, and for herself. She did not completely understand, and there was no woman on the fort who could tell her, but the ache was not for her papa or the indistinct soldiers; it was for James.

And now he stood above her and spoke harshly to her and told her to go away from him. Phillipa wished to cry then, but she wished also to be closer to her young man. She had waited and watched this long, she would not give up her anticipated pleasure without fighting.

"Say my name, James. Please. Call me Phillipa so I know that you care."

He was ready to choke on the familiarity of the name, a name he had spoken out loud to himself too many times. A sweetness collected in his throat and behind his eyes as he leaned closer to her, to give what she was asking.

"Phillipa. Phillipa Stockbridge." He saw the words run through her sweet face, and he could not bear the loss. He had to add all of what he felt.

"I love you . . . Phillipa Stockbridge."

He had no choice, the words flooded through him and forced their way past his frozen lips. "I love you."

He was real, standing over her, and the brightness of the unclouded moon revealed him to her. He had filled out in the chest and shoulders and was solid enough so she could rest in the protection of his arms. Phillipa came closer to him. She knew the color of his hair, she had seen him at a distance. It was darker now, and streaked a red bronze, thick and long, lying on his neck and curling around his ears and across his forehead. She wanted to reach up and push the forelock out of his eyes.

The eyes sparked their golden glow. Wide eyes, framed in black; perfect eyes, to add to the perfection of his face and form. Phillipa leaned against him then, overwhelmed by what she saw. And when he cringed under her weight, she stepped back, deeply hurt by the rejection.

"Have I grown so unlovely that you don't want me? Do your words of love mean nothing? Why . . . ?"

Her anguish sharpened the pain in Jim Henry, and he winced from the accusation. But before he could stammer out an excuse for the betrayal of his body, she was talking to him again, guessing at the cause of his distress. She was wrong, but the shared words were immeasurably sweet.

"It's the fight. Sergeant Fletcher told me about the fight. You must still hurt. Oh, James, is there anything I can do to help you, to make you feel better? . . . James?"

Let her believe she knew him this well, then she would not guess at the shameful hardening between his legs from her gentle touch. He had not had a woman yet, but he had seen enough, and he did not want to expose her to a man's dreadful lust. Let her believe his pain was from a fight; it was pleasing to have her worry so.

"I'm all right now, Phillipa. But I got places hurt some. Not bad enough to keep me from sitting with you." It wasn't what he wanted to say, and he cursed himself for the awkward words, but he could speak no other way. She would have to accept his manner as a part of him.

He pushed the dirt under the cottonwood with the edge of his old boots and scraped out a level spot for her. He removed his vest for a pillow and felt the weight of a small bundle that rode in the protection of the inside pocket—a bundle he had carried on all his trips to the fort. A bundle wrapped in smooth white leather and folded to be perfect. For her.

For Phillipa. A necklace inside the white leather that he had fashioned carefully from turquoise beads and crude silver balls that were traded in the compound. A necklace such as the one Rosa Ignacio sometimes wore.

Jim Henry shuddered. He did not want to think of Rosa, and Limm Tyler, and Phillipa all at the same time. Rosa and Limm were animals in their lust; he and Phillipa were different. Pure.

He placed his vest down near the cottonwood as a cushion for her. Phillipa leaned carefully against him, under the protection of his right arm. Her head fitted perfectly at his shoulder, and she could feel the comfort of his bone and muscle. It took Jim Henry several false tries before his hand took her wrist and turned her small white palm up to rest on his knee. Then he placed the white leather pouch in her hand and closed the slender fingers around its treasure.

She would cry if he said anything to her, and it was as if he knew and kept his silence. Phillipa held the pouch in her hand and marveled at its softness. She opened it and pulled out the silver-and-blue beads, strung together on a fine-cut thong of pale leather. The thin moon caught in the silver reflection, and the necklace glowed with its light.

Phillipa looked wordlessly at her James. If she could have seen him clearly, she would have touched the line of tears down his cheek. But she held the small beads in her hand, running them through her fingers and wondering at the perfection of their silver roundness set between the blue. It was a beautiful necklace, the most beautiful present anyone had ever given her.

They sat together for the rest of the night, and when Jim Henry felt the girl's breathing drop and even out to a slow sleep, he reached across with his free hand and brushed the dried tears from his face, wiping the salt dust on his greased leather pants. He had never known such a power of feeling; it filled and flooded him, gave him the strength needed to protect her.

The line of light above the horizon woke both of them. Jim Henry stood first and bent down to raise Phillipa from the cold ground. She came up easily and slid into his embrace as if she had always been there. He knew it was wrong, knew he was asking for too much, but he cupped her face and let her look at him before he kissed her gently. The immediate tension he felt in the girl he put down to a lady's resistance to such an attack, and he let her go, stepped back.

Unbelievably she followed him, stood up close to him and reached for his mouth with her own, pushing her hips against him, holding him in her power. It was a long minute before either of them felt the need for air.

Jim Henry broke the embrace; he was as frightened as he had ever been.

"Miss, uh, Phillipa. We can't do this. Ain't right, your pa, I'm nothing, we got to stay . . ." He couldn't finish any of the thoughts except that he wanted her. She did the tough work for him.

"I want to be with you, James. But we can't. Not here, not now. You'll come back for me, won't you? You'll come back and talk to my papa, and we'll always be together. . . . James?"

He didn't hear all her words, but he felt the pleading and knew its echo inside him. He did love her, he would come back to her, he would gather his courage and talk to her papa, make him know the sense of this, the natural run of feeling. But now he could make out a soldier walking from the barracks below them, could see the morning shadows become full daytime shapes. A whinny drifted up from the corral, smoke rose from different chimneys. She would have to go to her house, to her papa, who hated him so. Jim Henry mistrusted the confusion in his thinking and was glad of the shadows that hid his passion from her. There would be time enough.

"Miss Phillipa, you be sure I'm coming back. Next month and I'll be here again with Mr. Spencer's herd. I'll talk to your papa, maybe then we can—"

A thought he did not finish out of shame, and the terrible ache in his loins. Jim Henry shook his head, hands clenched together in doubled fists. He would not be like Limm Tyler, and his Phillipa was not Rosa Ignacio. They were not like other people, they were lovers to themselves, to no one else. To nothing else.

"I'll be back in a month, Phillipa. I promise you that."

"For someone short on sleeping, you surely are a cheerful cuss this morning, Jim Henry McCraw. Too cheerful, god-dammit. I got me a head like I been going through whiskey, and you know damn well I been doing nothing but lying here on this godforsaken bed. Jim Henry . . . I don't . . . well, hell, boy."

It took Jim Henry awhile to figure out the direction of Hap's vocalizing. The two range horses stood to the far side of the corral, bellies full, eyes bright, ears pricked at the men who came into their territory. The feisty speckled gray half-way reared, ears back, eyes showing a ring of white. Jim Henry found Hap against the railings, then looked back to the pot-bellied bronc. The horse stamped a hoof, raised a cloud of dust.

The short walk from the hut to the pens had taken a toll on Hap. A film of sweat glazed his normally dark face, and gray color pinched the corners of his mouth and painted circles under his eyes. The speckled horse reared again, bolder this time, coming to the center of the corral and waving newly shod feet at the intruders.

Tyler's old bay watched the performance and waited quietly. The bay had years and miles on him, he knew the energy put into such a display was wasted. He watched Jim Henry loop out his catch rope and snake it over the head of the prancing gray. The horse fought briefly, then gave in to his training and stood to Jim Henry's touch.

"Hap, I ain't never rode this horse of yours. You let me give him a try this morning? He's had a day or two of resting and might be kind of fun. That bay of Tyler's, he's no fun to set, just bogs his head once or twice and bellers. Then quits. Don't give much of a fight. You mind I ride out the gray?"

They both knew what Jim Henry was up to, but for once Hap did not have the breath or the gall to spin out his teasing. There was no way he could ride the gray; they both knew that. Hap leaned to a post, pushed deep into his reserves, and brought out a smile, gave his blessing, talking through the blood pounding in his head. This standing upright wasn't all he remembered it to be. Flat out on the bed looked real good to him about now.

"Well now, Jim Henry." He wasted a moment to search his memory, find the right way of speaking. "You think you can saddle that old plow horse o' mine? He ain't much of a ride, but I . . ." Hap lost it then, and looked away from Jim Henry, looked past the worry in his friend's face. Goddamn, he owed Jim Henry a lot.

Wherever the boy'd been last night to dawn, it sure perked him up some. Hap prayed it was a pretty girl, a Mex filly willing to lift her skirt for a peso. That was what Jim Henry needed, not a moon-eyed cavalry brat whose pa had blood in his eye—and his heart.

Damn, but his head hurt. The ride loomed up mean in front of him, and he knew they would be looking at hard traveling, fast moving. Them indios didn't pay much attention to the firepower of two men alone in the *despoblado*. He and Jim Henry'd have to ride hard and long, skirt the easy road, and never leave off checking their back trail.

"You go ahead, Jim Henry. Have you some fun, see if you can get that plow horse to buck. Then your granny can ride it home real easy like." It would be a battle; Hap wished he could see past the bright lights inside his head to watch and enjoy the spectacle.

The gray gelding was real polite about the saddle thrown on his back and cow-kicked at Jim Henry only once, when he bent under the flea-bitten belly to catch the cincha. The gray coughed and farted, snapped his yellow teeth when the strap was pulled tight and the saddle screwed down. The teeth snapped again and got fabric when Jim Henry fitted the bosal to the long skull, and the horse went rigid as the long-legged rider pulled his head around, hand snug in the woven bridle cheek. It was hard for a horse to buck with his head tucked to his shoulder, gave the rider a chance to settle in the saddle before hell came visiting. So the gray was patient as the new rider slipped up on his back. It wouldn't last much longer.

The gray quit waiting when the hand gave him his head, and he set out on his mission. Head curled between front legs, the horse squatted down slowly until his belly grazed the corral floor. There was nothing subtle about the horse; he bellowed once, wagged his head, and came up in a pile of fury to launch himself across the corral. Forelegs pawing air, hind quarters kicking at the hooded stirrups with each leap, the gray rose in a high arc and floated above the ground for a suspended moment in time.

Jim Henry knew what was coming. He leaned into the wiry mane, smelling the deep salted sweat of the furious horse, then whipped the knotted end of the mecate across the horse's neck. The gray came crashing down on bone-hard legs, jarring his rider back and forth with the effort. His head snapped back, his teeth clacked shut; Jim Henry bit down on his tongue and tasted blood. He spanked the gray again, and the little horse stepped into more furious bucking, up and down, hind legs kicking high, front feet straining for height. When Jim Henry raked spurs across the soaked shoulders, the mustang roared in anger. Blinded by insult, he spun in a tight circle, and his mouth closed on Jim Henry's foot, tail lashing with each contorted jump. The corral fence came up too fast, and Jim Henry felt the poles scrape his leg before he could swing free. The gray hit the fence hard enough to stun him and loosen his hold on Jim Henry's foot, but not hard enough to bring him down. The horse staggered and went to his knees, and Jim Henry grunted with the impact.

Then he slapped the gray with the mecate again, dug his outside spur into the flea-bitten side, and the horse leaped up into an uncertain rear that brought an involuntary gasp from the onlooker. Jim Henry felt the horse tilt beneath him, felt the off hind leg that had hit the fence give beneath the horse's weight. He slipped his feet loose and jumped free before the horse came down sideways and was laid flat out on the dirt floor. A dust cloud rose up over the fallen gray as his eyes rolled back in his head; all four hooves moved in a semblance of running, but the little horse was down.

Jim Henry lowered himself to sit on the hard skull below the ears and took his time finding a comfortable spot. Then he extended his long legs, feeling a rush of returned sensation to his right thigh and knee. He swallowed a groan and let his fingers look for something in his vest pocket.

When the dust settled, he was seated on the gray's head, smoke rising as he took a deep pull on the small cigar stuck in his mouth. The near forehoof of the gray lifted briefly, and the ragged tail thrashed across the soaked hide, but it was useless: The little horse was impotent under the weight of his new master. Jim Henry coughed and drew again on the cigar, letting the smoke drift about his head.

"Hap, I thought you said this here horse might put up something of a fight. He sure ain't worth much. Let me catch up the bay and we'll ride. Soon as I finish this here cigar."

It was hard for Hap to keep quiet about Jim Henry and his appearance. Blood smeared the rough face, the rim of his hat was broken, and dust matted his bronze hair and skin to a muddy brown. There was a limp to him when he finally tossed the cigar butt away and walked across the corral. And when the young fighter turned quickly to watch the gray sit up in the middle of the pen, Hap saw a grimace come across his face as he put weight to his right leg. But Jim Henry said nothing about it, so he left it alone.

That had been one hell of a ride. No getting around it. But the kid didn't want to talk, and his own head was banging away so damned hard inside his skull, Hap wasn't sure the sounds of his own words would be a hurricane he could ride out. Things was getting a bit tricky. But he knew he was almighty glad he didn't have to top off that damned gray before setting him to ride back. He surely did owe one to Jim Henry, more than he ever owed a man before.

Hap smiled, and Jim Henry slapped his hat against his pants leg and watched the dust fly.

CHAPTER 5

"**S**IR, CORPORAL AUSLANDER to speak with you. Sir. He's in the office waiting. You want me to let the bas—uh . . . the corporal in, sir?"

Murdoch Stockbridge barely lifted his eyes from the stack of paper in front of him. God knows he tried hard enough, but the soldiers out here under his command, the men with whom he and the colonel were expected to tame the flow of Indians, were uniformly foul-mouthed, unused to discipline, and hopeless in the rudiments of military protocol. Private Havercamp was a prime example. He'd coughed to hide the slip, but it was easy to fill in the words. No one had much use for Auslander, but that did not excuse Havercamp trying to call him a bastard. And Havercamp was one of the more responsible men under his command, that was what truly bothered Captain Stockbridge.

Auslander . . . another troublemaker, if he remembered correctly. Stockbridge ran his left hand over his face, patting the thinning strands of hair combed across his high forehead. Damn, he missed Evelyn, missed her so much the ache inside him grew daily. How could he know that leaving her in the safety of New York would find her dead of a fever? They had good doctors back east, the finest medical minds available, and yet she'd died of a fever brought on by the chill of a single night.

Murdoch Stockbridge pinched the bridge of his nose, coughed hard, and brought out a fine linen kerchief with which to wipe his mouth and the corners of his eyes. The kerchief itself was a painful reminder to have in hand; its corners were embroidered with his initials, its softly woven threads ineptly ironed by his daughter instead of the woman who had given it to him, along with the luxury of her love.

He would have preferred a colored square of cotton, like those used by the men in the fort and in town, bought from traders. But his daughter, Phillipa, their much-loved daughter, insisted in her quiet way that she wash and iron his kerchiefs for him. "Like Mama used to do. Please, Papa." He couldn't resist her pleading and her sad eyes, even though the daily reminder of his loss was sometimes more than he could bear. And time had made no dent in his mourning.

Murdoch Stockbridge, captain, eleven years in the army of the United States, graduate of West Point somewhere in the middle of his class, brought himself back to the business at hand. Private Havercamp was still waiting, in the semblance of a military man at ease.

"Yes, Private. Let Auslander come in, and I want those beef issue papers ready for my signature when he is gone. That will be all."

Sometimes even Havercamp did it correctly. The man came to an abrupt attention, pushed out his chest, drew in his considerable chins, and snapped a salute to his superior officer that would have done a Russian prince proud. Captain Stockbridge smiled slightly, bowed his head to his paper-strewn desk, and spoke softly to the departing man.

"Yes, Havercamp, that will be all."

Auslander was a different degree of soldier. Long and lean, shoulders and back slumped in a curve. The man came slowly to attention and saluted with an indifference Stockbridge did not appreciate. Another one of these western men brought into the army's rank by the promise of a monthly pay and a daily feed—too independent to ever make a reliable soldier, yet talk of his prowess in battle was already making the rounds.

"Now, sir, I come to request your permission, sir, to take me out a patrol. We got sign of them Indians you want us chasing, sir."

Stockbridge stirred in the hard-backed chair. A most peculiar request coming from a lackluster soldier. True, the man was a corporal, but it was a grudging promotion given to a natural leader. Auslander's slow, reptilian movements, the glance of his hooded eyes, had granted him an automatic ranking over the men in his company. Then, too, Stockbridge had been given to understand that the man was an active brawler, unbeaten in the ranks, possessed of a quick temper and a fast hand with a knife. It was not a military-issue weapon, but Auslander was rarely seen without his blade.

Stockbridge withheld his reply, using silence, as he had been taught, to goad the other man into tipping his hand. This time Stockbridge did not like what he was to hear.

"They's another reason for this here patrol. Sir. They was a younker to the fort this week. Come up with our beef from that Spencer. I seen him near your girl. Whole place knows you don't want that scum near to your girl. Sir. But I seen him come back a couple times, hanging round the spring, watching. And this morning, early, up to them springs. I saw him, and he weren't alone. No, sir."

Stockbridge let his anger through briefly; the man's words were a bitter poison. Phillipa was all that was left. He had been charged with her care by a dying wife and mother. She would have the best, even from a captain's meager salary. He would soon rise in rank and use his power to protect his child from the evils in this life. In the meantime, she must be kept safe from that young man: there was danger in his eyes—and more that Stockbridge did not wish to consider.

He opened his own eyes and looked into the sour face of Corporal Auslander. For the first time he saw the threat of what lay close under the surface of the man.

"Sir, that young'un and his friend, they riding out this morning. Saw 'em up to the corral, working up their stock. Friend's too drunk to ride his own bronc, so the kid rode it first. They going to be gone soon, but I'm betting they start out slow. That there friend's mighty wobbly.

"A patrol sent out could sweep wide for Indian sign. We got another report from Musquiz Canyon, Indians been raiding south of there. Them boys'll ride for home, won't be needing to follow the cattle trail. A patrol of good men, we could check out the canyon and follow them boys. Nothing would have to come back to the fort, sir. Nothing about soldiers. Be putting any blame to them damned Indians, pardon me, sir."

The man talked round and round and never said what he was truly thinking. Stockbridge felt a core of shame inside himself, setting this murderous man on an unsuspecting boy. And the rail-thin soldier was smarter than his harried commander had previously thought. Suspicion jumped into Stockbridge's mind full blown.

"Why are you suggesting such a maneuver, Corporal Auslander? It is only making work for yourself and others, dangerous work at that. You might well come across a band of Indians when you are out there. What then?"

"Sir, I just earned me these stripes, and I don't want to be going back to a private. Sir. I drinks more'n may be good for me. They ain't nothing much else to do up in this miserable place. Drinking and chasing Indians. Not much of a choice between them. Sir." Auslander sighed and shifted wearily on his feet.

He couldn't tell the truth to the captain. Hell, no one ever told the truth to a commanding officer. But Auslander had his reasons; that hard-nosed kid had beaten him in front of a number of his men in the tent a few days past. And Auslander had promised there would be revenge. Now he could make points with the captain, the dumb officer listening where he oughtn't to be, and the kid all at the same time. Auslander grinned, and the captain visibly paled as the lanky corporal began his spiel.

"Got me a bottle again last night and said me too many things about an officer I knew before," he went on. "He ain't too pleased with my mouth this morning. And God knows I don't want to be losing them stripes already. So I figured I'd make you a trade, offer you a service. That no one else could offer in this here camp. Then maybe you could soothe over that lieutenant and see me in a better light. I plan to be more careful in my drinking and talking in the future, sir. Never going to pick on an officer again. No, sir. Not ever again."

With that windy explanation, the corporal drew himself to his full height and produced an almost acceptable salute.

Stockbridge didn't like the bind, but he could see no other way to take the offer. With reservations. "Corporal Auslander, this is an order," he snapped. "Take a patrol out to investigate the report of Indians in Musquiz Canyon. But your patrol is not limited to the confines of the canyon. If you find it necessary to ride beyond the proscribed boundaries in pursuit of your duty, you may proceed with any military practice you deem necessary and prudent.''

It was a formal and lengthy order, but Captain Stockbridge waited near a full minute before he resumed talking. The words must be carefully spoken; there could be no room for misconception. Auslander must fully understand.

''At attention, Corporal! I want no confusion about this. If you and your men make contact with nonmilitary personnel other than Indians, you are to proceed with good conscience. The army must maintain its ties with the civilian population in this area at all costs. You will act accordingly, and there must be nothing to come back in the form of a protest to the authorities. Do I make myself understood, Corporal? There will be *no killing* of civilians.''

There was no further need for words. The corporal obviously understood, but Stockbridge did not like the smirk that passed as a smile across the man's drawn face. Stockbridge flicked his hand to his brow and let it fall back to the rough desktop, dismissing Auslander and his vendetta. He sincerely wished he could dismiss the fate of the boy and his daughter in such a simple manner. There was much to be said for the rules of military life.

Jim Henry was careful in his choices; he took speed over comfort. Hap needed to be at Spencer's Rancho, and Jim Henry knew the fast way. The land was brutal. The horses stumbled on bunched roots, stepped up and over deadly cactus, and wore their hooves and legs raw on hard-packed shale. Sometimes the earth held them, sometimes it gave way and the horses plunged into deep sand.

Water was the prime consideration. Back at Fort Davis, even down through Musquiz Canyon, it was high ground with streams and open springs. Once they angled out into the desert, they became dependent on what water they could carry in a gourd or canteen and the few springs that were safe. Jim Henry knew the Indians owned whatever they chose to in the desert. He could not challenge them with one active rifle and a sheathed knife. So he had to make careful choices.

Camp was spare: brush laid down for Hap's comfort, no fire, only jerked beef that chewed up slow in dry mouths. A short drink for Jim Henry, a few more swallows for Hap. The horses drank half a canteen between them. Much later, a dampened bandanna was laid across Hap's forehead, and it dried out immediately. That worried Jim Henry, until Hap opened his eyes and told a long tale about a ghost and a pretty farm girl. The day's ride hadn't taken all of his friend's strength.

Midday following, Jim Henry rationed out the last of the water to Hap. The horses had sucked eagerly from cupped hands in the morning, taking in less than they needed. Jim Henry's bay showed the effects of the rationing more than the younger gray. Eyes dulled, head low, the small horse kept to the trail but did not respond quickly to the rein.

This particular stretch of the *despoblado* was familiar to Jim Henry. He'd choused horses out of the narrow draw when Spencer tried raising them, and then he'd worked cattle from here, running them the length of the draw at full tilt. The powdery clay soil held little moisture, but from it grew an enriching grass the cattle loved.

He kicked hard at the coyoto bay and cursed the animal. There was a spring ahead, on the side of a steep-walled draw, tucked behind a roll of land and a screen of tumbled rock. The bare thread of a trail wound along the base of the draw, and there was no set direction for the spring. A man lost to this country could die less than ten yards from the spring and never know how close he'd been to salvation.

Set deep in the narrow canyon, on the edge of a steep wall, few white men knew of its existence. Small rodents and birds came easily to use the spring, but horses and cattle, and man, had difficulty making their way to the water. The Indians used the spring cautiously, but their passage did not show.

Jim Henry slid Hap off his gray and tied up the two horses. He was careful in his climb to the spring; he would leave no broken twigs or scuffed rock. This was a sacred place, and Jim Henry knew its laws; each traveler left no trace, and if a man were careless and marked his use, there would be a later reckoning.

He drank sparingly of the water, careful to put his face to

the small pool and not break back the shiny leaves. The smells tempted him: damp earth, rotting mulch, cold water. After he filled the gourds and the crude canteen, he drank again and let some of the water run down his chin to soak the front of his shirt. There was life here, given by the water held in his hand. He ran his tongue around the wetness in his mouth and inhaled deeply.

He returned by a different route, careful still not to disturb ground or crush grass. Hap was waiting eagerly. Both horses raised their heads, and Jim Henry saw the bay's nostrils widen. He was too slow; the bay whinnied, and the dry sound echoed off rock walls and sent shivers down Jim Henry's spine.

They had to hurry now. Jim Henry gave Hap a gourd and measured out water for each horse, poured into indentations in the rock. His fatigue had betrayed him, betrayed Hap, too. His need for a full belly of water and a face cleaned of dirt had put them at unknown risk.

Auslander's big bay heard the nicker, but the corporal's hand came down on the horse's muzzle and choked off the answering call. Auslander stared hard over the edge of the ridge, letting his eyes focus softly, never staring too long at one spot. Then he saw it—the outline of two horses and one man. Dumb kid.

"Captain says to check everything out, boys. We got something down there, we go check it. Mount up."

He played the game well. Three of the men who rode with him bore fading scars from a night not too long ago in a saloon tent. Auslander had his own grudge to settle; these men would eagerly do what was ahead of them.

There was only one way out of the narrow canyon, and it meant coming back through deep sand. The kid and his *compadre* would be prime targets for the picking. Auslander set his men well. Each one kept a hand over his horse's muzzle and the other hard to a pistol or rifle. Auslander was determined: that long-legged, hard-looking son would not get past him this time without a whole lot to remember.

The hard warning of a rifle being cocked stopped Jim Henry. The coyoto bay he was leading walked over his heels and stopped. Hap's gray sighed and rested its head on the bay's rump. Jim Henry crouched down, tried to see what was happening. His actions stirred Hap from his uneasy dozing.

"What you got, boy? You see something?" he asked, his voice soft from instinct and exhaustion.

"Hap, get down quick," Jim Henry warned. Then he froze from a new sound. "Hap . . ."

"Now, you two stay there a spell. Make me real pleased if you moved fast and I had to use this here rifle. You stand easy, Jim Henry McCraw. Get your hand off that knife behind you. I know it's there, I truly do."

The unseen voice continued, and the sound sent shivers through Jim Henry.

"I know a lot about you, Jim Henry McCraw, and I got you a message from a pretty lady."

Jim Henry froze. He could have slipped into the brush away from the voice, he could have gambled that the attacker was caught in his own talking and would be slow to fire. But the mention of the girl numbed him, left him wide open to the round end of a rifle that poked through the brush.

They had been waiting at the end of the draw, knowing the vulnerability of the men and horses and the need for water. Jim Henry cursed himself as much as the unseen man behind the exposed rifle.

"You, mister, on that speckled runt. Slip yourself down and be mighty careful how you go. One slip from you and you're dead, drilled plumb center and out the back."

Hap steadied himself on the gourd horn and slipped both feet free to slide down the off side. He thought to challenge the distant voice, until the broad snick of two more rifles sounded; then he just planted his feet wide on the rough ground and raised his hands in defeated salute.

A man finally appeared, a soldier in blue pants and tunic, high black boots, and loaded belt. A small man, wire-thin with a face blued by its whiskery growth, head covered with a very unregulation wide-brimmed straw hat. There was no mistaking the competence of the long rifle in his hands. Hap stepped back to the prodding, stepped back until he felt the sharp prick of a mesquite bush.

"Right there, mister. You ain't wanted in this here peace

talk. Mike, you lace him tight, set him down, and collar him to that tree. Make sure he's out of the action for the next few minutes.''

The voice of their tormentor was hard and clear, the order direct. Jim Henry could do nothing but watch as the small man named Mike bound Hap's hands behind him with raw-hide thongs and wrapped his ankles in the same manner. There was a strong taste of coppered fear in his mouth, and the unbidden sensation of his pa's hand laid across his back came to him . . . then the awful howling screams of the Indians, the cries from Benny, his father's anguish before a certain death. He didn't know where the flash had come from, he only knew it was binding him to the spot in terror. Jim Henry shook his head and stepped between Hap and the unseen voice.

The trooper called Mike moved to Jim Henry's left, and another soldier came out of hiding with rifle at the ready, a broken-toothed smile on his face. Jim Henry thought he recognized the man, but the pleasure in the crooked face at seeing him was obvious.

They knew who he was, they had been waiting for Hap and him in particular. He licked his dry lips and clenched and unclenched his fists.

''Hadden, you give me that water gourd from this one's saddle. Mike, you keep an eye on him. He can move faster than you'd think. Some of us know that already.''

There was a strange break in the slow-moving play, splintered with sounds Jim Henry could not always identify. Muffled cursing, low-spoken orders, a water stopper pulled from the gourd. A horse nickered nearby, and the gray lifted his head to answer. Overhead an angry bird called at the men below and flew to a less busy thicket to attend to business. Jim Henry shifted his weight, felt his belly roll over, and smiled anxiously at Hap.

''Grab him. Tie him spread to the rock, facedown.''

The man called Hadden butted Jim Henry with his rifle as someone else grabbed his right arm and yanked it up against his back. Jim Henry went to his knees.

''Watch it there. You break that boy's arm, we got us a nice young lady going to be something mad.''

Jim Henry didn't want to listen to the snake-oil voice or hear its message. He yanked his left arm free and swung blindly, felt his knuckles crack hard into rotting teeth. Wetness flowed over his raw hand, and then something slammed the back of his head and he was facedown in gravel.

He wasn't out, but he couldn't seem to move. He could hear, but the words made no sense to him. He thought to sit up and knew he was paralyzed because his arms and legs would not move. Desperation forced him to open his eyes.

There was the grain of a rock in front of him, a boulder worn by wind and rain to a narrow stance, wide enough to hold a man tied to it, arms strained around its waist, feet barely touching hard ground. Jim Henry couldn't move except to shift weight from one booted foot to the other. Bruises came alive, his wrists ached, his fingers throbbed with the beat of his heart. Twisting slightly, he tried to lift his head high enough to turn; a span of fingers held him against the rock. He felt the length of each finger, the cruel touch of nails skinning his cheek. When he pushed back, his head was lifted by the hair and slammed back into the rock.

His body went slack with the blow, and the rough hand that gripped him relaxed. Jim Henry waited and listened, and slowly recognized the voice that spoke to him.

"Boy, I guess you getting the message. And I got another one to go with it." The voice came closer, and there was a whisper in his ear he did not want to understand, a voice that would not let him alone. "You listen to me, boy. There's a pretty lady to the fort, and she's shamed by you. Shamed of being with you. And she's fearful you'll come back asking for more. She don't want the likes of you near her, so she asked us to come give you the word. Me, I figure this between her and you, no need to tell these soldiers or your slick friend. *Comprende?* You shake that head of yours slow-like and tell me you understand."

Jim Henry couldn't move, he couldn't do what the voice told him; he wouldn't believe she could be this cruel. He hung in his bonds and did not respond.

"And kid, she don't want that gewgaw you give her. No, sir. She give it to me to throw 'way. I want you to look at it close. Tell you real straight how the lady feels 'bout you. For goddamn certain you see how she feels.''

The sickness caught in his throat. It was a necklace of silver beads and worked turquoise—a necklace that flashed by his eyes before he could shut out the betrayal. Jim Henry shuddered and turned his head; the hand and the rough voice could not make him see.

"Now you listen, kid. I want you to remember this. She don't want nothing to do with you. No more. You remember I warned you.''

Hard laughter mixed with a whistling, then Jim Henry felt the bite of a lash through his shirt. As he arched away from the pain, the thongs holding him dug in and tore his flesh.

The whistle came again, and this time the laughter followed its descent. Jim Henry cried out; his feet scuffed the gravel, his hands jerked against the rawhide. Again came the laughter, and again the whistling and the fire. This time Jim Henry almost gave in to the blackness in his head. When the unseen man, the messenger, laughed and swung on him again, he yanked on the rawhide bonds and arched his back and called out his own cursing—until the rope hit again and his head came forward and cracked against the unmoving boulder.

The crack echoed, a few horses whinnied. Auslander let go of the wet reata and examined his work. The long-legged kid hung from his bonds, the tethered friend had nothing to say. Auslander opened his left fist and looked at the trinket, a blue-and-silver necklace bought for a few pesos. The dumb kid, thinking his was the only gift of its kind. It didn't matter, he would never know.

He checked the boy: breathing easily, not much blood, but a message delivered he would remember long past his healing. Auslander smiled and cut the other one's bond half-through. He fell sideways, the blanched face twisting in pain; the eyes flickered, but there was no recognition or interest in the half-lidded gaze. Auslander felt for a pulse: slow and strong. He guessed the kid's *compadre* would live.

He went back to McCraw and lifted his head off the rock, curious about the kid's face. White bone showed through the easy bleeding, but he would live. Marked up, but he were no beauty to begin with; a new scar would be no account and a good reminder.

Now that the work was done, he wanted to get out of the draw. "Get the bastards some water, Mike. Loose the cinchas on them broncs. Don't want these two pretty boys dyin' on us after all the care we took. Leave them canteens full." He laughed and picked up one of the gourd containers. "Fill these, too. Hell, fill all our canteens. It's a long ride back to the fort. Mike, get to it."

George Auslander had made his mistake. Mike Pettee was a city tough, driven west by hunger, working out a hitch in the godforsaken army. He had no understanding of the unwritten laws governing the spring, or any sense of the real preciousness of an unviolated flow of water. Pettee slammed his army mount up the fragile draw and partway up the hillside to the spring before the horse could go no farther in the tangled brush. Pettee dismounted and tied up the horse and continued on foot, holding to broken bushes and digging in his heels to make the climb. He left a trail a greenhorn could read.

Pettee filled the gourds and returned to his horse, tying the canteens to the saddle. It was easier mounting from uphill, and Pettee appreciated the ease. He had no love for the cantankerous animals the army provided, other than they beat the hell out of walking. He was city born and city bred. The *despoblado* gave him nothing.

Neither Pettee nor Auslander nor the whiskered Hadden, nor the other three men riding out of the draw knew that they were being watched. The small band of soldiers didn't feel the eyes following them, they didn't hear the unspoken curses as they laughed and drank out of refilled canteens and prepared to ride back to the fort.

Auslander knew better. He'd survived more than a year of Fort Davis and chasing the disappearing Indians. But he was loose-riding his big army mount, pulling at his second canteen, which was filled with whiskey instead of cooling water. Light-headed and relaxed, he was satiated with the experience of whipping the big-mouthed kid and watching him struggle against his rawhide bonds.

As he rode slowly back to the fort, Corporal Auslander

relived the past hour and pulled hard at his unshared whiskey and grinned to himself in complete pleasure. And forgot where he was and what could be in back of him.

It was a small band of Indians, no more than six or seven. Few words were spoken between them; gestures were enough. An arrow freed and fitted to its bow, a knife held in a dark fist. The leader carried an ancient pistol—a useless weapon—in his left hand, while resting a long blade across his pony's neck.

The small band had watched the invaders. First there had been two men on lean range ponies. They had seen that one was injured and that the other knew about the precious spring. The leader had stroked the rusted steel of the pistol's barrel and held up his hand when the uncle and the brother of Itaya Sol had recognized the tall horseman. The leader knew most of the Anglos who rode often on his land, and he knew the tall one. So he cut the edge of his hand through the air and chose not to see the anger in the eyes of Itaya Sol's uncle and his elder brother.

Itaya Sol had accepted what would come of his long-ago deed; he had known the vaqueros would hunt him for his cruel act. He had chosen to taunt the Anglos in a manner that would fuel their anger. When, years later, he and the young rider had met on ground Itaya Sol had invaded, they had fought with Itaya Sol's rules—and the Indian had lost.

To the leader of the small Indian band, the death of Itaya Sol had been clean and pure; there was to be no revenge taken on the young man. The self-proclaimed leader cut his hand in the air again and felt more than saw that the two restless members sat back on their ponies and let their hands hang free of weapons.

They would sit here, above the spring, and watch. They would wait to see what the tall rider and his companion would do. It was up to them, up to the purity of their hearts, the cleanness of their intentions, whether they lived or died.

The leader sighed deeply. He saw the tall young man's care as he approached the spring, he noted the tender brushing of the branches that did not break them; he watched the gentle manner in which the young man knelt in the damp earth and drank his fill, bathed his face. He approved of the return journey, when the young man did not retrace his faint prints but kept to a different route and did not leave sign of his passage.

It was Blanco who first saw the soldiers. Blanco, the youngest of the band, who was eager to prove he had earned his right to battle. The Indian had stiffened and spooked his untried pony. The lifted head, the widened nostrils, told the leader that there were more than the two riders.

He raised his fist, and Blanco eased back, allowed his pony to relax. A finger pointed, a head cocked, and the leader, too, saw the dark uniforms of the hated army. His hand tightened on the pony's line, he felt the muscles of his back and buttocks clench in anticipation of the awaited battle. The well-tried pony under him raised its spotted head and drew its quarters underneath in eagerness to run.

It took much effort for the leader to relax, and his pony wagged its head in disgust. But there was much he did not understand of the scene below him. The thin line of the blue army did not ride up to the young men. Instead, one man, a big man the Indian leader recognized with a flash of earned hatred, climbed down from his sweaty army mount and gestured for the others to do the same. They stayed at the mouth of the narrow canyon, hiding their horses so poorly, even a child could find them, and they put themselves behind bushes and rocks, unable to conceal their foolish blue clothing or their awkward, pale bodies.

The Indian smiled; he would wait now, and he would watch carefully. The small band looked to their leader and loosened their hold on their ponies and let their weapons rest lightly on their smooth legs. They, too, could wait and watch; they could wait a long time.

The action played out by the soldiers was easily recognized by the small band. A warning, a lesson of some kind. Brutal, quick, to be remembered. None of the Indians moved while the big soldier did his work.

It was when the single soldier crawled up to the spring and dug away the precious ground and broke branches, gouged great holes in the wet earth with his high black boots, that the leader gave his signal. With the motion of his hand, the band climbed higher on the ridge and disappeared in the cactus and brush thicket.

The soldiers, paid to seek out and kill the Indians, never saw the horsemen circle them. No one noticed the few unshod tracks, no one wondered at the flight of birds from the other side of the ridge. The soldiers were relaxed. One lit a rolled smoke and was allowed several drags before he was ordered to strip and bury the crude cigarette. No one hurried, each did his task. One man watered the ponies and loosened their gear; the big man cut the injured man loose, then went to the beaten Anglo and touched a hand to his neck, listening for life. He placed a knife near him, yet well out of reach, then loosened the rawhide bonds and laid the flopping head gently on the supporting rock. It was obvious that these two were meant to live and remember their harsh lesson.

The soldiers did not listen; they were sloppy in their actions, they wasted water poured over their heads and soaked in blue cloths. They gave their horses too much to drink. The leader of the Indians smiled; these soldiers would be easy prey.

Finally the soldiers mounted, but they did not see the warning flock of birds, and when a stout bay horse lifted its head to watch, its rider jerked and yanked on the bit, forcing him back into line. These men were too stupid to survive in the *despoblado*.

The soldiers rode out carelessly, directly into the Indians' attack. There was time only for them to feel the arrows pierce their flesh, time only to see the skinning knives flash down to cut deeply. The slaughter took a few minutes, and when it was done, it was the two unconscious riders and their alert ponies who lived.

The bodies of the soldiers were stripped and mutilated, then hauled into the brush, where time and chance would reveal their deaths. Finished, the Indians guided their mounts back over the top of the ridge. Only the uncle of Itaya Sol glanced down at the prisoner still tied to the rock. He thought of his murdered kin, but he held to the discipline of the band and thought no more of revenge. Itaya Sol had made a choice and had died from it. The Anglo child bound to the rock would live, for now.

The band of horsemen disappeared into the desert, and the small birds came back to the life-giving spring and began their songs again.

CHAPTER 6

IT WAS HAP'S turn, but he didn't know it when he first opened his eyes and tried to move. His hands were bound, but when he tugged hard, the rawhide fell away. He rolled to sitting and brought bits of the leather to his face and wasted a good deal of time coming to the conclusion that he had been deliberately cut free.

He sat down twice before his legs were steady enough to hold him. When he did stand, he needed to hold on to something but misjudged the nearest tree and got a handful of thorns. Hap sucked on the holes in his hand and swore.

The horses were content, tied to a scrub oak. Hap struggled past them until he was stopped by the obvious signs. Time had passed, a lot of time. The oak bark was stripped clean, the manure at each horse's quarters was stamped flat and partially dried. The gray nickered at him, the bay raised his head and licked his lips. Hap suddenly realized he was thirsty, too.

The gourds and the canteen were stacked away from the horses. Hap drank deeply, and, watching him, both horses whinnied. Hap shielded his eyes and looked hard at Jim Henry. The boy didn't move at all. A sigh escaped Hap when he focused on the long form strung to the awkward boulder; whoever had cut him free had not extended the same courtesy to Jim Henry.

A knife glinted next to the boulder like an offering; Hap bent to pick it up and had to put out a hand to keep from falling. He hefted the unfamiliar blade and finally pushed himself close enough to take a look.

It was a miracle, the kid was alive. Bound to the rock, arms stretched, knees bent, toes dug into hard ground. Hap stared a long time at the ground; one boot had scraped a shallow hole, and there were white marks scratched on the rock's surface. Jim Henry had fought back.

Hap used the knife to cut the rawhide. The freed arm flopped down, and he grabbed for it, bracing himself against Jim Henry's fall. There wasn't time to cut the other side; Jim Henry slid and pulled Hap with him. Hap gagged and almost let go. A ragged breath wheezed from Jim Henry's mouth, along with the sweet, rotted smell of blood.

He had to talk; he choked and swallowed and said anything he could to keep from puking. He didn't expect answers, but he liked the sound of his own voice. Then the head, resting on his shoulder, rolled toward his face, and he looked directly into an opened eye. Hap was conscious of the matted hair framing the gray face. The one eye watched him, the other was swollen shut. Hap stared back and stopped talking.

None of it made sense to him: his bonds cut, a knife waiting. Water, the tied horses. Didn't make sense; beating Jim Henry, leaving him alone. Whatever had happened, it had been meant for Jim Henry. Hap touched the side of his friend's face, and the open eye followed the movement of his hand. Looking into that one open eye, Hap realized he would never know what had happened.

And right then, reasons weren't important. He needed to stand up and cut Jim Henry's other hand loose; he needed to wipe the drawn face clean, feed water into the burned mouth, get his friend up on a horse, and get the hell out of the canyon. He wasn't too sure of the direction, but he had taken note they'd traveled southwest, angling into the falling sun. The old bay gelding would know the way back. His job was to get Jim Henry on top of a horse.

It took Hap a long time, and a determination he wasn't sure was his, to pull up the cinchas on the two broncs and water them again before he fitted the bridles over their unwilling heads. He tied the gray up to the bay with a piece of rope, then had to sit for a time and rest his head on the scratched rock. His eyes closed from the sun, and he must have slept. But Jim Henry didn't seem to mind.

* * *

They rode through a confusion of kids and donkeys and scrawny dogs and chickens and dark-eyed women before they reached the gates of the compound. At first no one took notice of their drifting, but as they passed more people, Hap became aware of whispering behind him. He turned in the saddle and thought to yell at the small groups of people who talked among themselves and stared at Jim Henry.

But it wasn't worth the effort, he decided. He had the energy to find Tyler, and that was about it. The questions and the curiosity would have to wait. He wanted water, to drink and spill down his shirt and soak into his pants. First, though, he had to leave Jim Henry with the old man and the Mex woman, and then he would find himself a woman and a whole barrel of water. It was a strong fantasy, and Hap forgot to direct the coyoto bay, which took him to the corrals and stopped. It took him a minute to think of what he was doing, then a hand reached for him, and he let go of the saddle and slid off and hoped he was caught. He did remember to tell his savior about Jim Henry. Then he went to sleep.

"Muy malo" was what he heard first. The words ran through Jim Henry's mind until he wasn't sure if they were real. He struck out at the offending sound and hit something as the words went around in his head. The words stopped when he cried out, and a different voice, a harsh voice, demanded answers to questions he did not understand.

At last the harsh voice went away, and Jim Henry slept. When he came awake again, there was a woman leaning over him, wiping his face with a wet cloth. Dark breasts showed under a loose blouse, and a sparking of blue and silver around her throat. In his fevered rage, Jim Henry reached up stiff hands to strangle the blue and silver. The string broke, the beads rolled over him.

He was pushed back down onto the bed, and the pain inside his head grew. He fell back into a restless sleep, unaware of the two figures that watched and worried over him.

Rosa's voice was blurred with tears, her dark hands trembled as the fingers picked up the spilled beads of her fine necklace. "Señor Limm, why would the *niño* do this to me? Why would he wish to choke me?"

Limm Tyler could do nothing but hold the crying woman in his arms and pat her back and mutter words meant to comfort her. "Hush, Rosa, he did not mean to harm you. It was someone in his dream he would destroy. Perhaps the man who did this to him. It was not you, my sweet Rosa. He meant you no harm."

He stayed with Rosa Ignacio and quieted her until she began to talk of more practical matters, such as the evening meal. Good strong food was needed to bring the boy back to health and to continue the slow healing of Tyler's busted leg. Only one more time did Rosa interrupt her work to confess her worries to Limm. "The boy has become too much like the Anglos who now move into the land. The ones who hate because of black hair and skin or the darkness of the eyes. He is like those, like the young ones who ride with the cattle and fight the blue-coated army. He hates, like these Anglos, he wishes only to kill. He is no longer like you, Señor Tyler. He has no love for those who love him in return."

She shook her head at her own words, and after staring at the long form of the boy laid out on the rough bed, she turned and left the hut to the freshness of the cool evening.

Tyler stayed with Jim Henry. His big hands wiped the dry face, and his voice soothed the boy when he moaned and thrashed in his sleep. Jim Henry woke twice, and each time Tyler was waiting with cooled thin broth and a wet rag. The second time, the boy took a few mouthfuls of the soup, then his good eye opened, and he looked straight into Tyler's eyes. The next instant he waved his arm, and the half-empty bowl went flying. Immediately the heavy head slumped on the loose neck, and the long body folded on the damp bed. Tyler cleaned up the mess and limped to the doorway to stare up at the brilliant sky.

The third time Jim Henry sat up, Tyler knew he was fully conscious. No words were exchanged, but Tyler offered him some cold broth, and Jim Henry finished the bowl, all the time watching Tyler through the single wild eye. And what Tyler thought he saw in the one eye did not please him: anger, hatred, scalded emotions that destroyed the soul.

He tried to console himself as he took the bowl and spoon from the extended hand. Perhaps, when the puffed flesh returned to normal, the boy would have learned a lesson. He doubted his own wishes but thought them anyway for the peace of Rosa's heart. There had never been ease in the soul of James Henry McCraw. Tyler watched the angry face now laid on a rumpled pillow, and he knew the world had grown darker for the boy. There would be no healing in his soul as his face and body scarred over to form their new shell.

Tyler went back to his doorway and took in a deep breath of the new morning air. It was as if the sickness had invaded even his lungs, and he had to cleanse himself of the hatred. He needed his Rosa right now, with great urgency. They had managed twice to make love around the bracing on his leg, and he needed her again.

That, too, was something more the boy did not understand. Tyler grimaced; there was much Jim Henry did not understand. What was between him and Rosa was good and natural, loving that had little to do with the wild fornications in a bawdy house or the loveless ruttings in a drunken town. His Rosa was special, and in a way it was because of Jim Henry that Tyler and Rosa had grown together.

Behind him the kid rolled over, and Tyler heard his painful cursing. The flow of desire eased in him some as he thought on the boy and away from the softness of Rosa Ignacio. The words grew in volume, and then Tyler heard his name being called.

The kid wasn't really awake; his face was shiny with sweat, and his eyes rolled wildly, but he was quiet and not thrashing. Tyler wiped his face clean and covered him again, making certain he was on his side to ease pressure on the sores of his back. Goddammit, no matter what went on between men, there was no cause for a mauling like this. It was a savagery past his understanding. Shaking his head, he reached for a clay bowl pipe in his pocket and drew a chair close to the door. He wanted the first rays of the sun to find him, he wanted to see the rooster hit the top of the dung pile and come out with his morning call. Sometimes the old she-dog belonging to Cleto would bring out her line of pups from their hole if she thought there weren't too many people moving around yet. They would dig through the refuse pile to the back of the main house, and the she-dog would watch their work carefully, quick to issue warning nips if one of the pups got rambunctious.

The parade would disappear soon as Armendiaz left his adobe and went to the brush corral for his burros. He led them to water first light, thinking there would be less danger then, wanting to start the day's work in plenty of time. This way, he said, the burros could have two more trips to water before the night's penning.

Tyler tamped the pipe and waited. Sure enough, a few minutes later Armendiaz ambled out his doorway. Bent with the years passing, white hair sticking through a ragged hat, the old man headed for the yard to begin the care of his animals. The burros knew he was coming, and one sounded the absurd alarm. That would wake the rest of the slow risers in the village.

Tyler drew hard on the pipe. Permanence wasn't something you counted on in the harsh *despoblado*. And permanence wasn't something a young man wanted. But now Fort Davis had brought a permanence of some sort. The Indians were slowly coming under rule, and the army was getting smarter and building more forts. They'd got Quitman built some time back and now Stockton over to Comanche Springs. The army was bound to settle the damned Indians, make it safe for all kinds of folk to come into the *despoblado*.

Tyler had a different way of looking at things. Make it safe and then folks'll start asking for more, building more towns, destroying the land. Tyler hated the settling; it was why he'd left Ohio and come out to this hellhole. At least it was a private hellhole then, with only those willing to take their chances and ask for nothing to be given them.

Sure it was a shame the boy's family was killed, and it were sad when any wife and child was murdered by them devils. But it was their land, too, and no white man worthy of his calling ought to bring a woman and child into such a hard life. He always wondered what drove McCraw to drag his family down with him. No business doing such a thing, no matter what the reason.

Now, man to man, you want something another man's got,

you look him eye to eye and you make your move. But you don't decide to drive out a whole nation because you fancy their territory. Spencer, he come here early to the river land, and he fought the Indians and anything else what wanted to take from him. Spencer, he could change with what flowed. The horse business lost too much to the Indians, well, he raised up herds of cattle and fed them to the army.

Tyler shook his head. Too much thinking, too much time while he sat waiting for his damned leg to heal. Deep inside he had the notion the leg weren't going to set right. So he'd been thinking and scheming. Spencer had a forge now, but the last man to work it hadn't stayed long. Got interested in a red-skinned gal and got his heart broke. Real literal. Thinking did no good, but Tyler guessed he could work out the forge, make his way as a smithy.

He was getting too old to ride the broncs. Best leave that to younger men. Tyler drew on the pipe, tasted the spoils of the burned tobacco, and spat out of the corner of his mouth. Tasted terrible, but it was a comforting habit when a man sat and thought.

The compound slowly filled with people. Thin lines of smoke drifted from chimneys, and Tyler thought about a cup of coffee, a slice of Rosa's good bread. A flour mill was going at Presidio del Norte, another improvement of the growing number of merchants in the area. Tyler damned the mill, and the people, but he couldn't get enough of the light bread Rosa made with the coarse-ground flour.

The people coming and going across the compound suddenly became precious to Tyler, and an unexpected mist filled his eyes, blurring the lines and the faces. Damn this pipe, damn the hot smoke.

A loud voice carried across the compound, but Tyler didn't listen. He couldn't get his thinking shut down proper. Spencer himself said there was a stir in the Congress of the country. Some kind of politics. Tyler had heard all the goings-on about states' rights and slavery and them abolitionists, but he didn't believe much of what he heard.

It was greed behind the palaver, hard cash to the man talking the longest and getting the most folks listening. No one went to war over the rights belonging to others. They went to battle for what they wanted themselves.

Unless you was a child, a boy, a young man full of fire and energy and ideals and thought you could change the world.

Tyler got real tired of setting and thinking right then. Nothing had a measure of sanity or kindness in it; a wounded man-child and a crazy outrider with a big mouth who knew nothing. And too many folks talking 'bout what they didn't understand, making a link between the *despoblado* and the distant city of Washington.

It was time for Tyler to quit thinking and find Rosa and the cup of coffee he needed. Setting all night without a bottle of brandy; setting and thinking and watching the boy and not getting anything straight in his mind . . . it weren't good. It was Rosa he needed, and Tyler admitted that to himself with a grin. Rosa and her seamed face, her strong hands around him, the warmth of her when they touched. He laughed at himself; the kid was all right now, wrapped in his silence and a mound of blankets, set to sleep away the day. It was Tyler who had the problem. Thinking did that to a man.

He pushed away from the rough chair and caught up his bent stick in one hand, leaning on it as he limped outside to find Rosa. He didn't bother with Jim Henry. He'd been from his woman too long.

Jim Henry slept in the narrow bed until he could no longer bear the smell of himself or the looseness of his muscles. It wasn't the injuries that kept him in bed, it was the endless, fearful argument in his mind.

When he was able to stagger across the dirt flooring of Tyler's cabin, there was no one to help him. No one to see him fall twice more before reaching the doorway and the brightness of the sun. He cleaned himself up, found clothes left waiting for him and a pair of boots that had been oiled and mended. Enough of his mother's hard-taught manners stayed with him that he sought out Limm Tyler and the woman and gave them his thank-yous before he moved back into his own dusty hut. It was lonesome at first and painful to sleep on the rough straw ticking, but it was his own place and safe from intrusion.

He was given little time. Spencer sent word he wanted him up to the house. Jim Henry waited a day, then dressed slowly and crossed the length of the compound to Spencer's door. This time, as before, the man did not acknowledge him as Jim Henry entered, so he took time to take in his surroundings. The plank flooring felt good underfoot. Some of the dark wood was covered with brightly woven rugs, more weavings covered the adobe wall, and there were high-backed, hand-carved chairs lined on the far wall.

Spencer sat at the back of a long table, legs pushed way under so that the tips of his black boots showed. He still did not look up, and Jim Henry shifted and heard his boots ring on the wood floor. If he could have seen Spencer's face, he'd have scowled at the small grin. There was little subtlety in Jim Henry, no need or understanding for anything less than direct action. And John Spencer was playing with him.

"Boy, I want to know what the hell happened out there. Not the brawl to the fort, I got word on that one. You did proud putting up those soldiers, covering for your partner. That was done right." Spencer looked at the pale face of the kid and nodded once, waited it out. But the kid gave back nothing, so Spencer attacked.

"Dionicio came in this morning, found himself the remains of five or six men, couldn't tell the number. Indians got to 'em. Near those springs where you was jumped. These men were army, sure enough. I sent word to the fort, kind of thing they need to know. We know it weren't Indians got to you, so I want to know what the hell went on, and why there was army involved."

It was a long, slow silence, and John Spencer had plenty of time to think. Loyalty was the prime consideration in the men who worked for him. Loyalty to him and the brand. Personal contact was a trap that took his energy and wasted it. The kid was a prime example. Family massacred, too damn young to work much in the beginning other than shine up Spencer's horse.

Spencer knew he liked the pa, but he couldn't remember the man's face. But he still remembered the pain at their death, especially that of the mother and the baby boy. But now he had the grown son, and the kid was causing too much trouble.

"Well, kid, you got an answer for me?"

The kid's going to lie. That was Spencer's first thought. *He knows what happened, and he ain't going to tell.* Close-mouthed son, that much he was, and it was lies he sure enough spoke.

"No, sir, I . . . I been over and over, I . . . There's no reason for what happened, 'less it be somethin' to do with Hap."

"It's you they worked over, McCraw. Not Railsford. He ain't been here long enough to get up hatred like that. Less someone took offense at his mouth. That may be likely, but not to get hisself almost killed. No, it was you the army was after. You tell me why."

He watched the scarred face carefully and kept talking. "It's serious. We got families living here, and children. I don't want anything coming to us we ain't ready for. You done a deed to bring down trouble, you tell me or ride on. I don't much care which."

"Mr. Spencer, I ain't real steady on what happened, but I would stake my life it won't come down to the rancho. That's about all I can say."

"Ain't just your life, McCraw. It's all of us. We may have the army around us in forts and on patrols, but we still got indios out there, and we still have their hatred. It's all of us, boy."

The kid only shook his head and didn't answer. Spencer drew his legs back under the table, planted his feet at the base of his chair, and half stood. Hands pounded flat to the table, papers scattered with the violent gesture, he glared at the kid. The boy met his fierce gaze, then blinked and dropped his eyes. Spencer shifted his thinking; let the kid fuss awhile, then maybe the truth would appear.

"Tyler's still laid up; that leg of his don't seem to heal. Says he taught you everything he knowed. There's a sorrel he started. I want it made into a finished bridle horse. *Comprende?* And that snaky, wall-eyed son of a gun that got Tyler, I want that bronco rock solid or dead. Won't have a

horse like that in the remuda, they all got to do an honest
job. Like the men I hire. . . . You understand me, boy?''

Jim Henry leaned against the corral wall and wanted to curse
the milling horses trapped inside. He could ride out now. He
had some money, enough to pick up a half-broke horse and
some supplies. If he was real careful, he could cross the
despoblado and head north, find out about the world beyond.

The track of his thinking took him by surprise. Never even
been to the town of Franklin to the north along the river,
never even considered a life past Spencer's Rancho and the
distance of Fort Davis. He'd heard they were calling Franklin
by the border name of El Paso now, said it was a city wild
and woolly. A crossroads of travelers headed east and west,
and some even coming down into the *despoblado*. Town had
its own vineyards; he'd tasted the wine Spencer had brought
down in great wooden barrels. Jim Henry grimaced and
wiped his mouth clean.

There was another memory flickering in his mind, one he
wanted to shut out—the warmth of her skin, the soft hand
fitted in his, the smell of sun-touched hair, the feel of burying
his face in its luxury and dreaming uncontrolled dreams. Jim
Henry's body jerked, and his hands became fists, nails sharp
in the calloused palms, knuckles ground white. The innocence almost reborn in him with the first touch of her hand
had now died and was buried deep inside.

There were no more dreams, no more softness and promise. It was the work now, the packed sweaty bodies of frightened horses. That was what he had. All that remained of the
dreams were shame and lies and lingering pain.

Jim Henry looked down to see his hands shaking. There
was a sour taste to his mouth, and his knees wobbled. Up
too soon and not fit to work. Not fit for much of anything.

''Well, by God, Jim Henry. Looks to be you caught yourself
a horse what don't care much for you. Maybe it's those snake
locks of hair you got waving about your face, or that devil's
brand over your eye. Whatever it is, son, you sure got yourself a handful of angry.''

If Jim Henry had had the strength left, he would have spun

around and thrown a quick loop at the speaker or shied a hat under the pot-bellied mustang and snapped the long end of the reata at its flanks. But he had neither the strength nor a free hand; both were pulled tight to the line snugged around the neck of an ugly, wall-eyed bay gelding. And he didn't need to look to know the man with the big mouth: Hap, hard at work digging in a man's mind.

The bay half-reared and squalled its fury. Jim Henry twisted the end of the rope along his butt and sat into the horse's pulling, yanking with both hands. The bay reared higher from the taut rope, balancing for a doubtful time on one hind leg. Jim Henry moved fast, loosened the rope, and scurried close to the ornery animal, coiling the rope as he ran. He reached high along the line and yanked as hard as he could, putting his own fury into the jerk. The wavering bay sat unexpectedly on its haunches and slid backward in a slamming fall, then rolled over on its back, legs flailing in the dusty air, mouth gaped wide, eyes wild in helpless panic.

The high bone of the withers stopped the roll, and the horse slid on its side, breathless for a moment from the outrageous tumble. All four legs still galloped in the air, and the long head banged intermittently on the hard-packed earth. Without loosening the rope from the drawn-out neck, Jim Henry wrapped the two forelegs in a quick hold, then picked up a hind leg and tangled it with the bound front legs. The free hind leg scratched at the corral dirt, kicking blindly at its rope prison.

Jim Henry ducked to the back of the horse and caught the big head with his hands, forcing the skull flat to the ground. He sat on the bony flat of the jaw and felt the animal rage helplessly underneath him. Sweat trickled down his back and mingled with the stirred dust to coat him in a fine mud. He'd sat down none too soon; his legs had their wobble back, and his hand shook enough to dump water out of a half-full bucket—something he didn't want Hap Railsford to see. He tugged the collar away from his itching neck and slapped at the dirt on his legs, then elbowed hair from his eye and felt the burning of the half-healed cut.

"How do, Hap," he said. "Been a while since I seen you. Got time to set a spell?"

Hap threw back his head and howled. Jim Henry McCraw was a good one to ride with, but he hadn't thought the kid capable of such a gesture. God damn the boy, another reason to stick around for some time. As the laughter overwhelmed him, he began to choke over violent hiccups—and had to struggle with the half-broke horse under him until they finally parted more or less in agreement. With the brown tied snug to a pole, Hap joined Jim Henry on the body of the wall-eyed bay.

"Seems to me we met here before, kid. Good to see you. Heard you was up and around. Spencer's got me out working the new herds coming up from the South, and I ain't been near the rancho too much. Alejo told me you was on the rough string now, but I didn't think this was what he meant. Said he'd seen you here the past three, four days. Not much goes on to the rancho without most folks knowing."

Both men were silent. Somehow Hap's words had touched on the beating. Hap dug his toe in the dirt and absently patted the bay gelding's jowl. The horse snorted in fierce resentment. Jim Henry drew in a deep breath and looked beyond the corral to the distance of rough sand and cholla, spindly ocotillo and squat mesquite. Blue mountains shimmered above the desert, hanging in the clear air as if in a separate picture.

He'd never done so much thinking as in the days since his beating. He could see Hap glance at him quickly, then look away, then shift his seat on the bony skull and almost speak. He paid his friend no mind but kept his fingers working a braid in the scraggly black mane, and his eyes held to the distant mountains. But Hap couldn't keep still.

"You know, I don't recollect much of that ride back, but it don't make no sense, them leaving me and working you. I heard Dionicio talking 'bout finding those soldier boys, what was left of them. Didn't sound pretty. . . . Boy, you tell me—what the hell happened out there?"

Sure enough, Hap got what he bargained for: goddamn blankness on the tired face. Jim Henry just shook his head and looked away. There was something live in the strange, brown-flecked eyes quartered behind the faded bruises and neatly stitched brow. Hap knew then he wasn't going to get no part of what was behind those eyes. The kid had changed from the ride, gotten real old in a short time. So he let go of his thinking, gave Jim Henry a grin to let him know he was giving up.

And then Jim Henry stood up from the bay's head, and Hap came up one step behind him. The skull lifted from the ground, and the wild eye rolled in its socket as Jim Henry unlashed the three feet and lifted the rope from the damp neck to set the horse free. The gelding did nothing more than lay its head back down in the dirt, showing no interest in renewing the fight.

It took slaps from the coiled reata before the bay took it to move, and as he struggled to sit up and then stand, Jim Henry and Hap took themselves to a less dangerous place in the corral. Jim Henry leaned on a post, and Hap climbed the rails to perch on top. He liked the view from up there.

"Hap, you ever think on riding out of here? I know you ain't been here too long, but you come from somewhere else, and this place can't be the end to everywhere. You think on riding out much?"

Hap just looked at Jim Henry. The kid had startled him with his questions. He had to think some before he tried an answer. "Well now," he said at last, "I set a part of each day aside to think hard on the subject. Thinking takes me some time, but I generally gets it straight. This here rancho, this here compound setting in the middle of nothing . . . well, it may be a long way from perfection, and then again it ain't too far from hell. But I been worse places. Folks here, they don't mind you 'less you cross them, and I like that."

Jim Henry watched the stiff-legged bay as he let Hap's confusing answer float over him. The gelding seemed little the worse for wear, but the angry eyes were quiet, and the big head didn't lift so high. Maybe he got the lesson, maybe sitting and thinking was good for maverick horses, too.

"Hap, you talk good for a man come in dry. This horse's done for now, and so'm I. Let's find us a bottle and drown it."

That was fine with Hap, although he'd never known Jim Henry to partake much of the whiskey flowing through Spencer's Rancho. But then, it never hurt to take a drink with a friend, never hurt to walk easy. Goddamn, it was hot. Hap almost had the energy to wonder about all the questions Jim Henry asked, all the effort and words and thinking been going on in the horse pen. But it took real thinking to wonder over such things, and it was too damn hot.

CHAPTER 7

"LISTEN TO THIS, Jim Henry: 'Texas votes to secede. On the fourth of March it became official, and the state of Texas placed its vote and its confidence in the justice of its cause and has seceded from the Union.' Why, hell, Jim Henry, we ain't a part of the United States no more. Listen to this. . . .''

Jim Henry couldn't help but listen, since Hap's voice rose a few more steps, and his normally careless pose was shattered. He hung to the paper, mouthing the words, reading them over, puzzling through them.

"I don't believe all this. Listen to this, by God. 'On March twenty-third this great state voted to ally itself with the Confederacy of States, reaffirming its constant belief in the supremacy of states' rights and its own sovereignty.' '' Hap read the rest silently, his eyes taking on a wild glow. Jim Henry enjoyed the quiet. His head ached, and thinking on Hap's words made it worse.

"Jim Henry, they even put in an army to chase out the Union forces here in Texas. Says we got us a Colonel John Ford with jurisdiction over the entire Rio Grande area. That's us, Jim Henry. You listening? And a man named Colonel Baylor's got the pleasure of chasing them blue bellies north of the border. By God, boy, we got us a war right here!''

Jim Henry finished the wine in his cup and put it down very carefully on the end of a barrel. As usual, he didn't understand a good amount of what Hap was spouting, but something was telling him to listen this time. And ask questions. Hap sounded too damned serious.

"What you mean, Texas secedes? Where'd you get that

paper? Can a state just up and leave the Union? Don't seem right to me.''

His tongue was well coated with El Paso wine, and the words ran by him as if he hadn't been the one to let them out. With a sigh, Jim Henry stopped talking.

"I reckon it's right. Says here that Texas voted to leave the Union on March fourth and joined up with the Confederacy on the twenty-third. Hell, Jim Henry, if they want to leave the Union, they up and do it. Says so right here in this paper Mr. Spencer got in El Paso, 'long with that wine you sucking on. Hell, I knowed the soldiers was moving out of the forts around here. Now it makes sense. Mr. Spencer, he says there ain't no more cattle going up to them boys to Fort Davis. You wouldn't know about that, boy, you been working the broncs too long and hanging around here rest of the time.'' He came up for air and glanced at Jim Henry.

"What's the matter now, kid? You got a soured look to you. Told you drinking wine ain't right for a man. Need a bottle of whiskey out of the mountains or some of that pure gold tequila to take hold.''

So the soldiers were gone, chased from Fort Davis. . . . That meant *she* was gone for certain now. The thought twisted Jim Henry's gut. The healed scars on his back itched furiously, and he scrubbed them on the chair but felt no relief. Hap talked on, and Jim Henry listened.

"This damned paper's more'n two weeks old, by God. We got some serious thinking to do, boy. They's going to be a war if it ain't already started. Things come so slow out here, we could have fought and won and nobody in this place would know the difference.''

He held out the paper to Jim Henry. "Look—TEXAS VOTES TO SECEDE. And now we got our own vote. I ain't going to set no nigger free to vote my rights and work my job. Tough enough down here with the Mexes wanting the same pay, thinking they can drink and ride with a white man. It ain't the way the laws was written. . . . You listening at all, Jim Henry?''

The kid had a bottle of wine stuck to his mouth and was off somewhere in his head. Hap didn't much mind the kid drinking, but he wasn't interested in nothing else, including women. Didn't even have the decency to listen about Texas. Hap found himself wanting to pick up the kid and shake him like a coyote would shake a dead prairie dog.

Then Jim Henry raised his eyes, and a rare smile split the burned face. Sullen son he'd been these past weeks, so when he finally did move, Hap was waiting. "Hap, you riding with me or you planning on sitting and talking about your Texas rights all day?"

"What you talking 'bout, Jim Henry, ride with you where? I got me important things here to—"

Jim Henry stood up, bottle of wine in hand. "Place where my pa built our house. Want to see it, ain't been there in nine years. Since they was . . . You talking or riding with me?"

Hap shook his head, bewildered by the sudden change.

"They come to mind this morning, real early," Jim Henry said. "Been at me all day. I ain't ever been to see what's left. You coming?"

Hap looked to the kid and saw deeper than he wanted; Jim Henry was a man full grown now, six feet of Texas leather and spit. Wine left its red mark in the hazel eyes, and the *despoblado* sun'd burned a map on his face. The boy was a true son of hell.

Hap pushed away looking into a man's soul and rustled the faded newspaper as he tried to fold it. "Jim Henry, you let that wine get to you, boy. You ain't said nothing 'bout a ride someplace. You want to go, boy, you know I'm with you. And I got 'nother bottle of that wine. Let's ride."

A yearling steer browsed inside the thicket, one hind hoof resting on a rotten beam. Powdered brick gave off pale red dust each time the animal stamped at a fly. Jim Henry aimed the restless bay at the steer and marveled at the animal's stubborn refusal to move until he'd slapped its flank with the butt end of his reins. The steer bellowed, swung its horns, and snorted as the bay spooked. Then it moved slowly from the rubble, and Jim Henry and Hap sat their horses to watch it disappear.

There wasn't much to let a body know there had been a house in this clearing. Spencer's men had pulled in the walls and shattered the roof, exposing what had been a home to the destruction of the wind and occasional rain. Hap slipped from the gray and tied up, then waited for Jim Henry's move.

It was a wonder to him that the place had been so small and yet held a family of four people. Little more than a squared room, the pile of dust and broken brick rose in a mound. It didn't look like much to Hap; the pens and corrals, and the low barn, all had fallen into the hard soil. Not much for memories. Hap found an edge of a wall for a seat and wondered what Jim Henry was going to do next.

Jim Henry stared at the mound of rubble. Underneath were his ma and pa and his little brother. He crossed his hands on the saddle horn, let his feet slip from the stirrups. The bay shifted uneasily, still doubtful of anything a human did. For once Hap had the sense to keep quiet as Jim Henry dismounted and tied and hobbled the suspicious bay.

Jesús's carved horse . . . Its shape came to Jim Henry, the careful drawing of the arched neck, the fine legs ending in delicate hooves, a rigid floating tail. Jesús had abandoned the McCraws to ride out to get help for his brother, but the horse had remained hidden in the ruins. Jim Henry began to dig, shifting through the piles of stone and moving the accumulation of manure and blown earth. The horse would be near where his pallet had been, in the small space partitioned off from his parents' bed.

The ground wouldn't give up fast enough, so Jim Henry tugged out his knife. He was careful in the beginning, digging slowly at the pile, chipping each brick gently. But the mound did not diminish until he shoved in the tip of the blade and flipped out a brick, and another, becoming impatient with the slowness of the chore.

Hap jumped when a rock skidded past him, and the bay gelding leaned on the hobbles' restraint and whinnied in alarm. Jim Henry kept digging, and Hap kept quiet.

Suddenly Jim Henry yanked at a buried shape and choked on the dust. He dug faster, fearful of what he'd found. There was a faint ring of metal as he touched wrapped cloth. The outer skin was greasy; when he peeled the layers back, memories flooded him, and tears stung his reddened eyes. He wiped them with his sleeve as he looked at the treasure, and he heard his father speak: *It's a rifleman's companion, boys.*

That's what it's called, Benny. Now, you two listen good to me. Don't ever touch this. I keep it sharp even when I ain't using it. No good having a weapon if you can't trust it.

A long, thin blade, charred and rusted, the handle half-eaten wood. From Tennessee, from the hills behind their cabin. Hard maple with a sheen to it, polished with love to a glowing warmth. Tiger's-eye maple, Pa had told them proudly. Cut special and fitted to the blade, rubbed and worked and oiled until it had its own life.

He remembered more; Pa's pride was buried in here, too. A swivel breech-loading rifle, a rare two-shot of medium caliber. A forty-four, if Jim Henry remembered right. The words flowed in his mind, coming to him in Pa's voice. Now he could understand the words that had no meaning to him as a child. The sound of his father rolled over him, the sight of the strong hands lifting the long knife and talking about it, polishing and honing the blade, rubbing the maple handle, enjoying its sheen. The rifle had to be buried near the knife's grave. He laid the knife carefully on two of the bricks, then went back to his digging, unmindful of Hap, the horses, anything around him.

The light on the long blade intrigued Hap. He was getting bored just sitting. He rose and walked over to the ruined hut. He'd heard of boot knives this length; his own pa had spoken of them. This looked to have been a good one, too bad about the handle. There weren't nothing in the *despoblado* to replace good maple like that had been.

Hap leaned down to inspect the treasure, and when he reached out to touch the metal, it was blocked by the tip of a dust-coated knife.

"You leave that be."

Jim Henry didn't even look up as he spoke. After a moment Hap shrugged and retreated to his section of the wall, snugged himself back into the most comfortable depression on the rotted adobe. The boy pure didn't want no one in his business. He pulled out a crudely carved pipe and tamped it down, struck a spark, and pulled in air through the bone stem. Nothing to do but set and wait. Fine by him, he'd just been a might curious.

The rifle had to be somewhere. . . . Jim Henry saw his pa

smearing something the length of the barrel and cursing as he wiped his hands on his breeches. It had to be here. Jim Henry grabbed a big chunk of stone, and it came free, filling his lungs with powder. His fingers slipped inside a long depression and felt a smooth-coated parcel, a heavy parcel, awkward and half-buried in the dirt.

It would be the old swivel breech rifle, coated in lard. Jim Henry remembered their mother's surprise when Pa asked for the grease. Remembered all the questions exploding inside him as he had watched with fascination. Benny was too small then to be much interested, but Jim Henry was drawn to the different make of the weapon—the feel of it in his hands when Pa let him hold it, the curious use of the rendered fat to insulate the weapon and protect it. John Spencer provided his men with rifles and bullets and powder, his pa explained. Provided anything they needed to insure the protection of the rancho. The swivel breech rifle was an extra now, as was the long knife known as the "rifleman's friend."

Jim Henry bent over his treasures. The sound from him was strange enough to bring Hap back from a half doze over the smoldering pipe. It was a cry, childlike and frightened. Hap glanced around him quickly. There were no birds he could see, no small animals provoked into fear, no restless horses or returned steers. He stood up and dusted himself off, saw Jim Henry cross-legged in the rubble, a long bundle on his lap, the dulled knife in his hand. He began to walk over slowly.

Blind eyes gazed up at him, unseeing eyes. . . . Hap stepped back, watched the sun shift behind the cottonwoods to the river. Anything to keep from seeing Jim Henry's face. It was sobs strangled in the boy's throat that produced the curious sound. One hand lifted and touched a long shape, the other held the charcoaled end of the old knife.

Hap dug out the bottle of wine and took a long drink himself before handing it to Jim Henry. It took half the bottle gone before the sobbing stopped. Jim Henry came up slowly, bent back to the careful laying down of his dust-covered treasures. "I got to get the horse, Hap, then we'll get the hell out of here."

Hap shook his head; no hurry. But the kid was lost in his

own world, as if everything—Hap, the sunlight, the empty bottle, the dust, and the sleeping horses—did not exist. Hap sighed and headed back to his seat on the adobe south wall.

And while Jim Henry worked, he smoked his pipe. Damn the boy for asking him to ride along, he thought. Damn the sadness inside him. He drew hard on the cold pipe and choked and spat into the thick dust. Memories were for the dead, not the living.

Jim Henry sat surrounded by his memories, bits of broken stone, charred wooden lumps, shreds of bright fabric dusted pale red. The bowl of a cooking pot with no handle. A leg of a chair half-burned, a once-shining hair comb dulled and rusted. And things in darker places he did not want to identify—long black shapes that rubbed clean and white when he touched them, curved and narrow pieces that lay together in soft symmetry. He patted the small horse in its new pocket, then layered dirt and broken ground over the wide, uncovered grave. The tears came again, but this time he did nothing to hide them or deny the crying.

When he was finished, he stood up slowly. Face smeared black and gray, with white tracks in the bearded line of his jaw, Jim Henry drew his arm in a farewell gesture across his face, and the grieving colors were blended with the river dust to become muddied and obscured.

"Hap, let's ride."

"I read that handbill you got put up on the cantina door, Mr. Spencer. Yes, sir, and I been thinking of joining up. That General Sibley, he sounds like a good man. We can hit up to the New Mexico territory, chase them soldiers. Free the territory for the Confederacy, and be closer to winning the war. That's what Sibley says in his poster, yes, sir."

Hap was uncomfortable in the big room, so he stayed right by the door, hat in hand, booted feet away from the pretty rugging on the plank floor.

"No, sir, I ain't seen Jim Henry for quite a spell. Last time I seen him he was saddling that rank son of a wall-eyed mother and had him a supply of bottles stuffed in his bags. Going to ride him out a drunk, I figured. If he'd wanted company, he would've asked, so I left him alone."

Spencer wanted to know about Jim Henry McCraw. Despite his own warnings, there was room for worrying about the kid. Dionicio had come to him with a strange tale of the two of them—Hap and McCraw—down to the ruined house. Dionicio had waited in the bush and, when they had gone, checked carefully for what was missing. What had been changed in the terrible, empty grave.

There was a lot of change in the *despoblado*. The Union Army was gone, taking Spencer's contracts with them. There were calls out across Texas for men to join the Confederacy. The Union and its new brother, the Confederacy, were at war.

Fort Davis had emptied out April 13, and Spencer read later that the Confederacy had fired on a fort in the east the day before. He'd figured to pull in his horns, fortify the rancho with his men and their families, keep track of the cattle best he could. Without the army, the Indians would return to their plundering ways. The Confederate troops moving through the *despoblado* would need rations; he could offer them contracted Yankee beef, and the roasted haunches would taste the better for not filling Union bellies. He could survive the war even if he came to growing crops along the river and pulling his own weeds. He would be here when the more civilized countries were ravaged and their men buried.

"Hap, you find Jim Henry, talk to him. I got mostly men with families staying to the rancho. Maybe you and the McCraw boy can hitch yourself to the army up to Fort Davis, or over to El Paso if you don't catch them to the fort. Whatever you do, it's best the two of you ride on. Don't want trouble here with the men, don't want the likes of you or that kid raising ghosts on me. I'll outfit you both, sure enough. And any of the other single men you take with you. Give you a good horse and furnishings, a weapon and ammunition. Sibley expects his men to come ready to fight, and by God, any man riding from Spencer's Rancho will have the best. So you find Jim Henry, and the two of you get started on your way."

Limm Tyler found Jim Henry first. Dionicio had talked to Josibio, who had said a word to Degado, who let his woman know, and she had told Rosa, who was upset and came to him. The boy had been to the grave of his parents for the first time in nine years.

Tyler found the boy down to the river, the wall-eyed gelding hobbled and tied in a circle of grass. The familiar dark bottle was in one hand, an empty bottle reflected itself in the high sun.

When the kid looked up at him, Tyler could not help himself. It wasn't as if there was pity in the blurred eyes, but there was a notion in the face that the boy was owed something. Tyler sighed again, feeling the old man inside him, feeling anger at his own weakness. He never did learn to speak what he thought to the kid, and he couldn't start now. So they made a pretty picture by the slow river: two men, one young, one old, tied to each other and pulled separate from the bond.

"Got something for you. Saw that old swivel breech of your pa's and figured you needed a horn. A good knife, too, always come in handy. Here."

The horn was a warm cream, finely etched with designs along its length. The texture was faded and smooth, but its polished surface drew on Jim Henry's mind. He put down the bottle, and Tyler placed the horn in his outstretched hand. The feel of it was perfect, the smoothness gentle under his thumb. Jim Henry allowed himself the pleasure of cupping the horn, holding it until the warmth of his palm was transferred to the horn and it became part of him.

"The knife, too, boy. Take your time. That horn was mine when I fought my war in Mexico. Yours, now."

The boy looked up and straight into Tyler, and the old man forgot what he'd planned out to speak. This was his boy; no matter he carried the name McCraw. Raised and trained and started by Limm Tyler. Like working a young colt, only the end weren't so easy to see. It was up to the boy now, and Tyler, confronted with the red eyes and bleached face, had his doubts. The skills were set, the knowledge in those sprung hands, the knowing how to work. But the part that made the boy a man was buried so hard, Tyler wondered if it would ever come to the surface.

"Tyler, I thank you. For the knife and the horn. I ain't . . . never seen a horn like this one. I . . . thank you."

The boy was trying; Tyler let his hand touch the arm above the elbow and felt the muscle flinch. Still gun-shy, still spooked bad enough to make a man wonder. "Good luck, Jim Henry. Come back if you can. You always got a home with Rosa and me. You remember that, you get going up north. Home is here."

Hap came along later and found Jim Henry passed out, back to a rock, head on his chest. He clutched a fine-carved horn in one hand, and a bowie knife with a fancy handle was laid across his chest. Hap shoved a foot in the sleeping man's ribs and laughed when Jim Henry toppled sideways and didn't stir. Out cold, with two empty bottles of wine beside him.

Hap relieved Jim Henry of the knife, curious as to the words carefully scribed on polished bone. It read easy, and he grinned at the message. He bet Jim Henry hadn't gotten those eyes focused close enough to reading, or he would be up wild and woolly: "Given this day, June 1861, to their son, James Henry McCraw, from Limm Tyler and Rosa."

"Well, by God, boy, you are a caution. We got to ride now; Mr. Spencer, he wants to give us gear and watch us leave. All the men here ain't taken a Mex woman to wife. We're headed to Fort Davis, boy, to find this Colonel Baylor supposed to come through with his Texas Mounted Rifles. We gone up to join the army, boy. The Confederate Army."

He spoke as if Jim Henry could hear him. "You coming along now, Jim Henry, or you planning to sleep out the rest of your life?"

The rifleman's companion fitted inside the new boots Mr. Spencer gave him, his first new boots. Jim Henry spent his time clearing the rust and honing the sharpness of the companion's blade. He gave his old knife to a boy down to the corrals—he had the heft and size of Tyler's carved bowie to keep in its place now. He worked on the companion, and oiled the swivel breech, and ignored the carving on the handle of the bowie. He could barely touch the words without a mix of anger and tears putting a taste in his dry mouth.

He quit drinking wine, and when Limm Tyler came to his small hut, he was pleased to ask questions and watch the old man pour out shot for the swivel breech and measure out the black powder. Tyler showed him the how-to of cleaning and loading the weapon, his blunt fingers knowing where to look for rust, and finally the rifle shined with oil.

Tyler talked while he worked, and Jim Henry began to listen. "We don't get much rain down here, but I know to New Mexico they got winter and storms and water. Man I knowed once, went up with the force in forty-one, he said the days were rightful, the nights cold. And sometimes wet. We got winter and snow here, but it goes quick, not like up north. Could be, you fight in the weather, others won't know what they's doing. But you listen and remember, maybe save your life."

The morning they left, a small company of men on eager horses, Jim Henry went first to the house Tyler shared with Rosa Ignacio and left a curved-handle cane at the door, oiled and smoothed, the rough knots scraped down and clean. The handle had a crude inlay of *L* and *T* with colored chips of blue stone.

They rode out the tenth day of June. Word came about their joining up, and there were others who rode with them. They would head north in an avenging column. They would come as Texans into the hard New Mexico land, and they would ride through and take the land for the glory of the new Confederacy.

Jim Henry rode by himself. Hap was the oldest of their company, an elderly twenty-five to an average age of nineteen. Hap talked and gestured, and the new riders listened and were awed. No one thought about Indians; they were invulnerable to attack, they were an army riding to conquer. Fort Davis was easily reached, and the soldiers stayed to their saddles as they rode in, quieted by the immense barrenness of the deserted town.

They had known the Union Army was gone. What they had not known or expected was the devastation left behind. Indians had come through in waves and burned and looted with impunity. Jim Henry felt his pulse beat in his throat when he saw the flayed stalks and torn ground that had been the garden by the spring. As if the destruction of the small plot of ground was the destruction of everything around it.

There was activity in one store, a general emporium run by Pat Murphy. The man confirmed that Colonel Baylor had sent an outrider to old Fort Davis, that his column destined for the New Mexico invasion would be arriving sometime within the next week. So it was said. They decided to wait.

The small band of young men turned to Hap for leadership, and he served them well. Stores of whiskey were scouted out, rationed to each man, and a camp was set up near Spencer's corrals. The time passed easily in the whiskey, but for Jim Henry it was a new version of hell.

He walked the ghost fort and found what must have been her home. The only signs of a woman in the camp—a white painted bed frame, a glass mirror behind an upright chest of drawers. A pale ribbon strung over an empty picture frame. He ran the smooth satin through his fingers, and his calloused skin pricked its fine surface, snagged its smoothness. The empty smell of the room, the echoes in the narrow house, the chairs placed neatly by the round table; he hated their soundless message.

Hap found the women, young girls who came up with an armed train of food and barter items, supplies for the Confederacy boys. They were Mexican girls, with black hair and dark eyes and quick to flirt for payment. Hap bought them with a coin and a bottle of wine.

The first night, and the second, Jim Henry stayed in the shadows of the fire. Hap knew he was there. The third night Hap was sodden drunk enough, satiated by his own high nature, to try and help the boy. Betting Jim Henry would watch, he freed a breast from its loose blouse, played with it in the firelight, and watched the nipple harden, deepen in color. He stroked the warm flesh, cupped his hand to his own groin, moved into the softness of the female buttocks. Laughing, he raised a bottle to his mouth. God *damn* the boy, this was living!

Jim Henry had no choice but to watch Hap while his body betrayed him with a fierce ache at his belly and legs—to watch as Hap's hand fondled the brown flesh, stroking and playing until the aureole and nipple stood proud against the teasing fingers.

Hap saw the tall shape move slowly toward the fire. He nodded as he squeezed the woman's breast again, delighting in her reaction when she looked up to him and giggled with the caress. He ran his hands down her side, cupped her buttocks, then caught the hem of her skirt and flipped it over her head. She wore nothing underneath.

That would bring the boy to the fire, Hap thought, grinning. That would get his pecker in a fighting stance. The dumb son of a bitch still thought women were special creatures. His fingers forced the woman spraddle-legged, and in the heat of the fondling, he forgot the boy and the reason for the public display. He pushed the girl to a pile of blankets and lay across her, fumbling with his britches' front.

Jim Henry looked away. Rosa Ignacio and Limm Tyler were there, firelight and a creaking bed, a woman's leering smile. Phillipa Stockbridge came to his side in the dark.

"Señor, you are alone? It is not right for one so handsome to be alone. I am Rosa Maria, and I would like you as my friend. I am not costing much, and it is so little payment for such pleasure as I can give."

The voice was wrong, but the small hand placed in his, the pressure close to his shirt, they were real. Not imaginary, like his dreams or his watching. Real hips that pushed against his, thighs opened to receive him.

"Only a peso, señor. And a bottle. So little for such pleasure."

The hand slipped from his and snugged between his legs. When it rubbed up and down his length, Jim Henry groaned. The woman smiled in the darkness and held out her hand for the coin that was now hers. Then she rubbed into the young man again, bumping him with her mound, drawing a deeper groan from his lips.

Such a handsome young one, she thought, with fine eyes that blazed a golden color to match his streaked hair. So young to have the scar above his eye, but it gave him a wildness she liked. He smelled less like a goat than some of the men near the fire, and he was kind to her, asking if she would like to lie on a bed. A real bed, inside the house of the soldiers. The padding was lumped in the cotton covering, and it had a damp smell, but it was more comfortable and more private than the hard ground or straw shucking.

He was a handsome young man. And so raw in his loving. He fumbled at her breast, tickling and pleasing her. But she had to take his hand and guide it to her center. His gentleness was a bonus; he was slow to ride her, willing to touch where she put his hand, shy about asking if he hurt her. *Dios*, he was a strange young one.

But he was worth her time. For lights flashed in her head, and she cried with the flow of her body. He cried with her, this strange Anglo with the scar above his eye. He cried as he drove hard into her, and she could feel his release in rapid spurts. He stayed with her when they were done, lying beside her on the narrow bed and whispering words she did not understand. It did not matter much; she had had her own rare pleasure, and there was a peso in the lining of her hem. She would sleep the night with him and ask for more in the morning. He would have the pesos to pay her, he would press them on her.

He was truly a strange young Anglo.

"Straight ahead, line up. No talking in the ranks. You wish to enlist in the army of the Confederacy, you will stand in line and answer the questions in turn. We have little time to waste here."

The speaker was a tired, whey-faced man who, when he removed his cap to wipe his face, revealed thinning hair and a sunburned scalp. Already Jim Henry didn't think much of the soldiers in the Confederate Army; already Jim Henry questioned his quick decision.

"Your name?"

"Railsford, Thomas Hapgood."

"Place of birth?"

"New Hope, North Carolina."

"Date of birth?"

"November 20, 1836."

"Next of kin?"

"Randolph and Amelia Railsford, sir, of New Hope."

"Good, soldier. Sign here. Next?"

"Sir, James Henry McCraw."

"Place of birth and date."

"I don't know where I was born. Sir. January 2, 1841. Sir."

"Next of—"

"None."

Jim Henry leaned down to sign his name and felt the table wobble under his weight. The signature, letters stiff and formal, didn't look like it belonged to him. But it meant he was firmly enlisted, in the new and great army of the Confederacy. He wasn't certain of the cause or the strength of reason that had brought him to this point. But he was signed up now, and there was no further need for thinking.

The same soldier who had spoken before they stood in line to sign up now faced the men. He drew himself up in a rigid stance, and Jim Henry found his own body responding in a semblance of attention. The soldier spoke in a crisp, clear voice, with an accent Jim Henry did not recognize, but the words were easy to understand, and the men surrounding Jim Henry shuffled into place, forming their own version of marching order. They were all in General Sibley's army of the Confederacy now.

"Line up, men. At ease. You will be marched to El Paso, where the armies are gathering for General Sibley's entry into New Mexico. As stated in the recruitment literature, you will provide your own weapon, your own horse and gear. If you have no access to a mount, you are now in the infantry. You will obey the orders as given by your commanding officer, and at all times you will act with the conscience of the Confederacy and the great state of Texas as your guide. That will be all. Dismissed."

PART TWO

CHAPTER 8

I T WAS THE cold that defeated him, taking all warmth from him as it stiffened muscle and bone. Jim Henry heard Hap cursing behind him and pulled the edges of his raw mouth in a grimace. His teeth ached, his lips were cracked and bleeding. There wasn't much to cheer about being in the Confederate Army.

They had marched from El Paso the first week of February; they had swept north along the Rio Grande, hard into New Mexican territory. Camp had been made on the tenth, seven miles south of the Union-held Fort Craig. General Sibley finally ordered an attack two days later, but the ragged army was repulsed by the cannon battery and consistent fire of the Fort Craig defenders. Orders came to try again; this time dust storms held the Confederates from their fighting.

Sibley tried a new tack; he sent word that his army was to cross the river, circle Fort Craig, and re-cross above the fort, at a place named Valverde. So the tired, bewildered men had crept out across the river and rode weary horses through the cold desert, back across the treacherous Rio Grande. Here, above the infamous Fort Craig, they began to fight. Here the untried soldiers met their first enemy, here Jim Henry had murdered in the line of duty.

The Battle of Valverde, Lieutenant Blackwell called it, a scattered four or five days of half fighting, marching, and regrouping that encircled the walls of defiant Fort Craig. The Texas boys had won; the New Mexico troops had left their fort unguarded and in ruins.

And Jim Henry learned new truths from the encounter. He remembered sprawling in the rough sand, spewing his guts into the river's sluggish water that now ran a colorless red. He had sighted on faces that did not know him and pulled the cold trigger, to blow bone and flesh and blood apart. But he offered death only to those who would kill him in return. He destroyed because he had been ordered to destroy, but he would cry again over the nameless deaths.

He heard Lieutenant Blackwell praise them for the Battle of Valverde, yet what he felt was the loss of his own imperfect flesh. There were no important words, only blank spaces in the long marching line. Men he'd known, dead and buried in a traitorous land; that is what had come out of the Battle of Valverde. Not glory, not the exaltation of victory. Just the dead and buried.

There had been a salvation in the momentary victory; stores left behind by the fleeing Union soldiers. Their own blue-dyed greatcoats, now to provide warmth for the enemy against the bitter nights. Jim Henry shivered deeper into his own coat, the gift from Rosa Ignacio he never thought he would need. He had a liberated coat pulled over his own, to give him almost enough protection from the night-chilled air.

Jim Henry sighed and pulled the burden of the coats closer. Soon he joined his own curses to Hap's steady stream; cursing the cold, the harsh New Mexican land, and most of all General Sibley and the futile promises of glory. He could not pull his thinking away from the past months, when he and his *compadres* had joined up with Sibley's valorous army.

It all lay with General Sibley. Jim Henry and Hap and the small group of boys who had straggled in to Fort Davis waited out the summer in the mountains with only Lieutenant Blackwell left to command them. They were to protect the remains of the fort and march down into El Paso early fall.

Initially they had laughed at the lieutenant's orders, moving slowly when they heard his words and fighting among themselves for amusement. They were rock-hard Texas boys who'd worked all their lives on their own, unused to obeying a man not much past their own years. So they waited through the summer in their own fashion. . . . Until one day the lieutenant hauled Jim Henry out to pull grass for the animals, and Ezra Massey talked back once too often and was muscled into stocks for the long day. Hap took to grumbling until the lieutenant beat him with a promotion to acting corporal and had him push the rest of the unbelieving boys into line.

At the start of each day, chores were handed out—"orders," they were called, begun in boisterous teasing and finished in silent compliance. It came slowly to the small band that this was serious business, that they had signed their lives on a line and the slender, grim-faced junior officer held their fates with the mark of authority on his shoulder and in his voice. Jim Henry said little and learned fast to toe the mark and do his job. Along with the others, he stood for drill each day, each of them holding a familiar piece chest-high to the marching orders. It was a sorry group at first, resentful boys, resisting the need to obey. But gradually they listened to the lieutenant and found their place in the line.

Toward the beginning of September the small band of new soldiers drifted into the El Paso encampment. They waited through a long fall until one afternoon just before Christmas, when the main body of recruits marched in. Sibley's army was now swollen to near thirty-seven hundred men, all ready to fight for Sibley's glory and their own greed. Between desertion, death, and wounds, there would be closer to thirteen hundred men to fight their Glorieta battle some months later. The violent mixture of Texans had little military discipline, and there was immediate disaster in the hot tempers and regional pride.

Jim Henry kept to the edge of the madness, uncertain with so many people, knowing only that he did not like the mob's closeness, the hard laughter and deafening shouts. A few of the summer's band stayed with him, but most went to the core of the gathering. Hap was their leader, and before he'd left he had come up to stand beside Jim Henry to look closely at his old *compadre*. The knowing eyes had traveled up and down the long body, then come back to the face in a slow, practiced movement. Jim Henry had stood quiet to the near insult, and he wasn't much surprised when Hap spoke his piece.

"Boy, you come far. But not far enough for this. See you sometime, maybe."

Then he'd disappeared into the mass of men, his followers close behind him. Jim Henry could see the dark head swing from side to side, could guess at the raucous stories, the tall tales. There was a brief flare of anger in him, then he bent to the task of making camp, beginning a meager supper over the fire.

There were but seven men around the small fire. Jim Henry was almost a part of the circle, but he kept his bedroll and gear two steps back from the ring, just enough to establish his own lonesome ground. The men settling in for the night knew Jim Henry by now and paid little attention to his peculiarities. They did wonder, briefly, at Hap's disappearance.

They were good men, solid Texas sons come to fight for a cause: Ezra Massey, converted from his day in irons to taking orders and now a corporal, blue-eyed and pot-bellied at nineteen, quiet spoken and quick to anger. Will Monkton and Cotton Belling, alike enough to be brothers, with bright red hair and pale, freckled skin, born a thousand miles apart yet comfortable with each other as if lost kin. Caleb Tanner, short, wide-faced, slow to anger, slow to speak, who watched Jim Henry carefully and disapproved of Hap, who moved in the company of men as if he were their father. And the Andrews brothers, as unalike as Belling and Monkton were alike, close in blood but differing tempers, Will already balding, Ben long-haired and full of pranks. Will's steadiness kept Ben from joining the mass of new soldiers, and the resentment in him was plain.

The main body of mounts was loose-herded past the big camp, well over two thousand head without adequate guard. Jim Henry's wall-eyed bay took offense at so many horses nearby and needed hobbling, with a sideline to the off hind pastern for safekeeping. As he tightened the line, Jim Henry ducked a swipe from the bay's yellow teeth and knew something close to affection for the opinionated gelding. He, too, didn't like the closeness of so many neighbors. Their restlessness settled in an itchy spot between his shoulders.

It was a long evening until Jim Henry lay down and wrapped himself in a blanket, his pa's old two-shot near to hand, his boots lined up by his head. The distant confusion slowed to a loud murmur, and he must have slept. The fire was down, the encampment quiet to almost nothing, when he woke. This new quiet was wrong; a smell hung in the air that disturbed him. He sat up to slip on his boots, caught the rifle as he stood, and went in a crabbed run for the hobbled bay.

Indians . . . after the unguarded stock. Confident enough to move through the mass of snoring men with insulting ease.

Jim Henry bridled the high-headed bay, freed the side-hobbled legs, and swung on the tense back. Caleb Tanner showed up beside him on his tough line-back dun, and Ben and Will Andrew drifted in on horseback, rifles braced to their thighs.

"What is it, Jim Henry? You see something—"

Gunfire answered the unfinished question, and Jim Henry raised his rifle free of the bay's mane. Gunfire doubled and redoubled as he drove spurless boots into the bay's sides. The horse bogged its head to pitch, and Jim Henry grabbed mane, knees clamped hard to the wide ribs. He caught up the reins, hauled the gaping mouth wide, drew the big head up. The bay reached a gallop in two strides as the rider let out a rising yell and rocked with the horse's speed. They were aimed for the main herd at a full-out run; Caleb Tanner was three strides back on the dun, the Andrews boys split right and left and answered Jim Henry's yell with their own.

The herd swallowed Jim Henry as he drove the bay straight in; blazed faces and white stars, wild eyes rolled back, dark shapes slamming into the straining bay. Jim Henry bent low to the mane, legs pinned to wet ribs. Indians, riding through the panicked herd, taking what they wanted. . . . Jim Henry saw a long shape rise over a small running horse. He slammed the bay into a winded sorrel and swung backward with the rifle butt. Bone gave, and a howl split the night. Jim Henry watched as the Indian slid beneath unsorted hooves with no further sound. The herd flowed up the sandy hills above the river, bodies slowing in the deep ground. The bay pulled through the treacherous footing, sprung ribs swelling with the need for air, muscles straining to lift each hoof.

A voice yelled at him, a white man's voice, in warning. He looked into the face of a screaming Indian, horse matching the bay's stride, rider frozen with a knife aimed at his back. Jim Henry kneed the bay hard left while the blade ticked across his ribs, and he lifted the rifle, butt braced on his thigh to fire dead on at the racing killer. The recoil shoved him sideways on the bay; the stunned horse almost lost his footing, then caught himself midstride and leaped back into the stampeding herd.

It was only a second's pause, but Jim Henry had seen the destruction from his shot, the blackness of blood against white bone of the shattered chest. A foulness rose in his mouth, his hand twisted on the hot breech, and he asked the bay for more speed. They were trapped in a frantic press of horseflesh, caught between animals racing in panic.

This time he saw the Indian who came at him, stolen pistol in one hand, eyes rimmed white above a thin, slashed mouth. Jim Henry and the bay were caught with the herd; the Indian showed white teeth as he slipped from one horse to another, making a trail to Jim Henry's back, confident of his prey's helplessness. Jim Henry read the wide smile and offered one of his own. For several strides the two men rode together, Jim Henry inches above the Indian quartered at his shoulder. The Indian spoke confident words in a garbled tongue, and Jim Henry understood, the pistol at his head the interpreter.

So he raised the rifle and brought it to his side, pointed it straight at his assassin's belly. The Indian's grin grew wider, and Jim Henry matched it. There was a long moment then, with only the sweated horse between his legs, the black night lit by peaceful stars, the taste of copper in his mouth, and the knowledge of the two-shot rifle's power. The opponents rode a hundred feet together, clinging to their horses and their anticipation with a joyous rage.

The Indian swung a leg over a new horse and brought the pistol to its full extension in his hand, aimed true to the center of Jim Henry's chest. Instantly the swivel breech rifle rose and fired and blew the grinning head apart. The ruptured torso disappeared as Jim Henry clung to the rioting bay. The herd splintered from the thunderous shot, and Jim Henry and his horse drifted to the outside rim.

At last the herd began to slow. Jim Henry drew the bay to an easy lope and guarded the right flank of the milling horses. Lieutenant Blackwell appeared beside him, clinging to a bald-faced brown. Three other riders grouped behind him, faces unseen, hands and bodies gripping their own tired mounts.

The stampede ended abruptly, the men gathered and collected their company mounts and herded them easily. Lieutenant Blackwell rode up beside Jim Henry. He was brief: "McCraw, I saw you. Looks to me you got two of them. Good work."

But there was little of congratulations in his voice, and there was a break in the stern military face. Jim Henry wondered, until Blackwell spoke again. "I want you and Monkton and Tanner to ride guard for an hour or so. I'll send out replacements. There's no need for this kind of thing to happen. Got to have guards out at night. Been guards, this never would have happened."

Jim Henry waited, but the lieutenant said nothing more and finally turned off from him and the herd. Jim Henry wondered at the look on Lieutenant Blackwell's face. The man had said nothing specific, but there was an implied condemnation Jim Henry recognized. Sibley again, a lack of leadership. Horses lost, men bruised and bloodied. Some of the enemy killed.

Monkton and Tanner drifted in beside him. Jim Henry stopped the tired bay, and the rest of the small herd settled gratefully. Monkton's eyes had a fire to them, dark streaks ran down his cheek, and his white shirt carried a new pattern of black stains.

"I got one of them savages. Got me an Indian, by God. Split his head wide open. You, too, Jim Henry. I saw that old swivel breech of yours take out that last one. Never thought much of you holding to that monster; it's a heavy bastard. But it sure do fire straight. Goddammit, Jim Henry, we got us our Indians!"

Caleb Tanner said nothing but sat his little dun and watched Jim Henry. There was a sadness in his face that Jim Henry did not want to understand, but he felt even less of a sympathy to Monkton's morbid pleasure. Men were dead, horses run off or recovered. Nothing more to the night than that.

He turned away from Will Monkton and found Caleb Tanner beside him.

"We got our introduction to war tonight, Jim Henry," Tanner said. "And it ain't no prettier 'n what I thought. Ain't pretty at all."

There was nothing asked for in Tanner's statement, but the words rolled through Jim Henry's mind. He felt his knife slide into the heart of his enemy Itaya Sol, he felt the pain in his own gut as the soft flesh parted and the man died beneath his hand. He didn't like the feelings that rode with him as he circled the tired herd, away from Monkton's crowing victory and Tanner's unsettling words. He didn't like the exploded skull that flashed behind his eyes or the shattered chest that lay down with him when he had his turn to sleep.

The next night, Jim Henry found Lieutenant Blackwell alone in front of a small fire. He made to lead his bay well around the lieutenant, to give the man his privacy. But Blackwell looked up and saw him, and gestured for him to come closer. Even the bay had learned the benefits of fire and was willing to stand quiet in the rare warmth.

Blackwell offered Jim Henry a tin cup of coffee, and its heat was welcome. But when Blackwell tried to talk, tried to explain his anger at the upcoming war, his distress at brother killing brother, Jim Henry thanked the man for his gesture, put the half-empty cup down near the fire, and walked back into the cold night.

The real cold began when they marched north of El Paso, to follow the winding banks of the Rio Grande. Sibley's promises were flawed; New Mexico in midwinter did not offer food and shelter to the long column of soldiers. And a two-year drought suffered by the land could not produce the promised grain for the horses. There was no cut hay, no graze for the trailing cattle.

Soldiers starved, horses faltered, the train moved slowly along the meandering water, sometimes making only ten miles in a day rather than go without water and kill off more cattle. It was the nights that brought new trouble for the men—freezing nights that chilled to the bone and destroyed the remaining spirit; cold that wound itself inside the few blankets owned by each man and robbed their spirit. After the first big encampment, more than three hundred of the horses had been lost, and their owners were now reduced to infantry. There was much grumbling, and the men who walked complained the loudest.

Jim Henry rode alone and managed to keep the bay gelding away from Lieutenant Blackwell's company. He spent his nights huddled in the hard woolen coat given him by Rosa Ignacio. It held the smell and the sight of the rancho in its warmth: the dusty air, the sweet sweat of dozing horses, the peculiar tang of burning mesquite that meant a meal.

Hap Railsford sometimes shared in the building of a fire, tending it through the nights, but his running comments on the nature of the fussy Ben Andrews and his dislike for Caleb Tanner forced Jim Henry to look between Hap and the men he raked with his words. Jim Henry was careful; he rode with his new friends and kept his distance from the officers.

The river was no comfort for the Texans. Even though it carried the name from the Texas side, it was not the same river. South of the New Mexico border the river was inconsistent and changing, sometimes wide and shallow, running between soft reeds and high bush or tumbling through narrow rock. It was not an expectant river or a gentle stream.

Now the river was wide, and the land it cut through was indifferent. The shallow trickle of water wandered in places across a wide, sandy expanse, rarely rising high enough to touch a rider's boots when the soldiers crossed its path. Those who knew talked of the years before the drought, when the raging river tore trees and houses from the land and swept everything before it on its run to Texas. Jim Henry frowned in disbelief as he looked on the river, flowing placid and sparkling in the overhead sun. It was the only water; the soldiers could not venture far from the river's banks.

The land, too, dictated their march: hard land, broken and endless, ringed with blue mountains that sometimes sloped to the river's edge. And endlessly cold at night. The days were warm and often beautiful, days when Jim Henry was content to follow the column's dust and look out to the distant clarity of color. But he resented the nighttime cold and the slow starvation that captured them all, man and beast. The bay's temper frayed quickly from the edge of hunger, and Jim Henry had gotten tired of dodging teeth and hooves.

One night, late into camp after pulling thin forage for the bay, Jim Henry found himself at the edge of a fire. He recognized the tilt of the lieutenant's head and the smell of hot brewed herbs. The lieutenant, too, knew how to forage. Coffee had long ago disappeared from the cache of foodstuffs for the long column of men.

Blackwell looked up and barely smiled, then offered Jim Henry the familiar battered cup and the free use of the liquid simmering on the coals. Jim Henry squatted on his heels, wrapped an edge of his greatcoat around the pot handle, and poured out the fragrant, bitter-tasting tea.

"You read any, Jim Henry? I know it's not my place, asking you a personal question like that, but so many of you men don't know how to read. It seems to me you must know how. Seems to me you think, at times, in other men's words."

Jim Henry didn't understand the lieutenant's question. He answered that yes, he could read some. But he did not understand what was in Lieutenant Blackwell's mind. The tea was soothing, and Jim Henry kept his uncovered hands around the tin cup, taking every bit of warmth he could find.

"You know, don't you, Jim Henry. We're starving to death on our 'glorious march.' Starving good men and horses, taking from others who are starving, all in the name of the Confederacy."

Blackwell looked up at Jim Henry with raw, red-rimmed eyes. "Why did you come along on this foolish endeavor, McCraw?" he asked. "Why you? What do you care about the issue of states' rights and slavery and the sovereignty of Jefferson Davis and his boys? Or did a couple of those books you read catch hold inside you and tell you different from your life south of here?"

As if the lieutenant finally heard his own words, he snapped his mouth shut, huddled deeper in his federal greatcoat, and waited for Jim Henry's reply.

But Jim Henry had nothing to say. Answers and anger and more questions boiled inside his mind, but he had nothing with which to speak them. He stared into the lieutenant's eyes and held quiet. Finally the lieutenant shook his head and poured out the last of the tea equally between their empty cups. Jim Henry drank the last swallow, spat out the leaves, and left the lieutenant's dying fire.

The next night Jim Henry found the lieutenant and offered him a skinned rabbit, along with a bundle of grass for his mount. They ate in silence, tearing at the seared flesh. Afterward Jim Henry sat back with a cup of the familiar tea and listened to the lieutenant's words. They parted easily; the lieutenant stayed to feed his solitary fire, and Jim Henry went to find camp with Caleb Tanner and the others.

The lack of food dominated the column's progress. In the very beginning, orders came down to respect the planted crops of the local farmers, to restrain the hungry horses from destroying the fragile winter wheat or a haystack. And each night horses would escape from their picket line and be found wandering in the morning, fresh grass hanging from their mouths, bellies full of a farmer's wealth. Orders came down again and again to picket the cavalry mounts and feed them only from purchased stores. Yet each morning more horses were found satiated, more fields and crops destroyed.

The local farmers could do nothing but stand and watch their destruction, and from what he saw in the dark faces, Jim Henry knew he would not want to ride back this way by himself or with only a few men. There was no love in the New Mexican farmers for these Texas invaders. And who could blame them for their hatred? The Texans were stealing food meant for their families, their horses and cattle.

The men had the same orders as for the stock, and they obeyed them as well. There were too many men, too many temperaments, too few warm blankets. And no one man was strong enough to keep the troops from moving into farmhouses wherever they stopped. The males of the family were moved outside, the women and children into one small room, and the soldiers crowded around the fire hearth, taking its precious warmth, often eating the family's prepared meal.

Sometimes the younger women stayed with the soldiers through the night. The officers were told these ladies offered no resistance—had even asked to stay—and sometimes this was true. Most often, though, it was not.

Hap took his first woman nine days out: a plump black-haired mother whose half-grown children fled when the band of soldiers rode into the yard. Hap went in ahead of his group. Jim Henry rode to the side, but he could see the moment's fear in the woman as Hap stood too close to her and placed his hand on the brownness of her shoulder where it joined the neck. He could not hear the words, but he saw alarm widen her eyes, then watched them soften as Hap produced a thin coin.

The quick transaction was lost in the shuffle of men and gear into the small adobe jacal. Hap commandeered a child's room off the back, while the family crowded in a lean-to. Hap's admirers took the main family room, eager to taste the plump woman's cooking, eager to share the fire's warmth.

Hap and the woman soon disappeared into the child's room. Jim Henry smelled the remains of the fiery chile and corn-ground tortillas and left the suddenly stifling heat of the adobe hut. He was more comfortable wrapped in his musty boiled coat and two blankets than he would be in the closeness of the flat-roofed farm jacal. He felt the division between him and Hap even more that night, and he stared at the sky a long time before finding needed sleep.

When he woke there were several covered mounds near him, the shapes of men hidden under tattered blankets, lightly dusted with a night's fall of snow. As the men stirred, Jim Henry recognized faces and nodded a morning's sullen greeting. Cotton Belling flicked a hand in return, Will Monkton grunted sourly and spat to the side. Ezra Massey rolled over in his blankets, and Belling nudged him with a boot toe. The Andrews boys nodded more to each other, then glanced sideways at Jim Henry. And it was Caleb Tanner who spoke the only real words, and who spoke for them all.

"Mornin', Jim Henry, boys. Guess we got our introduction to New Mexico last night. Ain't goin' to get better. Best get used to this pretty white blanket. I suspect we'll be sleeping under it a good deal on this trip north."

Then Tanner looked straight at Jim Henry. "Glad you didn't stay hooked up with Railsford, Jim Henry. I know you two been friends a good while, but what he's doing ain't right. Ain't right at all."

Jim Henry wouldn't give Tanner more than a quick shake of his head to acknowledge the statement. He was still bound to Hap in a tangle of events and feelings, but last night's doings lay sour on his belly, and he didn't want to go that path.

He didn't ride again with Hap, but he could not help but see the man flash in and out of the long column, riding the flea-bitten gray with a flare, traveling with admiring companions who listened to his tales and drank whatever liquor he could find. Jim Henry rode alone, outside the long line, eyes pinned to the banking along the river or to the sloping hills, the low scrub brush and pitted rock. If they were going to fight the enemy on this land, he wanted to know as much as possible about its temper.

Sometimes Caleb Tanner rode with him, or Will Monkton and the Andrews boys, once in a while Ezra Massey. Cotton Belling rode beside him for a half day and took to speaking to him at each night's camp. But given a choice, Jim Henry kept to himself at the edge of the long, slow-moving column.

He wasn't ready for the bright words or the smiling brown face. The bay jumped under him, set up by his rider's tension. Jim Henry took the time to steady the bay, then bit his own lower lip, pulled at the long hair curled around his ear. He didn't want to talk to anyone, especially this soldier.

"Well now, boy, you ain't much in sight these days. You got something stuck in your belly you need talking about, or you got yourself too fancy to ride with an old friend? Which is it, boy?"

There was no need to turn to the words. Jim Henry felt a chill run through him. It had been so easy to ride past in the column and not have to listen to the loud voice or watch the wild gestures as the man told another embroidered tale. Most of the stories Jim Henry knew by heart: full of hate and anger to a man's color, grown wilder and higher and stronger with each retelling. He was content to ride past and not listen.

"Boy. James Henry McCraw, you done forgot your friend, ain't you, boy? In this man's army, friends is all you got, and I see you ain't got too many. I watch you sneak off to sleep by your lonesome, and I seen them few fellows drift over to your private camp. Why, hell, Jim Henry, we done enlisted up together, rode in to that encampment on horses from the great Spencer's Rancho. Boy, you can't deny that kind of kinship; it's stronger than any blood tie. You hear me, Jim Henry?"

He wished Hap would shut his mouth, stop his endless talking, and ride silent for a change. Watch the smoky rock hills come closer to the river's course, read the muffled tracks to the side of the wide riverbed, smell the heat of the new day coming through the old night's chill. Anything but talk and talk and say nothing worth listening to. But the man didn't give up easily.

"Well, boy, you been off by your lonesome when them hooligan soldiers caught up with you, it'd be only your bones hanging by rawhide to that rock now. Be no one to cut you loose and bring you home if you'd been off by yourself. You forget awful easy, McCraw. You forget real easy when it suits."

The talk ended abruptly, and Jim Henry let the quiet ride a few more strides before he looked at Hap, matching the bay's big walk to the little flea-bitten mustang by touching the bit in easy jabs. He didn't understand; what did Hap want of him now that would bring him back in the long line to waste words and spend time slapping at the collected dust? What would Hap want from a Texas boy that he couldn't get from his new friends?

"You got yourself quite a reputation now, boy. Quite a reputation from that old two-shot of your pa's and those two dead Indians the night of that stampede. Lot of the men ain't too proud of themselves, same ones walking up the river knowing some Indians got their horses. But not you; you got your horse and a reputation to boot."

As simple as that; Hap wanted it known he was friends with the long-legged, sullen-mouthed kid with the old swivel breech rifle that blew away two Indians in one mad running fight. The sensation was strange to Jim Henry. He shifted in the hard wooden saddle and looked over to his right, to the flat-eared gray and the smiling man who goaded him at each step.

"Yeah, boy, you got yourself quite a reputation."

Words and thoughts came up in Jim Henry, words and thoughts he didn't know were in him. A rising anger at the callous need for killing, the quick blight of a story told about the deed that gave him brief fame. He shook his head hard, feeling the weight of greasy hair slap his neck. It was wrong,

that much he knew already. To glorify giving a man pain, to
fancy the flow of blood, the faded thoughts that slid into
death, and make those feelings a campfire song, a cruel re-
told tale. He didn't know how he knew the deaths were
wrong, but their overflow of anger flooded him, isolating him
from the marching column of intended killers.

Old Hap had it wrong. There were four dead Indians to
his name, one that night of the raid from the butt of the old
two-shot, the two blown apart by its furious powdered
blast. . . .

And Itaya Sol, on top of the ridge, near the wet spring. A
knife driven straight to the heart.

Four enemies dead. Jim Henry tried to slow the rush of
his thoughts, but he was helpless. But for having given his
word, his name signed to a piece of paper, he would ride
away now, before murdering more unseen boys somewhere
ahead in the waiting mountains. He was caught and damned
and too late to do more than what he was ordered. Thoughts
and words knifed through him as he rode beside Hap Railsford, but little of the conflict showed on his hard Texas face,
except the deep weariness and disgust that Hap would choose
to ignore.

The two horses walked stride for stride, heads bobbing
with the pull of loose river sand. Jim Henry had to try, knowing before he spoke that the right words weren't in him, and
that Hap would not listen or understand: "Hap, I done nothing more than what was needed. They was our horses, our
men up for killing. I was protecting what was mine, nothing
more. Nothing more than what the rest were doing. You see
that . . . protecting what was mine."

The words were said, and as he heard them spoken in the
cold air, Jim Henry doubted his own thinking. It was more
than he had in him to explain, and more than Hap wanted to
hear. Jim Henry shook his head, wiped his hand across his
frozen mouth. Words were useless, and thinking only brought
with it a nameless despair.

Old Hap didn't let him down. "Jim Henry, boy, well, now
you is a hero of sorts. A mighty reluctant hero, I'll tell the
boys. But you ain't riding away from this one. You killed
your men, you got some more killing to do, some long miles

to ride. Can't back out now, Jim Henry. Can't quit . . . you hear me?''

Hap's face widened in a dark grin; he reached out and slapped Jim Henry on the shoulder and as quickly reined the flea-bitten gray out of reach. He lifted the little horse into a run and let out a whoop that put more speed into the faltering gray's heart.

Jim Henry watched his old friend, saw Hap circle around his new companions and heard the voices rise and fall. He didn't understand, couldn't understand their pleasure in the kill. Somewhere deep in the long column were a few men he had begun to trust. And somewhere Lieutenant Blackwell rode in determined isolation.

Perhaps they both were too much alone. Friendship came hard to Jim Henry. He sensed a companionship in Lieutenant Blackwell's eyes. Perhaps there was talk that could ease the despair, but he didn't know what to say, didn't know how to corral the tumbling thoughts and raw emotion riding with him. He shook his head again; it would be simpler to give himself to the war, become one of the line of men. Fight when the enemy fired, kill his allotted share, and chance his own dying at the end of the aimless trail.

He found the lieutenant at his fire again that night, and this time Jim Henry brought no gifts of food or hay. This time he brought only his own bitter painful confusion and a stumbling question that prodded Lieutenant Blackwell into an angry speech.

Why, asked Jim Henry, did it hurt to kill another man—why did it pain so to give out death?

''McCraw, don't you play stupid for me. I know you can think, I know you feel what has been done in the name of glory out there. And you worry about what will be done. You signed on to kill, my friend. You signed on with an army born only to kill.'' Blackwell took a deep breath, and it shuddered out of him in an explosion. Jim Henry's bay snorted and backed to the end of his tether.

''McCraw, I'm not exonerated in this. I, too, have signed and accepted what I will do. I thought I knew why I was here. I thought I could see the reasons. But all I see is death.''

Jim Henry heard the words and saw the pale face and

understood what was being said even through the foreign sounds.

"You read, you told me about the books John Spencer got you. You've read enough, you ever find an answer in your books as to why men insist on killing men? You ever find an answer that agrees with you, or did you even think about the dying until it came your turn to kill? Can you tell me, Jim Henry McCraw, what you read that ever made a change in you, that ever helped you to understand?"

Jim Henry shook; the pictures of the death he knew rattled his lungs until he thought he would drown. His mother, his father . . . his little brother, Benny. The hatred, the taste of blood, the closeness of Itaya Sol. The breath stinking and foul as it carried out the bloodied soul.

Jim Henry shook and could not see the lieutenant's face.

"There was a poet who understood. An Englishman a long time ago. A poet, not a soldier or a warrior, but a poet. He knew, he understood. You ever read poetry, Jim Henry? You ever read the words of another man's heart?"

When Jim Henry said nothing, the lieutenant spoke again, less angry now, quieted by his own thoughts.

"This poet, his name was John Donne. He wrote against the war and killing. He wrote: 'Any man's death diminishes me. . . .' You know what that means, you know that each dying takes from the living. It's what hurts you now, Jim Henry. Even if you don't know. And what happens in the next weeks will tear you apart and destroy you. Don't think so much, McCraw. Good soldiers don't think, they kill."

Jim Henry walked out of the lieutenant's camp, leading the quiet wall-eyed bay, and he never went back to the small fire and the rare companionship of another man.

CHAPTER 9

IT WAS A woman's cry that stopped him cold. He was headed toward a small grove of trees near a bluff, figuring it would do to break the wind, keep some small warmth in him through the night. He'd seen the adobe jacal back from the banking and thought little of it until now. Until the sharp cry was joined by the wail of a child.

Jim Henry stopped long enough to withdraw the long knife from his boot top, and then he ran to the sound. No one had to tell him what he would find: another family pushed out into the cold, a woman facing her tormentors. He ran, knowing he would be standing to certain trouble.

She was beautiful. That was his first thought. Taller than most of the river settlement women, slender and long-legged, with that fine black hair freed down her back, spread in wings across her breast. She turned to the motion of Jim Henry, and her cry died as she recognized another Anglo. Her face stilled, and she gathered the wailing child to her side. She had accepted what would now happen.

A man's hands covered her fine breasts, and a man's hips were thrust to her from behind, a man's face buried at her long neck, face hidden in the luxurious hair. Jim Henry didn't need to be told to recognize the man. And there would be more like him around somewhere. The fight would be quick and deadly; Jim Henry's fingers found the knife, flipped it over in his hand, knuckles white on the bone-carved handle, mouth drawn fine from a bitter flaring rage.

Black-haired, dark-eyed Hap Railsford, who was the first to speak out about color, who was the first to take the women from their men. It was his body bucking into the woman. The child beside her looked up, and Jim Henry felt a dry-

122

faced shame. His own hands had slipped pesos to a black-
haired Rosa Maria, then fondled the thick hair and the breasts
that were exposed to the offering of his wealth. The soft
lumps of the mattress at Fort Davis, the warmth of her open
legs, the amazing pain of his first encounter with a
woman. . . .

He shed his heavy coat in a shrug and crossed the distance
to Hap and the woman. Her eyes widened slightly, her head
lifted in defiance. Jim Henry got to Hap before the man
raised his face from her neck, and he yanked at the arms
clasped to the wide, immobile hips. Hap spun into his attacker, and the two men hugged face-to-face. There was
complete surprise to Hap's eyes and an ugly, swollen set to
his mouth. No words were passed; Hap smiled slightly and
raised his knee hard into Jim Henry's groin.

The agony dropped Jim Henry without a sound. His gorge
rose in his throat, fire spread into his belly and down his
legs. He rolled into a ball, hands cupped to the blinding pain.
There was no air left to make a sound, but the fury trapped
in him turned him wicked. He rolled his head in the sand
and saw Hap's foot lifted for a killing kick. The woman was
quiet, head high, arms held protectively around the still-
crying child.

It was the face of the child that moved Jim Henry—a child
of no more than six or seven, the face of a helpless boy, a small
brother long dead. Jim Henry twisted suddenly, rolled frantically, and the hard-toed boot scraped his shoulder, the heavy
spur leaving a long tear across his arm. Hap's face grinned
down at him, then he went back to the woman and held her
again.

"Well, boy, after we done talking, I wouldn't have thought
you had the guts in you for this. She don't matter, boy. I left
my peso on a wooden chair."

Jim Henry scrambled to his knees, belly sucked tight,
pain dulled in his groin. He wiped his hand across his
mouth, spat into the dust, all the time keeping Hap's shifting body in view. Blood trickled inside the torn sleeve of
his right arm, and he wanted to rub it away. The long
knife lay in reach, its silver blade lost in a small pool of

melting winter snow. Now he dove forward, scooped up the knife, and came erect in one awkward lunge.

"Hap, I made my mistake. Guess it's your turn."

Hap lifted his hand from the woman's soft breast and grinned at the boy wobbling in front of him. "Boy, I didn't figure you for the balls."

He moved slowly from the woman as if the menace of Jim Henry did not exist. Then he dropped quickly, hand reaching for his own boot knife. But Jim Henry was already there, knife held to Hap's ear, tip pushed hard enough to draw a bead of blood. The threat was instant, and Hap eased his hand free from his boot top.

"You step with me, Hap. Real easy and slow. You remember this knife, you saw me dig it from the ruins. So you come along now. Real slow."

Hap rose to his directions, moved his fingers away from the tantalizing closeness of the bone handle against his ankle. The boy was quick and strong; he knew that too well. And he had a code Hap didn't understand. This was a Mex woman, probably got some Indian in her. A beautiful woman like this shouldn't be left to the pleasure of only Mexes; she should be taken and pleasured by white men, strong, healthy Texas men.

Hap lowered his hands, palms out, and walked with Jim Henry away from the woman and the wailing child. There would be other women, other times, when Jim Henry didn't have the edge. He kept on walking, even when the knife left his neck and Jim Henry no longer walked with him. There would be other times. Right now he didn't fancy fighting with a boy who would stand beside him in the coming battles.

Above all, Hap Railsford was a practical man.

There was nothing in his mind as Jim Henry slid the knife back in his boot. No feelings, no thoughts at all. Everything centered in his belly and groin. His legs had movement in them, his heart had slowed its pounding to a normal rate, moisture once again flooded his mouth and unlocked his lips. He straightened up and scratched absently at the blood congealing on his arm. He was cold again.

There was nothing in him as the woman walked toward him, nothing as she looked deep into his face as if to memorize him. Her beauty was nothing to him, the tears that trickled down her clear brown skin, her head bowed to the sobbing of the child; they were all nothing. He walked past her, blank-minded, sore between his legs. He blinked rapidly and shook his head as if to clear himself of a nightmare: Hap's face grinning at him, Hap's words mocking him.

"You got a reputation, boy. You done proud killing them. . . ."

Will Monkton showed in front of him, and Cotton Belling, bottle in hand, offered to Jim Henry, raised in salute to his refusal. And the Andrews boys, Ben and Will, quiet and watchful. It was Caleb Tanner, with Ezra Massey one step behind him, who came from a bunch of hobbled horses, carrying a small pan of water, a white cloth stark against the blueness of the heavy Union greatcoat.

"Let me wash up that cut, Jim Henry. It ain't much, but you've been rolling in a barnyard. It could infect. Here, I brought your coat, it's getting cold again."

Normal words, thoughtful, caring, everyday. The men clustered in a small group, Jim Henry at the center. Friends supporting each other, friends tending to needs, laughing at thin words, applauding brave acts.

"That was right, Jim Henry. You were right, you done . . ."

He turned from Caleb Tanner and his fumbling words, his pan of reddish water, the soaking cloth in hand, concern on his wide-browed face. Something bit deeply into Jim Henry, and he fought it hard before he spoke.

"I ain't done nothing, Caleb, but to lose an old friend. Nothing at all."

The woman stood for a long time on watch, to be certain the two men had gone completely. At first the boy clung to her skirts and continued crying, and her hands automatically wiped away his tears and held his thin shoulders. But her heart was not with him truly, and Tomás must have felt the lack, for he soon went off, to check the pens most likely, to see if his special lamb was sucking from its mother. They had struggled to keep that lamb alive, for it had come in the bad weather, and Tomás had sat up a night with the newborn wrapped in a blanket in his lap.

The shame of the Anglo's hands was still on her, the feel of them taking her flesh as if it were a piece of new bread, riding her skirt as if she were a bitch dog in heat. The black hair and eyes of the man, the short wideness of his body, had been familiar, but his hard-spoken words were Anglo words, harsh and unintelligible except for the mocking laughter.

She could speak some English, could understand if the words were spoken carefully to her and the meaning kept simple. She did not choose to use this skill, even when it could be of use to her and the boy. The blue-coated soldiers had come through their small village several times, talking to her as if she understood, laughing at her blank stare, and finally paying the price of their food and riding away, as she had wished for them to do.

These soldiers, these wild, uncurried ones, they, too, wore the hard blue coats, which had been her mistake, which was why she chose to speak briefly with the short dark one rather than pick up the rifle and point it at him in the universal language. Papa had told her about the Texas ones, when they had ridden north twenty years ago, when she was a child and did not remember. They had no mercy in them, they had no feelings. They were to be shunned. Or shot.

The young one . . . ah, he was different. The one who came to their rescue, who put his knife to the dark one's neck. He was different. He was a Texan, she knew that from the high boots and yellowed muslin shirt, the deep burn to his fair-skinned face, the bright streaks in the muddy browned hair. But the young one had been different.

She could close her eyes and see his face. There were tracings of scars on him, thin white lines that would not take the sun. And a new tear just healed in his brow, growing white hairs in the heavy blackness, bracketing the dull anger in his golden-flecked eyes.

He had a good face. Not a pretty face like some of the men who rode up to their door, but a kindness hidden behind the flat stare and a sense of honor. He had fought for her without knowing her, without asking anything of her. He had taken on his own kind, suffered punishing blows, and been kicked and stood again in his strength.

She ran her fingers through the tangled black hair and

twisted its heaviness back into a roped braid. Then she touched the corners of her mouth with the tips of her fingers and let her hands fall to her breast. It was her own touch that shamed her this time, a remembering of the hated man who forced her and the tall young man who fought for her. Tiredness swept her body, and she knew the remainder of the day's chores would take until darkness. There would be no resting for her if they would eat tonight and tomorrow.

"Tomás, you feed the sheep and the goats. I will milk. Hurry, Tomás."

CHAPTER 10

THE SHELL EXPLODED in the hard sand at his back and showered him with dirt. He rolled to a safer spot, then brushed the gravel from his eyes and came up behind a wide scrub juniper. He raised the barrel of the old two-shot, and its heat scorched his palm. He frowned then, having no memory of firing. The constant battle drummed in his ears, deafened him to normal sounds. One hand flew to his belt, and he felt for the fine leather pouch swinging on his hip. His fingers counted the round balls through the leather, and he was stunned. Three balls left. Only three . . . Pa's old swivel breech had been well used. Jim Henry ducked his head at a cracking sound, conscious of the shower of gravel just beyond his arm. He remembered nothing of what must have been repeated loading and firing, nothing of the past hour of war.

The company was surrounded, split in half and ill provisioned to make a stand. Major Pyron hadn't thought to engage the enemy here in the narrow canyon, hadn't thought Union soldiers were near the high-walled pass of La Glorieta. The army of Sibley's men wasn't used to an opposing force; they'd whipped the Irregulars along the river at Valverde, they'd hauled through the towns of Albuquerque and Santa Fe and called it a victory. They were on their way now to Fort Union, to take it for the Confederacy. They weren't supposed to be pinned down in this godforsaken canyon mouth, held by unseen troops that were something more than the New Mexico Irregulars they had battled and bested on the trip north.

It made no matter to Jim Henry that the enemy weren't supposed to be in the tight brushed canyon. It mattered only that he was low on ammunition, that he could see into the murderous barrels of the rifles aimed at him, that something hard and clawing held his belly in a vise and swept weakness through his body.

He wiggled deeper into the ground, sighted down the long barrel of the swivel breech, and fired. A cry pierced the sudden quiet; he counted a man down in his mind as he went through the motions of reloading the old rifle. The old double-shot would give him two more chances, then he was empty. A low moaning came from beyond him, a keening sound that carried hard in the stillness. Then bullets whined over-head, echoed in Jim Henry, and ricocheted off the high rocks. He ducked as chips brushed his face and tickled the back of his neck.

There had been only the one real battle before this surprise engagement, at Valverde, where the Texas boys fought out-numbered against the Union troops safe in their cannoned fort. They'd circled wide around the walls to break through the line in great numbers, falling easily before the patterned firing of the Union troops, rising again and again to charge unwounded. It had been a valiant and brave display, and it had the Union troops believing they were fighting ghosts or demons. Panicked, they'd fled their Fort Craig, leaving the wildly victorious Texans anything they could carry.

The sweet victory had been a partial payment for the Texans. But none of that mattered now; only the success of a bullet's path, the death of an unknown enemy, was impor-tant. Jim Henry pushed his thinking aside and grinned into the face of the enemy. This was close, too close. You could see shapes and eyes and know it was a man you were kill-ing—not a form or a color, but a frightened stare and a ner-vous grin. Jim Henry saw the glint of a barrel raised against him and fumbled with the carved horn, poured the powder, hurried the patch and ball. He was slower than the other boy at the end of the Union weapon, and he stood to pay the price.

Lyman Doble hadn't been raised to kill. His pa was a preacher, a minister to the small church back east. And his ma sometimes taught church school for the younger children.

But Lyman had come west looking for his glory and found payment in the mines of the territory of Colorado. He was hard fit now, wide-chested and blue-eyed, eager to march and fight, quick to sight and fire.

Lyman was soured by the bent-back labor of working his pa's small farm in southern Maine, eager to test himself against the western wilderness. He'd come out a child of nineteen and stood now a man of twenty-two, blond hair thinned on top, leaving a white forehead to peel in the New Mexico sun. The mining had taken his innocence, but he had taken up a tenet of his pa's, that no man had the right to own another. He rarely tested the belief in company, knowing in his eager righteousness that most men had come to fight for honor and excitement, for pride and boredom, for the monthly stipend, for almost anything excepting a cause.

Lyman kept to himself what he believed and fought his best, marched all day and lay silent at night, willing himself to sleep, already wearied of the fight. A mark of this particular encounter was the closeness, the same closeness that unnerved Jim Henry McCraw. The ability to see the face of your next victim and watch his eyes grow wide, his mouth gape with the bullet's entry. Each face made the trigger more difficult to pull, the act of killing more personal and damaging to the killer. Each man hid behind his own small bush or rock, each man of the Colorado force sighted down into the narrow pass, picked up on a target at will, fired with a certain knowledge of the death below.

Lyman picked out another shape doubled beneath a flimsy juniper, a long body hunched into its pretended safety behind the twisted trunk and spiny branches. He watched for a moment too long, saw the sun-dark face covered in sweat, a bony hand wipe at the salty liquid. Felt the soldier's discomfort as he squirmed to find powder and ball, reloaded in the confines of the fragile tree.

His weapon was an odd one, a heavy breeched configuration, lethal from its long barrel, twice the shot, twice the death in a short instant. Lyman had seen nothing like the weapon before. Or the face of its owner, a young face close in age to his own, burned into leather by years of sun but with something to the eyes, the lines bracketing the wide mouth that told Lyman more than he would want to know. As if the Texan were a human being, as if the dusty gray soldier had a life and a mind equal to his own.

He raised his own weapon, a new Sharps, and sighted and fired before he could think much more. No further thoughts, no further judgments; he was a soldier come down through the pass to kill. Lyman Doble fired straight at the suddenly grinning face of the distant Texan and knew as he fired that he could not kill the man. . . . So he lifted the rifle barrel and prayed to a merciless God.

Jim Henry grinned easily, quickly, knowing by instinct that someone above could see his face. Luck came to him as the Union bullet meant for his yellow-shirted chest glanced off the plated stock of the old swivel breech and rang out, before reshaping its spent path to slice upward, tearing a line across Jim Henry's chest and shoulder. The bullet's force was weakened, but it was enough to push him backward, burn him with its dying fury. The damaged rifle dropped from his hands. Jim Henry was stunned; blood flowed quickly from torn skin, bright red blood shining in the sun. He fought to breathe, looked down at the new pain, and was surprised and then frightened by the gushing red. He had to be dying, but he didn't want to die. His chest burst into flames; he coughed and lay back and shut his eyes.

Caleb Tanner saw the long body dented in the ground, heard the cry of a wounded friend. He threw away his rifle and scrambled to Jim Henry, remembering enough of the long summer's training to keep low, to drop his head and shoulders below an imaginary line. The Union soldier who fired the shot lay behind his rock and watched the scene below him.

"Jim Henry, you hit bad? Jim Henry, you hear me?"

The last words slipped in a pleading that Jim Henry could hear but not yet answer. His eyes widened, his hand rose to touch Caleb's face in slow movement. Caleb's mouth opened in more words, but Jim Henry heard only the ringing in his ears. Then Caleb rocked back from him, stuttered a curse Jim Henry heard, and stood up into the sun. Mouth wide, eyes rolled back, red thick on his stained muslin shirt. Red poured suddenly from his mouth, flooded his shirt, dropped onto Jim Henry sprawled below him.

Then Jim Henry was buried under the burden of a friend, smothered by Caleb's awful corpse. Tears soaked his face, then anger swelled in him to a blind fury as he struggled beneath the flaccid weight. He cursed the sharpshooter who had so easily taken Caleb's life, never to know the murderer was not the man who had fired on him, but another, less innocent Colorado volunteer. Caleb had been Jim Henry's true friend. Caleb was nothing more now than dead.

Jim Henry howled until he vomited from the tears, then vowed forever hatred to the unseen killer above him. The rage burned in him, scouring him clean and hard until a settling calm returned him to the war. He pushed aside the carcass smothering him, did not see the arm flop uselessly into a prickly cactus, did not feel the noise as the loose head struck rock. He could not afford to remember anything about Caleb. A quick exam told him his own wound was a slice, wet and tender and bloody, but not lethal. The cut already itched from drying blood. He did not acknowledge the source of the dried blood across his belly and on his hands: Caleb Tanner's death blood.

His swivel breech was useless to him, plate and stock shattered, metal curled around the bullet's glancing path. He went after Caleb's rifle, scrabbling on hands and knees to avoid the eyes above him. It was suspended above him, an old Kentuck rifle with richly oiled wood, barrel still warm. He saw Caleb's face for an instant until he scrubbed his knuckles hard into his eyes, blinding out the picture. He pulled the rifle free, returned to the corpse, and rolled it over to dig out the remaining ammunition. Unmindful of tears that mingled with the dust, he fitted each ball in his own pouch, fingers stumbling through the exercise. All the while he gasped for breath, hating the wetness on his face.

It was something more than Caleb's death that hampered his breathing, dried his mouth, and plugged the battle sounds to a muted thunder. Jim Henry knew the feeling, recognized it from years past: Pa's hand on his back, the sharp piercing catclaw thorns, the stirred dust from the ponies' legs. Fear . . . He raised the old rifle to his shoulder, sighted down the unfamiliar barrel, and pulled the trigger. The weapon jammed, the explosion lost in the shattered chamber. He threw the ruined rifle away from him and looked up, eyes blinking as if he had just seen the sun. A sharp whining crossed overhead, something tugged at his hair and plowed into the dirt behind him. He crouched in the shallow gully, grabbed handfuls of the broken dirt, and shuddered as if his muscles would part from their bone and destroy him.

Voices yelled above him, wild commands that were unintelligible, sounds that had no meaning. Jim Henry ran, spurred by the copper taste in his mouth, crouched low, weight shifting side to side in a brief attempt at dodging the enemy's fire. The fear held him completely, bit into his belly, drew his fluids to paste a solid stinking sweat under his arms, down his back, between his legs. His flight took him behind the battle, out of the marksman's range. Parting shots rang overhead, and he drew a burst of speed, head down, feet lifted in uneven stride over the rocks and clumped grass, until he stumbled and fell sprawling.

Unaware of the movement around him, of voices lifted and shouting, of the ragged volleys of fire, Jim Henry lay in the warm grass, open mouth tasting the salted liquor where he'd bitten his lip. Soaked by fear and blood, his blood, Caleb Tanner's blood. He shuddered in great spasms; he would run again, he was a mortal coward. He knew his fear, but he never knew he had run under direct orders, that he had retreated with the bulk of his company, that they had moved back under enemy fire to retrench their position.

His head came up, he loosened his stiffened legs and rolled over to sit and then stand. When someone spoke to him directly, he jumped blindly into a ragged attention.

"Soldier, pick a horse, a good one. Ride south, to Colonel Scurry's encampment, and give him this message. Return with his answer as soon as you can. Move, soldier! Here."

He saw the major then, eyes blazing red in a grim face, one hand extended with a canvas pouch. But he did not see the shadows moving in behind him, men with empty weapons, faces drawn of color, arms and bodies wrapped in bleeding strips of cloth. He saw only the gloved hand holding military canvas and heard only his major's voice.

"I've seen you, soldier, I've seen you ride. Get word to the colonel that we've met a force of Union soldiers in this damnable canyon, a stronger force than we've faced before. Ride hard and fast; the colonel will be our salvation."

Then, as if the major finally saw his appointed messenger, the strong voice softened to a query: "Soldier, are you wounded? Can you ride?"

"A flesh wound, sir. Nothing more."

Jim Henry wiped at the dried stains as if they would disappear. "It's not my blood. Sir. Not most of it. It's—"

But the major's back was turned to him; Jim Henry was dismissed without further thought. He sought out the line of horses, protected from the battle by tumbled rocks and a reluctant guard. A curious corporal stepped forward. Jim Henry waved the major's pouch at the man, who nodded back.

"How goes the war, brother?" he asked. "We sits here and listens, but we wants to fight. To get us a real Yankee, that's what. . . ."

Jim Henry paid the man no mind as he looked down the line of restless horses. The Texas men had ridden long through the country, and each and every horse showed the strain. He faced a line of hard-grass range ponies, flint-hooved and wiry, pot-bellied and goose-rumped. Bred not for their looks, but for endless endurance. It was the high-bred horses that had died on the march of hunger and exhaustion, starved on unpalatable weeds and incessant cactus. The Texas plains ponies walked on, roman-nosed head hanging, ears loose, bellies gaunt and ribbed. These were the ones that had endured.

His bay was deep in the line; Jim Henry could see the white-ringed eye, the blaze of temper. But he reached for a closer horse, a line-backed dun with short ears and ribs barely covered. Caleb Tanner's horse. He allowed a sigh as he swung into the saddle and thanked Caleb one last time before kicking the horse to a quick lope. There was no more time to think of Caleb. There was only time to run.

The Texas force had camped the previous night at a place called Johnson's Ranch, a small set of buildings with adequate water and good pens. When the enemy was engaged farther down the canyon, the horses had been pulled back to safety, far from the initial skirmish line, all the way back to Johnson's Ranch. At the mouth of the narrow canyon, hanging to a piece of flat ground surrounded by piled rock and hard slopes, it was a land of ridges and arroyos, with a few trails threaded through juniper and piñon pine.

Jim Henry pointed the dun south and let him travel at a trot. He stood in the saddle, legs braced against Caleb's stirrups, hand tucked under the swell for balance. Horse and rider wove through the small bush and scrub thorns. Often it was necessary to rein in the horse, set him to slide down a steep embankment, then half leap to the opposite side and pick up the trot again. He cursed the land and patted the dun's sweated neck.

Once the dun got caught in deep sand; Jim Henry drove in his spurs, and the animal bucked free, struggled for the crest of the ridge. There his rider halted the snorting horse and lifted from the saddle, weight on his hand at the swell, to gaze back at the blue puffs shifting in the dark foothills. All sound was gone, eaten by the distance, lost in the hard breathing of the dun. But Jim Henry could taste the smell of the gunpowder, hear the shooting in his mind, the howitzer's roar, the scream of downed men. He flinched from the close memory and rubbed his hand across his chest, fingers splayed to feel the edge of open skin under the torn shirt. The soreness brought back his shame.

He settled in the hard saddle, looked ahead at the ride rather than behind him at the vanishing battle. He goaded the dun with his spurs, and the horse jumped a small bush and bucked down the ridge into the next arroyo. Horse and rider resumed their erratic path between scattered rock and small cactus. The snow melted in patches and balled up in the dun's shod hooves; the half-starved beast was soon tired.

The sky turned suddenly dark, the air chilled. Jim Henry rolled up the collar of his coat and buttoned it to his chin. He had to look back one more time. The mountains lay bathed in a sun glow, the foothills dotted a brilliant green through the red earth. There was no sign of war. Jim Henry shivered and looked ahead, to a vast rolling flatness, a dull, green-spotted spread of land. Something touched his face, a white speck rolled in the dun's wiry black mane. Snow . . . by God, snow. Yet the sun glistened behind him over the battle-field.

The dun eased into a lope. The major had said fifteen miles or so due southeast from the canyon was the settlement of Galisteo, where he would find Colonel Scurry and the rein-forcements—ammunition and supplies, more men to bolster the faltering Texans and wipe out the Yankee force bottled in the narrow canyon. The snow came faster, bouncing off Jim Henry's face and sliding inside his collar. Damnable New Mexican weather. He let the dun run out, let his temper fly as the small horse hit good footing and bolted.

Soon enough, steam rose from the laboring horse. A loud roll of noise split the air, startling Jim Henry, drowning out the hard breathing of horse and rider. He hauled in the dun as the noise came again, muffled by the driving balls of snow. Thunder. Right above him, and again, a long roll of thunder. He risked looking behind him and could barely make out the distant mountains, rising high and clear in their own sun-light. He shook his head and slapped the tired dun.

"It's a crazy land, horse, a by God crazy land."

The horse spooked and jumped sideways, and Jim Henry clasped his legs to the saddle. Thunder rolled over them again and again, softened by the slowly falling snow. When the dun tugged at the reins, Jim Henry loosened his grip and let the animal run. Jim Henry had to duck his face against the stinging pellets; he and the horse ran blind.

Two things came to him at once: the dun was slowing of his own accord, and the snow had almost stopped. There were breaks in the sky ahead of him, bright patches of an intense blue. A stream sparkled through a cut in the land beyond him. Jim Henry slipped from the dun and led him into the deep gully. He let the horse drink sparingly, then jerked him from the water and walked in a large circle back from the stream, stopping long enough to loosen the horse-hair cincha and lift the saddle, slapping it against the steam-ing back. Heat rose in a cloud from the exposed skin, and Jim Henry replaced the rigging ahead of where it would set-tle.

Once again he let the horse drink, still sparingly. Then he lowered his own face to the thin stream and drank lightly, conscious of a new hunger in his belly, a pressure behind his eyes. He checked the cincha, pulled it snug, and remounted. A basin lay before him, wide and gently rolling, cupping to the deep-gullied streambed. The storm was gone, moved east and north to the mountains. He unbuttoned the heavy coat and almost shrugged out of it, then saw the lowered sun above the tree line and knew darkness and cold would be over them soon. He could push now, the run was almost over. The dun had a new energy and could easily take the soft footing and open miles.

At last the land rose in front of them; small hillocks blocked their run. Horse and rider angled south to where rock and ledge replaced the gentle ground, where hard slab rang from the dun's shod hooves. Dusk dimmed the shapes; the dun lifted his head and whinnied. Jim Henry let him go then, spurring the tired horse into a final gallop.

Two sentries challenged him as he approached, and he sat tall in the saddle, official in his reply: "I've a message from Major Pyron to the colonel. We've engaged the enemy and need reinforcements. Now."

It was over in a short while. Motion spiraled through the sleepy camp as men ran in all directions, voices rose and fell in shouted orders. "Move out, saddle up, hurry!" Someone handed Jim Henry the reins to a fresh horse, with Caleb's raw Texas rig cinched to its roached back. He had time for cold coffee and a biscuit wrapped in half-cooked bacon before he remounted. It was necessary to take the word back to Pyron immediately that his reinforcements were coming, that they must travel by the slower road with their wagons and long lines of men.

Nighttime doubled the ride, slowed it for the rock and sudden drops. Jim Henry trusted his memory enough to push the slab-sided horse into a jerky lope across the basin. He recognized the stream as the horse splashed through it, nostrils wide and blowing, head snugged into the hard metal bit. This time Jim Henry had to rein in a tight circle, step down, and walk his mount back to the water, to stand in its flow before the animal would drink. This would be the only water until they returned to Johnson's Ranch; the narrow river that wound into the canyon and out below the ridge had dug a deep protective gully, and it would be foolish to risk climbing down the sides in the dark.

It was well past midnight when he drew to a halt at the guard's query. He spoke quickly, and the guard's rifle lowered, a hand accepted the reins of the roach-backed sorrel. He walked to the major's tent and saw the shadow of a man through the canvas sides, blanket wrapped and at a desk, bent deep in study. The major came to the tent flap, red-rimmed eyes glowing in the kerosene light.

Jim Henry saluted as he had been taught and handed the major his pouch. There was no recognition of him; the pouch was taken, the flap lowered, and he was alone in the darkness. He stood for a time, feeling a sweep of tiredness flow through him. There was no silence in camp; horses shifted and whickered, stamped their hooves, kicked at a complaining neighbor. Intermittent groans and cries rose in the stilled air, reminders of the terrible day's battle.

The sorrel was gone, but Jim Henry found his gear dumped by a tree, with a blanket thrown over the cantle. There was a sheltered place by a rock; he scrubbed the ground to make a hole, rolled into the thin blanket with the blue greatcoat thrown over him, and dropped into restless sleep almost immediately.

CHAPTER 11

THE HIGH NOTE of the bugle woke him. The others around him came awake and sat up in their makeshift beds, faces pale in the predawn light. Bent figures passed from mound to mound down the line, shaking anyone who still slept. Jim Henry absorbed the moans that had sung to him in a violent sleep. The wounded lines, yesterday's war. His chest suddenly itched, and he scratched at it before remembering.

He coughed and spat at the rocky ground. "Put, you seen anything of Will Monkton or Ben and Will Andrews?"

He spoke to a barely familiar face, a San Antonio boy among the first to sign up with the general himself. A boy who rode away from Hap Railsford, a boy who kept his own company.

"Dead, Jim Henry. Monkton's dead, so's Ben Andrews. Don't know about Will. They's both gone when them Yankee horses jumped the arroyo. Was pure amazing, Jim Henry. We fired all day at them Yanks and hit nothing. They come at us like it were Sunday in a goddamn park, like that ditch was a shallow nothing. We did what we was told, we tore up that old bridge to pieces for the major. He said it would keep them back. He said it would hold their line." The boy grimaced. "Well, they jumped that ditch yelling and screaming and waving their rifles at us. They sure is devils, sure enough. Not like what we fought to Fort Craig." He shook his head and leaned back into his pallet.

"Yeah, Jim Henry, it's too bad. Monkton went down in the first volley from them soldiers. Ben Andrews, he took a head shot from a sniper early afternoon. We had us a bad day out there."

139

Jim Henry felt the words in his soul. Ben Andrews dead, Will Monkton gone. No sign of Will Andrews. Caleb Tanner left back in the high-sided trap, boneless and drained, nothing more than the earth he lay on. And all the time he'd been gone, running across the wide basin, taking flight while the others stayed to face the enemy. Under orders, yes, but orders given to an already running man.

Put Harvey went to rolling his gear, packing and stuffing as if he would be graded on the results. Careful, picky, hiding his own fears in the monotonous task of getting ready for the day. Three rifles were tripodded beside him, rifles belonging to others who had not come back.

Jim Henry moved from the line of waking men, and when he looked back he saw Put Harvey stop in his labors to touch one of the rifles. There was a sadness in his long face.

"McCraw, where the hell you been?"

The voice belonged to Lieutenant Blackwell, the curse a new note to the man's quick manner. Jim Henry began a protest, until the man walked past him and spun around, face empty and tired.

"I forgot, you took the major's pouch to Scurry. Sorry. Lafitte found your swivel breech rifle, ruined. We didn't know . . . there's too many out there." Blackwell made a vague gesture with his hand, then wiped his face and stared at nothing for a moment.

"Get some coffee, McCraw, something to eat," he said, rousing himself at last. "We need parties to go back into the canyon. The major's arranged for a cease-fire with the Federals, so we can get the rest of our wounded out. And the dead. They'll come at us by eight this morning, them Yanks, so get to it. . . ."

The words slid into muttering as if Jim Henry were not there. The lieutenant shook his head and gazed off into the ragged foothills and the flat entrance to the embattled canyon. Then he wiped his face again and stared at the shrouded forms tucked under a line of piñon trees. He had forgotten Jim Henry, forgotten the orders, forgotten everything except the blank corpses staring back at him.

Jim Henry left the man and found a line formed to the well back of the low-roofed hut. He took his place there, and when it was his turn he scrubbed the crusted dirt from his face and arms, drew in a gulp of water and rinsed his mouth, wiped his teeth with his finger, and spat to the side. It would be the coffee next and a sullen cook who offered the same biscuits and beans, salt pork a molded green. Jim Henry took the meager fare and walked away from groups of men gathered to share the meal. One of them lifted his head and stared at Jim Henry.

"Well, if it ain't by God the messenger boy come back to us. Where you off to now, Jim Henry? You got another ride in mind, one taking you out of here? You sure missed one hell of a fight, boy, when you left us. You surely did that."

The voice cracked in the attempted bitter humor, and a dry sorrow edged the words. Hap Railsford, shrunken in a dirty torn shirt, bathed in rusty stains down his left pant leg, hands trembling slightly as they held a tin cup and a half-empty plate. Hap Railsford, eyes a bright darkness in the wide face, hair matted and powdered to a pale brown.

"Boy, you had it good yesterday, riding out like that. You surely did."

It was Corporal Wheeler who got the men moving, who paired up teams and showed them how to make a litter. "It's easier than carrying a body, boys," he said. "Cleaner, too. Don't have to hang on to them bits and pieces. You take the time, find yourself a stout blanket got no holes, two lengths of tree, and you got a litter carry anything out there. Two of them bodies, or three if you have a mind, some of them blown apart so bad."

Wheeler's voice was a goad to the men, a prod to numbed minds, forcing them to walk on yesterday's horror and come back intact. Jim Henry saw a familiar face, Cotton Belling's, and touched him on the shoulder, looked to the rough litter lying between them. Belling said nothing but picked up the two poles and waited for Jim Henry to do the same.

They walked the battleground. Jim Henry saw a canvas sacking, initialed on the flap, belonging once to a friend, belonging once to Caleb Tanner. He didn't want to think; he followed Belling, stumbling through the rocks, caught on the uneven ground. Their trail wound past blasted juniper, small

oak wearing bright new gashes of splintered bark. The world
narrowed to the black boots Cotton wore, the feel of the
scratchy poles in each hand, the care it took to remain upright
on the shattered earth.

He stumbled once and opened his eyes to a booted foot,
encased in fine black kid. The sole of the boot was worn, the
leather cracked, but the fineness of the boot was still evident.
A crater yawned beyond the boot, darker earth drawn from
the rocky soil. Jim Henry and Cotton passed around its edge,
ignoring what they could not believe.

Words were shouted, men hurried to them. Jim Henry
made his way, part of a team carrying bloodied masses of
flesh and cloth, a hat placed over mangled features, both
boots attached firmly to their legs. They were nothing but
pack mules, thoughtless and empty of anything but the next
cautious step. This was not battle, this was not fighting, but
a mindless slaughter of close fire, rifles aimed two feet from
their target, hands and arms severed from smoking weapons.
Stacks of meat, nameless to the eye, known only by the face
missing at the nights' fires, the names and dates listed in a
company book.

Major Pyron came to speak to his men: "The armistice is
agreed on until eight this morning. I expect the enemy to
honor their word. We will be ready for this fight, we will
carry it to them until this foulness is done. There will be no
more slaughter such as we have endured. Our reinforcements
have arrived. . . ."

The words were fine and strong, the voice resonant, but
flies sang with the major's speech, flies that settled and lifted
from corpse to corpse, taking the best of the new blood meal
and coming back again and again. Jim Henry's chest itched,
his hand lay on the line gingerly, unwilling to touch the sore.
It was nothing; he was alive.

And Scurry's men were here, bustling with their importance. Dirty, tired from the night's march, but whole of arm
and leg, unbloodied, clear-eyed, willing to fight. They were
invincible, they were proud, they were untried against the
devils at the east end of the canyon. Jim Henry watched them
and listened to their boisterous laughter, their innocent
words, their light teasing. He did not marry them to the silent

rows behind him; they would not last as virgins in the day. As if he were a ten-year veteran of the campaign, he watched the new men and almost smiled.

It was a strange way to be disappointed. Pyron and Scurry and their cluster of subordinate officers talked together, aides around them in a protective circle. Then each lieutenant joined his group and ordered them to saddle and follow him, rifle ready, belt or pouch full. Jim Henry reached into the stack of unclaimed weapons and found a long rifle, balls that were compatible, a belt that had a stiffened place near the upside-down federal eagle.

They marched in force to the hated canyon, to yesterday's fatal spot. The lieutenants dispersed them into hiding as more men marched up to be scattered. Each soldier sat in his scant protection and waited. Scouts went out and came back grim-faced, with reports of nothing.

Jim Henry dozed in the new sun's warmth, face full to the light, mouth half-open, eyes folded shut. Around him others did the same, taking ten minutes, then a full half hour. The sun was a peace offering, light and comfort to exhausted men. The daylight dragged on, the men became hot and restless, bored and oddly frightened by the lack of a promised enemy.

Then they were pulled from their positions in the late afternoon, hundreds of men wild-eyed and stiff, teased and bored by the empty promise of the day. Scurry spoke to them again, hard words meant to build them for another fight: "Tomorrow we will break before daylight. The Federal forces must attack tomorrow. Our scouts have seen them at the far end of this canyon. They are there, they have been bringing in their own dead to bury. They are ready now and will attack in the morrow. And we will be waiting for them. Then we will march to Fort Union and final victory."

The words were stirring, the men cheered and yelled, waved their hands and their hats, looked into one another's eyes and refused to see the light of fear. Jim Henry shrank from the others crowded around him, unwilling to accept the mirror in their ancient eyes. He had a chore to attend, a chore shared by many other veterans of the day's waiting war.

He had taken an unfamiliar weapon early this morning, and it needed his attention; sand scoured the barrel, dirt was caught in the fine carving on the stock. It had been someone's prize; now he would clean it and claim it for the waiting fight. He could lose himself in the cleaning, the oiling, and lengthy preparations for morning. He could not see the slow drift of men around or hear the low voices, the eyes sometimes watching him. Men who had summered in the luxury of Fort Davis, men who'd ridden with him up the long river miles. Men who trusted the competence in his long hands, the ease of his few spoken words, the sorrow that lived inside him.

Will Andrews drifted to the center of the small group, and his friends held their grieving for him, for the death of his smiling brother, the hole left in their ranks. There were other holes, but no one to mourn in loud and strident words.

"We'll kill them all tomorrow," said Andrews. "Them sons a bitches. You'll see. They caught us short yesterday, and that won't happen again. We's the better fighters, and we know it. Pure luck kept them bastards hard on us. But tomorrow they'll know their own death, tomorrow they gets what they deserve."

The words were spoken for all of them, for Caleb Tanner lying in the row of unburied bodies, for the missing Ezra Massey, for brother Ben and all the murdered Texas boys. There was nothing to be added to Will Andrews's words.

"McCraw, you take first watch. Let these boys sleep some. They fought hard yesterday. Then you can sleep. . . ."

Jim Henry jumped to the voice, to the tiredness in Lieutenant Blackwell's unthought sentiment. There was no malice in him, only an abiding weariness. Jim Henry nodded to the order and took the half-cleaned rifle with him, climbed to the backside of a small boulder that would hide him as he watched.

Once again he was thankful for the abandoned stores from Fort Craig. The clear night was cold, even in the middle of March, and he snugged deeper into the warm wool. Horse sweat, man sweat, bitter fear, burned powder, all were woven into the fabric of the enemy's coat. Clear stars overhead gave off enough light to keep the mountains visible—heavy, swol-

len mounds that pressed on Jim Henry's turned back; pushed
on him, punished him. He could see out to where he had
ridden, could feel the presence of the great range behind him,
as if he were caught in a terrible trap.

The enemy slept out there, but a greater enemy ate at him,
tore his gut into shreds, and raced his mind in endless re-
gretful circles.

A hand on his shoulder brought him up fighting, fist drawn,
curses unuttered. He finally heard the soft-spoken words:

"Orders come down, Jim Henry. Them Yanks may already be waiting for us. The colonel figures to take the fight
to them, so we needs to be ready to march in ten minutes."

Hap's voice, Hap's hand that dug into him. Hap's casual
grin as he turned and walked around the kneeling Texas boy.
Jim Henry tried to stand.

"Coffee's to the cookwagon, and them damned biscuits,
too. Eat up, boy, going to be a long day before we get to
food again. Be the last day for some."

Jim Henry stayed on his knees. He hadn't been asleep on
guard, it was his worn blanket and the heavy Federal coat
beneath him. He'd come back to camp sometime in the night
and made his bed. The roiling in his belly eased, he found
saliva in his mouth and spat to the side.

The Texas boys were ready this time. Men moved in circles, sticking close to friends, preparing for the day. They all
knew the battle lost two days past would continue today. And
now they knew they'd been fighting a body of tough-minded
soldiers come down from Colorado, not the New Mexico
Irregulars. Jim Henry rolled his gear and stacked it, caught
his tin cup to his belt, and strapped on the pouch that held
the day's ammunition. He needed coffee, and then he would
be ready. He stretched tall, hands to the small of his back,
head tilted, neck exposed. The predawn light shimmered
gray, the hills and shadowed trees began to take on form and
line. He headed for the end of the cookwagon.

Hap found Jim Henry standing alone, big hands wrapped
around the doubtful warmth of the tin cup. Railsford squatted, rested his butt on his heels, and looked up the length of

Jim Henry. The dark eyes found the boy's face and pulled him down.

"Boy, we got our differences this ride. But we know each other, maybe too well. I want you near me today. Got a feeling. Stick to me, boy, and we'll give them Yanks a taste of what we learned to the *despoblado*."

Jim Henry was about to reply when a burst of sound took him and Hap by surprise; they whirled around, hands closed on their weapons. Sudden shouting, curses, a foreign ring to the squabbling.

It was a segment of the company brought up from Galisteo, hard-voiced Germans delegated to stay behind with the stores and the herd of horses. Men who wanted to fight, now accepting that they must remain behind. The sound of their protesting voices was almost enough to bring a smile to Hap's face, and Jim Henry knew a lift of spirit.

Then the order came to mount and ride. Jim Henry rode beside Hap, knowing he would honor an old debt and fight beside the man for the day. They headed to their posts. The cold early light halved the narrow canyon, one side caught in shadows and solid darkness, the other side leavened by invading sun. At times the soldiers' line came to a halt as men picked their way single file through rock tumbles and thick brush. The men were sullen, the horses restive under tight rein, tempers thin as they moved slowly out of the cold into hostile daylight.

The pass widened here, sloped away from the thin center-line path. High walls receded, pine and cedar covered, lined with rock ledges that overlooked the wandering arroyo. The line of soldiers proceeded, creeping forward on the ground's mercy to bring their fight to the waiting enemy. Colonel Scurry ordered them unmounted, to move faster through the impossible land, to breech the enemy lines.

Jim Henry moved with his companions, glancing from side to side. There were a few faces near him, heads bent to the ground directly in front, watching the treacherous footing, determined to stay in line. Without looking behind him, he knew Hap was there, dark head bent, eyes flickering. The line stopped, and unnatural sounds filtered through the harsh breathing.

Horses, from ahead of them, from the Federal end of the pass. . . . Bit chains unmuffled, hooves rattling on loose rock. Jim Henry knew the rhythm of the animals' walk. His hand shook as he fed his rifle, as if he could smell the hay-sweet breath, see the steam rise from fresh droppings.

It began: stirred voices, orders given, shots fired, horses screaming. Men screaming. Hidden by the thick bristling pine, plain to the sense of the ear. The enemy was engaged but not yet seen. A man rose in front of Jim Henry, dark coat a salt-rimmed blue. He waited to be certain. Then the retort of a rifle, and a branch overhead chipped and fell beside him. He sighted quickly and fired, prayed to the squeeze of his finger he was true. The agonized face that rose over the bush did not become a friend, the shattered chest was not a Texas heart. The Union solider was quiet, and Jim Henry counted a kill.

He was blind to the feeding of his Kentuck rifle when a soldier came into the clearing, and he didn't see the three more who wove in and out of the bush to find safe hiding. Their weapons fired in surprise, their bullets rang past him and brought sharp cries from behind. An unseen voice at his back called frantically: "Retreat, boy! We got to set us better. It's an order, Jim Henry—*retreat*!"

There was more. Jim Henry fell to his belly and wiggled free of his protection, came to his feet, and ran. There was a group of soldiers beside him, in back of him, eyes bright, mouths opened to draw in sweet gunpowder air. The small band of men moved into a new position and began again.

The hours were lost to Jim Henry, buried somewhere in the sounds of firing, the growing thickness of smoke, the cries of the dying, the silence of the dead. Fragments came back to him through stories told much later. He knew only two things on his own.

Hap Railsford stood to fire—midday, early afternoon, under hot sun and forced by a frustrated anger. He fired steadily at one man, received fire in return, both men missing their mark. Then Hap stood abruptly, arms wide. Jim Henry saw the rising form of the other man in the brush, counted the buttons on the open blue coat. He saw Hap aim and fire, smelled the flash of his weapon, saw the blue smoke curl up and around his grim face.

His eyes drew on the target and watched as the man went down, head erupting in bright red flowers, body loose and falling. Hap turned to Jim Henry and lifted his rifle in sudden victory, then stumbled and went down, eyes widened in surprise.

Jim Henry saw the bloodstain spread on Hap's body, saw the earth hold the liquid in a shimmering pool. Saw Hap roll side to side then, hands digging in the unforgiving dirt. The stain darkened, spread, disappeared into the greedy earth. Jim Henry rose, ran for Hap, hard-pushed by the constant firing to pick up his friend and drag him, boots scraping across rock and scrub . . . lift his head carefully, dig shaky fingers into each armpit, and literally tear him from the bloody ground.

He did not remember the bullets singing past, did not feel the sting of a bug across his shoulder or the closeness of tree bark torn above his head. He pulled Hap into cover, took him strides back from the fighting, and rested him against a shattered pine. Then he reached for the wound, slipped the confining buttons free, and touched the exposed bleeding. Hap's eyes opened and stared into Jim Henry's face. There was nothing said as the Texas boy let his fingers work an intimate path along the blood and find the wounded core. He sighed deeply, brought his hands to either side of Hap's neck, and rested them on the wide shoulders.

"It's not much, Hap. Plumb lucky, that you are. Bullet caught one of your buttons and shoved it in some, ran it around your ribs and raised hell with your shirt. But it ain't deep, you ain't dead."

It was as if Hap could hear him but could not answer, could not find the release of air to speak. He continued to watch the strong face hovering over him, eyes going from the opening and closing lips to the wide hazel stare. Jim Henry spoke his piece again, waited in the silence, and then did nothing more than smile.

"You ain't going to fight again, Hap. Not today. You set here, hold this kerchief to the wound. Sit and take the rest of the day. I'll be back for you when we got them Yankees licked.''

Hap nodded, and when his hand found the wadded cloth Jim Henry had put to the wound, there was little strength to his grip. Jim Henry sat back on his heels and waited for Hap to find the needed energy to hold in his life. The firing took on a distance and a pattern he ignored.

Finally the fingers beneath his palm took strength, then Hap's smile reached his dark eyes, and he found enough air.

''Thanks. Jim Henry. I'll . . . be here . . . waiting.''

He remembered all of that; he remembered Hap's grinning face, although it got tied up in another place, in the high mountains near Fort Davis, back in the *despoblado*. But Jim Henry knew he'd promised to go back for Hap, find him and bring him in.

There was another face caught in his faded memory: a Yankee face behind a rifle. A Yankee hand that fired at him repeatedly, that traced his run in the clearing and watched as he pulled Hap's body from the line of fire. He remembered that face too close, a hand waved in a half salute, a puff of smoke, a ringing in his head.

What he did not remember, what lost him hours of time, was the loud crack of a branch overhead—a tree riddled and dotted with a stream of bullets, loosened by a cannon's blast, that dropped squarely on the top of his head and stunned him senseless, ground his face on an unforgiving boulder that had been his cover. He lost the remainder of the battle, he forgot the Texans' defeat; he could remember nothing of the bitter, glorious day.

CHAPTER 12

LYMAN DOBLE BIT off a chaw from the leathered stick and worked it slowly in his mouth. It'd be enough to keep him going through the heat of this terrible day.

Yesterday had been spent in burial detail, digging deep holes and looking away when the bodies were slid into the depth. Too many familiar faces, too many gaping holes and spilled secrets. Lyman had had enough of the other man's fight, the other side's army. He wanted to finish his time and go home, go back to the high, damp farmhouse on the good bottom land, its wide front porch, the rock-strewn fields colored with bright grasses. He wanted nothing more of the West and its adventures.

Last night, and the night before that, there had been a parade of faces past his closed eyes, a single file of men in ragged butternut who stared down at him while they marched in quiet pacing. He'd wondered about the men he'd shot; mostly he'd wondered about the long Texas boy whose chest had shown blood from his aim. He hadn't stayed to see the soldier but had gone on to his next target, his own need to duck from the enemy and change position for safety. He would wonder long about that fateful moment, for he had connected with the boy; an intimate glance before dying.

There had been something in the face, something wise and hard and hidden, that he knew would belong to a friend. This was a hellhole war, where you could count the wrinkles of your foe, could see fear replace anger as the firing came too close.

Lyman had fought some in the Colorado mine fields, but there was little or no fighting in the small Maine town of his childhood. There you shot at chattering squirrels or a big buck half gone into the leafless woods. You shot for your dinner, for a roasted haunch of venison or a stewed carcass with apples and bits of Ma's winter onions. You never shot at another human being; it was against God's commandments.

Then come to Colorado, and you shot at your fellow man from self-defense—when he threatened to haul out your cache of nuggets or when he raised a hand to the bridle of your horse. Close body shots, knowing the face and manners of your opponent. One-on-one, face-to-face, accepting the dangers and the usual outcome. Handguns were less than lethal in the grip of a Maine farmboy. It was hard to fire accurately at a man whose name you could call out in anger.

It had been the deep eyes of the Texas boy that had looked straight to him while he sighted down the length of the barrel and thought to squeeze the trigger. Now instinct warred against hope that by lifting his barrel at the last moment he had saved a life, despite the picture of the long body thrown backward, despite the blood appearing as if by magic on the yellowed shirt. Instinct let him hope the enemy was alive and would come in the flesh to haunt him in this godforsaken canyon in this god-awful nightmare of a war.

He had thought a face was familiar when the sergeant had them carrying litters from the scene of the battle, to pick up the dying and the dead of the Colorado Volunteers. Lyman had twice thought he'd seen the rebel features ground into dirt, but the formless bodies had been other Texans, other dead soldiers with coarsened faces and shredded flesh. Not his boy, not the well-remembered long face and red-scarred eye. He'd wanted to ask the soldier about that deep crease in his skull, the hair grown white across the line of the brow. There had been nothing like that pattern in the littering of the dead and mangled.

Now, hidden comfortably in the high rock side of the open canyon, Lyman saw the telltale wound in the sun-dark face at the end of his sights. . . . And he heard himself sigh deeply. It was the Texas boy, the very same one. The same clean eyes, lanky body, careful aim. Lyman ducked as a rain of bullets sought his cover, and he took careless aim at the familiar face, lifting the rifle again to fire overhead. And he was pleased to see the young soldier duck down, hide behind a rock's safe bulk.

So the wound had not been serious. It was awkward to figure out, but Lyman was pleased to see the face again, know his shot had done little damage. They could be friends, they could live in the same small town and talk the same words to each other. As the boy shifted again in the arroyo, Lyman found it impossible to draw on the muslin shirt. Yet he could not sit and do nothing while the men below killed his comrades.

He moved his weapon's center to find a wide-chested man, older than the boy, dark-eyed and angry, mouth spewing steady, unheard curses as he primed and fired in rapid succession. This was a more willing target, a shape and form he did not care about. He was waiting when the man stood in a semblance of victory. He fired, and the wide arms loosened, the body angled and spun, and then fell . . . humped in the reddened earth, hands scrabbling for a hold, feet digging for a step.

Lyman readied his rifle to finish this enemy when he saw the familiar face come between him and his intended target. It was his Texas boy, running to the fallen man, sweeping him up in strong hands, staggering for safety. He could not fire again but aimed instead above the ground. The bushes leaped apart, the crest of the sun-bleached hair flew up, the proud head dropped. That was too close, so he fired into the arms of a stunted oak, putting all his fury into its destruction. Then he stopped firing, knowing the boy and his companion were safely out of sight, and turned instead to the next soldier in his line of fire.

He was there a time he did not remember, until word came to regroup, to fall back. The pass narrowed where they gathered, and Lyman began to have doubts. Word drifted back that the Southern boys had them running, had them cornered beneath the once-friendly cliffs of the canyon. The Colorado volunteers settled quietly and continued their fight.

It was almost done; where two days past the rebel bullets could not find a target, today the Colorado boys fired and could hit nothing. Pushed back, surrounded by Sibley's men, the remaining Volunteers fought their losing war. Lyman Doble felt an angry burning along the muscle of his right arm, felt pain and bodily fear for the first time in the encounter. His aim was rattled, he fired and missed, fired again and heard an answering yell, a whoop of survival.

At the last moment he saw the Texas face again and lifted his fire. Heard the heavy strike of a cannonball smash a spring-green tree. His fingers searched but found no more ammunition in the belt at his side; his quick glance told him he was alone, motionless, and exposed to the demented Texans. So he turned and ran, past the troops left in the sun to die, past the unrecognizable shapes and forms that had been human. Men ran with him. They were giving up the land hard fought for and won at great cost. They were close to surrendering to the Texans, they were close to defeat. Lyman ran with them, stumbling and falling in his haste.

The whistling stopped him—Lyman had no protection but the heavy sound of the cannon. He dropped to his knees, turned in the surprisingly soft sand, and had enough time, enough presence, to watch his approaching death. The soldier took careful aim at him. The young face of his unknown brother laid its cheek to the stock, the hands steady as they righted the barrel, the eyes clouded and remote. Lyman could only open his hands and spread them wide, hold them parallel to the ground and stay on his knees in the pose of a penitent. And watch as the brightly maned Texan prepared to kill him.

The cannon roared again, barely heard by the two men, lost in the dying sunlight and the act of Lyman's certain death. An oak tree absorbed its great punishment and split from the wound, trunk splayed in half, splintered branch dropping across the raised head of the Texas boy. He fell without a sound, sprawled in deep unconsciousness.

Lyman Doble could not stop the deep sigh that left him or the tug in his belly as he saw the branch roll twice and lie beside the stilled corpse, new spring buds shaking on the severed limb, dust rising and settling over the downed soldier. He wiped a hand across his face, looked at his fingers, and saw the wet film of mud. Mixed with tears . . . shed for the enemy.

Doble sighed again, then rose to his feet and began to run, never to look back.

It was a day the Texans fought wildly against the odds. Lieutenant Bradford's artillery was silenced, victims of the brutal Union firepower. But the Texans continued to push, driving their foe backward step by step. Colonel Scurry ordered one charge after another. Five times the remounted cavalry engaged the enemy, and five times they were driven back. But each charge forced the Federals to retreat a few feet, a short violent distance that had little value. Eventually the Federal troops found themselves backed to a draw, surrounded, cut off, and out of ammunition. Defeated. They turned to run, thought of raising a flag and submitting to the enemy.

In the growing dusk a horse and rider approached Colonel Scurry. The rider leaned down and spoke the message, and the colonel's face paled. His brief taste of victory, won at impossible cost, had given way to total defeat. A captured white silk scarf was pinned to a bloody saber and held high, for the stunned Union officer to accept.

The Texans had pressed their enemy hard and won the day's fighting, but something unseen had taken victory from them. A Colorado preacher and his volunteers had slipped past the lines and laid waste to Confederate supplies, slaughtering almost six hundred horses and mules, burning bedding and medical supplies, food, ammunition, and weapons. The move effectively stole what had come to the Texas forces after seven hours of continuous fighting. Less than a quarter mile had been taken by the rebels, and for this short ground men died, lives were altered and lost in the narrow canyon passage.

Scurry admitted defeat. The Texas regiments were hungry and cold, badly wounded, abandoned more than a thousand miles from home. The troops lay together for the night, huddled in the cold at Pigeon's Ranch. Those who were able foraged in the mired corrals and picked through day-old dung for undigested corn hulls. Roasted and cracked, it made a poor meal for the starving war survivors.

The Reverend Chivington had destroyed everything upon which Sibley's troops could depend. The rout was complete, the triumphant march north for the glory of the new Confederacy blown apart. Even the dead were lost to the destruction; Chivington and his men had taken the shovels needed to dig the graves and hide the dead. It was a long, black night for the rebel boys.

CHAPTER 13

JIM HENRY LAY still for a long time, and then shadows covered him. He was slowly joined by the others, parts of men who had stood to his side and fought with him, or against him. Bodies of too many of the enemy, now formed into grisly piles: young farmhands, plainsmen, Minnesota lads gone west, Texas boys. All a rich layer of the New Mexican soil.

Finally he was stirred to consciousness when cold hands picked at his shirt and rolled him over. He opened his eyes to nothing. Forms of men on two legs, forms that moved away from him, carrying what they could find from the rows of dead men. . . . Almost dark, yet there were no fires, no sounds of guns, no flashes of powder from behind trees. His last memory was of running toward the fleeing soldiers, his last thought of a final victory.

He sat up, hands pressed instantly to the sides of his face, desperate to hold in the pounding, contain it before it split his skull in half. His eyes saw only blurring forms, shapeless lumps under darkly stained clothing. Trees wavered in his sight; he blinked his eyes rapidly, groaned from the renewed explosion in his head, and stood slowly in the silence. A man walked past him, dragging a long rifle barrel in his fist. The man almost stopped, then looked at Jim Henry and shook his head, mouthed something between parched lips, and continued on, searching the torn battleground.

He had not heard the actual words from the soldier's mouth, but there had been a message from the man. Somehow they had lost, somehow the victory had been stolen from them. Jim Henry did not look down at the flesh piled near him, nor did he follow behind the wandering soldier. He had

156

found a memory: the face of Hap Railsford, the stunned and awful look to his eyes as he was placed carefully under the firm-standing tree. He didn't know where Hap was now, he knew only that a promise had been given, a promise he must keep.

His first steps were ragged. His fists grew distant from him, his hands dangled heavy at the wrists, his mouth turned to spongy pulp, bells and howling filled his ears. He walked with great care, picking each foot high to avoid unseen rocks, step over unnamed objects. He stopped, exhausted, after less than five minutes, lost in the confusion of red rock and clinging juniper. He would never find Hap in this wilderness.

The pounding in his head would not subside. There was something he must do, someone he must find. . . . He remembered running past a small cabin in the flush of victory, running toward the blue soldiers, exalting in their backward flight. Yes . . . the one he sought would be at that cabin. He walked on in the darkness, awkward and unsteady, putting out a hand to keep from falling. He must find the cabin. Maybe Hap remembered it, too; maybe Hap would be there.

The cabin was near where he thought, a small structure now punctuated by flowering holes, the door off its hinges, the floor unswept dirt. But it was intact, and it held the sleeping form of Hap, and other men. The cabin had been someone's home; there were stores of dried meat, a sack of flour. And a dugout shelter in the back that drew Jim Henry's attention. He knelt at the low doorway, put out a hand to brace himself, and fell halfway into the dark cave.

Warmth, the smell of fresh manure, heat from other living beings . . . Jim Henry tried again to stand, failed even to reach his knees, and rolled himself into a ball, hands wrapped between his legs, head rested on a wadded mound of damp straw. He slept easily, for the first time in days, comforted by the rank odor of chickens and the faded acid of cattle and horses.

"That you, Jim Henry? Them boots is yours, I know that much. Jim Henry?"

The voice was weak, but it was enough to rouse Jim Henry, move him from the cold comfort of the dugout flooring to

crawl back into the cabin itself. It was Hap, pale-faced, eyes
sunken deep in his skull, hands clutched to the shirtfront
stained brown.

"You come to find me, Jim Henry? You come to save
Hap? I am surely pleased to see you, boy."

"How . . . you . . . here? Hap?"

His voice didn't work right yet. The words twisted thick
on his tongue, the sounds weak and wrong in his ears. Jim
Henry tilted his head, craned his neck, and slammed the heel
of his hand to the side of his head. The pounding returned,
a thickening cotton between him and the world. He glanced
out the low doorway to bright sunshine, looked back quickly
at Hap—and could not see him. Could not see anything in
the room at all.

"We need us some food, boy. And some water. Got to
get me cleaned up, got some awful mess in my belly, can't
stand the sight of it. We needs to eat, Jim Henry."

There was no response to the demand. Hap wiped a hand
across his face and let it drop to his belly, grunted with the
result. Something was wrong with the boy. Something was
crazy to the look in his eyes, the set to his face, the stance
as he towered above the men on the cabin floor. He was
squinting as if there were bright sun hitting him, tilting to
one side as if his head were overloaded.

"You all right, boy? You got hit somewheres?"

A man's face appeared at the doorway. His voice wavered:
"You got room in here, friend? My buddy's hit bad, we need
shelter. Any room for us?"

Hap thought to speak first, to turn them away, but Jim
Henry stepped to the man and helped him draw in his friend.
Then he came to Hap's side, knelt to him, and spoke as if
the words pained with their sound.

"There's chickens in back, eggs, I think, an old broody
hen. Food, Hap, enough to keep us awhile. You know what
happened yesterday?"

Before Hap could speak, Jim Henry was gone, cautiously
poking around the cabin, looking for and finding meager
stores that would serve them as food, hiding the precious
meal from prying eyes. Hap wondered how they would survive; the boy was not quite complete. Then he heard ap-

proaching footsteps, tried to raise himself from the bit of straw that had been his pallet. Another head poked into the cabin, another voice intruded.

"You men doing all right? There's little food, no medicine, no help left at all. Them damned Colorado boys got everything. Those of us who can move, we're packing up to ride out. Sibley says we'll stop in Santa Fe, make provisions to send out ambulances, get you boys to a hospital. Hell, we ain't even got shovels to bury our dead. It'll take time, boys. But we will be back. The general won't forget you."

It was a corporal; Jim Henry saw the stripes sewn on the colorless coat, thought he knew the long face from another time. The name was lost in his mind, but there was a certainty the man could be trusted, would know what had happened.

"Corporal . . . who? What . . . ?"

He lost the words, swallowed in unexpected gulps of air. They wouldn't come back; the general never kept a promise. Jim Henry stood eye to eye with the man, furious at his own inability to put the words together, finish the simple question. He saw the man's face tighten, felt as if he were watched like a madman. The corporal stayed motionless until Jim Henry raised a hand, then he stepped back, hand quick to his belt, fumbling for something. There was a change in the man's face, as if he had understood what Jim Henry was trying to say.

"We lost, boy. We whipped them blue asses all day, and then we lost it. Some fire-breathing preacher and his men slaughtered our stock, burned all our supplies. We licked them Yankees and lost the battle. Goddamn."

The corporal leaned in to take a closer look at Jim Henry. "You're the McCraw kid. The one with that fancy shooting rifle. Remember you from the ride up here. What happened to you, boy? Word got out you was killed. Don't look shot, no blood to you."

When Jim Henry made no reply, he turned away, calling over his shoulder, "We done got licked, McCraw. That's all any of us needs remembering."

Then the man was gone, and Jim Henry didn't even know he'd left, paid no attention to the groans that filled the cabin as more men sought refuge in its blank walls. He looked once at Hap, saw the closed eyes, the soggy band wrapped around his middle. Still alive, still breathing in and out, but losing to the starvation days and the bullet path in his side. They were all hungry in the cabin, they were all wounded. Even Jim Henry, but he didn't know how or why. His head was fuzzy, his mind blanked and empty; the rest of him seemed to be in one piece.

Common sense told him to bury the sack of flour and hide the dried meat behind Hap's sleeping back. More men would be looking for food, and no one in the cabin could defend their meager supplies. Jim Henry did not consider himself. He could pick up things and put them down, but he held no weapon, had no fight left in him. He would not kill over dried beef and weevily flour.

The long knife, "the rifleman's companion," was gone from his boot. The corporal spoke of a fancy two-shot rifle, and Jim Henry knew it for a swivel breech, but he knew nothing of his ownership of the weapon. All was gone, but for a bone-carved bowie knife with *Limm Tyler* and *Rosa Ignacio* carved on it. He didn't know the names, only his own: Jim Henry McCraw.

His hands trembled as he lifted the old hen from her nest and gently wrung her neck. There were ten soldiers in the cabin now, sick and dying men who would rest easier with a belly full of broth, a taste of tough stewed meat between their teeth. It was for Jim Henry to do his chores and let the others look out for their own.

General H. H. Sibley acted true to form: His wounded lay untended for almost a week as a few were transported each day, traveling the almost twenty miles into Santa Fe. Sibley was gone, routed with his remaining soldiers far to the south, fleeing the Union troops of Colonel Canby, who retook Santa Fe with little fuss.

There were close to sixty wounded Southern troops left behind, men dying each day from lack of food, men left untended on the battle site, grown weaker and wasted by the indifference of their commander. It was the good women of Santa Fe who came out to nurse these men, led by Colonel

Canby's wife, herself a Southern woman true to her Union husband's cause. She would let no man suffer now for his allegiance. She arranged for the ambulances, devised slings across the high sides to cushion the men as much as possible from the rutted track. She visited and nursed the discarded men while the vanquished troops moved south and her husband returned to possess Santa Fe again.

Politics made little impact on Jim Henry and the small group of men in the cabin. Day by day the weaker survivors died, too far gone to live on the thin broth, too infected to make it without medicines. Jim Henry knew nothing beyond providing a crude meal, washing and rewrapping Hap's belly in clean, soaked cloths, watching the others die and removing their bodies. He did little for himself but eat scant rations, drink water from the well, and sit in silence.

There were times when he stood in the sun and felt a tug, a sharp dig of different smells, of brittle heat and thorned brush, of sweating horses and bawling cattle. And there were times when a sound came to him, a high, clear note that puzzled him. But he would go back in the hut and see Hap, count the men still alive, and try to forget the nagging sound and the sweet-smelling wind.

He slept when he could, easing quickly into its release and waking only when Hap fussed or one more soldier choked and died. He had no thought to leave the small homestead to seek out help or treatment, to let anyone know they were there. They were alive, that was enough.

A familiar face poked into the dark cabin, the lean man with corporal stripes on his blouse. He ordered the inhabitants to come outside, to join the last of the wounded back to Santa Fe.

Jim Henry vaguely remembered the city he saw, the pleasant outline of the adobe houses, the sweet thickness of the walls, the crowded street and people talking in quick accents. So much like another life in a hot country near a river. But it was cold here, the strong winds caught and held in the high mountain basin behind the city. Cold . . . and with too many people, too much confusion.

Too many men poured into the makeshift hospitals where

the wounded found little in the way of supplies or medication. There were physicians enough and ladies of the city willing to nurse them, but almost nothing to aid their healing. Word spread through the hospitals that Colonel Canby had reestablished control of Santa Fe, and the men waited for the sound of military marching that would make them prisoners.

The lack of supplies finally drove the Texas command to seek out Canby and surrender, whereupon they received medicines and nourishing food in return for their company names, their few weapons, and their acceptance of the status of prisoners of war. The imprisonment was enforced by a sentry at the door and a curfew for those able to move around, and their treatment came in the form of coffee and sugar, fresh eggs, and the blessed medicines.

Through all the confusion Jim Henry wandered untouched, whole in body, lost in his mind. To stay with Hap was his only constant. Hap's wound was not serious—the bullet had chipped off a rib and driven a piece of broken button into him—but it had become infected, as many untended wounds did. Hap was weak from fever with an open, draining hole in his side, unable to lift his head or tend to any of his basic needs.

Jim Henry would sit and wait through each morning after completing his chores, lifting Hap carefully onto the shallow waste pan, washing his face, drying his hands, spooning the morning meal in between slack lips. The attendants began to expect him, took no notice of him squatting on his heels outside the ward door. They became accustomed to his long legs in faded wool pants, the shirt too small for him, stained unevenly across the back, patched on the shoulder seams. They also accepted his blank response to their infrequent greetings, the vagueness in his eyes as he slowly stood to the ladies when they made their charitable rounds. His unending quiet, his undiminished patience, became part of the ward routine.

"What's your name, laddie? What are ye doing here? Ye look healthy enough to me."

"McCraw, sir. James Henry McCraw. I'm . . . I take care of . . . Railsford. Sir. I take care of Hap Railsford."

He knew not to salute. The man was a doctor with no signs of the military on him: skin ruddy-colored, face partially shaven and mottled a rusty stain with the day's blood; wild white hair above a high forehead, curled and pushed back and rearranged by the morning's operations. Jim Henry knew to stand quiet and let the man look him over. A good many people did this to him, as if he were a freak. Watched him thoughtfully, talked to each other in whispers while they kept him in sight. He didn't know what they wanted, but he learned to stand for their inspection, keep his eyes to a distant point, and answer what few questions they asked with simple words. It was easy; he found comfort in short words and long silences. The rest was all confusion, boiling in the top of his head and blinding him with light.

Dr. Alexander MacGregor, late of Edinburgh, soon to travel on to the vast California coast, watched the strange boy in front of him and tugged at his chin whiskers. He'd seen the boy before, but never up close. A tall young man, angular and too thin, aged by the recent fighting, lost somehow to the destruction run wild.

"I need particulars on you, lad. More than a name and a rank. More than just ye choosing to stay with an injured comrade, although I cannot find fault with yer generosity. Those of yer company who were able to travel have long since gone now, perhaps to be near their homes by this time. Don't ye wish to be with yer family, laddie, don't ye want to be headed home? Ye are not ill, as much as I can see, so it is a practicality for ye to remove ye'self and rejoin your friends."

Dr. MacGregor ran his fingers across his face, feeling the effects of the day's surgery: the tingling in his mouth, the scraped tenderness of his skin, the trembling of tired hands. So many had died under those hands, so many crippled once by bullets and then again by the inept saw and inadequate medicines. This boy in front of him had an entire body, both arms and both legs, functioning normally, well able to walk away from the horror. But it seemed he could not talk beyond mumbling to make his needs known.

Several of the Santa Fe ladies had questioned Dr. MacGregor about the boy, concerned by his blank eyes and scrambled speech. Now McGregor stepped closer to the Texan, put a hand on each shoulder, and watched the bleached face carefully. This was a man young in years but not experience. There were no recent blemishes on the staring face, no sign of a grave wound or hidden damage. Yet there was a terrible lack in the tough face, a distance in the hazel eyes that told of something broken.

That the boy had seen battle before this disaster was evident: the divided black brow, the bony hands and scarred joints and muscle. This hesitant, fumbling bewilderment was not a novice's terror from the sights and sounds of war; something more kept the youth a helpless captive. The puzzle intrigued Dr. MacGregor, a puzzle removed from the moaning bodies and endless blood.

"McCraw, come here. Lower yer head," he ordered.

He didn't like that—the boy doing what he was ordered with no change on his face, no curiosity or reluctance to the strange summons. MacGregor grimaced; he had to stretch to reach the boy's head, had to rise up on the toes of his hard-soled boots to touch the skull under the thick streaked hair. It was as he suspected.

"McCraw, laddie, I want ye to sit down and look at me, look straight into my eyes and try not to blink."

The long body folded onto a stool, the heavy-lidded eyes gazed up on command as the doctor ran expert hands across the skull. The eyes remained constant—unblinking with uneven pupils—no matter where the doctor pressed. There was a brief flinching when he found what he was looking for: a dent at the crown, a groove under unbroken skin. He deliberately dug his fingers into the depression.

"Can ye feel that, McCraw? What do ye feel? Tell me."

For a moment he thought he'd lost the boy. The eyelids shuttered closed, the face blanched pale, and the torso swayed on the three-legged stool. The doctor knew he couldn't hold the big lad if he fell, so he lessened the pressure. Slowly, very slowly, the eyes opened blinking against the dim hall light.

"What do ye feel, lad? What did ye feel?"

The command to speak loosened the white-rimmed mouth, relaxed the drawn shoulders. But the eyes stayed unfocused, glazed. "Nothing . . . sir. Till you pushed the top of my head. Then it was all . . . could feel. Like it took . . . whole."

"Could ye have moved then, could ye have said anything or done anything? Perhaps yer friend called, could ye have gone to him?"

"Hap needs me? Uh . . . I . . . no, sir."

Then the boy slumped beneath the doctor's grip, reached out to the adobe wall for support. Dr. MacGregor let the head fall back, took the stubbled chin in his hands, and lifted once again to peer into the wide-open eyes.

"It will be all right, lad. There's nothing much wrong with ye, excepting ye need rest and sunshine and lots of good food. And sleep, a place to sleep. I've been told ye live in this place, that ye sleep wherever ye can find a spot. We must do better than that for ye, James Henry McCraw, if ye are to recover from what must have been a nasty blow to the head. Ye don't remember anything at all?"

The face cradled in his two hands shook slightly, the eyes blinked open and shut. Dr. MacGregor took the response as a negative answer to his purely rhetorical question.

"Yer friend Mr. Railsford is doing fine now," he said. "We've gotten the last of the button fragments out of his chest, and the rib will repair itself nicely. It's time now to focus on yer own recuperation. It seems to me ye have carried out yer responsibilities quite well enough."

The strong face lifted slightly in the doctor's hands, a rare spark of interest brightened the eyes; there was a lightening of the harsh lines at the thin mouth. MacGregor guessed this came not from his words, but from something else, and he turned his head to follow the boy's gaze.

There was hope for the Texas child. Three young Santa Fe ladies, mere girls from their light walk and muffled laughter, glided down the hall corridor—three of the ladies brought to the hospital by the thoughtful Mrs. Canby, to entertain the healing men, pass out bunches of wilted flowers, and read fine literature and gentle poems. To give the young men hope and the return of sweet memories. One of these delicate flowers had obviously intrigued the McCraw boy. MacGregor watched the hazel eyes pick out the girl on the right, a slender child dressed plainly in dark cotton and uniformed in a white apron and starched cap. More of Mrs. Canby's attempts to modify the girls' individuality and turn both pretty and plain faces into a common sea of femininity.

Perhaps she reminded him of someone back home. The boy could only stare at the brown-haired girl, a young lady of no more than twenty. Close, the doctor surmised, to the age of the Texan himself. MacGregor was amazed: a smile touched the eyes, the worn face took color as the boy stood up, stepped back from the stool, and raised his right hand to his head as if to remove a hat. The words were stammered and soft, but undeniable:

"Good morning, miss."

The girls passed them by with little notice, and the boy showed no resentment or surprise, as if it was what he expected. So this could be his salvation, thought MacGregor—a young lady who ignored his awkwardness, a soft white hand raised over uncolored lips to hide a flattered smile.

MacGregor marveled at the innocence of the exchange and at what he had forgotten in the brutal aftermath of the fight. He would seek out the gentle Mrs. Canby and explain himself, ask her permission to know the young lass, to talk with her about a simple act of charity that might well aid the young lad's healing.

For Jim Henry, the polite impartial exchange of greetings went deep into his mind and touched a core of despair. He sagged against the wall, conscious only of the pounding in his head, the blank place in his thoughts. There was a name that went with the fine brown hair caught at the nape of her neck, the glowing eyes that hid so much in a simple glance. He knew their blue shining light, their changing green sparkle. The name was clear to be seen, written in the dirt by impatient fingers as he waited, spoken over and over aloud to nothing but the high stars and wind-curved trees. Where he did not know, nor why, only that she was a beauty to watch, a treasure to be guarded.

But there was the horror of another name and face, a different ache that grew in him and filled him. An empty, rough-built house, a sagging, torn bed, a woman underneath him and willing, in full cry. The wrong woman, a dark-haired woman paid to stare up at him and spread her mouth in a lewd, mocking smile. A woman who played with the dark hair that spilled across her and covered her fleshy breasts.

The memory mixed in him, confused and blown of everything except the name that would not come to him. The knowledge of the hot fingers on his body . . . Jim Henry dropped his head to the shame he felt and would not raise his eyes again to the doctor's command.

CHAPTER 14

MAELLEN WITTMAN HAD seen the young man before. With Patricia and Ada, she often walked into the small hospital and smiled at the rows of patients. For some reason, Mrs. Canby thought she could cheer up the men by her presence, help them heal their wounds. And Papa asked, so politely, that Maellen and her friends please the colonel's wife and walk lightly through the corridors, talk to the men, wave gaily, and leave small bunches of the prairie weeds that passed for flowers here. It was little enough to do for Papa and his career.

In the privacy of her room, she would admit to herself that the young man intrigued her. She knew he was a Texan; that was apparent from his lack of formal dress, his sun-darkened skin and halting manners. But it was manners that brought him to stand when she came near, sometimes with Ada and Patricia, sometimes by herself. The two girls were barely sixteen and only casual friends. There were only a few girls near her nineteen years in the confines of the city, so they spent much time together.

They saw nothing of interest in the tall young man who nodded to them as they passed in the hall. And she knew his interest was in her, not in their immature and childish giggling. On the days she was to go to the hospital, she took extra care brushing her red-tinted hair and pinched her cheeks, chewed on her lips to give them extra color. For the soldiers' pleasure, she told herself, for their day brightened by her walking past.

The Texan was most interesting, much more so than the larking young lieutenants who were her papa's choice, their hands clean and soft, their whiskers full-blown on smooth

168

cheeks, their eyes alert and eager. They had no mystery to them, no romance, no air of wounded secrets. They were like Papa, and Maellen did not want to become another military wife. Not after listening to her mama talk when they thought Maellen was asleep in the confined quarters of the fort.

Captain Butler was different sometimes. He had fought in the battle that her father called "the unfortunate incident at La Glorieta" and had come to the hospital with a slight wound in his shoulder—nothing bad enough to keep him from escorting Maellen and several of the young ladies of the city to recitals or to the foolishness of the vaudeville acts Mrs. Canby arranged equally for the bedridden Southern troops and the remaining Union casualties. The colonel's wife said that the poor Southern boys were taking longer to recover because of their terrible days of privation before being brought to Santa Fe and the safety of its hospitals. Maellen did not understand what this meant, but she found herself enjoying the interest of the men, the eyes that watched her as she walked—as if they could see past her demure clothing to how she felt beneath its exterior.

Captain Butler's wounded shoulder had healed nicely, although he sometimes complained that it was stiff and would ask one of the nursing staff to rub it gently and bring life back to its sore tissues. Papa had told her to do no such thing for the captain, and she had pleasured in the red flush that colored Mr. Butler's fair skin when she repeated Papa's words upon his next request. There was a delight in teasing men so, for they invariably stuttered and apologized.

This day, the Texas boy had been with the strange Dr. MacGregor. The doctor was sometimes hard to understand, with the odd way he spoke his words and the fire that blazed in him over some neglected act of medical care. He had been standing over the boy and had to step back as the soldier stood for her passing. She would have blushed and sighed at his stammered words, but for the quick glance Patricia sent her way. Patricia would not have the good sense to keep her thoughts and guesses to herself, and Ada would repeat anything she heard. So Maellen held herself stiffly erect and did not look at the boy as they passed. But her ruse did not work.

"It is that strange Texas boy, isn't it, Maellen? I've seen him look at you with those sad, sweet eyes. And I've seen you look back as if he were someone you knew. Really, Maellen!"

"Why, Tricia, my dear, I don't know what has gotten into you today, thinking I could notice a soldier, and a Southern one at that. Among all this suffering, to see only one person. That is not why Mrs. Canby asked us to help. . . ."

The bluff would keep Ada from thinking any further about the incident, about the calf eyes and fumbling words, but Patricia saw through her and would come back to the subject of the Texas boy and his obvious, unexplained adoration of Maellen Wittman.

The cover-up was completed. Tricia drew her arm through Maellen's, and Maellen touched Ada gently above the wrist, so as not to offend. In this fashion the young women continued their errands of mercy through the Southern boys, two of them holding a secret in their hearts.

Dr. MacGregor watched the three young ladies make their way down the crowded hall and knew it must have been his age, to have forgotten the healing powers of a lady's charm. The lad was in need of this kind of therapy as well as good food and a quiet place to rest. He needed to work his brain, wake up the slumbering cells scattered by whatever force caused the dent in his skull. Later he would ask the young women to seek out the tongue-tied soldier and make conversation with him, offer their good spirits and companionship.

He would have to counsel the young ladies about the lad's unsteady nature, that he would seem most strange at first, but that he was both harmless and well mannered. This would be the best type of medicine for James Henry McCraw, better than anything a sour hospital and inadequate knowledge could offer for his repair.

But more than a week passed before Dr. MacGregor remembered his prescription, and he remembered it at a most inauspicious time: one sunny morning in the ward, just as it was taking several hospital orderlies and a soldier and a broken chair leg to subdue the Texas boy.

MacGregor was a bystander to the scene, knowing immediately he had failed the lad and certain now—that after this wildness that would be talked about for several days—the young lady's parents would not take his odd request kindly. Still, he knew he must try, for the boy was disturbed in his mind. But he wasn't certain of the course he must take.

So the good doctor put Jim Henry out of his thoughts for several days, forgetting about the intriguingly unorthodox treatment he had considered. By then the young Texan had already come to his senses, aided by a knot on his head and the attentions of the inhabitants of the Santa Fe city jail.

They were picking up Hap to take him somewhere, some unnamed place. They wouldn't tell Jim Henry or let him go with Hap. They wouldn't say where or why. His questions were badly garbled, choked by the worry smothering him. Two men, dressed in the familiar muslin shirt and hard wool pants of the scattered Texas regiment. Two men who rustled Hap's wasted body onto a long canvas sling. Two men who didn't have any answers—men almost healed, on parole to help in the crowded hospital. The wild man confronting them was beyond their understanding. They knew something of Railsford's guardian, but they couldn't explain to the haggard-faced kid what they were doing. They were following orders; that was all they knew.

One of the tired faces looked familiar to Jim Henry. He could almost place the man with an empty rifle dragging in the dirt, near the doorway to a small cabin. He shook his head violently, raised his hands, fists clenched. The man stepped back, laid Hap on the fragile litter, looked at Jim Henry down the length of Hap's corpselike body. There was no remembering in the man's face, no understanding of Jim Henry's stuttered words, only a frightened anger and deep weariness in the pale eyes.

"Leave him . . . you can't take . . . I . . ."

Nothing fitted to his mouth; his head pounded unmercifully. Jim Henry covered his eyes, pressed hard into the sockets with the palms of his hands. Nothing eased the pounding, nothing fitted into his mind. But Hap could not be taken from him.

"You can't . . ."

He lunged for the man holding the foot of the canvas litter, shoved him aside, and didn't care that the man tumbled onto a sleeping patient. Hap and his litter dropped to the floor. The other man holding the end licked his mouth and watched Jim Henry carefully.

They couldn't take Hap. Hap was alive, Hap was recovering. Hap wasn't dead. It was Hap talking to him now— couldn't they hear his voice and know he was alive?

"Boy, it's all right. The doc told me, this morning. Earlier, when you wasn't here. They going to take this damn drain out of me, that's all. What the hell's wrong?"

Hap made no sense, the hand clawing at his shoulder made no difference. Jim Henry doubled his fist and struck at the smaller man with the faded eyes and dark red tear across his face. He welcomed the impact of his fist on the man's jaw and barely felt the blow between his own shoulders, barely noticed the impact as he stumbled facedown in the discarded bandages and spilled chamber pots. A weight lifted him, and he struck at it; a hand grabbed his throat, and he kicked high up, caught a foul breath as his knee connected between widespread legs. There was an echo to the fight, a distant picture of canvas walls and wild words and blue-legged soldiers coming at him. He did not understand at all.

Then his thoughts exploded in a blow to his head. Hap was the connection. Jim Henry turned from his gathered opponents, mindless of the shouting around him, of the women's voices raised in alarm, of the heavy sound of footsteps on swept tile floor. There was Hap's face, thinner than he remembered, lying wrapped in tan canvas on the floor, Hap reaching up to him, Hap grinning with his wide-stretched mouth, as if words were flowing from him that Jim Henry did not hear. Then he was aware of a whisper behind him, a surprise in Hap's face, and something clubbed him on the top of his head. He was unconscious before he hit the floor.

He woke to things crawling over him, light taps on his forehead, thin points tickling the corners of his mouth. He raised his head in defense, and the fleshy body squealed and scrambled down his chest. Jim Henry came awake fast.

It was easy to know where he was: thick adobe walls with

marks and scars and curses carved across the mottled expanse, small high windows with a cross of iron bars, the smell of too many bodies in too small a place. What had been darkness resolved itself to dusty light as his eyes adjusted.

"So, the pretty child comes awake. Now we will learn his fate. Will he stay here and keep us poor peons company, or will the fine Americans come and relieve him of this most terrible accident of his incarceration?"

The voice was thick in its accent, the words sly. Jim Henry muttered his own border versions of curses, then scrubbed a hand across his head and winced from the knotted bruise.

"Ah, the pretty boy thinks he may speak with us in our tongue. But he is one of the prison soldiers, one of the most blessed *Tejanos* who come here to ease us of our worrisome burdens. Our enslavement to the Union soldiers and its government, and of our crops, our women, and our warm hearth fires. This poor blessed child . . ."

The cell was no more than eighteen by twenty feet, yet there were thirteen men crammed in its confinement, plus the half-lying, half-sitting Jim Henry. They were all Mexican, and more than half wore a ball and chain, yet they moved constantly in the cramped quarters. The one who spoke was older, with gray streaks in his fine black hair and a heavy mustache covering a mouth empty of teeth.

"You do not like where you are, my friend. I cannot blame you, but you are a problem for us already here. There is not enough room before you came, and now we must rearrange our lives to include you. It is not something we will do easily, do you understand? *Comprende?*"

There was nothing for Jim Henry to say. The barrel-chested man smiling at him had all the questions and their answers. He could only nod his agreement.

"My name is—"

"Yes, we know. The young *Tejano* is called McCraw, ah . . . James Henry. Jaime, you will find room next to me. And perhaps we can do a little something about the food. These guards, they say you are not yet counted on the rolls, and they do not increase our allotment for this evening meal. But I will break a piece of bread with you, and even offer a small portion of the beans which I have saved.''

The food was offered, the bread dark and coarse ground, the beans congealed and spotted. He would not have eaten them but for the kindness of the gray-bearded man, his benefactor. It would be an unforgivable insult to refuse.

''Many thanks to you, señor. I am . . . grateful . . . for your . . . to a stranger.''

Once again his mouth and mind failed him. Silently Jim Henry offered his hand, looking straight at the smiling dark eyes, and felt his fingers caught in the grip of a wide, calloused hand.

''Ah señor, it is nothing. It is a way to pass the time while my daughter and her child seek to have my sins blessed and my honor restored. I am not a man of such cruelty as I am charged. The mule was dangerous; I sought only to pacify it by delivering such a blow to its skull that it would consent to listen. I did not intend to slay such a fine mule, but our generals so far do not listen to my tale. My child, my strong Josefina, will soon talk with the corporal and then the lieutenant and the captain, and she will continue her talk until the word reaches to Colonel Canby and he can listen to her words. She is a good child, my Josefina, and my grandson, her blessed son Tomás, he is my gem.''

Jim Henry was listening until the first bite, then the rest came so fast he lost interest in the story and struggled to find the tiny culprits attacking him, to squash them and rub the small welts they left behind. The fluent voice ran over him, washing him in pleasant sounds, and he scratched furiously until he bled. Between skirmishes with the invading bugs, he shoveled the cold beans into his mouth with his fingers and tore the black bread into bite-size pieces. He would have preferred a tortilla to shovel in the beans, but the army had not yet learned the benefits of the flat bread. The plate wiped clean, he sat back and belched; he had not known he was so hungry.

''Ah, to be young once again. Jaime, you come in here dragged by two angry men who leave you with parting kicks. Yet when you awake, you are content to eat what is given you and begin the ever-losing battle with our small comrades. Do you not want to stand, do you not want to know the extent of your bruises and your wounds? Or are you too well acquainted with their existence to wish to bother? You have the looks that says you would understand the ways of a vanished foe and that nothing would be of surprise to you from your abrupt entry into our world.''

The words flowed on and on; Jim Henry rubbed his eyes with the heel of his hand, ran his fingers through his hair and around the raised lump at the top of his skull. He could not hide the grimace, and the self-proclaimed grandfather and cell leader suffered with him.

"So, you do have a feeling; there is a pity in you, even if for yourself. Begin the process of standing, my young friend, and we will count for you the sighs and the groans. That way you will know how much to return to your kind jailers when you are released.''

He smiled as Jim Henry turned to hand him back his empty plate. "And do you know why you are here, or to what accusation you will answer? I could make no sense of the two who left you with us. They would not speak to one such as Eduardo. I could not get them to understand my questions.''

"Señor, Eduardo, I do not know, I can only . . .''

He had to shake his head and laugh at his own folly. Fighting again, in a place for the sick and the dying. Over what he could not remember. . . . But there were clear pictures in his mind, of the battle he had fought in the pass, the days spent in the hospital. Now if he could only remember what he was doing fighting over Hap's body laid out in a litter on the floor.

"I do not know, Señor Eduardo.''

"We are all innocents here, and it is good to know you are not an exception. All these men have done nothing, have lived their lives in ordinary ways and yet have brought down the wrath of an unseen force which pleases to keep them in this fine jail. It is the way of all worlds, is it not?''

Jim Henry grinned and tried to stand. At his full height, towering over the seated men, he nodded to them all, carefully lined along the cell wall, backs eased into the hard comfort of a chipped adobe *banco*. He received from each of them a nod and a grin, or averted eyes and a dark scowl. It was when he came back to the full face of Eduardo that he knew the extent of the man's power. The wide man did nothing but look at the boy and tilt his head, yet the men to either side moved closer to each other, leaving room for Jim Henry to sit against the wall, beside Eduardo. A place of honor for an Anglo.

"Jaime, take your rest. It is more comfortable, and much warmer when the nights become cold. There will be another day, another time to speak to our wardens and plead the cause of your food. Until then, we will each give you a mouthful, and you will not starve."

Eduardo shifted and gestured with one arm to the others lining the cell wall. "And now I will introduce you to your new family," he said. "This is Geraldo. He only took a burro that belonged to him, that his wife had sold for few pesos and that Geraldo needed once again. The authorities did not understand. . . ."

The man beside Jim Henry smiled at him, showing one plated tooth and wide red gums.

"And this is Bernardo, who wanted only to fondle the breast of a lovely lady. He did not think her cries were of fright, but of passion. He would not harm his own mother."

Another dark face, this one thin and smooth, black eyes close together, mouth full of shiny white teeth, a violet bruise fading at the temple. Jim Henry took the proffered hand and felt it move in his fist. The man muttered some words he could not hear and took his hand away.

There were more to face and acknowledge, a circle of men young and old, whose crimes were not crimes among their own people, who could not comprehend the new order of blue soldiers and rigid laws. He met them all, and they in turn stared at him, accepted him, because of the generosity of Eduardo.

He let his head rest against the rough plastered wall. The man called Bernardo uttered vague cursing under his breath, but it was loud enough for Jim Henry to hear and understand. He looked at the man and felt life returning to the lump of swollen flesh on his skull, a throbbing that moved to his temples, echoed in his ears. He was truly tired, yet he had business to finish with this one, here, right now.

"Señor, I want nothing that is not given freely," Jim Henry said. "If you have thoughts against me, please speak them to my face, and we can bargain with them. I am like you, I am here against my wishes, having done nothing but what I thought was right and correct. I am not wanting to take what is not given. Señor, if you have words for me, speak them so I may clearly understand."

The head rolled on the wall, faced Jim Henry, and he could see into the black eyes as the man thought over his speech, digested his challenge. Jim Henry let nothing show on his own face, none of the confusion and anger, but allowed his gaze to wander the pockmarked skin, let his mouth offer a consoling grin. He knew the game; there could be no fear showing in him, or threat. Nothing but a complacent waiting, a gracious gift of time.

The dark face lifted, the black eyes ground into Jim Henry, then a smile opened the bitter lips and the sullen look disappeared. "The young one is right, Eduardo. I will give as the others have given," he said.

The man nodded to the watchful Eduardo, then returned his gaze to Jim Henry. "McCraw . . . Jaime. Welcome. I am most pleased to offer you what little space there is and to share with you the fine repast these guards have allowed. It is little enough that has been done for me in the past. And will need to be done again, for this I am certain."

Jim Henry offered his hand again, watched the dark eyes lighten, the hidden smile come full bloom. He glanced around the mute circle of men as the two hands closed and held, felt the muscle in the outspoken man, saw the grin spread through the rest of his new companions.

He had been hungry, and they fed him. Now he was tired, with a numbing emptiness that overwhelmed him. His hand dropped to his side, and there was an audible crack as his head hit the adobe wall. His shoulders were weighted down, his mind closed.

"Ah, yes," murmured Eduardo, "the young warrior is finding his limits. It is time for him to sleep. It is time for all of us. Tomorrow will come, as surely as today. And there will be much time for words, and questions.''

Four days progressed in more or less orderly fashion. Two of the men were taken from the cell, one more entered in their midst. Then three men were released to the unseen noise of their families: children laughing, wives and mothers crying. Because of the sounds, their absence in the cell was more keenly felt. And there were tears on the faces of the men left behind.

For Jim Henry there was an accounting; his name was added to the daily roster. Food arrived for him, just as there was less food when the three men were gone. But no word came on charges, no grim face appearing at the door to announce his crime or the length of his punishment. Jim Henry had been added to the rolls, but he had not yet been accused of anything.

On the fifth day a guard stopped at the door and read Jim Henry's name from his list. Jim Henry walked to the door and did not hear Eduardo's words of warning as he held out his wrists for their shining bracelets and accepted the weight of iron around his ankles. He could only move in shortened steps down the long hallway, conscious of a growing pain in his belly, a knot beneath his breathing that constricted his bowels and brought a sour taste to his mouth. He could not stay in these chains, he would rot from their imprisonment; he would shrink to a small leathered doll before he would live in their entrapment.

By the time he reached the brightness of a high window and a door to his right, sweat covered his forehead, dripped cold from under his arms, nestled in his crotch, and chilled his legs. The hard rattle of the iron, the inhuman weight, the loss of freedom . . . Jim Henry fought to breathe, slowed his step until he could lean on a sunwarmed wall. His chest rose and fell rapidly, his eyes clenched shut under a heavy dampness. Tears stained his unshaven face and soaked into the grime of his collarless shirt. He could not take another step.

The Scottish burr to the words told him who was speaking from inside the small room: ''This is temporary, McCraw, only temporary. Until the colonel gets back and I am able to explain to him. I came to see how ye are doing, laddie, and to bring ye a book and a message.''

Jim Henry knew the voice but did not remember the name. He opened his clenched eyes and through the dancing white spots saw the ruddy face and wild hair of the hospital doctor. The round figure called to him with waving hands.

"Come in, lad. Sit down. I'll ask the guard to unchain ye. Ye are not a criminal, as are most of the inhabitants of this jail, but a young man confused and distraught. This most damnable war . . . I will make them understand, and they will release ye.''

When Jim Henry did not respond, MacGregor gestured again. "Come on, laddie, sit here, and I will get the guard. Rest, now. I will be only a moment.''

The roughly carved chair was a luxury, the sweet smell of a window open to the city outside, a long stuffed sofa with intricate legs, woven carpet under foot. . . . Small symbols of civilization. Jim Henry rested his bound hands on his thighs and wrenched his eyes away from the broad twin cuffs. He swallowed twice and made himself look out the window. He didn't hear the doctor come back into the room.

"It is a beautiful day. Yes, it is," said MacGregor. "The guard tells me he will be here in a minute. I have promised in your behalf that ye will give him no trouble. He has heard of why ye are here and was most doubtful of yer behavior. He's promised, though. He will be here shortly.''

Jim Henry looked at the good doctor. MacGregor, that was his name. Who had treated Hap and had tried some tricks with his own head. Talked strange, but would listen to the half-formed words he could put together. Jim Henry remembered his manners then and stood up laboriously as the older man settled on an armless ladies' chair.

"Ye don't look too badly off, m' lad. There is more color in yer face, and ye seem a bit easier. I struggle to think that jailing would be good for anyone, but it has done well by ye.''

Now he thought he knew. Jim Henry stood over the doctor and asked his question without waiting for the man to finish his statement: "What were they doing with Hap? What happened to him? I couldn't understand what they told me. Where did they take—''

"Mr. Railsford is fine," MacGregor assured him. "In fact, he is up and around now. Yer entire outfit is released, paroled on their word and sent home. Colonel Canby left orders before he rode out of Santa Fe. So tomorrow yer friend Hap and those able are on their way south, free of their captivity. From the looks of them, there will be few who will take up again the cause of the rebel South. I have never seen such a sad and crippled . . .''

The doctor's eyes closed. His hands trembled suddenly, and he placed them between his thighs, clasped them motionless. "Ye, James Henry, are the only one left. And the colonel is still not returned, not for another week or so. I have tried, but there is no one who may countermand his orders, or perhaps no one who has the courage to do the right thing and release ye to travel with your friends. I have explained over and over that it was yer devotion to Railsford that made ye attack the orderlies, that it was yer concern for a friend that brought on the wild fighting in the ward. But this Captain Butler, he is not willing to listen to me. He is not able to see beyond his training to know that ye should be going home with your comrades. I explained that there was an injury in ye, that you carry an unseen wound that constricted your mind. But he sees only the orders to incarcerate ye until the colonel returns.''

The doctor shook his head and sighed. "I am sorry, laddie. You don't remember, do ye? It was the final treatment for Hap that ye took for murder. And they, your esteemed hosts in this bloody war, took your actions as a direct threat to their command. I am sorry, lad.''

Dr. MacGregor fiddled with his vest pocket, took out a small bundle tied in pretty ribbon. "Ye Texas lads do fight, I will give ye that," he said. "But in the meantime, I have brought ye a book and a note from a young lady. One of them seems taken with ye, and asked me careful questions about yer actions that day. She was most curious. It seems ye may have taken a heart in this wild capital of the territory of New Mexico after all.''

He stood up, suddenly impatient, mouth tight with irritation. "Where is that guard? He said he would return to free ye of those terrible chains."

Jim Henry had forgotten about his chains, the good doctor's incessant talk. Memories flooded him, staggered him with their crowded impact. He heard Hap cry out when the bullet took him, he saw Caleb Tanner fall. He saw himself run from the first engagement. And he relived the hard run to a distant camp and the return through the cold night. The cold, the sweated horses, the fear, the endless fighting . . . As if everything was remembered now.

He looked out the narrow window. It was warm out there, sunshine and pleasant heat, leaves past budding on ancient trees, color in the doctor's round face, a light coat and open shirt replacing the heavy wool of winter.

It all came back to him; the cold nights and pointless battles, burying the innocent dead, then killing more to fill the open, pitted graves. As if there had come an end to his memory, a limit to what he could accept from that time, yet he knew he had lived through the months in the city, Santa Fe. The thick adobe walls, the smell of the hospital, all blurred in his mind, but he knew the memories were real.

"I guess I will have to ask the guard again," Dr. MacGregor was saying. "However it happens, lad, stand up and let me have a look at ye. That was a considerable blow ye took on yer head, and I wish to be sure there is no permanent damage."

Jim Henry stood to the examination. He did not flinch at the rattling chain or the way it constricted his movement. He did not pull back when the doctor held a match to his eyes, waved it back and forth, commanded him to follow its flicker.

Suddenly there was a commotion in the hall. Jim Henry barely had time to grab the book offered to him and snug it under his arm before the guard burst into the room. The stout man had no key with him and waved away the indignant doctor when confronted with a broken promise and the acceptance of a bribe. Still, there was enough time for the doctor to give Jim Henry a bit of lilac paper, a note folded and refolded, scented with unnamed flowers.

At the door to the crowded cell, the guard found a key to unlock Jim Henry's chains. Jim Henry let the manacles fall away and held to the book, the precious bit of scented paper. Inside were only four men now, the grandfather Eduardo and three new faces. Jim Henry was glad of the extra space; he had much to consider and needed solitude.

He placed the book down gently, laid the paper on its faded leather covering. Then he rubbed his wrists, worried at the ridged flesh with his fingertips, smelled the rankness of his body, and felt the lice picking at his hairline and groin. The small package of the book and the letter were out of place, lost in the layering of dust from restless men, the small damp quarters, the poor food. He touched the brittle leather boards, stroked the satiny, lilac-scented paper.

"Do not be shy, my young lover," murmured Eduardo from his pallet on the floor. "Open the pretty paper and read its message. You have a woman somewhere, a woman who waits for you. Eager for your return. She has been given the chance to write her feelings to you, and she has put her heart to this fine paper. Yet you are the coward for not reading it. If only I could read it for you. . . ."

After a moment Jim Henry unfolded the letter, angled it to the dim light filtering through the narrow window above, and began to read:

My Dear Friend Mr. McCraw,

Dr. MacGregor has told me of your plight, that you have been interred in the Santa Fe prison. He has asked me to give you some hope by writing to you. I trust his kindness and his honor, and am pleased to be of some help to you in your terrible time.

You are missed on the ward. Your devotion to your friend had been an inspiration to the inhabitants, and your presence most uplifting in its selflessness. I, too, had noticed you, and was distressed when the good Doctor explained your absence, although Captain Butler has said you were nothing but a trouble for him.

I do not wish to cause you further pain or embarrassment by my childish words, but I am concerned for your welfare and wanted you to know of another's thoughts. We will await your release, and your continuing kindness.

A faithful admirer,
Maellen Wittman

He remembered the girl in the hospital, long brown hair neatly tied, blue eyes hidden in a pale face. Much like the girl at Fort Davis, but without her life and laughter. It seemed logical, now, that he could see and watch the imitation girl walk through the wounded and smile at him alone, and remember the young woman in the Texas mountain fort.

The paper burned in his fingers, and he opened his fist, let the pretty leaves fall in soft waves to the dirt of the cell floor. He could understand, now, that he had seen one girl and pretended she was another, to give himself some hope, some pleasure, in the shrouded days of the hospital. He had not seen Miss Maellen Wittman: he had seen Phillipa Stockbridge.

"Give me the letter, Jaime, if you do not wish to keep it. I am able to enjoy its tenderness even if I cannot read the scribbling across its face. I know the words are private, but the woman will not know I am enjoying her gentle hands or the sweet spirit that brought her to writing you. Jaime . . ."

Jim Henry looked at the speaker, angered by the request, yet when he saw the deep, scowling face, with sadness in the warm eyes and a trembling mouth, he could not fuel the anger. It was another revelation to him, again something he could understand, that the fierce leader of this small pack of desperados, this hot-tempered old man, was lonesome, missing his family of the one daughter and her child. He wanted only to hold something of a woman's touch, to take what comfort he could from the few undecipherable lines on lilac-scented paper. His request showed Jim Henry a broken corner in the man's life, and yet the man was not too proud to ask.

So he said nothing, but handed the letter to Eduardo and watched the dainty morsel disappear in the murderous hands.

The paper was lifted reverently, carried close to the worn face, and Jim Henry blinked and turned away before he saw a betraying tear in the corner of the dark eyes.

Quiet settled in the half-empty cell, and Jim Henry found it a blessing. There was a high stream of sunlight coming through the window; he sat under its dusty path, and a deep sadness washed through him and left him clean and whole.

CHAPTER 15

"SHE DOES SOUND like my daughter, she is like my Josefina. But it is a son with her, not a daughter of her own. A son who has much laughter in him, and she loves him very much. Like this lady loves her child. I love him, too, my grandson. But I would take the man and . . ."

Jim Henry put the book down very gently, using a tattered bit of lilac-scented paper to mark the place. He had grown used to the outbursts from the old man, and he knew to honor them by ending the reading and waiting out the flow of angry words.

"My Josefina does not wear a letter sewn to her dress, but she has the mark on her, and the people we must live with, they let her know she has wronged them by her child's laughter."

Each time Jim Henry read something that spoke to Eduardo and took hold of his heart, the old man elaborated on it, expanded it to let Jim Henry and the others see more into his suffering and his love.

"My Josefina is a strong girl, a woman made for a strong man. She is much like her mother, and I am the father she has known, the man her son calls Papa. I am their protector, as God listens to me. And who will protect them while I sit in this blinding darkness and can do nothing for them. Who will protect Tomás, and tell him the ways of each day while I am made to pay for the death of a miserable mule, an unforgiving mule that could not be made to work the colonel's service. Who will take care of them while I rot inside these walls." The words were not offered as questions; they were statements made daily, an explosion of anguish.

Jim Henry touched the rough leather binding of the book

185

and looked up at the dimming light. There was only a short time during the daylight hours in which he could read. Light streamed through the high window in the early afternoon, long past the time for their morning meal, their hurried attempts to empty the overflowing pot and wash at the lice and dirt encrusted on their faces and their bodies. Sometimes, rarely, the guards allowed their five prisoners a chance to walk in the brightness, to stroll around a high-walled yard and remove their shirts, even stop and shake out their pants and feel the life-giving strength from the sun.

When this treat came to them, and they returned and the lice bit more frequently, as if to make them pay for their attempted escape, it was not often that Jim Henry read aloud from the book. It went unsaid in the group of men, because each feared he would not do justice to his thoughts, that they did not want to lose the special feeling of the sun to the overlapping sweetness of the words read from the book. One treat in a day's time was enough for the prisoners.

Jim Henry had not read the book before, and some of the words did not come out the way he would have supposed. They sounded false, jarring, wrong in his mouth, inadequate to fill the meaning of the author. Sometimes one of the prisoners, a tall, lean man with exposed arms and a hand missing two fingers, a mouth more suited to a bandit's sneer, would ask quietly if, perhaps, the word was something else, something other than Jim Henry's puzzled and elongated pronunciation. With the man's gentle prompting, Jim Henry would try the word again and find the corrected meaning in the new sounds.

Between them, they were making a slow journey through Hester Prynne's life, through the harsh judgments of *The Scarlet Letter* and the distant world of a time and a land none of the listeners would ever know. They traveled gently, and they did not know all of what they heard, but they suffered with the woman and were angry at the wavering minister, the old and ugly doctor. Each held his own thoughts when Jim Henry finished the day's reading. Only Eduardo, as the oldest and the natural leader, spoke out, wondering at a book written from a long distance that found something in each of their lives.

"It is about my child he has written. It is my Josefina. . . ."

Often there would be tears in the old man's eyes, slow-starting tears that stained him with their shame, with his daughter's shame. And the men seated beside him would turn their heads away to avoid his pain, to give him privacy in the small cell. They allowed him to deal with his grief and his love—the deep pain of his love that was felt by them all.

"Captain Butler will see you now, señor. Move quickly."

It was the thin-faced guard this time. Jim Henry did not move. He would not offer his arms to those manacles again.

"Jaime, hold out your arms or you will stay with us for the rest of your life," Eduardo warned him. "It is for your protection in their crazy world of rules and laws. Do not let them win."

The old man was right; Jim Henry lifted his hands and accepted the bondage, let only a small shudder escape him. It was Captain Butler, a familiar name written in a girlish scrawl across the scented paper. He remembered the name and the warning that went with it, but he could not recall the man's face. Perhaps this was his release, perhaps someone cared enough, knew enough, to set him free.

He did not offer a salute when the captain was able to see him. He recognized the hard face and scalded eyes, one of the few remaining Union soldiers who had taken part in the Glorieta battle and stayed to the city. Only a quick intake of breath, a stiffening in his back, betrayed Jim Henry's immediate anger.

This face had been in the ward when they had tried to take Hap, this face had issued the order to subdue Jim Henry, not to tell him what was going on, but to lay a chair leg across his head and leave him in the darkness of the prison cell. Now Jim Henry knew.

"It is you," Butler said softly, eyes narrowing. "I thought so. From Miss Maellen's description, her romancing of your character. She knows nothing of you Texans, McCraw, she knows little of your brutality and your cowardice under fire. I have accepted her directive, for her sake only, and have kept the letters intended for you. But she will not know I have read them first. You will not tell her. We both know you will not stay here in Santa Fe, we both know you will run with your parole as soon as Colonel Canby returns and your doubtful champion, Dr. MacGregor, is able to plead your case to the colonel's well-known generosity.''

The captain's words were casual and offhand, but he showed his distress by pacing up and down the room, scarcely looking at the captive Jim Henry. Captain Butler was a maverick, intent on making it through the ranks of the army to become what he saw as a righteous man in a world of chaos. A military girl such as Maellen Wittman would do him proud as a wife, and a dirty-skinned Texan was nothing more than a bug to smack and sweep out with the trash.

''So I have allowed your letters, and you will understand I will read your reply, if it is possible you are able to write at all,'' he went on. ''The guards tell me you are stumbling your way through a book, so I must assume you have skills in writing as well. You will respond to the kindness of Miss Maellen, but you will choose carefully what you will say, and you will say nothing of affection.'' He paused to fix Jim Henry with an icy glare. ''Do you understand what I am saying, James McCraw? . . . Prisoner McCraw? There is no need to have a young lady as fine and generous as Miss Maellen suffer the likes of you. But you have become her pet, and I will not tolerate her suffering when she finds out your true worth.''

The letters were a small pile of lilac, shy of the flower scent but still startling in their daintiness. Jim Henry felt his wrists thicken, his fingers swell as he tried to pick up the packet. The letters slipped through his bound hands and spilled on the floor. Jim Henry knew the beginnings of a terrible rage: if the captain laughed at him, he would attack, manacles or not, guards by the door, pistol slipped in its military holster. He bit hard on the inside of his mouth, drew a deep breath, and knelt to the floor, inches away from the shiny black boots.

He gathered the letters, then rose slowly to the red face of the man who was his unwilling captor. For one brief moment he saw into the hot eyes of the man and felt a stiff mercy. The captain was not much older than he, a battlefield officer, a misfit in the regimented protocol of the military life. Just as much a misfit as Jim Henry in his life along the river.

His hands trembled of their own accord as he unfolded each note and slowly read the contents. He sat alone in a corner of the cell; Eduardo had done nothing more than look into his eyes and shake his head, and the men in the crowded room left him alone. Jim Henry put one hand under his thigh as he tried to make out the pretty words. His whole arm shook, his mouth was dry, his vision blurred.

There was nothing in the letters, bare descriptions of a day's events, a sweet mention of new flowers, a beautiful sun setting across the mountains. Nothings, a girl's poetic thoughts. Yet they were bursts of pleasure to read, reminders of a different life. There were five such notes, each one the same, each asking about his health and state of mind, with a careful complaining about his prolonged stay in the jail. The captain must have suffered to read these words, knowing it was he who kept Jim Henry under key, he whom the girl blamed.

And there were words Jim Henry did not understand, words he would not share with the pock-faced man. The pale lilac letters were impersonal, yet they were his alone.

There was nothing in the letters to worry the captain, and Jim Henry would not go back on his word and try to make contact with his benefactress. He would write Miss Maellen a short note, thank her for the kindness. But he would do nothing more. She was not the brown-haired girl of Fort Davis; she was not Phillipa Stockbridge. He had separated them in his mind and was grateful for the division. This girl was less direct, more gentle than Phillipa Stockbridge, yet she was able to wield the same daggers of deceit and dismissal.

Jim Henry did not feel the skin rupture as his teeth clamped down on his lip, nor did he taste the blood that flowed from the cut, to be smeared on his chin by a back-wiped hand. He was wholly absorbed in the task before him, that of replying properly to the sweet attentions of the brown-haired girl from Santa Fe:

Miss Wittman,

   Your kindness to an enemy prisoner is most gratefully
received. I don't know why, but you give me a taste of
your fine city and its pleasant air.
   When I am released from prison, I will go back to
Texas. Thank you for the time spent in cheering me.
Capt. Butler has allowed me to use pen and paper to try
and repay your kindness.

                         Yrs,

He knew the attempt was childish, the words unable to give
meaning to what he truly felt. But she had no right to know;
just putting a few lines to pretty paper did not give her the
right to lay claim to his feelings and his private thoughts.
Anger swelled in him, and pain; she was not a girl for him,
just as the other girl had not been. He had not known writing
down words could tear into a person, open him to sense and
sound and smell that blotted out the day's activity. The words
were innocent, the thoughts and feelings smothered.

   Jim Henry kept the small packet of letters, and his short
attempt at a reply, until the following morning. He slept with
the papers bunched in his hand, he slept curled up to the
back wall of the cell. With only five men inside, there was
the luxury of space, the ability to stretch out and truly sleep.
Jim Henry fought and rolled endlessly in the dark and awoke
panting and damp where his head had lain on his arm. The
lilac papers were soggy, his reply was wrinkled but still recognizable. Toward morning, he found an hour's rest.

"Colonel Canby, I am Dr. MacGregor, one of the surgeons
attached to the hospital. I know I am imposing on yer time,
sir, but I have a request of ye that can wait no longer."

   Dr. MacGregor found himself talking fast to cover his ner-
vousness, and he knew his Scottish burr was thickening,
making his words almost incomprehensible. He tried to slow
down. The colonel was a good man, a fine man, of good
character; there was no reason to be nervous.

   "It is about a prisoner in yer jail," he went on slowly,
carefully. "Or rather the city's jail. A Texas lad, to be sure,

who has been there for over two weeks now, while ye were away. It is a mistake for him to be there. I told the captain, but he has no power to release the lad. His name is James McCraw, one of the Texas survivors. And he's been at the hospital for over two months. But it was not he who suffered the injury, at least not an obvious one. A friend came in, with a strange wound badly suppurating, from a button hit and splintered by a bullet, a most unusual—''

MacGregor broke off and drew a deep breath.

''But I digress, sir. And for that I apologize. It is McCraw who concerns me now. A fine young man, who I think must have taken a blow to the head in the heat of battle. It would account for his behavior these past months, very strange behavior. He stayed to nurse his friend, although the man was not of the character to warrant such devotion. McCraw refused to leave his side when ye most kindly offered parole to the healed to return to their state. He stayed behind to care for his friend.

''But that is not the behavior for which he is in jail,'' MacGregor continued. ''And sir, I do apologize for my digressions. Yer wife's great kindness to these lads has been most beneficial to them, and to our small corner of this most tragic war. But the lad, James McCraw, languishes in the Santa Fe jail, imprisoned for the sin of caring, Colonel, imprisoned for striking out at strangers whom he believed endangered his still bedridden friend. Now, I have talked to the lad since then. He is of good character and well respected by his comrades. There is no need for him to continue his confinement. I believe his senses have been restored these past few weeks, and that he is well enough to return home. If ye would consider releasing him, Colonel . . .''

Five minutes later Dr. MacGregor bowed himself from the room, the official paper in hand, his mind caught up in the drama of the moment. Alexander MacGregor, defender of the innocent, liberator of the unjustly imprisoned, savior of one hot-headed Texan. It was enough for the day, enough for his smothered soul to hide in and ignore the dead and dying and the butchery around him. There was one in the continuing war who would go free, to ride south out of the struggle with all haste. Dr. MacGregor was pleased with himself, pleased with the day. Pleased for James Henry McCraw.

"I have heard this. That it is said you will soon be free of our cozy home. The colonel is returned, and your doctor is talking to him. Perhaps even now they are on the way to our small part of this prison, to open the door and call your name. This time you will walk out without your irons, Jaime. How do you think on that?"

The broad face twisted and wrinkled as Eduardo spoke. The old man was not yet beaten, not yet admitting to the drain of the cell's confinement, the poor food, the constant battle with rats and lice. His grin refused to fade, his eyes kept a brightness that Jim Henry envied. He had to smile at the man; Eduardo would not be beaten.

It was three days since the book was finished, since the final sadness of the graves dug together. For two of the men the reading of the words had meant little; they had come to the cell almost at the end of the volume and at first had refused to sit in quiet while Jim Henry read aloud. It had been Eduardo and the long-faced man with the skull-hard smile who silenced them and allowed him to finish.

Eduardo had said little at the book's ending. The long-faced man had grinned and nodded his appreciation to Jim Henry, said, *"Gracias,"* in a husky voice, and returned to staring out the high window. Jim Henry waited, but the old man said nothing, showed nothing on his strong brown face.

But now Eduardo talked of Jim Henry's freedom. He had sat in the dark cell for a long time, looking out the window, waiting with unending patience for his turn at the colonel's ear. Yet he had the grace to congratulate Jim Henry and be pleased his Anglo friend would be escaping what still confined him.

"I have a favor to ask of you, Jaime. I must ask it of you, as you are one I would trust."

Jim Henry looked to the source of the voice, hidden in the shadows, with only the now-familiar wide bulk of shoulder and belly outlined by the darkening light.

"I would ask of you to take my Josefina home. To take her and her unfathered child to our small farm south along the river. It is little for you to do. You must travel our road, pass our house, on your return to Texas. We farm land you and your companion soldiers crossed on your trip north to defeat."

Jim Henry was not surprised by the bitterness of the last words, and shame flushed his face and neck at the unrepentant actions of his fellow soldiers. Eduardo had no need to tell him particulars, Jim Henry had seen them in the days along the river.

"She is a good woman, my Josefina. She can cook your meals and mend your clothes. And the boy is small, not yet a man, who will ride with his mama and will hardly be noticed by you. This is all I ask of you. To return them to their home. I am trusting you, Jaime, as I would trust few other Anglos, to ride with my daughter and her son, and leave them at their house."

CHAPTER 16

S HE SMOOTHED THE softness of her new curls and lin-
gered there to stroke the skin at the base of her neck.
Lightly, a gentle touching of her own flesh, an unfamiliar
caress that let her gathering emotions well up.

He had been so different, this young soldier, from what
she remembered, what she had built in her mind's eye. Captain Butler had been behind her, watching from the office
doorway, and she could almost hear his words, see his mouth
form the "I told you so" that he was thinking. She held
herself erect, furious at his impertinence, even more angry
at the figure striding toward her down the hall.

James Henry McCraw had not turned out to be what she'd
hoped, what she'd expected. But then, she had taken on his
cause only at the urging of Dr. MacGregor, because she
wanted to do her part for these sad young warriors. So she
had written her letters, many of them before he had the politeness to return her efforts. And such a poor letter, badly
misspelled, smudged, the paper stained and wrinkled.

She was a slow learner, and too much of a romantic. His
dull response to her packet of letters, and the quality of his
writing, should have warned her that he would be more of a
disappointment in the flesh. But there had been little else to
occupy her fancy, and she had teased the captain into letting
her know the time of his dismissal from the miserable Santa
Fe city jail. She would be there waiting for him, she would
surprise him with her caring, she would wait for him to see
her standing at the end of the hall and enjoy his hurried steps
to her, his stammered thanks. It was something to do, better
than speaking polite phrases to the few wounded left, or sew-

194

ing with the ladies, or talking to Patricia and Ada. Something to do.

Maellen wound her fingers in the loose curls, finding solace in their clean shininess. He had been filthy, like an animal. Bearded, but not curried and groomed like the Union officers with their side whiskers and flowing beards. The hair curled around his ears, dull and matted and unpleasant even to consider. His face had a grayish, sickly pallor, and his eyes were dull. But they brightened when he saw her, and she called his name. Then he had stopped, had not come to her but kept his distance.

At first she had been mortified that he did not return her greeting. As she looked him over carefully, she did believe he stayed his distance not to offend her sensibilities. But his smell drifted down the hallway to her, and she wrinkled her nose and covered it with a lace dainty before she realized his distress. The look on his face told her everything: the hazel eyes narrowed and dropped away, the red shine of the face, the hands fiddling with nothing.

It could not be considered her fault. She had never known a man who had come out of prison, had never corresponded with a felon. Or a Texas boy, if she thought about it. She was a well-bred, well-schooled young lady, and had the war not been engaged this far west, she would never have had to know the sight of blood or hear the cries of dying young men. Or look into the face of a proud Southern soldier and know the shame she caused as she flinched from his condition.

There were small mercies; he walked by her then, long strides that hurried him to the outdoors. She barely glimpsed the loose, collarless shirt, one of the good doctor's, she supposed, and turned away from the small white things crawling at the base of his neck, held in her breath from the horrid stench of his passing. He was nothing but a crude country boy, an enemy to her father's army and her way of life. That he had been hurt by her refusal to speak to him, or acknowledge him, she could not help. She had done her part.

It was the final freedom, to be on horseback, looking out over the open desert. The paint mare shifted restlessly, and

Jim Henry touched her heavy mane, spoke soft, wordless sounds that brought back an ear to listen. The mare shook her head, jerked at the rattling bit chain, then settled under him. Horse and rider continued to wait. For he had made his promise: he would sit on the ridge and wait for the daughter named Josefina and the grandson named Tomás.

The promise had not been given lightly, nor had the old man asked for something easy. A lifetime ago, Jim Henry had come north along the course of the river in the safety of over a thousand marching men, knowing that the power of their numbers would enable them to capture the New Mexico territory. They had been wrong about their absolute power, but they had marched in confidence and had almost succeeded.

Now he was the only one left, other than a dozen or so of the badly wounded who still were not fit for travel. The doctor had said it would be beating the odds if even four of those dozen ever made the journey. So it was Jim Henry, healthy and eager, ready to move out alone.

But he had promised to wait for a woman and a child. He could hear the words of old Eduardo, worry pushing him to repeat himself many times: "You will stay away from the river, Jaime. Especially at night. Do not camp along the water, for it draws everyone and everything, evil and animal, and the indios. When it is safe, you may ride down to the water and allow the animals to drink their fill. And you may drink, fill your canteens."

The old man rambled on with his advice, and Jim Henry let him, accepting the torrent of words as a grandfather's hard-earned concern. Jim Henry had lived his life on the river, he knew the *despoblado* like he knew nothing else, and this was the same river. But if it gave the old man comfort to lecture him, it was a small price to pay.

"Jaime, you already know what I am telling you, and yet you give me the room to tell it over and over. It is the curse of becoming old to never believe the young could know. Even though as a youth, I, too, knew how to survive on the river's shore. But remember, you have lived your life thus far, but I have gotten much further along and am still alive, still strong. It is only because I have downed a mule that I am not able to return to my farm. Remember my words. My eyes have seen years that yours have not.''

So Jim Henry made the promise, and now he waited in the chill of the high desert for the darkened sun to push through low clouds and spread color over the flat land before him. They would ride down the land, to a deep gorge and a wide wash, landmarks he remembered from struggling to climb them so many months back.

The mare shifted her weight underneath him, sighed deeply, and tossed her heavy mane again—letting him know she was impatient, but still mindful of her master. Jim Henry slapped her brown-and-white neck and crossed his hands on the broad horned pommel. Streaks of sunlight caught the tips of black-leafed bushes and brought new life to their bright spring green. As the mare's head drooped lower, Jim Henry let his eyes close, felt the gravel tiredness behind his lids.

The woman had been told to be here by noon; the sloping land below him showed the brilliant colors of the high sun. Jim Henry's back itched between his shoulder blades, his scalp tightened. The mare must have felt his tension, for her head lifted and her ears pricked at nothing.

It was good to be mounted. Jim Henry thought longingly of the bay gelding, the stout barrel and hard legs, the rolling white eye and nervous head. This little mare was nothing much, and he had an Anglo's distaste for paints and for mares. But she had appeared at the hospital for him, saddled with an old Spanish hull over two beautifully woven muted blankets, bridled in a hair-braided headstall, and bitted with an inlaid curb. He appreciated the old Hawken in the scabbard, had pulled it out and rubbed his hand over the plain stock. A powder flask and cap and balls in a leather pouch were tied to the flat horn. There had been no explanation for the mare's appearance, but there were papers to say she belonged to him; and that was enough.

The mare snorted and sidestepped. Jim Henry let his body go with her, put a leg against her ribs, and settled his hands on her neck. She quieted again, swiveled her head, and gazed off into the hills. He looked with her; there was nothing visible, but he would trust her instincts. He waited, cautiously, hand to the Navy Colt stuck in his belt.

He had never appreciated a bath, or a haircut, as much as the one given him on his release. Water was a luxury, always a luxury. The river had been all the bathing he had ever needed. But the swirl of graying water over his belly, the teasing warmth of its soapy sheen, had been a treat this time. At last he'd stood in the private courtyard while the doctor had poured bucket after bucket over him, sluicing away the lice and ticks, the ingrained blackness that had darkened his skin.

Then clean clothes . . . Not clothes to his liking, but clean and even pressed. Heavy wool pants too short in the leg, too wide in the waist, another collarless shirt brightly striped with several buttons missing. A short canvas jacket and a flat-crowned hat. The doctor had burned the prison clothes, with Jim Henry's blessing. The boots were his, along with the bowie knife.

The washing did not entirely erase his shame or scrub out the picture of the girl with her hand raised in horror against him. Jim Henry swallowed hard, shook his head. The mare shifted uneasily, stamped a hoof, and swung her head. He touched the reins, and still she did not settle.

The mare heard them before he did: a heavy tread crossing the rock slope. Two horses, two animals ridden in single file. Jim Henry slipped from the mare and ground-tied her, disappeared behind the thick bush of a piñon, hand steady to the rim of his knife. The paint mare whickered and was answered in kind, then a woman's fluid voice called out impatiently:

"Señor, we are here. You need not hide from us, señor, my father, he—"

He stepped into sight, walked to the mare, and held her by the bit shank. He lifted his gaze to the woman, noting the dun mule she rode, the swayed brown pack horse carrying nameless bundles and a child perched in the middle of the load. She wore a brimmed hat tied with a yellow scarf beneath her chin; the boy's face was protected by a hat much too big for him. As he made out her features, his mouth fell open and his hands opened of their own accord, releasing the paint mare to whinny again to the familiar brown gelding.

* * *

This she had not expected. Her papa had said a young man, yes, a *Tejano*. And they had looked at each other carefully, knowing the pain and trouble the *Tejanos* had given them. She knew the stories Papa told of the other invasion, many years back, when she was a new baby and her mama was alive. So it meant to her that this man would be special or Papa would not entrust her, and Tomás, to his care. Ah, what Papa felt about Tomás! How he loved her boy, even though they would not discuss his parentage other than to curse the *Tejanos*. She had no love for their breed.

But this one . . . she remembered him. Remembered him well. He had changed, as all men change who fought a war. Thinner and much paler, but that would come from his time spent in jail with Papa. The hair was short now, dulled a common brown, no longer streaked bronze by the sun. The eyes had changed little; there was still a sadness to them, perhaps grown stronger from past months. Gold-flecked eyes that looked to her and to the child, then back to her with a growing confusion. He would be a rare one indeed if he recognized her. To most of the wild-eyed *Tejanos*, another dark-skinned woman with black hair and a brat tugging at their skirts would be no different from any number of women they had taken and terrorized.

But this one was truly different. Papa had thought so, and now, as she watched his face puzzle through the pain of finding her in his mind, she could almost sympathize with his confusion. Papa trusted him; she would try, she would be polite. "Señor, I am Josefina, and this is Tomás."

She wanted to say something to ease the tightness in the young man, but she, too, had her fears and her doubts, despite her papa's recommendation. For Papa had been in jail, she must remember that. And this man had been in the jail with him. There had been something said about a book, and pretty letters on colored paper. She had paid little attention to what Papa had said of those days, only that he would be kept in the jail longer, that she must return to the farm and work it so they would live through the winter. And Tomás, he wanted to return to his pet lamb, to see if there were other lambs newborn.

Josefina dropped her gaze, lowered her head, and let wisps

of dark hair cover her face. She would not look at this man
again; she did not like the sudden heat in his eyes, the pinched
whiteness of his wide mouth. Pale skin, lank hair, bony and
awkward, ugly in his wide pants and prim shirt. Nothing—a
boy come north in prideful anger, taking what he could from
the people of the land, believing in his special rightness. She
wanted to turn her head and spit at the grim face. Instead,
she reached for the comfort of Tomás piled on the old horse's
wide back. She drew the child to her, balancing him on the
spiky neck of the dun-colored mule, and would not look
again at the man still staring at her.

The knot in his belly tightened, threatened to cut even deeper.
Jim Henry drew in a short breath and held it, let it out in
quick puffs. Hap's woman . . . the woman he'd rescued from
Hap's eager hands. He had forgotten about her, forgotten
about the small boy clinging to her skirts and the evening
chill, the feel of his knife at Hap's neck. The sullen surrender
of his one-time friend, the bitter anger between them. Hap,
who had accepted his ministrations from the battle's destruction, his attendance in the army hospital, and then had gone
south without a note, leaving him to rot in the Santa Fe jail.
He had not expected to see this woman again.

She was more beautiful than he remembered, sitting on the
lazy dun mule, holding on to her child as to a precious object.
Face half-hidden by the flowing black hair, eyes turned from
him in their secret knowledge. She had been told by her papa
to trust him, to go with him back to the farm along the river.
She would do what her papa had told her.

What else had she been told? About his shameful paper
romance, his ignorant stumbling through the thin leather
book? The desertion of his friend? The horror his exit from
the jail had caused in a refined young lady? What all did she
know?

"Ma'am, my name is James McCraw," he said. "Your
pap called me Jaime. We best get moving. Losing time just
standing here."

He recovered enough to find his manners and tipped his
hat to her, waited while she kicked the mule into a walk, still
holding the boy in front of her like a shield to his presence.

He slipped a foot in the wooden stirrup bow and swung up on the mare, letting her step into a walk to catch up to the mule.

"Ma'am, best to let me lead."

It was only when he realized she had said nothing back to him, had not reined in the mule and let him pass, or given her name and a few pleasant words to introduce the boy, that he realized he had spoken in English, *Tejano* English. He searched his mind, found the sounds, and repeated his statements in her tongue, a clumsy attempt at border Spanish. Time in the cell had reacquainted him with the choice of words. He took the almost invisible shrug as her acknowledgment and gigged the mare to pass the brown pack horse and the dun mule.

CHAPTER 17

THE PAINT MARE had a quick shuffling walk, the mule would not be prodded out of his deliberate pace, and the brown pack horse took every chance to grab at the sparse vegetation. Within an hour Jim Henry's hold on his temper had frayed to near nothing. He yanked at the mare's mouth, and she half reared, flattened her ears, and spun in a tight circle. The other animals merely pricked their ears; they were in no hurry. Jim Henry settled the mare and took another deep breath, eased his butt end in the hard saddle . . . and waited while the mule and the brown picked their way to him.

Santa Fe spread itself up against the mountains—dulled adobe walls shadowed between dark piñon and bright red soil. Thin plumes of kitchen smoke revealed the individual homes. Jim Henry was glad to have a distance between himself and the city. Only a few miles, but it made a difference to him. He patted the mare's neck, lifted the heavy mane, and let the strands slide through his fingers. He hadn't seen Santa Fe like this before. He'd been too close, too caught up in the smells and sounds of the hospital, the need to do for Hap, the confusion in his own brain. And his stay in the city jail had given him a different view of life altogether, one he would not choose to repeat.

Still, he had to admit that the collection of houses and walled compounds gave the settlement a pleasing air. The columned building known as the Palace, with its internal square that formed a courtyard, offered a sense of permanence beyond his experience. Leaton's Fort, back along the river near Presidio, had been the most imposing structure he knew, and it was only a few years old. Mud huts, woven reed walls, and ocotillo roofs were common in the *despoblado*, yet as they came north along the river he had been intrigued by the collections of red houses with old walls, parts of ancient communities. It was a nice thought, that a house could be part of a man's life, part of a stability to bring him home each night.

"Señor, the little one is tired and thirsty. We must stop, and I will find him a sweet packed on the brown horse and a drink of water. He is tired, señor."

Goddamn. Jim Henry kept the blasphemy quiet in his mind; he couldn't swear in front of a woman and a child. His pa had taught him that. But he felt his temper slip another notch. He would never get home this way.

"Lady, we got no time to stop now. Haven't come but a mile or two. That boy'll keep another hour or so. Be too hot to ride then, you can baby him all you want."

Jim Henry knew little about children, but he recognized the flash of anger in the child's eye as he sat in front of his mother on the dun mule and was called a baby by a stranger. He thought to take back the word, but then he looked at the boy and knew it was too late. The child pulled away from the softness of his mother's breast and straightened in great dignity, lifted his head to stare at the Anglo. His voice was thin and high, but the words were strong, words of a grown man.

"You do not need to baby me, señor. I can ride until your fine paint mare will no longer carry you."

Then tears spilled over in the angry eyes, and the boy let them flow, jerked away from his mother's tender hand. The woman looked at Jim Henry, accusation heavy in her face, then kicked the dun mule, hard. The sleeping animal picked up a hoof and put it back down but did not move. It was enough to make Jim Henry laugh, but he had insulted these people too often and too soon. He best keep quiet; it was a long trip.

"We will ride, señor. And we will keep up with you. Tomás, bring me a switch for the mule."

She lowered the child from the mule, and he sorted through a series of broken limbs and twisted rock before finding a long, knobby branch. The mule sensed the coming attack and lifted its head in anticipation. Before Jim Henry could dismount to help, the mother, Josefina, leaned down and clasped the boy's hand in hers; she pulled him from the ground until his foot could rest on hers, and he slipped up on the mule's back.

"We are ready, señor. And we will not slow you down again."

They moved away from the mountains slowly, out to the sloping plain dotted with piñon, cut by narrow washes, pocked with holes and rocks. The air was calm, the sun high overhead and brilliant; it was without pity, sucking precious moisture from the three riders and their mounts. Time and again Jim Henry licked his lips, and the saliva dried immediately, taking with it what wetness had been in his mouth. The land continued its gradual slope, yet he could see ahead to the blue mountain peaks on his left and the rounder, more gentle swell of hills dotted green on his right. They looked soft and close and inviting, never coming nearer or retreating, hanging just out of reach across the wide gray and green of the plains.

The paint mare was grateful when he stopped her; a moment later the dun mule caught up beside him. Jim Henry wiped his face and glanced up at the woman. She did not look worn by the heat or the traveling. He cursed again under his breath.

"Lady, your pap said you knew the trip home, said for you to tell me where we stop for the night, how long it is to water, the rough spots in the trail."

He did not pose it to her as a question, so she sat the dun mule silently, watching his face, eyes bright in anticipation. She could not fully understand this man's anger at her, or his refusal to speak her name. But her papa had chosen him, so she would follow his directions. Tomás rested his head on her back, and she could feel the warmth, the closeness. His arms were wrapped tight around her waist, and sweat collected under the heat of his skin. She waited for the man to ask his questions.

"Lady, where the . . . where are we? This a good place to stop, or is there water, shade, up ahead I can't see? Land's breaking up, I can see cottonwoods, maybe bottom of a draw. You tell me, lady—there a stream we can rest near, water the animals, or best we take what we can out here and wait out the afternoon sun?''

He was not a polite man, had little manners to speak thus to her. But he was a Texan, and Josefina would give him the benefit of her father's trust. ''If we push hard, señor, we could make La Bajada today,'' she told him. ''But the boy is tired, and it has been some time since I have ridden these miles. Ahead there is a small community, well fortified against *los indios*. My papa has many friends there, and he has said we should spend our first night there, protected and welcomed. Papa and I, and Tomás, often stay there when we make the journey to Santa Fe.''

He gave little, face bland, hands crossed on the horn of his old saddle. Josefina had to smile at his direct approach.

''How far is this place, and what is La Bajada?'' he asked.

''Señor, if we rest now for an hour, we will ride to La Ciénaga easily before the evening meal. And you must know of La Bajada; you would have fought her great walls on your march north to liberate us from your enemies.''

He wanted to take offense at her tone of voice, the barbed words, but he could not blame her for being bitter. The Texans had marched onto land not their own to try and claim it for a new government. She had suffered her own encounters with the troops; she had the right to be sharp with her tongue.

And he did remember La Bajada—the steep-walled fortress they had faced once out of Albuquerque, the impossible rock wall that rose magnificently above the insignificant soldiers and the path of the river. La Bajada, the long rock rim that stretched for miles and halted the advancing army. It had been a nightmare.

''There are trails down La Bajada, señor. I know them well. I can guide you, so you need not worry. But they will not be easy. Nothing about La Bajada is easy.''

Jim Henry did not need reminding. Two horses had panicked and fallen on their cautious climb up the face, and several men had limped to the top, cursing a fractious horse and a sliding backward fall. He looked at the woman with new respect. But he would not let her know.

"How far to this village you talk about?"

She shrugged. "Señor, we rest here for a bit, let the horses take air, let us walk our legs to see if they still work. Here you may roll a smoke if you wish, and Tomás may have one of the sweets his grandpapa promised. Then we will ride on, and we will come to the farms in good time."

They had come to a halt in a small stand of piñon, bent and twisted trees, stunted from the strong mountain winds. Their twisted shapes offered flat ground and low shade. It was a reasonable place to stop for a breather. Jim Henry did not acknowledge the validity of her suggestion but swung a leg over the paint mare and dismounted. It came to him as he placed one foot on the ground and tried to stand that he, too, had ridden little over the past months and was in poor shape. He would have bent over, stretched his back, eased the burden of his weight, but for the señorita and her child.

He shook his head; he was little more than an escort for the woman and her son. It was she who controlled their traveling pace, she who picked their spots. He carried the weapons, he brought in wood for the fire, he stood guard and took care of the horses. But it was the woman who led the way. It was a new situation for him, and he wasn't sure he liked the shift in power.

He walked to the dun mule and helped the woman dismount. She smelled good to him as he held her briefly and let her slip to the side. The child was little more than a feather, light and fragile, bone barely padded with flesh. He could never have been a child such as this, helpless and frail. A disturbing moment of hooves flashed in his mind, visions of black-haired murderers, bodies spread around the sandy yard, a corner of the house burning slowly, blue smoke billowing up in clear air. The images stunned him, and he backed away from the woman and her son.

Something must have shown in his face, for the woman drew the child to her, arms across his chest for protection, eyes watching him carefully. He wiped a gritty hand across his forehead. "Lady, you got a good idea we rest here," he said. "That mare's ganting up some, the pack horse breathing hard."

He turned to the brown gelding and unwrapped a canteen,

watched the grayed head come up as he poured a cupped fist of water and held it to the eager mouth. The horse gulped the handful, licked Jim Henry's palm with thick mustached lips. He did the same for the mare and the mule, careful to keep an eye on the woman and her son. She paid little attention to him but spread a blanket under a nearby piñon and took the child with her to lie down.

Jim Henry felt the heaviness in his eyes, the grit under his lids, the sun-baked heat of his face and neck. He found his own place away from the other two travelers and lowered himself carefully to the pebbled ground. His eyes closed, but he could not rest. Each sound was magnified in his mind, and once he came half erect at a crunching behind him. The dun mule looked at him down a long nose, lips holding the broken end of a brittle bush. He had to grin at himself as he loosened his grip on the old Navy Colt. There were worse enemies in the world than a spiteful dun mule.

That middle space between waking and sleeping held room for thinking, and Jim Henry drifted in and out of the drowsy time. Images came and went in his mind, interwoven and tangled thoughts he tried to avoid when fully awake: the reasons for his parents' death, the lifeless body of his little brother, the unreasoned anger at Limm Tyler and Rosa Ignacio. The names startled him; still mostly asleep, he rolled his head, felt the rocks grate into his skin. *Damn.* . . . Then he must have dozed off again, for he didn't hear the small boy until the words were spoken, close upon his booted feet.

"Señor, my mama say perhaps it is time to move on. We have a good ride before we come to the village where we will spend the night. This is what my mama says, señor."

The voice startled him, but Jim Henry caught the reaction of his hand and grabbed hold of his belt rather than the butt end of the Colt. He was half-asleep and stiff from the riding. His legs did not move as he wished them to; his left arm still cradled his head, and he raised his right arm from near the Colt and blocked the sun from his eyes so he could see the boy. The knowledge that he had been caught unawares twisted his gut; his belly shivered, and a spasm rattled his knees. He had forgotten much with his time in the hospital, the community of the cell; he had to reawaken his body and his senses. A year past no one could have come to him as this child had, and spoken to him, before he was fully awake and on his feet. He knew the lesson without thinking: if he did not find his edge again soon, he would never make the harsh lands of the *despoblado*, he would be wasted coyote meat, stripped and left naked, the paint mare and his rigging led past him in the hands of a quick-moving scavenger.

Jim Henry was up and to the horses with no words for the boy. He rewatered each animal and offered water to the woman and the child, denying himself in punishment. They mounted and moved into a line along the shadowed edge of a newly started wash. The woman rode the lead, carrying an old musket across her lap, hand resting easily on the burnished stock; her son once more perched on the pack horse.

"Señor, we will be coming into the settlement soon. And here the people are careful, and do not like *Tejanos*. Papa says for you to speak very little, and to stay near me. There is a man who is Papa's great friend, and Papa has hoped to send him word before we arrive. Since we do not know if the message has been received, it is best you stay with me."

Jim Henry took a hold on the words that bubbled in him and wanted to bust out. He tugged the brim of his floppy hat, pulled at his left ear, and spat to the side. That gave him time to grab his temper.

"Lady, your pap and me, we talked this over," he said. "He told me, so you don't need to be using a whip to my hide to make me understand. This is your show, lady. I ain't got doubts about that."

"Señor, my name is Josefina. You may call me by my name, it is more polite than your 'lady.' "

After their stop they rode for an hour without speaking. The trail wound down into a low-walled arroyo filled with soft sand and piled brush. The paint mare worried the bit, and Jim Henry leaned over to touch her behind the ears. The banks on either side showed him more color than he'd seen in the winter march; the land was almost beautiful. The thin wiry brush had pale brilliant green stems topped with bright flowers, the grasses grew in rich clumps, and even the piñon seemed a darker, richer green against the coarse red soil.

Puffs of pale red rose from the horses' hooves as they broke
into the crust. Small yellow flowers lined the banks and
peeked from under the brush, heads moving gently in the
slight air.

They followed a definite trail that wound up and down and
through the brush. At one point there was a man-made ditch,
set into the side of a sandstone cliff, a ditch carefully banked
to hold the water flowing through it. The paint mare spooked
when they crossed a narrow wooden plank bridge, but the
mule and the old brown only lifted their heads and snorted
in appreciation of the water's cold, clear scent.

There the woman led her procession away from the flat
land, and Jim Henry felt the mare grunt as they climbed a
steep hill. The ground sloped away from them at the top, and
in the distance he could see red mud walls and woven corrals,
familiar signs that told him there was a ranch down the slope
and in the cover of old cottonwoods. He stayed behind the
woman and child, conscious of the Navy Colt tucked in his
belt and the old musket the woman held.

The three animals bunched at a high gate; the brown gelding lifted his head to whinny and received a thin cry in response. Then the paint jointed in, and the mule lowered its
head in futility. Jim Henry was ready when a man stepped
out of a nearby hut and worked the latch to the gate.

The man swept off his wide hat and bowed to the woman
and the boy. He was most careful not to look directly at Jim
Henry. The boy wiggled free from the lumpy pack and slid
down from the horse, and the man was there to catch him.
He spoke rapidly to the woman in a soft voice, but Jim Henry
could understand much of what was said.

"Ah, Eduardo's grandson, how you have grown! Josefina,
we had word you would be with us today or tomorrow. Enselmo is most anxious to see you both, to have word of your
papa and how he fares in the jail. It is good to have you here,
even for so short a visit."

A child close in age to Tomás appeared, and two more,
then a tiny girl with twin braids and an older girl who held
her hand. The children talked quickly, laughter came from
them in bright sounds, and then they all disappeared. Jim

Henry leaned on the horn of his saddle, attentive to the rapid-fire speech that passed between the woman and her admirer.

"Your papa has sent word from his cell that you would be here, and that you would be bringing an Anglo, a *Tejano*. Whom we are to treat as if he is one of us. We do this, Josefina, only for your papa. Antonio and the one-eyed man are here, and I cannot promise what your papa asks of us. We are but farmers, and you know Antonio. . . ."

The man looked quickly at Jim Henry, and his face registered the knowledge that the Anglo understood him. Jim Henry nodded to the man, kept his face expressionless, and answered in the man's own tongue:

"I understand, señor. And I will do my best to stay out of this Antonio's way, as he worries you so. But I cannot go against my promise to Señor Eduardo to return his family to their land. This promise must come first."

There was a hint of a smile on the brown face, and the man glanced up quickly one more time to the *Tejano* mounted on the range-bred mare. Then he looked at the woman.

"The señor speaks true," he said. "I will do what I can to keep Antonio to his word. He is our guest, he must not dishonor us. But Antonio, he can be most difficult."

The widespread hands, the slow shrug, the eyes rolled in the dark face. . . . Nothing more would be said of the matter; it was out of their hands. Jim Henry didn't bother to take in the wide, dark face bordered with a ridged forehead and heavy mouth; he wanted nothing from these people but to spend the night in sleep and ride out unharmed in the morning. But the dark eyes stayed too long on him, and he turned restless under their gaze. He cursed under his breath and dismounted from the paint, took the reins to the mule and the brown, wanting to be doing something, anything.

"Pleased to know where I put up the stock. And get them a drink. They're in need of watering." The less he said, the better he would feel, and the less chance of starting trouble.

As if the other man understood, he walked to a low-roofed building and passed through an open gate, not looking back to see if the Anglo would follow.

It was a wide courtyard, with half-walled openings and

poled sheds to hold wagons and carts and field implements to work the land. Jim Henry looked down the direction of the man's outstretched arm and saw a narrow doorway, a slip gate with a long-eared head poking out over the skinned poles. The man turned unexpectedly to Jim Henry, eyes bright with an unfinished curiosity.

"You will find feed and water for them there, señor," he said. "And you may store your gear in the room where we leave all things waiting for repair. They will be safe, Señor Jaime."

The use of Eduardo's name for him brought words to Jim Henry's mouth, but the expectation in the man's face smothered the impulse, and he only nodded. The expectation died slowly, the grin lost in a shake of his head. The next moment the man walked away as if Jim Henry did not exist.

He put up the horses and the cranky mule, watering them slightly at first, tying them and scrubbing their wet backs with a twisted wisp of hay, then leading them back to water to drink their fill before letting them attack the loose pile of good hay. He would come back later, and catch up the mare and the brown, and fill a morral for each with the oats he had seen spilled from a bin. But to hell with the mule; catching it once in the morning would be trouble enough. It could live the night on its stolen meal from the ancient burro and the lamed buckskin that shared the corral.

"Señor Jaime, my mama says you are to come with me. It will soon be time for our meal, and she does not want us to be late. It is not polite, so my mama says."

The boy made no move to leave the corral railings but climbed to the top pole and hung his elbows to secure himself.

"I have ridden that burro when I was a baby," he declared proudly. "And I did not fall off, not even when Grandpapa let me ride alone around the corral. But the burro is old now and can no longer see to not stumble on the bad ground, so it stays here to be company with whatever is sick or lamed. This is what Alonso tells me, and he is a good man. My grandpapa says so."

The child talked more than Jim Henry wanted, but he

could not look at the smiling face or turn his back in rudeness. He grunted, as if that were answer enough, and picked up the matted wisps of hay, sticky now with sweat and coated with unshed winter hair. He went back to work on the brown gelding.

"Señor, I have watched you with the mare, and now the brown. Will you show me what you do with that straw that makes them wiggle their lips and have such a funny face? It must feel good to have you rub them where they cannot reach. But why do you not do such a kindness to the mule? It, too, has worked hard and deserves the attention. It is only fair, Señor Jaime."

How did you explain to a child the problem of catching up a miserable mule, the unlikely chance of skinning its back and sides without receiving a kick or a bite for the effort? Jim Henry thought about an explanation, looking at the broken wisps in his hand. Then the shy child was standing beside him and laid a woven rope across his palm. Attached to the other end was the dun mule, eyes half-closed, ears comfortably loose across the gray-striped neck.

"Would you please show me, Señor Jaime? I am needing to know what you have done."

They were late as Tomás hurried him to a brightly lit room. The boy crossed through doorways and passed long, empty halls as if he knew where he was headed, and was confident Jim Henry would follow. The child turned a sharp left and opened a carved door, then stopped at the edge of the room and waited for Jim Henry to catch up.

The Texan did not expect the number of people who turned at their entrance. He had not known of the families in the compound, he had not bothered with the evidence of numerous horses and goats, sheep and spring lambs, the winter crops stored and mostly used, wagons and harness and rope half spun out and braided. He had stayed within himself, conscious of the three animals in his care and little else.

The boy, Tomás, went straight to an older, gray-haired man and dropped his head to his chest as he offered an apology for their lateness. Jim Henry did not follow the child.

His gaze swept the room, and he found his enemies, waiting for him with expectant grins.

The one-eyed man was there, black hair bound in rolled cotton, milky eye loose in its scarred hole, hands spread to the plate of food before him, knife point buried in beans and shredded meat. Jim Henry dipped his head and moved his gaze to the one called Antonio, who, having already made known his threat, graced Jim Henry with a smile and a pleasant nod as he shoveled beans onto a tortilla and bit off the rolled end. As he chewed the food, his smile broadened, and bits of food escaped his broken mouth.

Jim Henry continued his circle of the room and saw a frown of concern on the face of Tomás's mother. It would be for her son, for his lateness. He would not let himself think there could be any concern in her for an Anglo Texas boy. Then a voice broke into his bitter thoughts, and he returned to the room filled with faces and hushed expectancy.

"Señor, please. To come here. Tomás tells me of what you have been doing. I am wanting to know more."

The labored words were English, the voice gentle and weak, but the fire in the old man's face had not lessened or been diminished by the pain that bent his neck and the age that stiffened his once-strong hands.

As if there had been a signal, the rapid talking and clattered sounds of the meal resumed. Jim Henry sat at the old man's side, the boy perched on a stool to his right. The plate left in front of him was piled generously, and the cooled wine in a wooden cup was delicious. He felt its release immediately, as a complement to the spiced beans and goat meat, the damp green shredded leaves and red sauce. In halting Spanish he answered the old man's inquiries and filled out the boy's version of the day's ride. He did not take note when the man named Antonio lifted his fingers to tug at the gold cross around his neck and hold it in his closed fist; nor did he see the same hand stray to the belt and finger a long, murderous knife.

Jim Henry was most polite when he refused the offer of a bed in the old man's house or a pallet near the side doorway. He would not be caught off guard this night; there was more here than a small child full of mischief. He bowed to the old man's kindness but remained firm in his insistence that he sleep outside, somewhere in the compound, somewhere near the barns or beside a corral fence or near a brick baking oven.

Antonio had not looked directly at him after the introductions, but he had felt the heat of a stare through the evening meal and knew a sharp quickening of his senses, an edge to his thoughts. It was as if the man's hatred were a glowing, burning thing of its own, naked and wild in its lust to kill Texans. Jim Henry willed himself not to look for trouble from Antonio or the one-eyed man. He would not deliberately violate the village hospitality, but he would be ready to defend himself. And he sensed those skills would be needed soon.

The night cooled slowly, but there was the sweet hint of summer warmth spiced with freshening hay and sweated animals, the rise of odor from the packed red dirt. The night air teased him, fired a restless anticipation that kept him from lying down on the woven blanket and putting his head on a wadded shirt as he looked up at the bright stars and passed slowly into sleep.

Instead, he walked the compound, finding many similarities with Spencer's Rancho. It was not yet a year since he had ridden out of the walls on the high-headed bay, with Hap and the others beside him. He knew there had been a reason then for signing up to fight, but he could no longer remember anything of why he had come north in the long army column.

Instinct took him to the back corral, where he'd left the two horses and the mule. The paint was easy to find in the dark; white streaks bisected her ribs and swept down her neck, and the white end of her tail flipped lazily at a few persistent flies. Jim Henry leaned on the skinned pole barrier, letting his chin graze the wood, watching the brown gelding consider him carefully before going back to the scattered pile of hay.

When he heard the voices he stepped into the shadowed protection of an overhanging roof. It was late, well past midnight. No one expected to find him out with the horses at this time. He slowed his breathing and held his body tight to the day-warmed adobe wall. He almost started forward when he heard the voice again.

"But Señor Antonio, I have told you again. I am not one of your women, nor will I give away my child and my papa to become one. I am Tomás's mother, and that is what I choose to be. Nothing more. I have told you this."

The man interrupted her, voice harsh, unforgiving: "Josefina, you do not listen to me. I have no more women, only you. I am to be yours alone. This I have known since the day the *Tejano* bandit rode through your farm and left you with the child. I will avenge you, and I will wed you."

Jim Henry drew in a hard breath and thought the two heard him. But it was the sound of struggling he heard, not their steps toward his hiding place. He touched the hilt of his knife, drew it halfway out, then waited as the sounds diminished.

"Antonio, I do not love you now. I will never love you. Or any man. It will do you no good to paw at me or follow me as you have done. No!"

Her voice was sharp and loud, but there was no fear to it. Jim Henry eased his shoulders, let the knife fall back to its sheath, rested his head on the comforting wall. If he intruded now, the woman would turn her anger on him, there would be words with the slighted lover, and it would come to nothing but trouble. This was not the way to return the woman and her child to their farm as he had promised.

"Tomás and I leave tomorrow. We will travel as Papa has asked. We go under the guard of this Señor Jaime, a man Papa has trusted. You will not be our guardian; Papa knows you and did not ask you to perform this task. It is for Señor Jaime to finish, and for us to follow."

There was a long moment of tense silence, and then she continued: "As for being a man . . . the señor is cold and quiet, but he means us no harm even though he is a *Tejano*. He does not see me or the child. It is best this way."

The man hiding in the shadows, a reluctant listener to the heated conversation, flinched at the dispassionate voice and the picture of him that it drew. It was not a kindness to hear what others thought of you. The woman was wrong, far from the truth; he could imagine her face in the darkness, the lift and swell of her body, the strength in her straight back, and the tenderness in her worn hands. And now he could see the man beside her, confronting her. Again he slid his fingers to the hilt of his knife, forcing himself to wait.

"Ah, Josefina, but you are wrong. No man can look and not see you. Your beauty, your fire . . . You are lying to yourself to have things as you wish. The young *Tejano* is still a man, with too much time in war and prison. He will see you, and then you will find out about his honor and his word. You will have need of Antonio then, and I may well not be there waiting for your command."

She must have shaken her head, for Jim Henry could hear a silky brushing before she found the words she wanted: "Antonio, you know only what you feel, and think. That is all. And you think the world is the way you are. But this is not true. There are men who keep their promises, who do not pester a woman with their swollen ideas of love. There is nothing to this boy, there is only a quiet sadness. I have taken his word, and I will trust it, for Papa already knows well his honor. It is something you cannot understand."

Jim Henry burned in his head, choked off and swallowed a meaningless sound. Another word from the scalded Antonio and he would leave the safety of the roofline and bring his knife tip to the man's throat and be damned to the test of his word, the kindness of the village. He could no longer bear to hear himself discussed as if his feelings could be taken out and examined like a lead ball or a piece of wood, to suffer pity and scorn. He would have no woman feel pity for him, he would not suffer the laughter of a man like Antonio. He put his weight on his right foot, leaned from the wall.

But the woman walked away from the shallow doorway where she had stood, and Antonio followed her for a step until she turned to him and lifted her hand for him to stop. Jim Henry strained to listen.

"There is nothing more, Antonio. I have been clear to

you. Your protection is not needed, and your declaration of love is for yourself only, not for who I am. Now I will go to my son and you will leave us alone. Good night, señor. Goodbye.''

CHAPTER 18

THE PAINT MARE stood saddled and eating breakfast. The mule was cornered, long ears flopping, hind end shifting as it sought to elude Jim Henry and the catch rope. He heard the woman and the boy come in behind him and smiled when Tomás took the rope from his hands and slipped it over the mule's neck without being asked. The brown gelding came to a shake of a pan of oats, and Jim Henry took care to smooth the blanket on the dark back before setting the wooden pack saddle into place.

It was not yet true dawn, but the sky had lightened enough for shadows, and Jim Henry could see the woman's softly colored face. She, too, was smiling, although when he looked straight at her she frowned and turned away. He bowed his head to the brown's belly and tugged the cincha. The anger came out in his voice and fired the heat rushing his face and neck, burning his ears:

"Lady, I don't trust that Señor Antonio, or his choice of riding companions. Once we get past the village here, we ain't riding with old Enselmo's blessing. So I figure we best move out early, get a stick for you to carry, keep that mule moving. If there's trouble, run. Don't think about me or the pack horse, just run like hell. You'll have the boy with you, all that's important to you."

She said nothing to him, yet she had shown up before dawn, too early for the rest of the village to be stirring. The boy's face appeared at her side, and it was he who asked the questions:

"Señor Jaime, why would this man want to hurt us? Why must we run from him? He knows my grandpapa, he has shared a meal with us. Is it because of you . . . of being a *Tejano*?''

It was close enough to the truth that Jim Henry allowed the question to stand as its own answer. And he knew the woman would add nothing to change the boy's opinion. She waited in the soft light, looking straight into his eyes until he had to pull away.

''Señor Jaime?''

''Yeah, boy, guess it's because of me all right.''

He hated the half lie, but there was little else he would tell a child about his own mother. Last night and its revelation stuck in Jim Henry's gut.

''First light's here. We got to ride. Lady, you keep hold of that switch, use it on the mule if you got to. Boy, you ride up with your mama.''

Traveling was slow; the ground fought them with piled rocks and clumped grass, steep washes, low cactus that spiked the horses, quick uphill scrambles over baked red ground. As they worked slowly through the scrub, there was a conical hill ahead of them always to their distant right, a landmark Jim Henry instinctively kept at his shoulder. He cursed the slow going but held quiet and stayed behind the shuffling mule. It was an hour out before he sighted the men following them. He kicked the mare into a trot and drew up alongside the mule.

''We got our company,'' he said without looking at the woman. ''Don't look back. Two men, maybe three. You got a notion 'bout this, lady?''

He regretted the words as soon as they were out, but he owned their truth. She had no right to put all this to him. It wasn't his life that got them in trouble, it was her and her pity, her casual beauty and superior airs. Given a chance, he could come to hate this woman.

He regretted the question even more when he saw the shock on her face, but he didn't give her time to answer as he struggled to cover his tracks: ''I figure it this way. If they mean us no harm, if they's only traveling same way we are, then they won't push their mounts to catch up. Won't be bothering them if we pick up our speed. But''—and he worked over the thought before coming to a conclusion—"if they're after us, then when we move out some, they'll keep pace, when we stop, they'll keep coming. We got to find out which."

He could see the black-faced wall they had faced on the march north months past. A nightmare then, and one they would have to go down to get away from the men following them.

"Lady, that rim we got to cross, it's ahead, right? Real close? Do you know a quick way down? These men probably figure they can catch us there, otherwise they would've come out last night and been waiting to ambush us."

There was more than that: There was Antonio's arguing with the woman late into the night, there were words passed and tempers frayed. And when she spoke in answer to his question, her words did nothing to ease his fears.

"There is no fast way down La Bajada, Señor Jaime. But there are choices, an easy way that is long and smooth, and a fast way which is most dangerous unless you have a good horse and much nerve. There is a small village at La Bajada's base. It is home to some few indios and a priest. The priest is expecting us, but he will be looking to the road and not the trail. If you think we must, then we will go down the trail. Head toward the peak, for at its base is the way down." She hesitated. "And the choice to take that trail is yours, señor."

He did not look at her then, but he could see her face with its dusty skin and black eyes, the shiny hair pulled back and stuffed under the wide straw hat. "It ain't just my choice, lady. It depends on what them three want. Me, I'd take the easy ride and hit the river, go past the village, and head on home. But . . . you punch up that mule, pick up a little speed, but not so those watching think we know why they're behind us. I'll give you a lead, and you keep me going to the peak. Once we hit the ridge and get out of their sight, we move out. How far from the ridge to the rim—La Bajada, you call it?"

"It is easily another hour to the ridge, señor," she replied, "and then only a short distance to the rim. You will see the black rock as we climb to the crest, and the trail will be down to your right. At a run it will be less than a half hour to the edge of La Bajada.''

Jim Henry looked to the hills ahead, squinting in the sunlight. ''Lady, it depends on them fellows behind us, but I figure we're going to head down that ride faster than it's been done before. If them gents follow, then we make it a run. Unless you want to go back and reason with that man and his *compadres*. He might listen to you.''

The words had been calculated to hurt, and he had succeeded. But she gave him nothing in return: ''We will do as you say, señor. And God have mercy on us, for La Bajada will not.''

The land rose slowly to the ridge line. The woman prodded at the mule with every step, forcing it to keep up with the mare. Jim Henry let the paint move out and had to tug constantly at the brown's lead. They traveled smoothly, kicking up little dust on the grassy plain, while the wind blew small storms around them, taking what dust they did stir and blowing it away.

Jim Henry could not look back, but he knew the men were following without having to see for himself. The distant peak moved farther away, and he knew it was a distortion of the heat and the wind, but it raised a knot of worry that they wouldn't make the time, that the riders would feel their suspicion and circle around them to force a standoff.

Jim Henry bit into his lip in frustration—they were exposed and underarmed. He wanted nothing more than to turn and take the fight to Antonio and his companions, but the woman and the boy were his charges. They would be the ones to suffer if he failed. It was not a decision he could make.

The mule slowed in spite of the switch, and Jim Henry laced the dun animal with the braided end of his reins. The mule leaped into a sluggish trot. ''How much more to the ridge, lady?'' he asked. ''A guess, a good guess'll do. What you . . . ?''

''It is less than an hour, Señor Jaime, if we keep to this pace, and then a gallop to the rim. Then you must decide.''

"It's been decided for us. We ain't fooling our shadows. They got their own horses walking out, keeping pace. We're going down the fast trail. This mare's good-footed, and I ain't seen the mule step wrong yet. The brown'll have to take care of himself. I'll let him go once we're over the ridge, give us more speed. If he keeps with us, fine. But it ain't a ladies' party waiting for us back there. Those gents're dead serious about their intentions."

The wind took the last of his words, and he touched spur to the mare, leaned over to chouse the mule. The big ears flopped back, the hind end lifted, and the mule caught the paint mare square in the ribs. Jim Henry stuck to her as she bucked sideways, but his hat was caught by the wind and flipped endlessly until it caught on a tough piñon branch. It hung there, way off to the side, out of reach.

Jim Henry wanted to turn the mare and rescue his hat. It was ignorant, and courting death, to ride the desert without one, but he did not have the time to waste. He almost put a rein to the mare's neck, but the woman stopped him.

"Señor, don't. The priest will have a hat for you. A good hat, señor. He is a friend of my papa's. Please."

She drew close to him, and the mare shied sideways, wary of the mule's intentions. Jim Henry yanked on the brown's line, picked up a narrow thread of a trail, and rode toward the peak. The land dropped into a narrow gully; single file, they slid down the banking, hopped across the bottom, and scrambled up the opposite side. Jim Henry almost left his saddle when the brown stopped to inspect the ditch, then jumped beside the mare.

He risked a backward glance then and saw one rider pass in front of a piñon. Two more were clearly outlined by the mountains far behind them. He yanked again at the brown. They had to ride hard now; it was time to make their run.

Another wash dropped them out of sight, and this time the land rose steeper when they climbed out the bank. The hills to their left were smaller, and the bare outline of other mountains in the distance became clearer. The paint mare coughed, and Jim Henry felt her ribs rise and fall in hard breaths. The sun sucked at them now, the wind dried their sweat instantly. He narrowed his eyes against the glare and ran his tongue over dry lips, glancing over as the mule shuffled ahead under protest. The woman's face was hidden under the tipped brim of her hat, and he envied her the protection. The boy looked asleep, leaning against his mother in complete trust.

They topped the ridge, the peaked hill to their right. It was a short sweep to the blackness of the rim, yet Jim Henry knew the distance was deceptive. He risked a look back and could no longer see their trio. Then he let their own animals walk until he was comfortable that they could not be seen over the ridge.

He spoke to the woman, keeping the words soft, holding in the taste of his own fear: "All right, lady, pick the line and take us to the rim best you can. A trot'll get us there and leave something for the horses to make the climb down. Let's go."

She nodded and spoke to the boy, gentle words that woke him and that Jim Henry could not understand. He shut his eyes, conscious of a burning itch on his forehead, a prickling sensation on his face and around his mouth. He'd been in a hospital and then in jail. It had been a long time since he'd tasted the sun's power; he wiped the salt from his lips and scratched his chin.

They moved out while his eyes were still closed, and he felt the mare jerk into a trot to stay with the mule. He rode blind a few steps, swaying with her strides. Then his eyes snapped open and he rose in his stirrups, steadied himself, and hauled on the brown to bring him up to the mare. Leaned sideways, the brown head near his knee, he wound the lead rope around the wooden saddle and let the brown go. The mare hurried to catch up to the mule, and the old brown gelding slowed, finally returning to a walk.

They rode for a good ten minutes at a trot, keeping silent. The paint mare paced the mule while Jim Henry rode balanced over her back to help save her. Sweat lathered white on the mule's shoulders, foam rubbed underneath the breast collar and breeching. As the mare labored for breath, Jim Henry touched spurs to her sides.

Gradually the ground smoothed out, the piñons thinned, small rock and clumped grass woven with cactus gave way to rusty dirt and black pebbling. There was only the hard breathing of the animals and the heat pounding at them. Jim Henry twisted in the saddle, hands pressed to the pommel for balance; three shaded forms topped the ridge behind them, slowed to stand together. He could imagine the talk, the quick questions and bitter curses. Then the riders came rolling down the slope, tempting Jim Henry to goad their own mounts into a frantic gallop.

He chewed on his cracked lip, saw the woman whack the mule hard on the rump, the boy held tight by one arm across his chest. The paint mare rose and fell in her strides beneath Jim Henry, stumbled on a skidding rock, and shook her head, whinnying. He looked back again and sighed to see the men pull up to a trot. He knew they would keep pace until their quarry reached the lip and dropped down, then they would gallop to the rim, dismount, and take their time shooting at the target he and the mare would make. It would give these men much pleasure to bring down the mare and the hated Anglo *Tejano* riding her. They would laugh at his death on the treacherous slope called La Bajada.

Josefina reined in the mule sharply. "We are here, señor. This is our trail," she said.

Her voice told the story. Jim Henry looked out and down, almost shook his head, but was conscious of the child's anxious face, the dark worry of the mother. The trail was little beyond a thin line wound in black rock. If he waited too long or looked too closely, he would not make the attempt. If he hesitated, the woman and the child would not follow. And the men behind them were closing in. He was losing their slight advantage.

So he nodded casually to the woman and drove spurs into the mare. She flattened her ears and jumped forward, slipped on a flat rock, and went to her knees in a mad scramble. Jim Henry pulled on the bit for support, closed his eyes, and drove the little mare forward. The mule followed as the woman wielded the stick on its rump without mercy, and the narrow hooves clattered over the same loose slab.

The trail went sideways at first, between flat-topped boulders and black rock spires. Jim Henry could look up easily and see their pursuers, could almost make out the fury distorting their faces. Then the narrow track switched back quickly, sharp angles that left the mare's head out in space as she tried to make the bend. Jim Henry heard rushing hoof-beats above them. He pushed the mare into a jog, and when she resisted from common sense he lashed her with the rein ends, driving in his spurs to draw blood. The mare lowered her body, hocks deep under her, head and neck stretched flat, belly almost touching ground. The trail dropped away for a good five feet. They couldn't take this much time; Jim Henry spurred again, and the mare jumped, landing awkwardly and slamming her rider's leg against a rock. Jim Henry grimaced and spurred again. His right leg did not work, but the mare plunged down the next step, frantic from his cruel goading.

It was a gamble, a big gamble. Shouts drifted down from the rim, barely heard through the rushing wind and the blood pounding in his ears. Then Jim Henry could make some sense of the cursing and beat at the slowing mare. Antonio wanted the woman. He would not fire at the mule, he would concentrate his hatred on Jim Henry and try to bring the mare down. That was why Jim Henry had taken the lead, why he drove the paint so relentlessly on the impossible trail. If the mare went down, it must be well away from the mule's fragile double burden.

He heard the crack after the rock near his shoulder splintered and chips stung his face. When the mare startled beneath him, he drove her forward. Three shots broke ground ahead of him, a fourth nicked his arm. He risked a backward glance and saw the woman prodding the mule, intent on keeping up with him, unaware she was putting herself and the child into the line of fire.

Then he looked down and shuddered. They were almost halfway, but the track crossed the face of La Bajada for a hundred yards, presenting him and the mare as broadside targets for the snipers above them. He could see the flat roofs of the houses below him, and the irrigation ditches, the leafed cottonwoods near a pond, the regular lines of a planted field. La Bajada, quiet and peaceful, oblivious of the battle raging along the high cliff.

Jim Henry swung the mare's head out into space; a bullet

meant for the bony protrusion between her ears winged off soundlessly, digging up dirt on the unused trail. He lifted the mare's head so she could not see and drove in the spurs, tearing hide and drawing blood. The little paint jumped blindly from the punishment, dropped down beside a boulder, went to her knees, and staggered to her feet. Above him, Jim Henry heard the woman scream, and he yelled meaningless words at her to stay on the trail, take the safer way down. He was the target, she was the prize.

Again he dug into the mare, jumping her without mercy into a loose field of black rock. She scrambled for balance, sliding on her haunches and belly until Jim Henry's feet scraped the ground. Two shots passed his ear. He yanked the mare hard left and yelled again—wordless, high-pitched sounds; he was as frightened as the mare. He leaned back in the saddle, forced his legs under him, lifted the reins for balance. The mare skidded to a halt, front legs braced wide, sides heaving. A slab of red rock moved under her and began its descent, spooking the mare wildly. Jim Henry watched as the two-foot-square piece picked up speed on the slope, rattling smaller rocks and pebbles before it, tearing up grass and small cactus. Then it lifted into air and almost floated down, gaining speed, shattering on the hard ground far below horse and rider. The mare trembled, and Jim Henry bit back the taste of fear.

The woman yelled again. He looked up to see that she and the boy were off the mule, huddled against a leaning boulder. Two of the men had started their journey down the rim, while the third stayed on his knees at the top and fired as Jim Henry stared at him.

The old trail turned back on itself below Jim Henry and the paint. He put the mare to the thin line of the trail and gave her rein to move out. As she began to trot, he yanked her head around and drove her again to jump across the trail, his weight held back to help her fly. The pair wove through the black rock, stumbled and went down, then came up and made another flying leap. A hail of bullets marked their passage, chips flew, dust rose and settled.

Finally the mare reached her limit—tripped over a sliding rock, went to her knees again, and could not regain her balance. She slid over on her side and dragged Jim Henry with her, tearing the length of his leg and slowly bleeding her own hide. Jim Henry grabbed for something to stop his slide, dragging his hands over rock and cactus until he wrapped himself around a struggling bush and held on, leaving the mare to continue her helpless descent without him. A moment later the loose-rooted bush broke free, and Jim Henry began to slide on his back over the mare's path. He rolled sideways, dug in his toes, clenched at anything with bleeding fingers to slow his fall. He could hear the mare whinny, the woman above him scream, and he realized the screen of dust from the sliding horse gave him life-saving cover.

His heel caught on a pointed rock, his hands found a hold in the broken half of a boulder, the trail turned back below him. He dropped down to it, came up from his knees, and scrambled along the path, running for his life. The little paint mare had found her footing and stood trembling. Red streaks covered her sides; the near stirrup on the old saddle was gone, and the rifle was missing from the scabbard. The slip bridle hung around her neck, one rein trailing at her legs, the other torn in half. She whinnied again wildly, her entire body shaking from fear, then picked her way down the hill to the widening road at the bottom, where she trotted slowly, head high, tail thrashing.

Jim Henry came to another turn in the switchback, near to the bottom. Someone from the village must have heard the shooting or seen the mare's frantic tumble, for a figure was coming quickly along the road, almost running, with the long outline of an old musket held in one hand.

It was all confusion. Jim Henry didn't know where the woman was, didn't know how close the two riders were. The bottom of the old trail widened slightly, evened out to a straight line—close, but not close enough. He took the mare's scraped path, leaned back on his heels, and skidded down the slope, throwing out a hand to push off from a boulder, grabbing at any rooted vegetation to slow his progress and keep himself upright.

Suddenly his fingers lost their hold, his boot heel skidded on loose rock, and he fell—hard on his side, rolling over the sharp black rock, head slammed repeatedly on the rough edges, back scraped raw. He fought for balance; then, as the ground gave way under him, he wrapped his arms over his head in vain protection and closed his eyes, praying to something while he gained momentum. At last his feet hit and stuck on a rock, his body flipped over, and he sailed the last few feet of La Bajada. He had a fleeting glimpse of a brown face, mouth wide in surprise, a pair of brown hands spread apart in motionless support. Jim Henry hit bottom on one foot and a shoulder, folded up, and was slammed to the hard rock ground.

Close to senseless, he could think only of the woman and the child. The fight wasn't over.

He remembered seeing an old musket somewhere near him, and when he opened his eyes a figure leaned over him, hat in one hand, the precious musket in the other. The browned face was seamed with bewilderment.

"Señor, are . . . ?"

"I need the musket, quick. Powder, too, everything you've got."

He spoke in English, and the puzzlement on the strange face grew deeper. Jim Henry shuddered at the effort it took as he struggled to his feet and reached for the weapon in the man's hand. He corrected his error, fumbled for the words:

"*Gracias, señor.*"

The dark face smiled, then the man crossed himself in an ancient blessing. Jim Henry had the vague thought the blessing would be for him, for his need of the weapon. He shook his head, took a deep and painful breath, and looked at the great height of the wall. His first step brought him to his knees as his ankle gave under him, but he came up and used the butt end of the old musket as a crutch to carry his weight. As he hobbled he checked for the enemy, conscious of his exposed position.

He was out of range for the man on the rim, who had already started his treacherous way down La Bajada. Two of them had reached the woman and child; one had worked his way by them, picking his trail carefully through the ruins Jim Henry left behind. He could not look more than a few feet ahead of him; could not lift his head and see Jim Henry. The small bay horse he rode stumbled often, tired from the harsh run up on the high desert.

It was the other one who worried Jim Henry. He held the dun mule at the bit and stared up at the woman, one hand fingering the knife at his belt. The woman sat tall and silent, her son clasped to her breast. The sight of her distress moved Jim Henry as his own thoughts could not. Her face and the sense of the child cleared the mist slowing his decisions, and spurred him to settle on a plan.

He knelt beside a boulder, rested the musket on its slanted surface, sighted down the barrel, and lifted the weapon to make the distance uphill. It must not be near the woman and the boy; he was too unsteady for shooting close to them. He touched the trigger, felt the pull of its rusty parts. His target would be the small bay or the long-legged rider urging it on. The shot barely registered in Jim Henry's ears, but he could see rock shatter and the bay horse spook from the flying chips. Slowly he aimed again, fighting a buzzing in his head, conscious that the man holding the dun mule had turned, hand dropped to his own pistol. Jim Henry knew he was an easy target, that he knelt exposed and helpless, but he could not let these men take the woman. Not without a fight.

He found his fingers had reloaded the old musket without his being conscious of the act. He wished then for the old swivel breech of his pa's. He wished for the two shots that could make the difference. He focused on the bay and its rider, white-faced, reaching for a scabbard and a rifle on the off side. He tried to sight on the bay, but his eyes blurred, and his head pounded. So he pointed and fired, feeling the strain of the weapon as it slammed out the shot. He was as surprised as the rider when the bay buckled and fell sideways against the hill trail. The rider catapulted over the downed horse, rolled twice, and hit a boulder headfirst. The sound echoed. . . . Jim Henry's gut churned, his mouth went dry. He didn't need to look at the stilled form; the man was out of the fight.

It was the woman's scream that brought him back. He looked up to where she now stood. There must have been time unaccounted for, moments gone where he had not been awake. The dun mule came slowly down the trail, the boy clinging to its brush tail. And the woman stood alone, a knife in her hand, its bright blade dulled a dark brown. Jim Henry saw the figures in the tableau, and his mind worked over what it could understand until it became clear to him.

The one-eyed man sat near the woman, rested against a boulder, hands folded neatly over his belly. The slowly growing red stain, the dulled tip of the woman's knife, told Jim Henry what had happened. He shuddered, then glanced up at the rim, straining to lift his head, feeling for the first time the damage done to his back and side. The man at the top, the one who had started down last, was gone. He had left his companions to their problems. It would be Antonio who had escaped, for the dead man with the bay horse was unfamiliar to Jim Henry, and the one-eyed man sat dying or dead near the woman.

Jim Henry rose from his crouch by the rock, rose slowly, aware once again of the sun's constant power, the thirst in his mouth, the soreness of his entire body. He forgot his leg and took a step, went down to his knees on sharp rock, and grunted in surprise. He stayed kneeling, too tired to make another attempt, until the long face of the dun mule loomed over him and the cry of the boy pushed him to try one more time.

"Mama, he is fine. Señor Jaime. He is here, and so am I. Please, Mama, come down. Please."

The boy's need would bring the woman back. Jim Henry was able to stand and watch as she stepped over the sitting man, pausing only to lay the knife beside him on a flat grassy place. Then she began her descent, picking her way carefully down the ruined trail, leaving tiny puffs of dust in the churned ground as she passed. Jim Henry watched her, conscious of her grace as she walked, knowing she would not be crying when she reached the bottom of the rim.

Then a small hand touched his palm, and Jim Henry looked down at the serious face of Tomás. The boy was much like his mother. There were no tears streaking his young face, but there was a brightness in his eyes and a gentle trembling in the hand that clung to Jim Henry's. He closed his fingers over the much smaller ones given to him and marveled at their slender length, their baby strength. Then he shut his eyes to a feeling he had never known and waited for the woman to reach him and the child.

CHAPTER 19

THE SHAKES STARTED and loosened his knees, dried his mouth to cotton. He had to open his eyes. The woman was more than halfway down the hill, and no priest had come out to greet her. Instead there was a growing band of men surrounding Jim Henry, black-haired, black-eyed men with skin coppered from the daily sun and their heritage.

She had told him it was a small village of Indians who had converted, and one priest to lead them, who would be their host and welcome the daughter of Eduardo Iberra and her son, and their protector. In place of the absent priest were men holding various weapons, men with no friendliness in their faces for the sudden invaders. Jim Henry recognized the seamed face of the man who had given up his weapon earlier, who came to stand in front of him now, both hands outstretched, eyes grim as he gestured for the return of his rifle.

Jim Henry shook his head to the request, as he let the musket drift carelessly over the growing crowd. He felt the heat of the old musket, and realized he could not remember reloading. There were no women or children present. They would be hidden safely in the squat adobe jacals of the village, protected from the unwanted visitors. He knew a threat would be enough. Jim Henry picked out his first target and let the musket waver across the man's chest. The action was recognized and the band of men drew together, stepped back from his hostile act, and continued their stubborn wait.

Fear caught in his throat, and he took a half step sideways when someone put a hand on his shoulder. Then he smelled her scent and knew who stood beside him before she spoke.

"Señor, be most careful, do not shoot. They have never

harmed us before, but the priest has always been here to greet us, to guide them.''

The brightness of the sun numbed him, the scrapes and bruises from his fall began to reawaken. Jim Henry couldn't hear what she was telling him; he could only see the groups of men, in twos and threes, who joined the crowd around him, faces blank, menacing. He knew the tightness of his belly, the touch of his finger to the trigger of the musket, the anticipation growing in him, the fear and its companion, anger.

When the knot of men loosened, Jim Henry eased back on the trigger. These men were farmers who worked their crops and dug the ditches to water them—not fierce, untamed warriors, but men who had chosen to settle under a priest's blessing and live a different life. He saw someone striding toward him down the road, leading a paint mare, talking softly to the horse, stroking her neck as he led her past the rushing acequia. They were returning his horse to him; there was no malice in these men.

The now-familiar face of the musket's owner reappeared. Jim Henry looked at the man and raised the long barrel. The crowd stepped back, and voices hissed a muted warning. But he let the musket slip in his hands and offered it to the owner butt-first. He thought the woman beside him jerked in surprise and almost touched him as he laid the stock across the man's outstretched hands. But he could not be sure, and this was all he could figure out to do.

The gesture loosened excited talk in the group, words Jim Henry did not understand at all. He risked a glance at the woman, who shook her head as if he had actually spoken his question. He let out his breath slowly, stabbed in his ribs by a bruise, feeling the length of his leg throb, his ankle swell. If these men chose to fight him now, there was no doubt in him as to the outcome. He wanted to wipe his forehead, dig at the itch behind his ear, shift weight from the sore ankle and leg, even sit down in the comfort of a shady tree. Then the noise of the talking died quickly, and tension filled him. He sighed deeply and closed his eyes, winced from what could happen.

Something tickled his fingers, and he heard the mare snort

before he saw her. The crowd had melted away; it was one man who gave him the mare, an older man with gray streaks in his bound hair, an opaque film discoloring his left eye. There were no words in their exchange. Jim Henry bowed his head twice, and the old man slipped the recovered Hawken into its scabbard and stepped back to wait. It took Jim Henry much time to put weight and turn on his good leg, to balance with a hand on the mare's rump and reach back for the mule. The woman came to him then, gathering her skirts around her and holding to her son. She mounted the mule quickly, and Jim Henry gave the boy an awkward push to settle him in front of his mother.

Then it was for him to climb back on the mare and lead their group out of the old man's village. Someone had taken the time to pin a length of leather to the broken rein, the stirrup was gone from the near side, but the sturdy Hawken settled in the scabbard, and the leather pouch stayed tied to the horn. If he ever believed in miracles, he would believe now. He reached quickly, instinctively, to the small pouch around his neck. It, too, remained secure. Now he knew, now he believed. Jim Henry hobbled to the mare's chest, ducked under her neck, and held to the breast collar for support. He had to put his weight on his left leg when he stood erect, and the knee buckled under him. The ankle blossomed into violent throbbing as he slipped his right foot into the wooden stirrup and braced himself to swing up and over. The woman caught his torn shirt at the neck, yanked as hard as she was able, and he used the momentum to lift himself onto the mare.

It took him what felt like minutes to steady himself in the hard saddle, find his breath, settle the odd bits of pained cuts and scratches, before he could again face the old man, who had been joined by the savior with the ancient musket. The gray-haired Indian blessed Jim Henry and the woman, and her son—this time slowly, with much dignity, putting a spirit into the halting words in almost comprehensible Latin.

The small trio bowed to the blessing, and when the old man was done, they moved off slowly, picking their way through the crops and cross-ditched waterways, splashing through a small stream and enjoying the short comfort of the cottonwood shade. They rode away from their rescuers and did not look back, did not trust the spirit that let them go. Behind them the men knotted together again, this time with their women and children. They watched the man who had held the musket on them and had returned it, the woman who had taken the strength of a man with his own knife, and the child who did not cry but stayed with his own and kept his silence. They watched the three riders disappear from the deep shadows of their village and ride onto the heat of the flat desert plain.

The old man was politely crowded by the villagers; he carried their burdens now. The priest had told them nothing of welcoming strangers to their home, yet the woman's face had been familiar, the small boy had once played with the old man's grandson, Domingo. They had come with the older man, who sat and laughed much with the priest. They often stayed one night, or more, on their journey back to the farm way below them on the great river.

The priest had warned them of strangers, yet the tall young man had shown great bravery in his running fight down the terrible wall of La Bajada, and there was a correctness in his returning the rifle to Isidero in the face of great odds. The old man had decided then: the two and their child would be allowed to continue their journey across the lands of the Indians. It was his to decide now, and the old man bowed to the necessity of making such a decision.

If the priest were here today, they would have offered aid to the Anglo, medicine for his scrapes and cuts, and something to help him breathe against the bruises of his ribs. A poultice of yucca root on his fair skin would draw out the sun's burning, and there would be stewed meat and good broth to put muscle on him for the long hard journey ahead. The woman would help in his care, and it would be several days before they would ride on. For as strong as the young Anglo was—and his strength was in his eyes and his soul as well as the muscle of his back and the length of his hand— he would need the days to regain what he had lost to La Bajada. The child could run again with Domingo, and when the young Anglo recovered it would be good for the men of the village to sit and talk with such a warrior.

But the priest was not here. The priest was buried in the slope of his La Bajada, at his favorite blessed spring, where he had fallen with a hand raised to his chest, his mouth opened in silent agony. They had washed and tended his body as he had taught them through his years of guidance; they had tried to speak his foreign words over the white flesh of his body. Then they had dug him into the earth as he would want, to become a part of the earth surrounding him.

The old man stood proudly as he watched the horses disappear into the vastness of the river plain. He did not expect the woman, or the man, to look back and see him watching. He scratched his head, puzzled by the return of thoughts banished by the small battle and the unusual excitement: the firing of weapons, the horses running, men dying. It was for him now to make the decision again, the choice the villagers would follow. They were here because of a foreign man and a foreign belief, the sanctity of the high-walled church, a vague acceptance of the power of a new god who owned that church and lived inside it, and the dead priest who now rested in the land of La Bajada. It was the old man's choice now, and its importance awed him.

He had no more time for the man and the woman and her child. He had his own thinking to attend, a host of thoughts that must be examined, a village of people waiting for his conclusion. He turned away from the vastness of the dry plain and walked to the mud wall of the church. Inside lived a god, outside lived the village of people; he worked over the conflict and tried to forget all about the events that had stirred up the day.

The mare stumbled occasionally, but her limp disappeared, smoothed out by the slow walking. The ground was easy for her, soft dirt and clumped grass with little variation in its levels. When at last Jim Henry looked back, he could not see the village or the immense mountains that had loomed over him for the past months. A sense of loss saddened him, even though there were other blue peaks to his right and to the far left. But those distant mountains had become special to him. He wiped his face on his torn sleeve and sighed, regretting it instantly as his ribs bit deep into his flesh.

Josefina heard the sigh and its abrupt ending, and thought to bring the mule beside the paint mare and talk to this strange Anglo. But her hands shook on the reins, and the dun mule would not listen to her commands. She knew there was a stream ahead, she remembered it from the thickening green of the trees, the singing of the birds above her head. At the water she could wash her hands, wash them clean of the stain embedded in her nails, dried dark in the lines of her palms, ingrained deeply in the work-calloused skin of her fingers. It was almost enough to make her cry, the dark stains in her skin, but the weight of her son resting on her breast and belly would not let the tears run clean. She would have to explain them to the boy—that they were from the pain in her heart and the memory in her fingers, the sight of life leaving a human because of what she had done. A man, sinking to his knees, hugging to himself, leaning back to wait, dying from the blade still warm in her own hand.

She knew the hard reality, knew that that one man would have taken her with no thought but his pleasure, that he would have gutted the Anglo with a wide smile and left her son to watch the horror and suffer with it for the remainder of his life. But the knowledge did little to ease her conscience, and she grabbed the mane of the dun mule, wound her fingers in its comforting wire stiffness, and clamped her legs to the sweaty sides. She bit the corners of her mouth, tasted the copper salt of the thin trickle. They would ride to the water, where she would bathe, and then they would continue riding until they reached the familiar crossing of the river, the slow spread of crop land, the comfort of her papa's sprawling farmhouse, and the safety of her own home.

The bruises opened their protest more quickly now. His right ankle blew up to fill the boot top, hot lines ran up the leg into his groin. His pants were shredded on his left leg, and he could feel the individual droplets of blood slide down his calf, wet until the sun dried them to a crust. None of the cuts were serious, nor were there broken bones or severed tendons or muscles. Jim Henry had been part of a hospital long enough to know the limits of his damage, and it was nothing compared with what he had seen. What he himself had caused.

The ribs were the most vocal, aching steadily, jerked to painful flares whenever the mare stumbled. But he could ride, even with the awkward loss of the near stirrup and the crudely patched rein. He wished there had been time to pick up his hat way back on the rim, or that the old Indian of the village could have seen his need and offered something, even a square of loose woven cotton. He lifted his arm to wipe at the sweat stinging his eyes and groaned again at the pull across his ribs. *Goddamn.*

She would not hear his sounds or feel the sympathy they stirred inside her. It was she who was injured, not the slow-riding *Tejano* with the blurred face and glassy eyes. She hated him now, hated what he was asking from her. It was all she could do to touch the smooth skin at the neck of her son, feel the rush of tenderness it brought, and not weep great fountains of tears. She did not need the claims of a pale-skinned Anglo to take her pity. Or need her help which she could not give.

She kicked viciously at the mule, wishing for the long stick the Anglo had made her use up on the rim to hurry the poor animal's walk. She must get to the water, but the trees were no closer, the water only a vivid memory. She must wash herself and her child soon, bathe each in the clean water to take away the horror, to take away the sin.

The mule lifted its long head; Josefina felt rather than heard its attempted bray, the dun sides rattling between her legs with a strong shake of the clumsy head. At the answering whinny she hauled savagely on the reins, terrified because there was a man waiting in the brush ahead, waiting to finish what had been started up on the rim of La Bajada. It must be Antonio; she had not killed him, nor had the Anglo with his shot that destroyed the bay gelding.

She wanted the knife in her hand, the warm wooden stock of a rifle that her papa had taught her to aim and shoot. But there was nothing for her as the mule lifted its head again, and this time its braying sounded loud and clear in the thicket of trees.

Jim Henry and the mare were way behind when the mule stopped and brayed. Quick thoughts of retribution filled him, but he could not take them to heart. There was no fight left to him, no organization to his thinking. So he was not surprised when a brown head thrust its way out of the bushes and the old pack horse nickered gladly to the mule's welcome. Even the tired little mare pricked her ears and stepped out a few strides before slowing again.

There was no halter and lead on the grayed head, but the packs had held to their lashings and the horse was glad for company, pleased to fall in behind the mule. Jim Henry knew the presence of the brown was good, but he could not remember why the brown had disappeared or if something had driven it off. He knew only that his mouth was dry, and his head ached, and the sun took all moisture from him, and he wanted to drink a long time from the river and lie quietly under a tree.

It was little more than a shallow trickle, shiny in the overhead rays of the sun, lost in the wide expanse of sand that had been a bed for the spring's snow off the mountain. Josefina had known they were close to water when the mule hurried its step willingly, carrying them from the brush onto the heavy pale red sand. Blessed water, waiting to cleanse her, offering its healing to one who was in great need.

She kicked at the mule, and it lumbered into an awkward trot. It, too, was needy. The brown gelding followed, though not as eagerly. There were recent tracks where the brown had already been to the river to drink. He stayed with the mule for company but had little interest in more of the muddy water. It was the paint mare who suffered the most; her shoulder was lame again, and her foreleg dripped blood. Her rider swayed dangerously in the high saddle, throwing off her stride, making her stagger in the depth of the sand and taking the edge off her eagerness to drink.

The woman was off the mule in an instant and kneeling in the wet sand, hands digging in the fine grains and scouring each other, rubbing the tough skin to a bright raw pink. She went through the pattern over and over, digging the damp sand and rubbing it endlessly between her hands, then letting the slow water bathe them, sluicing them of even the finest grains but not yet leaving the hands clean. She repeated the washing and rinsing until the boy spoke to her and broke into her concentration.

"Mama, come quick. It is Señor Jaime. Help me, Mama."

Only her Tomás was important enough to bring her out of the small world she had created; only her Tomás meant more than her own life. She looked around her frantically; he was kneeling by the long form of the *Tejano*. The horses and mule were together, heads hanging, mouths pursed to hold the precious taste of water. But the man was down far from the water's purifying salvation. And he was motionless and alone in the hot sun.

"Mama, please come help me. I cannot move him. He is too heavy. Mama, he is crying."

She stood over the man for a long time before she knew what to do for him. It was the eyes of her son that finally moved her. Frightened, shining eyes, in a thin face with its childish softness lost. Suddenly she could see the man he would become, and she was proud that he was of her body. His small hands cupped the head of the *Tejano*, and his young shoulders strained with the burden of the fallen weight. It was more than a child so young should have to bear alone.

First she must have something in which to carry water. She and the boy could not move Señor Jaime by themselves, and he had great need of the water's special magic. The tears that had been squeezed from under his eyelids were dried in salt lines down his face, and there were bright red blisters oozing around his mouth and eyes.

She must give him water first and bathe his face, then she would look to the rest of his injuries.

The three dozing animals did not move as she hurried between them and lifted out the blackened coffeepot tied to the pack saddle. She gave Tomás the pot to hold as she dabbed water from its black belly onto the man's face and between his scabbed lips. Again and again she soaked up water with the torn corner of a brightly colored skirt pulled from her rolled canvas, squeezing the drops onto the scaled lips several times, then gently wiping the dampened cloth over his forehead and cheeks.

It was several minutes before the *Tejano* stirred and the closed eyes came open. She saw fever in their glazed blankness, and for a moment she let the worry slow her. But she gave him the corner of the soaked cloth, and he sucked at it like a baby, drew in the moisture and worked his mouth until he could form words. She had to drop closer to hear what he tried so hard to say.

"Señora . . . señorita . . . Miss Josefina, I . . . that tastes almighty good. I thank . . . "

His determination gave out, and he closed his eyes, but she finally understood. His stumbling attempt at thanks told her he had not known all this time how to address her, whether she was to be called señora although he knew there was no husband, or whether there be an insult in the correct address of señorita. So he had used "lady" because he had not known anything better, and she had taken as an affront what had been his try at manners.

"It is Señorita Josefina, Jaime. Or Josefina, as my papa calls me, and I would be honored if you would call me so. You must lie still now and rest. I will give you more water, and we will wait until its strength has gone through you. Then we will all go back to the brush and make our camp."

He raised his head away from Tomás's hand, and something flitted through his eyes that she thought she understood. "I know, Señor Jaime, we are too close to the water and all those who would use it," she said. "We will be at their mercy. But none of us are strong, and we must trust to God's kindness and protection and remain here. I am not yet clean, and you are much too weak to think of traveling this day. We will take our chances here by the river, and pray to our God. There is nothing you can do but obey me. You must rest, and I must stay by the water. . . . We will wash you and give you sips and take care of you. Tomás and I. And God."

She watched for the signs she knew would cross the reddened face. She saw the white lines draw around the mouth, the lips move in protest, but she did not lean near to hear their sounds. Then his eyes closed and there was a slackness about him that told her he was asleep. Or dead. There was little more they could do now, so she and Tomás let his head fall back to the soft sand. She told the boy to get more water in the black pot while she checked the Anglo's body to learn of his injuries. They would make their camp and wait for the *Tejano* to awaken enough to help himself to its comfort—or, if he were to die, they would find the strength tomorrow to bury him in a shallow grave.

Her examination was done quickly, with little mercy in her probing fingers; she was calm and distant as she tore away sticky clothing and picked at scabbed wounds. There was little of a serious nature to the collection of scrapes and bruises, yet their impact on his body had been severe. The right ankle had swollen to fill his boot completely, and she knew only a knife would release his foot. This was worrisome, for the flesh above the boot was hard and turning black. The skin would break and fester, and he would lose his foot, and perhaps his life, to the resulting infection.

The condition of his face also drew her attention. The sun had beaten it, burned it to small blisters and peeling skin. And the rocks of La Bajada had left their mark in dark bruises and raw flesh. She would have to layer him with the crushed roots of the yucca to soothe the skin, but he must have a head covering of some kind if they were to continue their journey. She could fashion something from the remains of her festive skirt.

It was obvious when she tried to lift and turn him that there was pain in his ribs, for he gasped in surprise and pressed his arm to his side, face pale and eyes open in shock. She hushed him gently and let him lie back in the sand. This, too, she could heal, by binding his ribs with the torn skirt—unless there was a broken end inside; then he would heal or die on his own strength.

Truly there was nothing of major importance in the sum of his injuries, but she knew that together they had taken a toll on the *Tejano* boy that left him as a baby.

Jim Henry opened his eyes again, fought to move when the woman spoke to him. She talked to him slowly, as if he were an idiot, yet the words made sense and he struggled to do their bidding:

"Señor, we must move you out of the sun, and you are too heavy for Tomás and me. So it must be that you help. You will stand, we will be your legs and walk you to where I have chosen a camp. But it must be you who stands, for we cannot do this ourselves."

They made a strange picture as they worked their path across the deep sand, the tall man, loose and stumbling, hanging between the slender woman and a small child. The woman offered her strength and her height to the man as a crutch; the child gave his courage and determination. And the Anglo, Jim Henry McCraw, made his way to the crude shelter of the camp.

A bizarre trail was drawn in the sand, one that would take days to disappear and would cause great puzzlement to three Indians when they came across it. They had not been in the village of La Bajada yet, they did not know of the trio of strangers crossing their land, nor of the great fight that traveled the wall of La Bajada and left behind two dead and one man sorely injured.

But they rose from the indecipherable prints and returned to their village, heard the tale of the events of that day, and they looked at each other and nodded at the completion of the story.

CHAPTER 20

HE SLEPT THIRTEEN hours, from before sunset to well after dawn. Josefina bathed his face often and let water trickle into his mouth and even offered him a plate of beans when his eyes opened once near midnight. But he was not truly awake then and had no memory later of her efforts and his abrupt refusal.

The camp was simple, beds dug in the soft sand, a small, almost smokeless fire. The horses were picketed to the trees, where Josefina had hobbled them one at a time to let them browse for food and drink from the river. But it was the child who worried her, who allowed her little sleep through the long night. He curled in his own sandy bed and slept for an hour, then began to cry, long gulping wails that woke her and brought her own fears to the surface as she held him to her and cradled him, sang quietly, and talked of nonsense that soothed him. Then, when she tried to sleep herself, the cries began again.

In the long hour before dawn the boy's crying eased and he slept warm against her hip. Josefina sat with her back to a rotting tree, eyes wide as if she could see into the lifting blackness. The warmth of the boy comforted her. The sounds of the horses moving in the trees, stamping the soft ground, shifting and pulling against their ties, these also were a comfort; familiar, homey noises in a frightening place. When at last her eyes closed, she saw only the wide face of the one-eyed man left on La Bajada, the horror of his blood staining her hands. And when she reached to touch the child, she knew why the killing had happened, and she came slowly to her own dreamless sleep.

* * *

244

Jim Henry woke in panicked stages. It took time to identify the sound that roused him. A gentle snoring, a soft, fluttered intake and exhale of air. Before he opened his eyes he knew it was daylight; the warming air and the fine light behind his lids told him he'd slept the night.

His forehead burned and itched painfully, and he tried to bring up his arm to touch the soreness. Muscles strained across his ribs, and he heard the cry escape him before he could bite down. Then he remembered. His eyes came wide open, his head lifted from the wadded cloth where it had rested, and he surveyed the small clearing where she had put them, partially hidden among the heavy brush and rotting trees.

They were too near the water. That was his first thought, and he came halfway erect with the immediacy of disaster. He caught the cry this time and muffled it. Slowly, carefully, he moved in awe of his bruises and was able to sit up without crying out. He could see the protection of the camp, he could see the mound of the boy and his mother huddled together near the broken trees. It was the woman who snored, rolled away from him, legs drawn up to her belly, black hair fanned out around her head. And it was her son who awakened with Jim Henry's movement and watched over his mother, reluctant to look at the stirring *Tejano*.

The animals were tethered in the trees. The mule stood patiently on a line, rope tangled around a foreleg, ears hanging loose, eyes half shut. The paint mare had found enough line to lie down, and she rested like a dog, muzzle propped in the sand, snorting and puffing with each breath. The brown was nowhere in sight, but the packs were opened and gear spread out.

Jim Henry stood in jerky stages, conscious of being quiet for the woman and yet urged on by the pressure of a full bladder. He smiled down at the boy, who watched him as he stood; then he tried a step, staggered from the weakness of his ankle, and went down. The woman's snores split and stuttered, then went back to their rhythm. Jim Henry knelt in the soft sand, felt the reawakening of each bruise and cut. The boy watched, then slowly pushed out a limb broken from a tree, offering it as a crutch.

So he made his way to the river, stopping first to relieve himself well out of sight from the camp. The short journey left him with shaking hands and a circle of white spots at the edge of his vision. He lowered himself gratefully on the damp sand of the river and inspected the damage and what had already been done as repair.

The ankle was the worst; he drew the leg up across his knee and grabbed the boot, jerked hard, and almost passed out. Biting hard on his lip, he jerked again, and again, until the knife-slit leather parted completely and the foot came free. He allowed himself the luxury of a groan as he lowered the ankle into the water, then lay back and let his head sink in the damp sand. His belly roiled and heaved, and he closed his eyes against the nausea, waiting for the fire to recede, for his mind to clear. Then he sat up and began to inspect his ankle.

The skin was dark blue and black-mottled red, pushed to cracking from the pressure of contained fluid. Water was the best treatment, so he slid closer to the river's trickle, hollowed out a small pool, and let the collected water bathe the sorry leg. As he worked the soreness eased some in his bruised side, so he knew nothing was broken, only battered like the rest of him.

He must have slept a little, for his eyes opened to a much brighter sky and the shrieking of birds overhead. This time he sat up with less pain and saw that the cool water had reduced his ankle to more normal proportions. But his inspection was not yet over. His legs were covered with cuts, scrapes, and bruises, and there was one gash that needed to be stitched, over two inches long and showing wide-lipped flesh. His pants were pretty much torn away; the cloth hung in shreds from the waistband down his hip and leg, and each move exposed white skin and private flesh. Jim Henry surprised himself by flushing with shame as he thought of the woman hauling him to camp, laying him in the shallow depression of his sandy bed. She would know every part of him from the raggedness of his clothing. There was a disturbing edge to his shame he did not like.

Using a torn corner of the pants, he soaked up the river water and washed the gaping cut as best he could. The skin's whiteness was shocking against the dark brown of his hands, and the rough cloth left behind a ladder of reddish sores and darkened bruises. He worried over the gash. Bright red streaks coursed up his leg from the wound, and he had seen men die for less in the days after battle—men treated for simple gun wounds, killed by gangrene. So he washed and rubbed at the cut until it throbbed in time with his ankle and the flesh was a cheery pink. If the woman had a needle with her, or they could find a long thorn, he would boil horsehair and stitch the wound.

He poked and prodded at the cut, anxiety building with images of the men he'd known, men rotted and dying, surrounded by torn trees and fragmented rock. Cannons fired loud inside him, bitter smells and horrible screams tore into him. His head twitched side to side, trying to erase the memories, trying to bury them one more time.

Josefina came partly awake with the *Tejano*'s struggle to stand, and she chose to retreat back into her sleep and not deal with his stirrings. It was the boy's gentle hand on her shoulder that brought her out of sleep. Unwillingly she rolled over, opened her eyes, and thought about the day ahead. There was water to boil for coffee, and folded tortillas, a packet of beans, a slice of goat cheese. Enough to fill their bellies for breakfast. But the man had not yet come back from the river, and she wanted to talk with him, check his wounds, and perhaps make plans to travel later in the day. She smiled at Tomás and patted his head as she prepared the food. They would take a meal to the river, to the man who would be waiting there.

Mother and son carried their plate and cup easily, both refreshed and willing after the long night . . . until they came to the edge of the thick brush and could see the river's flow. There, laid out beside the water, was the long body of the man. It was as if he had been taken by a devil, for his white skin was bright against the damp red sand, and his head dug a trench as it rolled side to side on the stretched neck. The hard-boned hands tore at the earth and threw up clumps of pack sand into the air. He had shed most of his torn clothing, and the long line of injuries on his left side could be seen and counted: great red-and-black patches on the ribs, iso-lated red lines and dotted bright cuts down the thigh and bone of his calf to the untouched soft leather of his one boot.

He thrashed and flopped on the sand as if he were a mon-ster beached by an unknown force, and Tomás cried out in fear. Josefina ran to the man, dropped to her knees, and felt the blow across her shoulder from a wildly flailing arm. It angered her, and she slapped him hard, slapped him again as his head turned toward her, eyes shut tight, mouth drawn back to sand-encrusted teeth. She pounded on him then, fists rattling on his chest, doubling their efforts as he fought back in silence, fought her as if she were the enemy he had lost to in the past few months. Fingers tore her shoulders, yanked her from her knees to fly across his chest. She screamed then and kicked her legs, feeling them thump on the tenderness of his ribs.

Then he groaned, eyes opened from the end of a horrible fantasy, and went limp under her, sagging deeper into the churned sand. She thought she saw a shaking in his mouth, a quivering along his throat, and she knew there was trem-bling in the body underneath her.

"Ma'am—" He coughed. "Señorita Josefina, I truly am sorry . . . I ain't, you're not . . . the enemy."

She rolled off his quiet flesh, pushed herself back to kneel-ing beside him. She looked down at the pale whiteness of his face and exposed body, and smiled—as much for herself as for the Texas boy and his shameful glance. "Señor Jaime, you were ill, and we have cared for you," she said. "That is all. It was a nightmare for you, and now it is done. There is nothing for you to apologize, nothing you have done wrong. We are safe, and that is of the most importance."

But she had the feeling she was talking to herself then, and to the worried child beside her, more than to the half-naked man who stayed motionless, partially in the water, buried still in the violence of his dreams.

"I have found you a pair of pants, señor. They will not be your length, but they will cover you. And a shirt also. I have figured out how to make a covering for your head and neck. It will not be much, but it will help save you. But before we think of travel, we must finish cleaning you. You have washed well, and your leg is clean, the ankle less swollen. We must sew up that cut or it will infect. Señor, I believe you know all of what I am saying. . . . Señor?''

His body no longer betrayed him in panic. His hands had relaxed, the fingers and palms open to the wetness of the sand. It was the eyes she knew to watch as she spoke, and they had calmed enough for her to know he had returned. Golden brown eyes, with specks of green and black, a dark rim surrounding their color. Eyes unlike any she had seen so close, eyes innocent and beautiful in their ageless sorrow. She drew back then, feeling a constriction in her throat and a heat in her body.

"Señor Jaime, the boy and I will help you to stand, then I will take you to the clothing. And the needle and thread for mending you. Then, if you feel it is safe, you may eat your meal, and we will talk of the day's travel. But first we must see to that wound.''

But they chose not to move on that day. Josefina Iberra slept through the midday heat after she packed yucca and herbs on the stitches of the Anglo's leg and soothed his burned face with yucca paste. She was only the slightest bit tired when she lay down for a short rest—and it lasted past three hours. When she awoke, the boy was nestled up against her, tears streaked on his face, hands tight on her wrist, holding her to him with all his strength.

She thought then of the *Tejano* and saw him resting, his back to the rotted stump she had earlier chosen. His face looked like a mask through its covering, and his body was clothed decently in the soft white shirt and stained pants of her papa. But there was a length of skin from the end of the pants, and most of his forearm and hand dangled past the sleeves. The *Tejano* was involved in sewing a band of his torn pants to the cuff on his left leg, and his right ankle was bound in layers of soft white bands. He indeed made a strange and sorrowful picture to her eyes.

Then he looked up at her and grinned, a quiet show of pleasure as she rose from her nest and moved around the boy. She was beginning to believe he was a gentle man despite his part in the war, despite his being in the jail with her papa. She would not think of his shooting the bay gelding and the death of the rider, no more than she would consider the one-eyed man's death at her hands. There was an honor to this *Tejano*, shown in his returning the rifle to its owner and standing defenseless before the village of Indians.

And now, as he looked at her while he put the thread to his mouth and bit it clean, she saw the honor in him. Then he lifted a piece of the old brown pants and motioned that he would sew it to the right leg and then add a cuff to each sleeve. She nodded at his cleverness and smiled, knowing he would look away from her. He puzzled her with his sometime shyness, sometime arrogance, as if he did not know how to treat her as she was, as if he could not find her a place in his world of thinking.

Then she thought she understood. He was, of course, a *Tejano*. And to that breed of men, the dark-haired women of the border towns were to be bought for pleasure or taken against their will. He did not know of her pure heritage, of the lines of her family that went back to the ancient Spanish explorers. He did not understand the pride of those in the New Mexican territory, the strength of their Spanish blood.

So the poor Anglo could not fit her into his world; so she must feel pity for him. Anger flared abruptly, and she surged to her feet with no regard for her child. It was Tomás's cry that brought her to her knees. She cradled her son's head against her breast and began to cry.

She did not see the amazement on Jim Henry's face, nor his bewilderment as he watched her rise up in blazing fury and drop down in tenderness in the next moment. The spiral of emotions in her confused him and caused nothing but wonder and distress in his mind.

Jim Henry moved from the comfort of the old stump and the shade, far away from the woman's fury and the crying child. His ankle held his weight now, if he used a crutch, and he could make distance with his hobbling. When his bare toes touched ground, the stickers and hot sand reminded him he would need footwear to ride out of camp. So he went back to the water and found the knife-cut boot. He widened the pool where he had soaked his foot earlier and let the bandaged lump rest in the water while he worked the boot. He cut several gashes along the sides to help it accept the extra width, and made a kind of sandal that would cover the sole of his foot and still support the ankle in some comfort.

The next day they broke camp, straggling across the narrow thread of water. They had eaten two small birds caught in a snare, for Jim Henry would not risk a shot, nor would he waste ammunition with his shaking arm. He thought of the old Indian who had kindly returned the lost Hawken to the scabbard on the mare's saddle before handing over the reins. The gesture had almost been enough to give him faith.

They were a silent group as they rode out; the woman did not speak to him, and the boy stayed huddled to her side. There was little energy in any of them for talk. They ate and slept, and avoided contact with one another. The face of unexplained anger rode with Jim Henry, and he kept to himself, reining the mare away from the dun mule. He was confused, bothered, tired, and still sore, and there was no spare time to waste in wondering about the strange woman and her son.

They had ridden less than half a day when Jim Henry knew he was in trouble. His head and lower face had been bound by the woman that morning with pieces from her long skirt, but the sun burned through the worn fabric, and he had new blisters at the corners of his mouth, and his eyes swam with a yellowed haze. The clothing he had stitched with great care did not hold, and the heavy bulk of his old pants pulled through the loose-woven material to expose bare calf, pale forearm. He was burned in stripes down his leg, and his arms and hands were a bright new pink.

There was a town below them on the riverbanks; he remembered it well from his march through in midwinter. It was Albuquerque, which had surrendered to the Texas forces with little argument and was now back in Federal hands. He had a parole from Colonel Canby, wrapped in oiled parchment and tied in the pouch around his neck. But he did not want to ride into Albuquerque armed only with this piece of paper and in the company of a black-haired woman and a whimpering child. The town was filled with soldiers, survivors of the winter's march, the early spring rout in Glorieta

Pass. There would be little compassion for a Texan in the army town. But the sun beating down on him, and the shredded condition of his clothing, gave him little choice.

For the rest of this day they would be surrounded by tall brush and no water; at night they would have to camp dry, then endure another day's riding, pushed hard into the afternoon, before they would see the red walls and irrigated fields of Albuquerque's river settlement. Jim Henry spoke to the woman of his doubts, the first words they had passed since the camp by the river. She shared his concerns, more for herself and the boy than for his *Tejano* hide. But she had seen his deteriorating condition, and she hid her worry behind care for her son.

Albuquerque had been a quiet town when the Texans came north, a town Jim Henry remembered little, but now it held a garrison of men, blue-coated soldiers who walked the narrow streets and challenged strangers. There was no choice but for the trio to ride straight to army headquarters as if they belonged in the busy town.

Jim Henry drew back his shoulders and stretched in the saddle, wincing against the pull of his ribs, the stitching of his leg. It would not do to show weakness to these curious men who milled around him and the paint mare, men who watched the fineness of Señorita Josefina and smiled at the bravery of the boy. Jim Henry was first of all from the *despoblado*, a Texan now in a foreign land. And he would show no fear.

The folded paper in hand, he dismounted awkwardly from the mare and leaned into her shoulder for a moment's rest. Then he motioned for the woman and the child to remain with the horses and grabbed at a nearby post to hobble up the steps. There was a walkway in front of the small building that said it belonged to the commander of the Union troops. The Union flag flew above the army seal, and two guards stood with the door open between them.

As Jim Henry hesitated, one of the guards stepped forward and held out a hand. He looked into the soldier's face, held his gaze to the other man's eyes long enough to satisfy his pride before he gave over the paper that explained his presence. It was what stood between him and more time in a jail. The soldier quickly read the words, refolded the paper, and hesitated almost too long before returning it—as if he knew something about Jim Henry that was a secret, important and yet unsaid. It opened a raw area of doubt in the Texan that left him unsteady.

He did not return the man's salute but limped into the narrow room, ducking under the lintel before he stood to full height and once more presented his papers to a man bent over a desk. Again the paper was unfolded and read, this time more quickly, then refolded and handed back to him. No words had yet been spoken.

Something was wrong, and it dug into Jim Henry's confidence. He had not come this far to fight over the Glorieta Pass battle. Perhaps the man outside had been in the battle, perhaps he still held a grudge. The puzzle gnawed at his gut, until he heard someone speaking and realized a man was talking to him, asking questions he could not answer.

". . . is it that you want from us? By the looks of you, it has been a difficult trip, and I can offer you little encouragement from here. Most of your comrades have passed through here on the colonel's parole. Although several misjudged the temper of the town and left their lives here, instead of returning to their home on their given word." Silence for a beat or two, then:

"Again, soldier, I ask you, what is it you wish from us?"

Jim Henry stirred himself to speak. "Clothing, sir. At least pants and a hat. I am traveling with a woman and her son, at the request of her father. We are headed downriver, to return them to their home above Fort Bliss. From there I will ride on to my land, where I hope to find work. I have given my word. But for this trip, I need pants and a hat, and possibly a shirt and a neckerchief. And even boots, if that is possible. Although at this point, I cannot yet wear much on this foot."

It was a long speech for him, and it felt as if the words had taken something from him, something private and hard-shared. There was a luxury in speaking English to someone who understood, who did not tilt his head in bewilderment at the flow of foreign words or giggle over his broken attempts at Spanish. It bothered him; if he stood here much longer, he would ramble on and tell everything to the disinterested captain who sat before him in barely concealed impatience. About Hap Railsford's wound and his fear, about the long corridors of the hospital and the days of confusion that had not yet left him. Of the time in prison, with the reading from the leather-bound book and the unexpected sympathy from its words and his listeners. There was more, too much.

Jim Henry began to shake, exhausted from his thinking. The Union soldier saw the long body standing before him shift and waver, and he thought of the man's exposed wounds and gave in to an easy sympathy.

"Doble, come in here. Sergeant, get Corporal Doble in here right away."

The loud voice of command brought Jim Henry to attention, and he saw the strange soldier from outside on guard. The man entered the small office and saluted his commanding officer, stood at attention while the captain gave his orders:

The commanding officer hesitated, and Jim Henry saw the weariness in the drawn face. The seated man shook his head, as if beset by unsurmountable problems. A deep sigh escaped from the prim mouth, and Jim Henry winced with the pain of the sound. Then the officer spoke, and Jim Henry was released.

"Doble, take this gentleman to our storeroom and outfit him the best you can. Not in army issue unless it is all you can find. Make certain he has a hat, a good one, for this sun will blind you without protection. And then see that he and the woman he is escorting have enough provisions for their journey. Or any other arrangements you may be able to make for them. He has been paroled by Colonel Canby, and is obviously in dire need of our help. That is all, Corporal Doble."

CHAPTER 21

NOW LYMAN DOBLE remembered the soldier. The sun-bronzed Texas face was burned a new red, the strong hands and long body were leaned down and battered, but he knew the bones of the face, the hard light in the hazel eyes. He'd seen the man's soul at the end of his rifle sights, had seen those hands lift a downed comrade and carry him from danger.

Doble guessed that the odds of meeting this man were beyond comprehension, yet he had known stranger things to happen. A stroke of luck, a meeting of chance, or a power greater than all of mankind wanting to finish out a segment of a daily life. Whatever it was, Lyman Doble thanked God for letting him be the one on duty by the captain's door, to be sent with the ragged soldier and to talk with him as they walked. Perhaps, perhaps he would gain an understanding of some part of the broken days of war and the line of senseless deaths.

Doble's unit had lost all but two of its men. Doble himself had escaped being wounded but had seen the deaths of his friends. He chose to remain in New Mexico with a segment of the Colorado Volunteers, to clean up the campaign while the fuller strength of the Volunteers headed east, to the major struggle. Doble's heart was no longer in the fighting, and it had been the face of the soldier walking now beside him that changed his beliefs and lessened his will.

This was a priceless opportunity—to talk with a soldier, to walk with the enemy and ask about his reasons for joining the fight, to search even deeper into the man's soul, to find his God, to begin to comprehend a power that dealt with the despair and death wrought by battle. Doble felt an excitement build in him, a pressure on his heart and lungs, and he cautioned himself to move slowly.

For the battle had changed him radically, and he had made a promise: to finish his enlistment in the Union Army, then return east to civilian life and take up the studies as a minister of God. He would no longer bear the bitter wilderness of Colorado, the lawless fighting, the rapid and unsought dying that came to so many of the innocent drawn in by gold. He would make sense of the destruction, even if it were only to bow to a blind faith and accept the life hereafter as its final reward, leaving daily existence to its immeasurable disaster and pain.

Doble walked stride for stride with the lanky Texan, stretching himself until the man faltered in his steps and put out a hand, blindly seeking support. Doble offered his shoulder, and as the man's bulk pressed down upon him, he came in contact with the flesh ill clad to withstand the desert and understood the extent of Jim Henry's weakness.

The pants were laughably short, hemmed across the bottom with unraveled brown wool. Dots of rusted red traveled the length of the left leg, and the right foot was encased most awkwardly in an open half boot. It was obvious the ankle was painful, for the Texan lifted it from the walkway and sighed as he leaned heavily on Doble for support.

A sudden shyness kept Doble silent, and he let the man use him without word or question. To be so close to one he had tried to kill, to murder on the command of an unseen, unknown officer, to feel the man's fragile humanity touch his own, was unnerving. Doble was a dead shot, a practical fighting man, and many were the bodies at Apache Canyon and Pigeon's Ranch that could be added to the list of his sins, that would await him on Judgment Day. He did not care that the oath he took inducted him into a corps of men whose job it was to kill and maim, all in the name of God and country. This was no longer his God. These deaths were on his soul, and he was thankful to his new God that at least one man's death had not been added to his shame.

The Texas voice was cracked and hollow. Doble knew it was from the past days, the exhaustion written in the man's face, and he waited politely while the slow words were formed:

"Mister, I . . . thank you. Forget sometimes . . . bad leg here. Give me a minute. . . . I'll be walking again . . . fine. Thank you."

The stumbling words spoke of almost-forgotten manners. There was good family behind this man, good quality. Doble stared at him, found he had to look up to see into the shadowed face. The man met his gaze without apology, and there was an arrogance hidden in the Texas grin that almost brought a smile to Doble's lips. His was a natural state for those who claimed Texas heritage. Doble knew that, even as he knew the difference from his own Maine upbringing, or of the tight morality of the violent abolitionists who shouted their politics to any who would listen.

Doble would not fight this boy again, he would fight none of them. But he would try to understand what would bring a young man like McCraw to such a lonely town along the shallow river, looking for all the world as if he had died yesterday and been dug up this morning.

"There is no hurry, Mr. McCraw," he said. "The captain, ah . . . he allowed me some of the details of your situation and your name. We have a limited supply from which to choose, but there is enough in the warehouse to cover you decently and shade your head from this damnable and ever-present sun. I am not originally from these parts, as you may have surmised, and I find this sun to be an abomination in its unholy power."

Jim Henry was constantly puzzled by the quick tongue of the man who walked with him—as if he could not speak the same words, although he knew the corporal spoke in English. The man had a spit and snarl to his words, and he kept looking at Jim Henry as if he were a true oddity, not just a casualty of war. As if he'd been washed up on the river. Jim Henry drew away from the strange man, unwilling to continue using him for a crutch. He was vaguely ashamed of his distaste, knowing the shorter man meant no harm, had offered out of kindness to help a fellow soldier. But still, Jim Henry was wary.

Doble spoke again, and Jim Henry was caught up in the foreign sound to his voice: "I have heard a small party of soldiers has been ordered out to ride with a number of travelers headed to Fort Bliss and beyond. Perhaps you, and the lady with you, who has a child, so the captain said . . . well, perhaps you could all travel with this group of wagons. It could be arranged, and it would be much safer for all of you, given your rather dilapidated condition."

Doble's words took a long time coming from his mouth, and when they were out Jim Henry still wasn't certain he knew all their content. But the flow died down when the two men came to a high canvas wall with *USA* painted across its tied door.

"Our supplies are inside here, Mr. McCraw," Doble said then. "At your disposal. Follow me if you will."

It took almost two hours to sort through the ill-marked containers and find clothing to fit Jim Henry's length and breadth. The pants had to be winter-weight woolen, but the shirt was a warm-weather dress blue with bib and golden army buttons. Doble suggested, rather slyly, that they have the eagle-embossed buttons replaced, as it would not "look proper for a repatriated Southern boy to appear in public dressed suchly." Jim Henry agreed with the sentiment, although the vocabulary set him back some.

During the time of fitting and measuring, of quick bursts of laughter at the picture Jim Henry made primed in formal hat or draped with a general's frock, a slow sympathy grew between the two vastly different men. Doble was extra careful as he held shirt and pants against the Texan, wary of the wrapped ankle and exposed thigh covered in dark bruises, the skin slashed with a terrible-looking sore.

"You might have our surgeon look to that, McCraw. The sewing is crude and could well suppurate and infect. It would take up little of your time."

Jim Henry shook his head and lifted a pile of folded shirts in silent response. The leg itched now, tender to his touch but no longer painful. The little man was a worrier, and Jim Henry appreciated his concern. But the Yankee did not know the toughness of a man grown up in the *despoblado*.

So they chose a shirt, and even found an undervest and set

of long drawers that covered Jim Henry most modestly. Doble had to stifle the laughter bubbling in him at the pale white legs showing beneath the flimsy knee-length cotton pants and the contrast of the red neck and throat, the dark face above the pale V exposed under the loose sleeveless vest. The man was a caricature, a veritable Ichabod Crane.

When it was done, and McCraw was clothed and hatted, the two men walked awhile through the small town of Albuquerque. Jim Henry had questions about the place he had passed through so briefly on his northern march. Doble had some of the answers, but he knew little beyond the town walls. There were Indians to the south, he'd heard, and east and west, all along the banking of the river, although they chose to stay distant from the Union forces. But it worried him still, and he let his opinion be known to Jim Henry:

"This is why I would suggest you ride with the train of wagons going out in three days' time. I am fairly certain we can clear the idea with the captain, and your lady and the boy will be much more comfortable in the security of the soldiers, and the pleasure of traveling with other people. I have no doubt of your abilities and worthiness, McCraw, both as a guide and a pleasant companion, but there will be plenty of guards against the Indians, and other women for visiting, other children for play. Wagons for ease in traveling and the blessings of a man of the cloth. The lady is of Spanish descent, am I right? She will be most Catholic in her beliefs, and there will be a priest traveling, also. It would be an honor for one such as her to be traveling with such fine people."

Jim Henry was mindful of a funny taste in his mouth, felt an edge sliced between the pleasure of his new clothes, the comfort of a new friend—an edge drawn by the flow of Doble's words. There was a lack in him, a realization of words he did not have, a want of the familiarity and confidence needed to pick through the long-winded speech and dig out what bothered him. The suggested segregation, the superiority of Doble's earnest mind, broke Jim Henry's stride, and he slowed, letting Doble step ahead of him. And in his innocence Lyman Doble could not see the distress sweeping his newfound companion. Jim Henry frowned, worked over the barely understood lesson in his mind, stared way past Doble's turned, blond head.

Josefina Iberra was Spanish pure enough—Mexican to him, but he had listened to her explanation of the northern territory people and their differences in blood and heritage. To border dwellers like Jim Henry, it was all dark skin and black eyes, with a fluid, fiery language and a temper to match. These were the people who betrayed him as a child, who had sold themselves to many others, who had listed him among the victors, and the vanquished.

The confusion was his undoing. Josefina was as proud of her background as his pa had been of his. As his ma had told her stories of ancestors and lineage, Josefina would tell the same types of stories to Tomás, as he would to his own when the time came. It was all wrong, somehow, and Jim Henry could not think through the mixture to sort it out to his satisfaction. But he could react to the bland, thoughtless words that Lyman Doble spoke.

"Well, McCraw . . . this can all be arranged. I will speak to the captain on the morrow, and we will work out the necessary details. As for tonight, I would like you to dine with me. There are more questions I would ask, and I am certain the captain would not mind, or we can try one of the eating establishments in town, although they are mostly of the type of fiery food these locals enjoy, and I have not yet . . ."

Jim Henry allowed the confusion to surface then, used its magnified power to move him from beside Doble to the dusty road off the board walkway. Used the pressure in him to let loose words he would otherwise be cautious in speaking. His position in this enemy camp was precarious, and he knew well enough to pick his way carefully; but there had been too much said, spoken too lightly, for him to keep still.

"Doble, you go on too much. I ain't a friend, I'm a paroled prisoner, a goddamn enemy of you and every man in this Yankee town. Not your friend, Doble. Not ever your friend," he said, the words portioned out slow and careful. "That woman you don't think much on, she's more of a friend to me, and I damned sure trust her more. She's fought for me, Doble, not against me. And I ain't never going to forget that. You understand?"

He took a deep breath, frightened by the intensity of what boiled in him. "I ain't hearing nothing spoken against the señorita. Those words ain't worth your life, Doble. You think to it."

Jim Henry left the man at the top step of the walkway, stunned, mouth open, eyes widened in shock. He did have the courtesy to turn around after he was far enough away and offer a half-raised thank-you for the clean clothes and the time spent.

He walked off his anger, going to the army corrals and checking on the stock, circling the line of army remounts, picking up and putting down the battered gear he had ridden. Anything to keep him from thinking. But he kept running over the one thing Doble said that made some sense—about joining the wagon train leaving in a few days. It would be something to talk over with the woman. It would be safer for her and the boy, it would be all those things that Doble listed; but he would be damned if the idea didn't ride hard in him. As if only he could protect the woman, as if only he could understand her strengths and her fragility.

She was coming too close to him, finding niches in his thoughts that gave her importance. Jim Henry slammed his fist into the slatted corral fence and felt the skin split over a knuckle. *Goddamn.* . . . He would talk with her later, when his temper cooled and his thoughts settled back into a safer privacy.

There was no surprise in her answer, and no hesitation. Of course she would choose the safety of numbers and an armed escort of soldiers. So he offered to ride on and leave her, but the woman would not yet give him up. He must stay with them; he would be needed for the ride into their small village and the final trail to the farm tucked in beside the river.

The practicality of her thoughts dimmed a sudden cheerfulness in Jim Henry, and he left the woman with a promise to speak on her behalf to the captain. It would mean another day or two in Albuquerque, and he knew his body could use the rest. But his mind drove him to endless walking, and it was only the renewed throbbing in his ankle and a companion pounding in his head that slowed him enough to stop at the captain's small quarters and demand to speak with him.

Doble was not on duty, nor was the man who had taken and read his papers yesterday. So he had to retrace his story, wait the interminable time while the new officer read the parole, asked his questions, listened about the woman and her son, the father's request and Jim Henry's attempt to honor it.

In the end, after more than an hour of answering and waiting, explaining and restating, Jim Henry received permission for him and the Señorita Iberra and her son to join the escorted train leaving in two days' time. They would have need of a wagon, and Jim Henry was given further instructions which he ignored. No one would care about a Mex woman and her child, no one would question her appearance. To hell with the continuous rumble of words from the round-faced officer. Jim Henry stood abruptly and left without bothering to say his thanks. The officer snorted once, thought of several choice epithets to follow the ungrateful Texas scum, then went back to his paperwork and forgot about the incident.

Jim Henry chose to spend the remaining time with the paint mare and the dun mule and the old brown gelding. The mare's shoulder was fine, the scabbed cut well healed, no doubt aided by the woman's repeated applications of mashed yucca. He begged some scrap leather from the hosteler and dug his knife out of their gear. There was a bent stirrup tossed in a discard pile he could use, and he spent a half day repairing the old bowed saddle. He even redid the Indian's crude repair of the broken rein with a neat splice and a soft length of leather.

The work was a pleasure, the sun a healing warmth, the time slow and peaceful. He could leave the heat when it was too much and find shade. He could return to the brightness again and take its healing power for himself, and leave again if and when he chose. The time passed quickly, with repeated trips to the wooden water barrel and a slatted outhouse. Midday he was asked to share a lunch of tamales and warm beer with the hosteler and two grinning friends, to share it in a companionable silence, with only the sounds of chewing and the swallowing of the tepid beer to break the desert silence at the tail end of the town.

He saw the woman once that day; she passed the open stable with the boy by her side. Jim Henry lifted his hand to acknowledge her, but the señorita did not turn her head, and he let his hand drop casually, stung by her stubborn indifference. She would be busy and excited by the necessities of the wagon trip. She would be in a hurry, and her mind would be full of preparations, and she would not be able to see inside the dark stable. These were the excuses he found for her behavior, yet her refusal to see him left a small pain he would not identify.

That evening there was a half moon; the air came up, and a slow breeze took the day's warmth from the town. Jim Henry was restless, unwilling yet to spread out his woven mat behind the stable and try for sleep. He had rested after the noontime beer and now found himself full of a new energy. He walked the busy streets, head bent, hands clasped behind him, unaware of the drunken, off-duty soldiers, deaf to the laughter of the women in one of the canvas-sided saloons. He had little interest in the pleasures offered by a soldier's night.

So he ended up by the corral, leaned against the fence to watch the white splashes of the paint mare glow in the moon's light. A voice sounded near him, and he half crouched, spun quickly, knife fixed in his hand, heart pounding in almost pleasurable anticipation.

"It's only me, Mr. McCraw. Lyman Doble, whom you did not see fit to dine with these past days, or to come and visit. I do not know what it is you suddenly found distasteful about me, sir, but I am curious about you, my friend, and have something to speak of with you that may well pique your interest and give me the room to ask questions I would otherwise not find answers for. We will not cross paths again, so I am taking this chanced opportunity to try one last time."

Jim Henry kept the knife loose in his fist but let himself relax against the cut poles of the corral fence. He took the time needed to sort through Doble's speech and decided he would listen. He owed the man that much, for his time and his suggestion of riding out under the soldiers' guard tomorrow. But he didn't think he would find much to interest him in the stocky man's reasoned madness.

Doble must have felt the man ease, for he leaped into the middle of his own conversation as if it had not stopped in his mind, even though the start of it had not come through his lips:

"For we have much between us, Jim Henry. A bond, if you will, that you and I have forged, that you feel, you must feel, but do not understand. Please listen to me, hear my words, and think them clearly before you dismiss them as you would do now."

Jim Henry was startled to hear Doble put out loud what he was thinking. He nodded his head, not knowing if he could be seen by the moon's light, but his continued silence at the fence gave Doble enough encouragement.

"Do you remember the first day of our engagement—La Glorieta they call it now?" Doble asked. "Of course . . . Well, do you remember a bullet that creased your chest, that should have killed you? I do, for I was the sender of that bullet, the marksman who lifted his rifle barrel at the last instant and let the shot move away from your certain death. I was your murderer that day, McCraw, and again two days later when our companies rejoined in battle and many more were killed and finally buried. On that second day, on that day I had aim on you once again, and had to fire, for it was my sworn duty—to protect my country and my fellow soldiers from your disloyalty, your terrible disobedience. Yet something moved my hand, something caught in me, and I found instead one of your companions. A dark-faced man whose only recommendation for my bullet was the blackness of his hair, the burned brown of his skin, and a sneer I put on his face to compensate for my choice of his death."

He paused to draw a deep breath, hands clenched at his sides. "I would ask you now, McCraw, if you can see the reason for my choosing—if your man survived the wound I gave him, and if there was damage to you from the cannon's final fire and the branch you lay under," he said. "For I saw it all, Jim Henry. As if it were meant for me to see, as if it were a lesson, a warning we would meet again somewhere.

It started for me when I aimed true the first day, and saw the white line drawn through your dark brow. When you were sighted in my eyes, targeted for death, I wanted then to ask you about that scar and its story, I wanted to talk to you as one young man to another, one companion in arms to a stranger destined to be a friend." He held out his hands in a helpless gesture.

"Jim Henry, I am trying to find that in which I believe, and your appearance here, in this miserable and dusty town of Albuquerque, has given me a renewed hope. That there is a higher power in which I may believe and entrust my life, and find salvation. I need your answers, James Henry McCraw. I need your words for my faith. Please . . ."

The smooth, endless flow overwhelmed Jim Henry; he could not catch his breath or understand what he was hearing. The mouth moved in the sunburned face, the eyes flashed under the lank blond hair, the lips thinned and pushed and rounded in spoken sounds, but Jim Henry could not understand any of it. He wanted only to escape, to move away from the hardness of the knotted pole dug into his back and run. Not look back, but run hard and fast, putting all his fears and the edge of these terrible questions into the striding of his legs and the high distance of the mountains left behind him on La Bajada.

He was truly frightened of the man standing beside him, the man asking him an impossible collection of thoughts, drawing fearful images with the complexities of his words. He shook violently, stunned into immobility as Lyman Doble stopped his talking and waited. A black and tearing silence shimmered between them for an endless space of time. At last the words struggled past his lips, as if chewed and mutilated in his mind before escaping:

"Don't make sense, mister. I ain't never heard such talking. Nothing is right in a war, nothing is set up ahead, by no one, man or God. There ain't no faith alive in a battle, nothing but bad luck and good luck and no luck. It ain't got a connection to me, there ain't no knowing, before or after. I was one of the lucky ones, mister. You pulled your shot that first day 'cause you was scared. And you aimed wrong that second day, taking a better target."

He stopped then, mouth drawn tight, eyes glittering. "You son of a bitch . . . Hap made it. You was off—goddamn bullet drove a button into him, infected something bad, but he made it. You probably talked to him right on this street and didn't know it. Didn't have no mystical connection to him at all. Or there would have been a sign for you to read, one of them signs you looking for now. The skies would open when Hap rode by, and He would've talked to you right then. Your God, I mean. Not old Hap, he ain't much of a talker to Yankee scum."

A fury rose in him, possessed him . . . and he would have struck down the man in front of him. But the silver light of the half moon let him see the longing in the rounded face, with its thinning hair spiked wildly around the globed skull, the placid eyes glowing with a pain deeper than any Jim Henry could match with his fists or the familiar carved bowie knife he still clung to. Everything drained from him then: the blazing fury, the blinded fear. He could only shake his head and move his foot in a tight circle in the red sandy soil. He was tired, more tired than he had ever been, and he coughed twice before speaking:

"I don't know what you got in your head, Doble. I don't really know. This cut you saw . . . got that from an Indian pony, I was coming eleven. Lost my folks then. Got slammed there again 'bout a year past by a man delivering me a message I didn't want to hear. Nothing heroic about that scar, just more of man's kindness."

The tension left him from the impossible exchange, and as Lyman Doble sagged against the pole corral, he let his shoulders slump and his head lower. He thought of the luxury of a rolled cigarette, a vice he'd picked up from Hap and the others down in the *despoblado* along the march north to their defeat. Tobacco had been scarce; he could taste the tang in his mouth, the clean, bitter smoke curling through his nose into his lungs, could see himself rolling the cigarette, lighting the crumpled end, drawing in that first deep breath, sharing its taste, handing it carefully to Doble so that none of the precious contents would be lost.

He stiffened abruptly, wondering where such a contradictory idea had come from, how it had snuck into his feeble mind. The man standing next to him had just confessed to his own attempted murder, not once but twice, and to deliberately choosing Hap for a bullet. No doubt he had watched Hap's supposed death and cheered for the loss of one more rebel.

It was more than Jim Henry could stand. It should be in him to kill this man, not to think on sharing a smoke with him. He sheathed his knife, and his hand shook with the effort.

"Doble, you talking to the wrong person," he said. "You got to find you your own faith, your own belief. Me, I ain't got nothing but a paint mare and a hope to ride home. You got the schooling, the family waiting on you. You got all the words to do the thinking. Me, I can't answer for you. You got to do your own work on this one. But, Doble . . . I got to wish you luck."

Jim Henry had thought he was done with the man and thanked him silently for not keeping on with the talk, asking for what was not in him to give. He took three steps away from Doble, then waited, wondering if the man would follow. There was nothing in Doble's shadow, no movement, no sound. He could walk away free. . . .

Jim Henry hurried his stride then, careful to step easy on his ankle. He turned once and could almost see the vague outline that would be the soldier. Still by the corral, alone in his darkness. The words came to him, and he knew they had to be said, but the sound of them in the still night drove deep into his heart:

"Doble, I do thank you, for not killing me those times. For that act, you are a friend."

CHAPTER 22

TWO DAYS LATER a short line of wagons and a patrol of soldiers headed south along the Rio Grande. Jim Henry was relieved to know that the strange Lyman Doble was not one of the blue-coated guard. None of the uniformed faces were familiar to him, and he planned on keeping it that way for the trip.

Dust covered everyone instantly. Puffs rose under the heavy hooves of the draft animals, the yoked oxen, and the outriders pulled up their neck rags to cover their faces. Jim Henry reined the paint mare to the outside of the line of wagons, upwind and able to breathe more freely. He heard someone yell, saw a soldier wave him back, but he paid no mind. He wasn't one of the blue-bellied Union boys.

Albuquerque had finished him for good folk; he couldn't wait to hit the desert, to ride back to the *despoblado*. Too many wandered the streets of the town, standing too close, smelling one another, giving orders and directions even when they weren't asked. He needed to ride on, needed to get home. But a promise had been given to a man, and he would see it through before he turned south, back into his own desert lands.

A horseman came up quickly on his left. Jim Henry saw the blue-and-yellow coloring and kept the mare reined to a walk. It was a soldier, one who knew Jim Henry's name.

"Mr. McCraw, lieutenant's order. You are to ride in with the column, sir, or alongside the wagons. We cannot have civilians left unattended. Too many of them savages out here, sir."

The man was older than Jim Henry by a good number of years, and his voice had the same flat twang as Doble's, but he was calling Jim Henry "sir." It was something to study on. Jim Henry rode the mare on a straight line, holding her steady with his long legs to her sides.

"You tell your officer I ain't riding under his protection, soldier," he said. "You tell him I came along with the Iberras, and I know right where they are in your line. Got my eye on them, my rifle handy. Saw Indian sign back half a mile, though. Day old, or older. Nothing more than that. You tell your officer. I can take care of myself—you tell him that. *Gracias*, señor."

He bowed politely, tipped the brim of his hard-rimmed soldier hat. If he staked his claim now, got it set in the lieutenant's mind, then there would be no more questions come the rest of the ride. So he stated out his piece and watched the soldier boy ride with it to his commanding officer. Then he let the mare out to run on pretense of checking her shoulder and the condition of her foreleg. She snorted and threw her head, dropped forward into a buck and then into a quick-strided gallop. Horse and rider needed no excuse; they'd had several days of rest and food, of attention to various wounds and concern for their well-being . . . days of confinement and good behavior. That was all the excuse needed.

A hundred yards along, Jim Henry drew in the reins and felt no resistence in the mare's response. Their recovery was a sham, a false trail. The running battle down La Bajada still had them cornered. He felt a familiar light-headedness, a deep throbbing in his ankle where he'd stood to lift his weight from the mare's back. And the little paint's ribs heaved in and out, her ears drooped, and white foam lathered under the saddle. Jim Henry dismounted, held the mare's muzzle in his hands, and felt the force of her breathing.

He looked down the embankment and saw the bulk of the wagons, shrouded in dust, moving slowly along the wide path beside the river: three wagons belonging to families, one to a trader eager to share his pricy goods, and supplies for the soldiers in an army ambulance. Twelve cavalrymen rode beside the train, led by their lieutenant. Not a frightening show of force to scatter the enemy Indians, but enough men and rifles and supplies to make the pickings hard work. Jim Henry had to admit it to himself: he liked the security

of the blue-jacketed riders, the comforting presence of ammunition and weapons, the military determination to protect
civilians at all cost.

He needed to find the woman and the boy, see if they were
comfortable, if they had need of anything. He knew Josefina
had found a two-wheeled cart, a *carreta* with awkward, high
wood wheels. A tired harness held the reluctant dun mule
between the shafts. It was a clumsy affair, but it would take
them home.

He spurred the mare back down the embankment to join
the brown gelding. Tomás grinned from high on the old gelding's back, proud of his independence, secure on the wide
saddle. The mare reached over and snuffled at her traveling
companion. Tomás grinned at Jim Henry, and the *Tejano* felt
a quick lift of pleasure in the boy's obvious delight.

"Señor Jaime, we have missed you today. Mama has said
you have been busy in the town, repairing your saddle and
the bridle, and finding yourself new clothes. You look more
like a soldier now, señor, than you ever did before. But it is
the wrong side of the war, is it not, señor?"

He would not have thought a child could see so much,
understand such complexities. The buttons on the blue tunic
had been replaced, but its cut and style were unmistakable.
He smiled at the boy and made as if to slap the brown gelding.

"Tomás, you have a quick mouth for one so young," he
said. "You have taken care of your mama these past days, I
trust. And you will of course be of no trouble these last few
days of our journey."

The boy nodded. He was content to have Jim Henry ride
beside him, happy to see his mama look back once, then
smile and tap the reins to urge the mule forward.

Jim Henry turned his head and spat to one side, tasted the
coated dust on his mouth. The deep sand tired him, the sun
sucked the morning's ration of water from him. He wished
for the clear air past the wagons, but he would ride with
Tomás and his mother for a distance more before leaving
them again. The woman had only glanced at his arrival near
her wagon, but it was enough for him that the boy would grin
and talk.

Then she surprised him by dipping her head, freeing the heavy black hair, and staring up through its thickness as if it were a shield between them. "Ah, the señor *Tejano* has returned to us now that the town is behind us and only the wide-open land is ahead. Señor, you have returned to our small family for what purpose this time?"

So she was still angry at him. Jim Henry had thought she would be well pleased to have him gone from her days. She could visit with her own friends in the town, take some time to relax and talk, laugh and gossip, without concern for his backward behavior. He did not understand, and he let his confusion color his face as he stared down at her.

"Señorita Josefina, have you talked with the people in those wagons ahead? I seen signs of women and children. So you and the boy won't be stuck with just me and the mule for company." He was trying to be polite, to make small talk that would amuse her, but it was a tough chore. So he shut his mouth and let the mare step out ahead of the wagon. When the mule shook its head stubbornly and remained behind, Jim Henry reined in the mare to keep stride.

Josefina Iberra looked again at the tall Anglo riding the little paint pony. Was he so ignorant he did not see the women and the children of this train? Did he not see their pale faces and white-collared dresses and clean hands? Did he not hear the resonance of their harsh-sounding names? She had met Mrs. Pease and her two daughters, traveling to Fort Bliss to meet with another group of ladies returning east during the unpleasantness. And she had been introduced to the two sisters traveling with a man—the Miss Dorsey, with faded brown hair covered by a bonnet, her sweet face shy behind the whiteness of her handkerchief, and her married sister, the Mrs. Howard. And the sour-faced husband called Mr. Jack by his timid wife.

There were more of these people, good Anglo folk who suffered her traveling to the rear of the train, who accepted her need for the soldiers' protection but would look no further than that. She knew that she and the boy would not be taken into their camp and made welcome around their fires, to share their meals and their gracious talk. She had not yet met the trader, nor did she wish to; he looked at her with a familiar gleam in his eye, and she held her head stiff as he passed her. There was another wagon, one more, but she knew nothing of those who rode in it.

She would laugh at the hundred little slights given her and the boy over the days of their journey, but even that much acknowledgment raised its pain. She had met them all, whether she knew their names and their faces, lost to the accumulation of ancient distrusts. She would not cry, for it would disgrace her child, her father. Josefina could trace her family line back two hundred years, yet these pale-skinned ladies took a position of superiority because of her black-as-night hair, her dark eyes, the browned copper of her skin, and the shame of her work-hardened hands.

And she knew the *Tejano* did not understand; he could not, it was not in him. She would like to know more of his early years, before his time in the *despoblado*. She knew he would have grown up with a mix of fine Spanish blood and the hard twist of Mexican and Indian. And, too, he would have lived with the Anglo discards, who sought out the land to hide from their past mistakes.

Her *Tejano* was the product of a torn land, a suspicious and proud breed of men, yet he rode beside her and thought to ask about new friends. Josefina would laugh at his innocence, except that it raised a tender pain in her heart. Instead, she waved him past, unable to look at the fineness of his new clothes and the excitement building in his hazel eyes. He was as her son Tomás, eager for the traveling on, the new places, the feel of the horses and the peace of a new night's camp. She could only shake her head at the sweet eagerness of his bright smile and flick her whip over the dun mule's back.

The deep sand along the riverbank slowed the train, tiring the heavy draft animals, straining their muscles and tendons. The train managed less then twelve miles that first day out. Camp was made in early dusk, after the stock was taken under guard down to the river to drink. Guards were carefully placed, and the same soldier who had earlier come calling for Jim Henry now walked over to give him orders from the lieutenant that he would be expected to stand his share of guard. Jim Henry had no quarrel with such a practical idea, so he nodded his acceptance.

They ate separate from the camp, and Jim Henry was surprised by the isolation. A grain supplement was brought for the mule, a gift from the army, but there was none of the neighborliness Jim Henry had expected. The woman kept her distance and spoke only quiet, murmured words to the boy as she prepared their brief supper. When Tomás finally asked if he could please go see the other camps, she looked a long time into her son's face and then hugged him tightly before he struggled free and left their fire. Jim Henry did not understand, but he could feel her distress, and it found a home in his hesitant words:

"Ma'am . . . Señorita Josefina. That boy'll do fine. He's a good one, got him a good head for thinking. You'll see, ain't nothin' going to happen to him on this train. They's good folks out there."

"Señor, you do not know of what you speak," she snapped back at him, a suspicious shining in her dark eyes. "We are of different worlds, and have suffered different truths. So you will let me care for my child, as you will care for your promise to Papa. When you have finished, your concern will no longer be of importance to you, or to Tomás and me. Do you understand?"

Jim Henry reared back like a spooked bronc. The woman spoke as if he had somehow joined forces with her enemies, as if his acts—riding alongside the Howard wagon and exchanging words with the man holding the lines, or bowing to the tired woman who poked her head out in curiosity—had made him a traitor. He knew his place, and it was beside the dun mule and the high-wheeled *carreta* and the old brown gelding. Those ahead, who drove the matched teams and had fine hats to shade their skin, they were not his people. Josefina and the boy were his.

The thoughts spun through Jim Henry. He looked carefully at the woman bent to her routine chores. He would walk up the line now, casually, and he would see to the boy, see that nothing harmed him, that nothing hurt him. Then he would come back to their camp before taking his turn at guard.

He stopped just out of the small camp to break off a twig and chew on its greenness, tasting the pungent flavor as he scoured his teeth. His left leg itched over the cut, and he rubbed gingerly around the flesh, pleased that it was healing so quickly. It was a beautiful night, one lost to the brilliance of the stars and a cool, freshening wind. The twig quickly shredded in his mouth, and he spat out small bits, slowed his steps, listened to the rustled brush as the night animals hurried for their survival.

He passed the trader's campsite without a glance: a heavy wagon pulled by a mismatched six-up of big-boned mules and a spotted saddler with a wall eye and sloping croup. A man headed to the quick money outside the confines of Fort Bliss, eager to take advantage of the soldiers' boredom. The trader's voice came loud over the braying of one mule, and Jim Henry let the sounds drift past him. He'd heard too many men like this one down along the river—loud, demanding, quick to take short payment for poor goods, with a half smile at the ignorant bargain.

He looked for the boy and heard bright laughter from the farthest wagon, the one he had not gotten to during the day. But he'd been told it held a preacher and his wife, and a child or two. So much for Lyman Doble and his priest for Josefina. Tomás would head straight for this wagon, with a child's instinct to seek out his companions. Jim Henry was not prepared when two shadows leaped out at him and slammed into his hip. He staggered from the impact, hand quick to pull his knife free, when the high voices and shrill giggling eased into him and he let the knife fall back to its sheath.

"Señor Jaime, it is me, Tomás," cried the boy. "We are Indians, can't you tell? And we have captured you and will now torture you until you tell us everything."

Jim Henry didn't like the game, didn't like the mixture of border Spanish and stiff English. He was jealous of another person teaching Tomás, laughing with the small boy. But he let himself be pulled to the small fire, a reluctant captive to the small wild band of Indians.

Tomás's new friend was a pale-haired child, a boy slighter than he was, too thin and wobbly, yet with bright, shining blue eyes and a quick grin that gave him a strength. The brightness to the eyes disturbed Jim Henry, as did the slight cough as the boy ran past the fire to the adults seated near their wagon. Then Tomás tugged at Jim Henry's arm, pulled him forward, demanded that he meet his new friends.

"Señor Jaime, this is Christopher, he is a year older than me," he said proudly. "I can run faster than Christopher, but he can spit a big distance, and he has a box that makes music when you squeeze it."

Jim Henry listened to the boy and was aware of the other people who came near the center of the circle. A square man, black-suited and white-faced, head completely bald, hands folded across his ample belly, who looked intently at Jim Henry. There was a woman one step behind him, a plump, soft woman who looked much older, with a kind face and gray hair pinned tightly to her skull. She was wide like the man, with the jutting chin and bent nose of the man softened by her sex and her years. Jim Henry looked at Tomás, lifted his arm gently from the boy's grasp. He was uncomfortable with the man's eyes hard on him.

There was another person, a young woman, who finally joined the group—pale, like the boy, thin-faced, and with the same bright eyes. Her blond hair was pinned much as the older woman's, and her eyes shone from the fire's light. It was this young woman who spoke first, who knew her manners in company. She smiled encouragingly at Jim Henry, as if to make him feel more at ease.

"Young Tomás has already introduced himself to us, and has spoken well of you and the journey south from Santa Fe. We are impressed with his English, perhaps he might teach Christopher," she said, then brought herself up quickly. "We are the Appletons. This is my father, the Reverend Derek Appleton, and my grandmother. This, of course, is Christopher, and my name is Josephine. We are brother and sister. And your name is Señor Jaime?"

It was evidently a long speech for the young woman, for she coughed at its completion, coughed most gently to the back of her hand, then took a white kerchief from her sleeve and held it discreetly to her mouth. A flare of something showed in the older woman's face, but the man did nothing but stare at Jim Henry. The girl continued as if there had been no interruption:

"Won't you sit down, join us for a cup of coffee? It is real coffee, a treat out here, so I am told. . . . Señor Jaime?"

The Spanish title was strange in her mouth, flat and empty, but her eyes sparkled as she tried the language. Jim Henry smiled at her efforts and seated himself on a turned stump.

"It's James Henry McCraw, ma'am," he told her. "The boy here calls me Señor Jaime, but most just stick to Jim Henry. Pleasure to meet you all."

He bowed then, slightly, remembering his mother's voice, and heard the sweetness of the older woman as she spoke for the first time:

"We've all come a long distance to meet here, Mr. McCraw. Let us hope it continues to be a pleasant journey."

Jim Henry smiled at the soft slurring of her words; a Southern woman, with a dumbstruck son and two grandchildren with the clipped words of Lyman Doble. Northerners, with a grandmother Southern-born and bred . . . mixed families, mixed loyalties. Much like him and the woman and child, and the *despoblado*.

"Sure enough would enjoy that cup of coffee, ma'am, you still offering."

The father said very little during the visit. Jim Henry found he could chatter away to the old woman about almost nothing and she would smile back at him, pass on her memories and her nonsense. He spoke some of the *despoblado* and its power, of the small animals and how they lived, the horses and the people and the toughness it took for everything to survive. She in turn gave him Georgia, its sweet air and gentle ways, and the sharp coldness of the North. There was a slight reference to the death of the children's mother, the wife of her dear and silent son, but little else of the family gathered around the dying fire.

The man spoke only twice. The first time was to interrupt and state that they were traveling to Fort Bliss to bring Christian comfort to the soldiers and the papist families. Jim Henry thought then the man was mad, but it was not his place to offer such an opinion. It took almost an hour before the man spoke again, to interrupt his mother's description of the peach orchard in back of the house where she had grown up. He told Jim Henry that his wife had died from a lung ailment and that they were frightened the children had inherited her weakness.

While the adults sat and talked, Tomás and Christopher had tired, and Tomás had come to sit beside Jim Henry and lay his head on the length of Jim Henry's thigh and close his eyes to the sounds. The child was dreamily awake, not listening to the words, but absorbing the sounds at the soothing edge of sleep. The other child went first to his father for such comfort as Tomás enjoyed; finding none, he had come warily to Jim Henry and sat down, a feather barely touching the Texan's long leg, a sadness in the brilliant eyes.

The girl did little but start the coffee and listen to her grandmother and Jim Henry. Her eyes watched the Texan, watched him so carefully he could not look at her in the light of the fire. There was a beauty in her fine features, a highbred and pale beauty that belonged indoors, in a fancy candlelit home with servants at the door and music hidden in a garden. The picture slipped full-blown into Jim Henry's mind, and he could almost heard the sounds.

Josephine . . . He said her name soundlessly and thought of Tomás's mother, the black-haired Josefina. It was this type of woman she feared: the polite manner, the well-bred form, the hesitating shyness that gave to the world a sense of fineness. When the girl spoke to him, Jim Henry started at her words, which echoed true inside of him as if she had known his thoughts:

"I understand the boy's mother, the señora, is named Josefina. I would so much like to meet her—she must be a wonderful woman to have such a fine son. And it is lonesome on the drive. The good Mr. Howard shields his sister-in-law so much I have not yet met her, or Mrs. Howard. And most of the ladies of Albuquerque have removed themselves to a more suitable place because of the sad state of war. So I have been alone a good deal."

She hesitated, as if unsure of how to continue without giving offense. "I understand, Mr. McCraw, that you were a combatant in this tragic affair some months back. It would seem to me that you escaped relatively intact from the horror, with only your limp and that intriguing scar over your eye. And now you are headed home . . . to the *despoblado*, you call it?''

She stumbled over pronouncing the heavy foreign word, then smiled at Jim Henry, expecting him to pick up where she had ended. She couldn't know what images and memories her polite questions stirred up, or how wrong she was about the injuries. Her short words brought forth the long march and the repeated fighting, the dead and dying, the confusion of the hospital and the strange rest found in the local jail. It was a lot to bring up in a few words; Jim Henry could only shake his head and agree with her, dumbfounded by the complexity of trying to explain.

''Yes, ma'am, I'm headed home once I get the señorita and Tomás safe to theirs.''

Jim Henry didn't much like being the one to talk, but it had to be said, to be laid out where these good folk could see and hear—that it was the señorita, not the proper and acceptable señora. He saw the sour face of the Reverend Appleton, the confusion in the daughter's pale eyes. He would bet, because he couldn't see her but had a sense of her mind, that the grandmother had taken his mistake in stride. He had damned Josefina in front of these people, but damned her with something that was best spoken by a stranger and not let loose through a new friendship. He knew he was a constant innocent, planning and hoping for miracles in the human spirit, but he'd be damned if he'd let anyone hurt Josefina to her face.

All the doubts and angers of the long days got to him then, and Jim Henry rose to his full height, waking the boys rudely from their half sleep, restless with his own thinking. Miss Appleton rose with him, as if she understood somehow.

''Mr. McCraw, these two are asleep,'' she said softly. ''I shall walk with you back to your camp, where his mother may put Tomás to bed. Perhaps I shall have the chance to meet her. Perhaps, if nothing more, there will be the enjoyment of the cool evening and the most beautiful stars. Papa,''—she turned to her silent father, and there must have been something in her face Jim Henry could not see that kept the older man from protesting what was a most unusual act on his daughter's part—"please take Christopher and see he is comfortable. I have space for him in the wagon, to keep him from lying on damp ground. I shall not be gone for very long. Mr. McCraw will escort me through the camp, so you have no cause for concern."

They walked slowly, Tomás cradled in Jim Henry's arms. They spoke little, except to comment on a quick shooting star and to avoid a high cactus. Jim Henry had a new respect for the slender lady who walked beside him, and he barely felt the weight of the sleeping child.

Josefina Iberra had found herself a place near a broken stump, a spot that let her see beyond the camp to the great ridge that rose above the river, and beyond that to the dark wonder of the night sky. She felt a nagging worry about Tomás but told herself that Jaime was out there, Jaime would find and care for him and see to his return. She did not have the heart to deny Tomás his excited pleasure in exploring the camp, although she felt an old anguish in thinking of the prejudice he would discover among the white faces and fine manners.

She heard their soft talk and saw their indistinct shapes before she could truly identify them: a tall man carrying a small burden, a slender woman walking beside him. They stepped easily together, the man's head bent to the woman's words. Josefina rose quickly from the stump's comfort, lowered her head, and swung it violently, loosening the blackness of her hair to shimmer in waves down her back. It was a reflex action, and she went proudly to the man and the woman, head high, conscious of her body under the shabby skirt and loose blouse. She was no less a lady for her wealth of hair and her bright, patched clothing.

Señor Jaime must have known some of her disquiet, for he placed Tomás in her arms gently and smiled at her, pleased to see her, thanking her for letting the boy have his adventure. He spoke to her then, in a mixture of English and Spanish, searching in his memory for the correctness of the introductions as he motioned for the fine lady to come forward and meet the señorita. Josefina could not help but treasure his Anglo awkwardness.

"This is Miss Appleton, señorita. Josephine Appleton. It is her brother that Tomás played with—"

"Ah . . . Miss Appleton, this is Señorita Josefina Iberra. Mother of Tomás . . . I, uh . . ."

So, the *Tejano* had told them of her child and her unmarried state. That would have caused him much discomfort, yet this prim and proper lady chose to come back with him to meet Tomás's mother. Josefina looked carefully into the blue eyes, darkened by the night's low fire but still brilliant in their color. She saw no condemnation there, no instant assumption of any superiority. Perhaps, perhaps this one would be a friend and companion on the trip. Perhaps . . .

Jim Henry felt his awkward uselessness and fumbled with the stupidity of his thick mouth and unwilling mind. He would rather face the guns of Señor Antonio than stay between these two women for much longer. He took the boy back from his mother and used him as a shield.

"Señorita Josefina, I will put the boy to bed," he said. "Then I got guard duty, be out for a while myself. This one needs his sleep for tomorrow's travel. Them two, they sure played hard tonight."

He would have gone through more words, but Josefina pushed him gently and looked somehow as if she were pleased with something. It sure weren't him, that much Jim Henry knew. He found it tough going to look at Miss Appleton, confused by the ease of walking next to her and talking, and fearful of Josenfina's temper, worried that the pale-haired one would not see her fine spirit, but only her browned skin and rough clothes. It was all more than he had bargained for in taking the mother and son to their home.

He wanted to run, but the boy's weight kept him to an uneven walk. He wanted to find a lonesome spot and roll up for the night, but guard duty and walking Miss Appleton back to her wagon got in the way. And the stock needed tending, the fire had to be damped and put out. Josefina still needed his protection; that promise wasn't emptied out yet. He'd thought getting past Albuquerque would make life simple. Now it was all wrapped up in families and new faces.

The boy slept through being laid out on a pallet, and Jim Henry found a moment's ease in the half-broken stump, conscious he sat where Josefina had been sitting and oddly comforted by the shallow depression left by her body, the scuff marks in the sand pushed by her feet and legs. There were voices distant from him, the two ladies making quick acquaintance. And then a man's voice broke into the pleasant sounds, calling past the fire, looking for Jim Henry for his turn of duty.

He walked Miss Appleton quickly to her wagon, striding out in the heavy sand, half carrying her with a hand under her elbow. Then he turned away, leaving her with just enough breath to thank him for the interesting evening, and disappeared into the sweet night's dark air.

CHAPTER 23

THE WAGON TRAIN moved slowly, hampered by the heavy river sand and the daily needs of the travelers. The six-up hauling the trade goods lost a wheel horse to an unseen hole. The trader refused to leave any of his goods behind, and the remaining mules and the angular spotted saddler showed the strain, ribs jutting through their coats, heads lowered to the windblown ground.

Jim Henry found the sluggish rhythm of the train a punishment. Every night on guard duty, every day responsible for harnessing the mule and saddling the horses, watching for the boy during the daylight hours, waiting each night for the two women to finish their shared meal and settle in for the night's rest. Routine bored and angered him; he stifled the urge to let the paint mare run until the wagon train was a dusty ghost. Instead, he kept to a placid walk and tried to answer Tomás's questions about whatever caught his eye along the way.

Small incidents broke the monotony, like the fight that broke out with a red-bearded corporal who thought the señorita should pay for her army protection with some fancied loving. Jim Henry wore a black eye and a split lip from the fracas, and the corporal took his guard duty three nights running. It was poor payment for the insult, but there weren't enough men to keep on under constant guard.

Also, there were sightings of the enemy; rarely did the wagons see a distant Indian, but at times a figure appeared on a ridge, horse immobile in the bright sun, rider motionless and watching. It was more common to find fresh tracks ahead of the wagons or behind them. And one morning, only five days out, there were tracks along the army's picket line, and a bay gelding was missing, a mule's line half undone. After that the lieutenant brought the stock into the wagons' circle and doubled the guard. They were not bothered again.

Places along the route were familiar to Jim Henry: a bluff that dropped quickly to the river's edge; a shade tree isolated among scrub brush; a deep, narrow wash where the wall-eyed bay gelding had jumped across instead of picking his way down and almost unseated Jim Henry. Sometimes it seemed to him there were voices caught in the remembered places, young, unworried voices still alive, voices with the dying battle yet to be fought. When they came to the site of Fort Craig and its ruined walls, there were harsh words passed about Jim Henry's soldiering career, several blows struck, and an apology offered under the lieutenant's command.

It was best for Jim Henry to isolate himself. It was easy to rise to the bitter words and strike at their speaker, almost a relief to trade the blows and feel the sting of a fist against his cheek, know the soreness in his shoulder after sending a man to his knees. But Jim Henry could not keep his anger built at the men who wanted the fight; he was their enemy, sworn by his allegiance to destroy what they embraced. So he found his isolation with a quiet mind and kept the paint mare well off to the side of the moving train, ignored by the officer in charge and suddenly hated by the blue-coated men.

The women added to his isolation, and their defection hurt more than the soldier's blows. They had banded together after that first night; the boys were rarely apart. Christopher finally received permission from his worried father to ride behind Tomás on the steady brown. The careful horse walked to the edge of the wagons, and the puffs of dust raised by the large hooves blew quickly away in the clear air. Hidden by a straw hat and well protected by a long-sleeve shirt and light jacket, the frail child developed some color in his face and his cough lessened, occurring rarely at night and never during the day. Once in a while Jim Henry would ride with the children, but there was something about the two faces, one toasted dark brown, the other pale cream and carefully shaded, that bothered him, something that dug into an unspoken rule written in his core.

That same feeling kept him from joining the women at night. He would sit apart from them and listen with half his mind to their never-ending conversations. Josefina was teaching Miss Josephine Appleton the new language of the territory, and Josephine was working with Señorita Josefina on the better use of her fundamental English. Jim Henry could not keep the rapid-fire talking straight and often got up and walked away when he heard their special laughter. The growing trust between the two women was a bond that exempted him from their company.

He lost time and days, lost in the routine steps, the packing and unpacking, the work of resetting shoes, mending worn harness leather, standing guard. He talked less and less and was close to becoming the sullen boy who had ridden north from the *despoblado*.

He walked a good part of one day, leading the mare, conscious at every step of the shoe pulled from her hoof, the cracked and broken wall. The tools were packed in the army's kit, and there was no reason to expect the army to pull up and lose time for a Southern boy to reshoe a range-bred mare. So he walked, striding easily at first, then tiring from the constant pull of the loose sand on his muscles, the incessant sun beating over him. He fell way behind the train and found the two women with their camp all set, their meal bubbling over the fire, when he finally came in. But the long walk gave him a greater respect for the mare's energy and willingness to carry her burden each day. He did not speak to the women but reset the shoe, taking extra pains to fashion clips to hold over the broken wall; then he went to his nighttime guard duty without supper. Worn out from the day's effort, dust still thick in his mouth, uncertain muscles trembling in his legs, he lay on the blankets rolled out for him and was unable to sleep.

He could count the stars, he could taste the day's walk, he could feel the tension in his belly, but he could not sleep that night.

He was unprepared when Josefina came to him one evening, before he had finished his meal, and spoke to him of her plans for the following day:

"We are less than two days' travel from our home," she said. "Señor Jaime, it has been said and settled, tonight we will share our meal with the Appleton family, and tomorrow the boy and I, and you, will take our leave of the train and cross the river, to make our way home."

Hesitating, she watched him carefully, eyes keen in the dark face.

"There is a choice for you. It is here that I am safe, and it is here that you may leave us. Nothing will happen to Tomás and me, for this is our land, our people. You have fulfilled your promise to Papa, Jaime, and you may begin your own journey home, knowing you have kept that promise as any good man would."

Jim Henry could hear the English lessons from Miss Appleton in Josefina's speech—the hard bite of the sounds, the corrected pronunciation. He wanted to take her by the shoulders and shake her, bury her new refined speech in the rotted sand. He had lost her, and he was jealous. He was jealous of a pale-haired woman and shared laughter and spoken words. It was more than he could understand.

"Ma'am, I got guard duty tonight. Señorita. You and the boy enjoy your fine dinner. I'll be at camp come morning, never fear."

"Jim Henry, why, I do believe you are shy of a party!" She was laughing at him, teasing him with her gloried manners. "But I have already talked to the lieutenant, and he has given permission for you to be relieved for the night's duty. So you may join us in our meal and the conversation."

She must have seen what her words were doing, for she softened her voice and returned to her native tongue. "Please, Señor Jaime. Please to join us this night, or you will disappoint many people. You are a part of this journey, Jaime, whether you wish to be or not. And you must come to bid good-bye to friends. . . . Jaime?"

She was too close; she was asking too much of a bumbling Texas boy. And there was more, a fear growing in him of what he had seen in the early mornings before the fine mist lifted from the river and the camp had not yet come to life. He would tell her now, disturb her easy composure, keep her off balance. It was cruel, but he knew no other way.

"You ain't home free yet, Señorita Iberra," he said. "Been tracks these last few nights, white man tracks. Riding a big-footed mule. Tracks such as the ones your friend Antonio left when he came into that village long way behind us. I seen him on that mule. It's a big son, standing close to sixteen hands. Not a common size for a mule out here. So I reckon you got Antonio on your heels again, lady. And he don't set with me the forgiving kind, like your new preacher's family. You got me with you tomorrow, and the day after, until you and the boy's safe in that house your papa built and I can find a man or two to keep watch. We ain't come all this distance to lose now to a single son of a bitch."

The harsh Anglo curse, spoken to a young woman, was unforgivable, and Jim Henry felt the sting inside him, regretting the words as soon as they were said. But they were needed to catch her attention. So he held his gaze to the woman's face and would not let his eyes drop away in shame. She would listen to him now and be properly frightened. It was his duty, to her and to her pap.

But when she spoke to him, her voice held none of the fear, the meek submission, he'd expected: "Señor Jaime, I am thankful for your concern. And I, too, know Antonio is waiting out there for me. I have dealt with the man and his declarations before. He will not come to harm me. It is you now he wants. You, for killing his men, for outwitting him on La Bajada. If you stay with the wagon train and take its protection as far as El Paso, Antonio will be lost to you, and I will have reached the safety of my farm and my village. Then we both will have escaped his senseless wrath."

"Josefina . . . you have not listened, you no longer understand. It was you also who killed one of Antonio's men. You who took a life on the side of La Bajada. He will not forget, he will not let you be."

The words were bitter, spoken as gently as Jim Henry knew how, and he saw their impact sweep the easy grace from the señorita. He shuddered at what would be racing in her mind, and he almost took a step closer to offer his hand, his body, to be some comfort for her. He remembered seeing her wash her raw hands over and over in the river's slow water, and he knew what went on in her mind as she tried to work the impossible. There was no scrubbing away the blood of a dead man.

So he bowed his head in a mimic of a gentleman's manners and accepted her invitation to the evening's celebration, knowing he had destroyed some of its pleasure for her, knowing also that it had to be done.

He let the evening meal wash over him, and he drank heavily of the brandy supplied by the lieutenant as a parting gift. The women had brought their considerable talents to the minimal varieties of food carried on the wagon train. In this way the minister and his mother, the daughter and the young son and their guests, Señorita Josefina and her child, Tomás, and Señor Jaime sampled what different cultures could do with the same basic ingredients.

Jim Henry was aware of being impolite but was almost helpless to change. The elder Mrs. Appleton tried several times to regain the easy conversation they had enjoyed the first night, but this time he had no words to swap with her, no stories of the *despoblado* that were fitting for a woman's ear. As if the older woman finally accepted his remoteness, she stood away from him and patted his face gently with one soft hand before she spoke to the boys and asked Josefina a question. Jim Henry sat down. He had been dismissed.

As the evening passed beyond their bedtime with no word from an authority, the boys circled the small fire with manic energy, driven by the knowledge that tomorrow they would be separated. Offers for visits and letters had been exchanged, but the individuals in camp knew in their saddened hearts that the closeness they shared would be broken by the distance of time and memory.

The boys gradually tired, having run through all their energies, and they came shyly to Jim Henry, watching him as they walked to him, ready to run from his uncertain temper. Hope shone in their faces as they came close enough to be able to smell Jim Henry's breath and see the expression in his eyes. They waited, hesitant, expectant, hopeful.

A warmth welled up in Jim Henry he did not know lived in his world; a sense of gentle pride and love. He reached out and touched each child on the shoulder and drew them to him carefully, as if they were wild deer to be stroked and tamed. The boys moved into his arms and leaned on the bulk of his shoulders, laid their heads down, and closed their eyes. Bodies relaxed, trusting, ready for sleep.

Jim Henry did not understand. There was no comparison for the wealth of feeling in him, the knot in his throat, the salty wetness in his eyes. He would have rubbed away that shame but for the weights resting on each arm, the light touching of thin bodies against his ribs. He blinked his eyes and dropped his head, brought the children closer to him, and made to stand, disturbing their balance ever so gently until the two pairs of eyes opened, and the dark and light heads came up, and he could remove his support and step away.

"It's bedtime, Tomás. Long day for us tomorrow."

His good-bye to the Reverend Appleton and his mother, and the young lady named Josephine, were short and barely civil. He gave Tomás to his mother, let the boy Christopher hold his sister's hand, and was gone from the closeness of the fire, the demands of too many people.

But he took a near full bottle of the lieutenant's brandy with him, with the neck fitted in his hand, the rounded shape banging along his thigh as he walked away. He found a lonesome stunted tree, one half bent to the ground from the unchecked wind, and cleared himself a place under it where he could relax and watch the stars, sip at the harsh liquor, and let the whirling night enter his mind, spin inside him until he had to lean to the side and vomit, gagging and spewing the half-eaten dinner, spitting and hawking to clear himself of all the good feeling and wallow in his immediate sickness.

The mule headed away from the other wagons with a renewed life to his stride. Josefina did not have to encourage the sour animal to move into the traces, and she smiled at its stubbornness. Just like Señor Jaime in its own way, set on what it knew, plowing through good common sense to keep its imaginary straight line.

The mule was headed to its home. She guessed that the Anglo was on the same track, for today he did not ride next to Tomás on the brown but stayed back a good pace from them. She had seen the redness of his eyes, the pallor of the skin on his face, and she thought she understood why he kept his distance from them. But she looked ahead of her, to the familiar track into her valley, and did not see the constant shifting of the *Tejano*'s eyes, the worry on his face as he held the paint to a slow walk, rifle in his arms, pistol stuck close in the waistband of his pants.

Josefina had her mind fixed on other items, important to her, fresh and sweet in her mind. She would miss the company of the frail Josephine Appleton, recently from New York State, now to reside in the dubious comfort of Fort Bliss. There would not be a great distance separating them in miles, yet each knew they would rarely, if ever, meet again. They must once again take on the burdens their respective societies would demand.

If there were trouble, Miss Josephine Appleton would respond; if there were disaster, Señorita Josefina Iberra would somehow appear. But the day-to-day routine of their lives would stand no more closeness, no more confidences. It was so, and the ladies accepted the painful standard, smiled at each other, and hugged closely, bodies touching until there was a unified beating pulse, a shedding of mingled tears.

"Ma'am . . . uh, señorita, I think we got us our tail. Ugly man on a clumsy mule. 'Bout a mile back, thinks we ain't seen him yet. Or the son's planning to ride close enough to spook us. Just wanted you to know."

Josefina came back abruptly to the bright daylight, the rattled jerking of the old *carreta*, the constant slap of the mule's brush tail, and the immediacy of the *Tejano*'s words. "It is of course Antonio," she said. "And it will be a mistake to believe in his carelessness. He is letting you know that he follows; he will do nothing but what he wishes."

"I figured on that, señorita. If I ride out now, the son . . . he'll follow me, sure as . . . be counting a quick kill. You and the boy head home, or if you need, find a good place and defend yourselves. Maybe I can draw him out, set my own trap."

Josefina frowned and shook her head.

"This is his land, Jaime. He knows every changing ridge and broken gully. He will fox you and tease you and then allow you to come close enough that he may kill you at his pleasure. But if we can make it to our farm, we will be on our ground, where I can guide you. The farm can give you strength; from it you may return the battle to Antonio.''

Her words were all wrong, and she knew it. But she had no other way of expressing herself. So his answer was of no surprise.

''Lady, you don't know nothing about fighting. I can take this son of a . . . that son anytime, anyplace, his choosing or mine.''

The bragging came naturally, from the heat of his belly and the anger riding in him. No man was going to run James Henry McCraw to a woman's protection. He hauled savagely on the paint mare, spinning her in a tight circle until he could drive her forward in a bucking run, away from the guaranteed safety of the Iberra farm, straight back to the prints of the oversize mule and its sour rider. He let his pride push the mare fast out of sight of the wagon before he heard her labored breathing and reined her in. The mare lifted her head to whinny for the brown gelding and the dun mule, and he cuffed her on the ears, cursing her dependent sex. Females were unreliable, and too goddamn bossy.

North were the distant blue mountains, to the east ran the river's course, to his west were more mountains, dark green and flinty. The ground he stood on was a scabby tan, rock strewn and hard, covered with leg-breaking holes lost under heavy-rooted scrub. The land was slashed at differing angles with deep gullies washed open by the spring runoff from the mountains. The man Antonio and his big-footed mule could be anywhere out there.

From the few tracks Jim Henry had found, the man tended to stay to the back right of the wagon train. That would put him due north now, somewhere dropped out of sight in a wash, picking his way carefully, knowing that the woman was headed to the farm and that the Anglo would be riding with her.

Jim Henry steadied the mare and cursed himself. If the bastard had seen his wild burst of temper in running the mare flat out, he would be waiting somewhere with a long rifle aimed and ready. That had been a pure stupid move on Jim

Henry's part, spurred by angry pride. But if the son hadn't seen him race the mare, then he would still be picking his way along, easing toward the Iberra place and smiling to himself at the certain death ahead. Jim Henry planned to make it Antonio's death, not his own or the woman's.

Even if Jim Henry did no more than bring down the mule, he would have an advantage. He shook his head, saw the trembling of his hands crossed on the wooden horn. Back to battle, back to fighting an impersonal enemy. He hated himself at the moment, hated the weakness that turned his belly. So he drove spurs into the little mare and lifted her into a easy gallop . . . straight ahead, reaching to find the right wash and face the stalking man. Dead on at the enemy.

Antonio Encinias watched the pitiful Anglo and let his breath ease out between spaced front teeth. He could not deny the admiration he felt for the wild rider, the sorry courage that brought the man blindly into range. And he might feel a stab of pity when he shot into the great heart of the racing spotted mare, more pity than he would feel as the blood drained from the Anglo's wounds and the man died buried in the desert wind. So he sat the big-headed mule and crossed his hands on the flat horn of his high saddle, waiting for the Anglo to come to him, to bring him much-needed and anticipated pleasure.

The running mare disappeared into a wash. Antonio held his breath until she reappeared, ears flat, foam at her mouth, drawing her strength to crest the top of the bank and find her stride again. Twice more horse and rider dropped down into an arroyo, and twice Antonio waited in his cover of twisted juniper, anticipating the course of their slowed run. Then it happened much faster than he could comprehend.

There was a deep arroyo in front of him, one that would take the tiring mare much time to cross. Antonio could wait; she would bring her rider to the point of his bullet. He saw the little horse drop down the opposite bank, saw the last flick of her tail as she sat on her haunches and slid. Then he picked up his smooth-bore muzzle-loader and sighted on where he knew horse and rider would reappear.

But they did not come up where they should. Too many

minutes went by with no sign of the pair. Antonio dropped from the mule, rolled in the warmed sand, wrapped his arms around the bulky weapon, and prayed to keep its barrel clear. The hard crack of the expected shot came a second after the big mule leaped backward, brayed once, and then sank to its knees, blood streaming from its unhinged jaw, tail thrashing, ears loose, body sinking. Finally the great animal rolled on its side, the swollen ribs lifting one more time before it died.

Antonio skimmed deeper into the heavy growth and drew the weapon in with him. Burying his face in the coolness of the shaded sand, he prayed again to his God that must keep him alive. The Anglo was more clever than he had thought.

Luck had ridden with Jim Henry in his rush across the land; luck had kept the mare upright through the endless holes, then steadied Jim Henry's arm as he picked up on the mule when the mare bounded out of a wash a good ten strides down from Antonio's waiting muzzle-loader. Jim Henry had let his eye fix on the spot and he'd fired, aiming for the hated rider on the towering mule. But the man had thrown himself clear, and the bullet could not be stopped. The hasty shot had brought down the mule—and Jim Henry's luck died with it.

The mare shied from the gunshot and went to her knees. Then it was Antonio's turn. He saw the stumble, heard the sound of the shot strike his mule, and took aim in quickened anger. A clump of grass behind the hated *Tejano* exploded and Antonio cursed as he fumbled to reload his weapon. His chance was lost in haste; he cursed and rammed in the powder and ball.

But the crazy *Tejano* raised himself from the safety of the high grass and let himself be seen. Antonio knew a deadly fear as he himself tried to steady his arm and take a more careful aim. This Anglo's courage was strong, stronger than Antonio's need for revenge.

A bullet whined too near Antonio's skull; he winced and flattened himself into the safety of the warm earth. Fear knotted Antonio's belly, sweat washed his face. Then he found his own brand of courage and raised his head and shoulders enough to fire his own shot, grinning as he saw the Anglo's body flinch from the impact.

A horrible stinging carved flesh from the top of Antonio's shoulder, and he fell back to the ground, crying from his pain. The wound became a burning fire, a wetness that stained his woven shirt and flooded him with a new fear he did not want to know.

Got him. . . . The son of a bitch was down, and blood flowed from his neck. Jim Henry rolled from the protection of a tall grass hummock, then cursed the man. Sand ground into the wet slice across his hip, reminding him that the enemy had taken a piece of his own flesh. But the bastard was stranded now, wounded and perhaps dying. The mule was dead; a darkening patch of black circled its uncovered teeth, and flies had already settled into the gaping hole back of its shoulder. It was a clean shot, a killing shot meant for its rider. Jim Henry cursed.

There was no movement in the brush hiding Antonio. Jim Henry gambled and raised his head. The paint mare was well off to the side, tail sweeping back along her sides, head lowered. She had cover from a nest of tall cactus, and there was little chance the man could see her. He would kill her if he could.

Jim Henry let time pass, careful to keep his hip out of the sand after once touching the wound and finding its depth. A goodly deep furrow, more bloody and painful than serious. He thought of his pa then, heard his pa's voice: "A long way from your heart, boy." The wound had torn what little flesh there was from the high part of his buttocks. More embarrassing than serious. But the loss of blood would tell if he did not get the hole plugged and wrapped soon.

His hat lay a good fifty feet away. Jim Henry ran his tongue over the corners of his mouth and felt the sun take what moisture was left in him. The flow of blood from his butt slowed, also thickened by the heat. His heart pulsed, his head pounded, his chest rose and fell too quickly. He was lightheaded, the taste of last night's liquor soured in his belly and his mouth.

He would have to gamble, make a final gesture of contempt to draw the man out—if he were alive, if he were watching for such a move. . . . Without thinking Jim Henry rose quickly from his cover, took two steps, and fell to his knees, then went down flat in the sand. It was only partially an act for Antonio's benefit: his head swam, his eyes blinked and blurred against the sharpness of the sun. But there had been no shot, no reaction at all.

It was too easy—the man dead or dying, the mule downed by a random shot. Jim Henry lifted his head from the sand, saw the mare turn to look at him. There was a great distance between horse and rider, a distance he did not yet trust. He showed his head and shoulders, held motionless for a moment, offering a target that was not taken.

He called to the mare then, chirping through dry lips, clucking in his throat and watching as the mare pricked her ears and took one step. Still no shot from the brush. Jim Henry called again, working his mouth for wetness. The paint mare took three steps this time, then caught a trailing rein and jerked her head against the pressure. He clucked to her, told her sweet nothings to entice her. The mended rein separated, and the mare took more steps in relief, head high, eyes wide.

Then she caught sight of the dead mule and snorted. Eyes showing a ring of white, muscles bunching to flee this new terror, she stood there trembling. Jim Henry called to her, extended his hand and wiggled his fingers, bribing her with curiosity, tantalizing her instincts. The mare came to him, walking freely around the slapping of the broken rein. She lowered her head gratefully to accept his pat when he could reach her face.

The mare shook under him as he mounted, and he felt the wound on his butt reopen as soon as it hit the saddle. He gasped, and the mare sidestepped violently, trying to run from the dead mule's body. Blood ran down Jim Henry's leg, and he cursed its wetness. He tried riding the mare closer to where he thought Antonio's body would be, but the paint would have nothing of the mule's presence, and he lacked the strength in his legs to push her forward. So they swung around, exposing his back, if the hidden man had the life left in him to fire. There was a twitching between his shoulder blades, but no bullet. Antonio must be dead.

Now Jim Henry needed a destination. There was a stand of old cottonwood trees in the distance, their color pointed straight to the bright blue sky. The woman and boy would be waiting there, waiting confidently for him to return. He aimed the mare at what he guessed would be their camp and let the sun's power and the slow loss of blood ease him into a floating sleep.

It wasn't long before pride alone kept him to the saddle. There was no pain, no fiery cutting, only a weak lassitude that reduced him to little more than a bundle of muscle and bone wrapped around the paint mare. He lost every sense but the rocking gait of the mare and the high confines of the old saddle.

When the mare lifted her head and quickened her stride, Jim Henry slipped sideways and nearly fell. He forced open his eyes and saw the woman by the old two-wheeled *carreta* and the harnessed dun mule. The boy rode toward him on the high-withered brown, a welcoming smile on his thin brown face, his hand outstretched with the gift of water. Jim Henry pulled himself erect and fought the nausea in his belly as the grinning child rode to his side. He took the water, sipped it, and spat out the muddied contents of his mouth. Then he lifted the canteen and let the water flow through and over him, down his chin and into the dryness of his mouth. He grinned back at Tomás, looked over his dark head to the woman, who had made no move toward him.

"Got him, I think. Got that . . . mule, at least, and I know I put a bullet in Antonio. Waited a long time 'fore I rode out, gave him time to wake up and take another shot. Even gave him the mare and me as a target, and he didn't take us."

He shifted painfully in the saddle. "Betting you can go home now, señorita. With no more troubles than thinking about the next crop you got to get in. Antonio won't be botherin' you."

He liked the recognition in her eyes—that he had fought for her and come back the winner. He would put out of his mind the broken mule and the bright red shirt. It was done for this woman and her child. It was worth the price. Then his wound reminded him that it wasn't a clear victory, nor was there a corpse laid out to be the final tally.

He winced as he spoke, but there had to be an understanding: "I at least slowed him, Josefina. And we can get you and the boy to your farm without having to run like blind mustangs."

Then he had to admit his pain and his weakness. He felt the red shame flush him as he looked at the woman. "If you got the mind, he did take a chunk out of me I can't get to, to clean up," he said. "Be right thankful you could help me some."

The embarrassment was something fierce, but he steadied himself. He knew this woman's heart, trusted her compassion. So he lifted himself from the sticky saddle and allowed his legs to slide down the mare's side. The intake of air, the sharp cutoff of the laugh, told him she saw the position of his wound. He could feel the bite of fresh air on the torn seat of his britches, and he laughed with her. For certain, his ass was hanging out this time.

It was tough letting her strip down his pants and wash his buttocks clean, then fill the groove with a heavy salve she carried for harness sores. But he wasn't going to let her sew up the trousers while he sat around in the long-legged drawers that Union soldier got him back in Albuquerque. He could do his own sewing, something his ma taught him years back. So he settled away from the fire, isolated by his red-faced pride and his long, bared legs and the soreness of his butt, and he stitched and darned the tear in his pants and kept to his lonely silence.

He did not fully understand that the woman felt his shame and spoke quietly to her son, warning him to leave the señor alone, that he was tired and upset and needed to have his own company for the night. Tomás fussed, for he, too, was lonely, without the eager child Christopher Appleton to play with. But he looked at his *mamacíta* and then to the Anglo half-hidden under a juniper, and he decided that the paint mare needed a good currying, and that the brown gelding and the mule could use some of the same attention. Between the mother and the child, they left the white-legged *Tejano* the remnants of his pride.

Antonio Encinias finally came out of hiding, well after dark, well after the Anglo had ridden off on his fine paint mare. He stared a long time at the bulk of the dead mule. His prized mule . . . taken from him by the hated, sunburned, long-haired *Tejano*. Then he moved too quickly and felt the sting of the crease along his neck at the junction of his shoulder; he laid a finger gently in the hole and winced from the bite. Something else the Anglo had taken from him—some part of his pride.

There was more that Antonio would not think upon: that the Anglo had come riding straight at him, offering to battle face-to-face, and he had chosen to lie in wait and not accept the challenge. He would not admit to the disgrace. There was no one here to see him and remember, except the Anglo himself, and Antonio would soon settle that matter.

He would turn the anger at himself into a bigger hatred of the Anglo, and he would use its energy to walk through the night, dragging the length of the old muzzle-loader. He would cut steaks from the rump of the mule and chew on them raw while he walked, holding them in his mouth and tasting their bitter memory.

For he knew where the woman and the child called their home, he knew the paths and the trails that led to the quiet valley. The Anglo would be brought down from his fine horse, and he would pay in the loss of his life for the shame in Antonio's.

The woman, too, would receive no more forgiveness. Or the child. No longer would the shallow friendship offered by the father hold Antonio, no longer would he deny himself the pleasure of the woman. He would take her, as she had been taken by other men. First he would kill the crazy Anglo and tie up the small boy, and then he would take his pleasure from the woman until she cried from his passion.

It would be the Anglo first; that was his promise to himself as he walked, as the blisters burned his tender feet and the sweet taste of the mule turned sour in his mouth. The long body would be spread across the desert valley as a warning to all other men, that it was Antonio and no one else who ruled the hot dry lands at his pleasure and his whim.

He feasted on these thoughts, and they pumped him full of false energy. They kept him awake and on his feet when his body cried out for sleep. Everything was gone from his mind but the need for the killing that awaited him.

CHAPTER 24

THE LAND WAS becoming familiar to Jim Henry, a small and secluded valley with its own spring flowing into narrow strips of plowed land. Green furrows already showed the tips of their planted crop. He had been here before, he could remember admiring the valley and its careful planning as he rode in back of Hap Railsford, rode with his new friends on the long march—Ezra Massey and Cotton Belling, the two Andrews boys. And Caleb Tanner. He felt the day, the lust on Hap's features, the woman frozen in fear, the child clutching her skirts. The short and bitter fight that freed her.

Now he was here again, riding past the tree where he had camped that night, reining in the small mare past the spring where the wall-eyed bay had snorted and played like a sea monster. Many men had ridden here with him, some known dead, some alive and on their way home, some disappeared as if they had never been born. Lost in fragments, buried in separate places. Jim Henry bit hard on his lip and pushed those thoughts aside.

In another day he would be riding back out of this valley, alone this time and headed back toward the *despoblado*. Alone . . . without the curiosity of the boy's words, his smiling face, without the teasing laughter of the black-haired woman or the bite of her quick tongue. Without ever knowing what he felt for her and her son. He could get lost here too easily, and there was a safety and comfort in the thought that slowed him, muddied his reactions.

He pulled the mare out from behind the wagon and sent her flying into the depth of the bushes, then let her run on, caught up in the web of his thinking. There was nothing to tell him what was next; no birds flew away in scattered fear, no small animals scurried across the trail, anxious about their own disturbed homes. There were no smells to slow the mare and raise her head. But there was something circling him, something threatening the woman and the boy, that ate into Jim Henry's confidence.

Antonio could not be here before them; without a mule, wounded and alone, he would sleep the night and be just now staggering in circles in the heat of the day. Jim Henry slowed the mare, watched the trail with quick eyes, worried about what he did not understand. He still saw nothing, yet the hair at the back of his neck rose and stiffened, and he yanked the mare to a sliding stop and reached for the pistol jammed into his waist.

The mare's slide saved his life, but he did not know this or anything else. There was a sharp *crack!* as something slammed into the side of his head, and he was knocked senseless before his body hit the ground.

Antonio stood over the Anglo and kicked him hard in the ribs, watching absently as the enemy was lifted and then dropped, rolled over from the force of his booted toe. There was nothing left of this fierce *Tejano*, nothing but blood smeared on the bleached face and more blood flowing from the sun-bleached hair. This was nothing more than dead flesh, to be left for the scavengers.

Antonio stepped over the carcass with no more thought to the man it had once been. The woman waited for him now . . . finally to become his, earned by his long night's walk, bought and paid for with his wounded shoulder and angry thoughts. He would take her as many times as he wished, then he would put a knife into her black heart, the final act of vengeance before he torched the farm and erased his deeds. It would be he who took the word to the father, he who would fashion the tale of the Anglo's incompetence, the quick strike from *los indios*, the painful death of his beloved daughter and child before he, Antonio, could reach them and offer his protection. He would expose a creased shoulder and perhaps a burn or two on his hands and arms as proof of his bravery and his loyalty.

It would mean murdering the boy, but there was little else

to be done. So it was decided, and he would now complete the acts.

Josefina heard the muffled boom of the old smooth-bore and knew it was not Jaime who was firing. It could be any number of people, perhaps one of the few farmers who stayed in the valley, or a wandering soldier, or a packer headed back to Fort Bliss with a week's supply of game. But she knew it would be Antonio, and the fact that there was no return fire told her Jaime was down and unable to continue the fight.

She did not need to explain anything to the boy; she stood up in the *carreta* and whipped at the tired mule, urging it with sharp blows to find enough energy to run. Gradually she got a shambling trot, and then the boy came alongside on the brown gelding and whipped at the mule with a broken stick. Ahead was their safety: the small adobe jacal, the carefully piled mesquite corral. Home. Papa had arranged with the neighbors to keep their flock of sheep and goats, and Ernesto had agreed to put in the crop and tend the small garden until such time as the Iberras returned. A farmer could not afford to lose the season, even to a term in jail over the disposition of a stubborn army mule.

Josefina jumped from the *carreta* as it passed near the adobe hut. She stumbled on the hard-packed ground and fell to her knees, aching with the closeness of the shuttered door, knowing that Antonio was too near. And she was not surprised when she looked behind her and saw the man running across the yard, black hair freed and flying loose behind him, wide feet splatting on the solid earth.

But where was the boy? She screamed his name and stood up as she caught sight of the bundle of rags dropped by the corral, a faithful brown horse standing guard. Her son, her Tomás, killed by this animal, this beast who would now think to use her for himself.

A piece of firewood, laboriously cut into chunks, was the nearest weapon. She stood up to meet Antonio as he rushed toward her and swung hard when he came within reach. The blow connected with his ribs, drawing tears to his eyes but not downing him. Josefina would have no other chance, yet she drew back her arm and widened her stance, put all of her fury and strength into the swing of the stick, and laid open Antonio's cheek in a savage blow.

Antonio respected the woman then, praised her courage as he went through the swing and grabbed her upper arm, squeezed with all his might until her hand went numb and her fingers opened to drop the bloodied bit of wood. She fought him wildly, flailed at him with her fingers clawed until he caught the other arm and bound her helpless. But he could not silence her tongue before he mounted her and proved his manhood. So he suffered her words as he struggled to pin her to the ground.

"You fight well with women and children, you are a man with no *cojónes*! Where were you yesterday when the Anglo looked for you? He would fight you, a fight between men. But you knew you were not a man—you, you can find your strength only with the helpless!"

Tears streamed down her face, yet she was not crying. She spat full in his eyes and glared at him, so close he could feel her breath on his mouth. The glow of her hatred fired him.

"You are mine, Josefina," he told her. "I have waited long enough. You have spurned me yet taken others. I will no longer be treated so."

"You do not have the *cojónes* to take a woman unless she is bound and helpless before you. You are man enough only to kill small children!"

"I have killed the Anglo you have fancied. Do not forget that, Josefina. I have killed your *Tejano*."

But the woman was lost in her own words and did not seem to hear him. For a moment Antonio thought she would give up the struggle, and he loosened his hold. Instantly she raised her knee and caught him full in the groin, sending a weakness flooding through him, drawing all blood from his face. He would have dropped her arms and hugged himself, but she challenged him by pulling away and scratching him again on the side of his neck. He could not bear the pain below his belly, yet he could not let the woman go, for she would do worse. He did not know what to do, so he hung on to the fury blindly, crying from the pain in his crotch and letting the blackness inside him grow.

* * *

It was a wooden-handled knife that protruded from Tomás's back—a bright, shiny blade that rose from his ribs and fluttered back and forth with the effort of his breathing. Antonio's knife, thrown carelessly, bringing down the boy from its weight and the shock, but not yet killing him.

Tomás had once been with his grandpapa, last year, when they found the antelope pinned to the ground. A small knife such as this one had gone through its flesh to find earth, and the young animal could not move without tearing itself. It lay on the ground, panting and bleating as Tomás and his grandpapa came to help it. Grandpapa showed Tomás how to grasp the knife and withdraw it quickly, freeing the stunned animal from its prison.

"If this blade has touched something vital inside the antelope, Tomás, we will surely kill this poor beast by our helping, for it will pour out its blood too quickly onto the ground. But if we do not try, it will die from a long day's bleeding, from a lack of caring."

His grandpapa had run his hands over the wounds, then leaned back to let Tomás look.

"See, the blade has touched only bone on its path. There is nothing cut that cannot be healed, nothing severed that cannot grow again. We will let this poor child go and hope that it will heal itself. But we will not have killed it by our efforts."

Tomás had not understood everything Grandpapa had said, but he remembered the antelope struggling to stand, finding its legs and then suddenly leaping past them, hurrying back to the safety, or a death, in its herd. So now he reached behind himself and found the shaft of the knife protruding from between his ribs. A good place to be so wounded, his grandpapa would say. But touching the slippery shaft pained him, and he cried out, chewed the sand near his face to smother the sounds. He was a child of this land, and he knew the enemy would hear what sounds he made. So he bit hard into his own lip and jerked at the unseen knife.

It was the very thinness of his body that saved him from much pain. The knife slid its inches and was freed. Tomás lay in the sand, feeling the warmth pooling along his side,

knowing now he was in a different danger. The cries of
his mother roused him, reminded him why he lay here in
the hot sand, bleeding. Why Señor Jaime had disappeared.
Why his mother fought bravely against the ugly big man
who sometimes came to the farm and sat through a meal,
staring at his mama, talking rudely if at all to his grandpapa.

He crawled first on hands and knees. It was easier than
trying to stand. He crawled across the hard-packed yard,
conscious of the sand cactus in his palms, the hard-edged
stones scoring his knees. Yet, he drew strength from the cries
of his mother—cries that weakened instead of growing louder
as he inched nearer.

At the last minute Josefina knew her rescuer. Tomás had
found the same piece of wood she had used and had wrapped
his small hands around it, taking comfort from its bloodied
end. Slowly, very slowly, he raised himself from the stained
ground to stagger toward the pumping buttocks of his enemy.
It was his mother's face seen past the man's shoulders that
hurried him, that gave him the strength to raise the stick high
over his head and bring it down with all his small-boy fury
onto the back of Antonio Encinias's head.

The sound it made sickened him, and Tomás could not
raise the stick again. The man on top of his mother groaned
and slumped, and did not move again. Tomás wanted to cry
out to his mother. Then her beloved face showed under the
man's weight, and her legs began to kick, and her strong
hands began to pound on the man's back. Tomás was stunned
to see the fury that was his mother emerge from the beast
who rode her. She half sat up, held out her hand, begging
silently for the stick from Tomás's hand.

He watched in terrible fascination. Then his mama finished her escape from under the man and pushed his body
to one side. There was a smile on her face as she came
toward Tomás, and he wanted to stand up and go to her.
But suddenly he was tired, too tired to do more than sit
and wait.

When Jim Henry staggered into the yard of the Iberra farm,
he found the woman still seated on the ground, holding the

boy to her breast, rocking him and singing gentle sounds to quiet him. Jim Henry tried to hurry when he saw the woman and child, frightened by the blood covering them. But he sank to his knees and knelt in the dirt, gagging against the bile that threatened to choke him. He stayed kneeling for a long time, and the woman did not once look up to see him there.

When he finally got to her, she was covered with the child, both of them hollowed-eyed, horrified by the remains of the man, terrified by what had been done. Jim Henry wobbled on unsteady feet, stared at them, and then looked away to the body of Antonio Encinias.

It took time for his addled mind to register what he saw. The man's pants were down to his knees, the exposed back and buttocks lewd and white in the cleanness of the summer sun. There was shattered bone and tissue at the base of the skull; ants crawled in and out of the open mouth, flies buzzed a circle around the drying red pools. Jim Henry had to force himself to step over Antonio's body and go to the woman.

They were both covered in blood, but he quickly saw that it was the boy who bled. He pried loose the woman's grasp and lifted the child in his arms. The burden made his head swim and blurred his vision as he passed the woman, and he had to stop when he came to the front door of the house. He had to fight to form the words, and the sounds echoed in his head until he wanted to cry from their force, but he had to yell so she would understand and obey.

"Open it. Open the door. I can't let go of the boy. Lady, get the latch and open this goddamned door. Ain't got the life to kick it in. . . . Josefina, for God's sake!"

She must have heard him, for the next thing he knew he was inside. The darkness was soothing, and he more than anything wanted to lie down on the rope-woven bed and sleep. Instead, he put the child down gently, turning him on his side to expose the great hole in his back.

"Make a fire, Josefina. Boil us some water. Cloth. Some kind of dressing. I . . . uh . . ."

He sat down unexpectedly, weakness forcing his knees out from under him. But whatever he had said, it had started something in the woman, for she began the chores. A fire was quickly laid, and Jim Henry heard the tearing of cloth bandages. When the fire was high, he took up an empty bucket and made a trip outside to the well, as she told him to do. The sunshine grated on his eyelids, and he walked a dizzy line to the water and back, concentrating on stepping carefully.

Then he sat down again and was immediately asleep.

It was dark outside, and the woman was speaking to him: "Please, I need more water, but I cannot leave Tomás. Please, Jaime. Wake up."

He was lying on a pallet of grass, his head wound scabbed over, with hay matted and stuck to his scalp.

"The boy must have some herbs, and I need to bathe his forehead. Jaime, you will get me a bucket of water. Now!"

He rose to the command, knowing she would call until he answered. The cabin was barely lit, one candle burning near the bedstead. The boy lay there, bundled in quilts despite the warm summer evening, head nestled in the deep pillows. The small face burned a bright red, the half-open eyes sparkled, the mouth worked and gave forth tiny cries. Jim Henry looked to the mother, saw the glaze of exhaustion in her face, and picked up the bucket.

When he returned it to Josefina, full of crystal-clear water, she poured some of it over a pot of shredded meat and hung the pot on a hook over the fire to simmer. Then she wetted a cloth and handed it to Jim Henry, wetted another and went to the boy. She spoke to Jim Henry as she knelt by the child and touched his face so gently.

"Jaime, you must clean that wound to your head. I have done nothing for you, as the boy is restless, coming to fever, and I am watching him while you slept. I have washed him and picked out the dirt from his wound and packed it with the herbs that will heal him, but he worries me. He is so small to be so brave."

Jim Henry knelt by the woman and drew her to him, offered his body for her physical comfort. It was all he knew to do. She did not cry, but she placed one arm around his ribs and hugged him to her, fiercely, with a great shudder that went through her and rocked him. Then she pulled away, as if she could give up no more of her emotions to the strange *Tejano*.

"He is my son, Jaime. And he is my savior. He must not die."

She looked straight into Jim Henry's eyes. Their faces were inches apart, and he could taste her breathing, feel her anguish.

"Do you understand, señor? He is my life, and he must not die."

The night widened out before them. Jim Henry followed orders and washed the side of his head, rinsing out the cloth in the shallow water pan, marveling at the pale pink swirls that turned a ropy red, at the bits of hay and dirt he cleaned from his skull. There was a hole in the skin above his ear, and a trough of torn flesh that parted the top of his hair. He could push and pull the skin around the wound, move it over the bone underneath. There was little pain save a deep throbbing behind his eyes, and the wound had no exit point. It was a wound he did not understand, except that it was not fatal.

The night blackened; the boy's cries rose and fell, and the woman stayed by his bedside, ignoring any efforts Jim Henry made to help her. He stirred the boiling broth over the fire, replenished the small bundles of wood, and kept the flame going. Somewhere past midnight he dozed off again and woke with a start to hear the woman crying. But when he reached the child's bed in three long strides, her eyes were dry, and the boy's head lay firmly under her hand.

"He is burning, señor, and is much restless, as if something is chasing him. He will never forget that man, or that day. But he will live to try and understand."

She ignored Jim Henry again, gave him only the sight of her long back and the sound of her quiet murmurings as she soothed her son. Jim Henry made a pot of coffee, letting it boil too long before he offered her a cup. She took several sips and made a face at him, then went back to the boy.

It was close to four in the morning when she finally broke down. Jim Henry came awake once more to the sobbing and

felt the deep, unsettling fear in his gut—a fear worse than
any he had known before. But it was not the boy's dying that
had claimed her, it was the clear gaze of the child as he
looked up at his mother and spoke words she could not hear
over her tears. It was her own exhaustion that denied her
strength.

"Mama, I am thirsty. . . . Mama."

The woman could only cry harder, and it was Jim Henry
who lifted the small head, marveling at its light weight and
the smoothed skin, and let the child have a few sips of cooled
water laced with sugar. The woman watched the act as if it
were a miracle, then she began to move again. She came to
her son with a bowl of the broth and signaled for Jim Henry
to raise the child's head again. The boy took the first spoon-
fuls eagerly, then tired and closed his eyes. Jim Henry laid
the head back carefully among the pillows and stood tall
above the child on the bed, watching the black lashes flutter
on the pale skin.

It was his turn now to do the nursing. He lifted the woman
from her stool and brought her in his arms to the grass pallet.
She did not struggle when he placed her on the torn quilt,
nor did she protest when he covered her with a woven blanket
spun from the wool of her own sheep, and she listened when
Jim Henry told her sternly to sleep while he watched over
the boy.

He sipped absently at the bitter coffee and spat out a few
chunks of grounds. A gray false dawn lined the edge of the
horizon, and the slow light brought into relief the body of
the dead man, left among the splintered pile of winter wood.
Jim Henry shook his head and looked back at the woman.
She was sound asleep; the boy too was quiet, hardly able to
be seen in the pile of soft pillows and quilts. Asleep, not on
the edge of fever, not drifting into death, but comfortably
asleep in his own home.

Jim Henry dragged the stiff corpse by its shoulders down
a gradual slope to a place well down from the small farm.
He buried the body in the side of an arroyo, where hopefully
next year's spring runoff would not spill the bones into the
rushing water. Then he went back to the cabin to check on
his charges and to sit down in the tilted chair by the door and

sip again at the coffee. The colors of the new sun found him dozing in the chair, coffee spilled at his side, mouth open, head thrown back in silent snoring.

CHAPTER 25

THE OCCUPANTS OF the jacal slept until midmorning. It was the plaintive whinny of the paint mare that finally woke Jim Henry. He moved too quickly, and the tilted chair threw him backward, sprawling him across the dirt floor. No one else woke to see him fall, and he replaced the chair by the wall and went out to the animals. He did not look down at the dark stain by the woodpile but lifted his feet carefully to avoid stepping in its reminder.

When the animals had been seen to, he found an iron pick and a worn shovel in the shed near the corrals. The ground at the front of the cabin was hard and at first resisted his weak efforts to break it apart. But he was persistent, and an hour's work erased the blackened spot. He hid the scoured ground in the manure pile and was careful to replace it with dirt similar to its surroundings. The less seen of that night, the easier it would rest with the boy and his mother.

Yet he could not keep his mind steady on his work, and the basic and inescapable thought that held him drove him to work harder at breaking up the ground, cleaning up the evidence. He didn't much like himself this morning, didn't take pride in his actions of the past day or two. His decisions had been wrong, his plans off kilter and ultimately dangerous. He'd let pride take him where common sense would have cautioned not to go. And it had come down to a child finally doing his job, protecting the woman where he could not. The child had acted where Jim Henry had failed.

The anger blossoming in him would not let him rest. At the stock pens he put the restless edge to work grooming the sweat marks from the paint mare and the child's brown gelding, and even the mule. Then he spent another hour shoveling out the accumulation of droppings from the pen, driving himself until his legs trembled and his head spun. But the thoughts would not go away, and he could not slow himself down.

"Jaime, the boy asks for you. Please come."

The woman's words came as he took a moment to wipe the sweat from his eyes. He lifted his head enough to look at her; she was smiling at him, and he winced from the gesture. It would be almost impossible for him to look at Tomás's face, knowing that the child had killed a man because of James Henry McCraw's incompetence. But he could not deny the boy's request.

Still, he could not bear the pressure behind his eyes as the small hand fitted into his and the childish voice cut the silence in the cabin: "Señor Jaime, you are safe. Mama says that Antonio is gone and that we have nothing more to fear. I am glad you are with us, señor. That Grandpapa found you as our soldier. Mama says . . ."

The voiced faded, the eyes closed, and Jim Henry was released from the pressure of those small fingers to hurry outside before his stomach could betray him into disgracing himself once again. But the clarity of the air, the vision of the steep mountains surrounding the tiny valley, and the sounds of the animals eating peaceably in the cleaned corral settled him, let him sink to his haunches and draw lines in the loose dirt and occasionally lift his head to the blue sky.

Josefina came out sometime later and gave him a plate of beans and folded tortillas, a scrambled mass of green chile and dried beef, and asked nothing more of him than he sit with her and eat. There was a new light in her eyes, and she would share it with the Anglo who had come so far with them.

"You will stay with us, until the boy wakes up and can move," she said. "You are a pleasure for him. He talks much of you, so you will stay."

She saw the quick tension around the Anglo's weary eyes and guessed at the reason behind his refusal to look into her own, but she would leave him alone as long as he stayed for the boy. It was easy to know the *Tejano* had too much gnaw-

ing at him, but she did not care. It was her son who needed
her, not this awkward, whey-faced, half-grown child who
worried more over things he could not affect. She did not
understand the *Tejano*, but she was glad for his company,
glad that he had been their "soldier," as the boy had called
him. She touched his hand and felt the fingers jump from her
caress.

"Jaime, you are welcome here," she said softly. "You are
a piece of our family. *Gracias*."

The boy slept much of the afternoon. Jim Henry napped
fitfully outside, under the shade of the shed roof, comforted
when he awoke to the sounds of animals, settled by their acid
smells. Once he got up and went inside the cabin, pulled by
a nameless worry, disturbed by Antonio's black face. He
found them asleep, Josefina curled up in a heavy-slatted chair
beside the bed, her face soft in sleep, gentle as he had never
seen it. The boy slept by her, motionless in the bed cover-
ings.

Restless again, he drew water from the well and scoured
out what pans the woman had used, rinsed out the pile of
bloody strips, and hung them from a thorn bush to dry. Even
these simple chores tired him, and he went back to his shaded
roof to sleep.

The second time he awoke, he was driven to the house by
fitful dreams and was almost back outside when the señorita
joined him. The shadows of the day drew long streaked lines
across the yard, and the air tasted cooler, promising nighttime soon to come.

"Ah, Jaime, it will be a beautiful night," said the woman.
"Look, a rabbit. As a child I would chase them when they
came into our gardens."

Her voice faded beside him, and they stood quietly to watch
the slow and miraculous changes that brought night. There
was no edge to Jim Henry now, no restless pushing at his
gut, no tight knotted hands. There was a soothing to the
sense of the woman beside him.

"I will begin a meal for us, Jaime. You will take care of
the animals?"

Simple chores, simple wants and needs, part of the eve-

ning air, part of the life of a man and a woman. The boy was
the focus, and the land, its crops and the life they gave. The
solid warming smell when the clumped dirt was raised and
sifted through spread fingers. A taste that was left in a man's
mouth.

The stock needed watering. Jim Henry carried the heavy
yoke from the well to the wooden trough and watched the
horses drink. The paint mare finished quickly and played
with the water, the dun mule laced back its ears at her fri-
volity. It would be simple, Jim Henry thought, a pump set
into the top of the well, a spillway to the trough, a lessening
of one daily chore instead of the hard work of drawing a
bucket from the well and carrying it to the stock.

Even the wet wood of the trough pleased Jim Henry, sending a pungent scent of dampness to contrast with the acid of
fresh droppings, the salty rime of a day's sweat dried on the
animals' coats. He lifted his head, jerked back to the time
by an insistent whirring; then he laughed at himself. Cicadas,
nothing much more than crickets starting their evening's
news. Caught him napping, caught him thinking on other
things and scared him silly.

Then it all flooded through him again, yesterday's horror.
He unknowingly brought a hand to his head and felt the fresh
scabbed wound above his ear. The remembered pain, the
throbbing blackness of another time . . . the misjudgment,
the futility of his grand gestures, the ultimate tragedy half
unfolded, and the courage of a small boy. He, James Henry
McCraw, had done his best and been consistently wrong. He
had nothing in this life but his skills as a cowhand, a paid
baby-sitter of cattle, a hand with a rough string of broncs.
He made a poor soldier, and an even poorer bodyguard; he
would do best to live away from people, where the mistakes
he made could touch only animals and not human lives.

Despair held him mute and motionless; he had taken to
the boy Tomás, enjoyed the questions and the innocence, the
shy hand of friendship. And he had almost killed the boy.
Jim Henry shook his head violently, reawakening the pounding ache behind his eyes, taking it as punishment for his sins.
He would not think on the woman, what he had almost taken

from her, what Antonio would have demanded as his rightful and victorious prize.

Jim Henry, Señor Jaime, was sick then, bent to his knees and vomiting in the dust, wretching and gagging in his weakness. Shivering swept over him, then a flush of warmth that raised sweat on his forehead, water that trickled down his back. He gagged again, leaning forward on all fours. Head hanging, eyes swollen with tears, he was swept up in self-pity and could hear nothing, see nothing, but himself.

"Jaime, it is your head wound," came the voice of the woman, slow and soothing. "You have cared for us all this time, and we have done nothing for you, to ease your pain. Here, let me wipe your mouth, let me give you a bit of water to wash away the taste. Here . . ."

He would have howled with the anguish, but her hand was busy washing the stinking foam from his mouth, and her arm rested on his cheek. He could smell her sweetness through his shame, and it kept him silent. So he let her guide him to the cabin and made no protest when she pushed him gently to lie down on her soft pallet of grass. He was asleep instantly, barely conscious of her efforts to remove his boots and loosen the buttons of his pants. The sleep was dreamless and hard; he moved only once, to take pressure off the side of his head.

Five hours he slept, straight through the boy's restless questioning of his mother, through his first tentative steps with his mother holding him, so he could relieve himself properly at the small outhouse behind the jacal. He slept as if he were drugged until past midnight, when the soft rustle of a scurrying animal woke him. Then he lay on his back and let his eyes adjust to the simple light of a candle, amazed and surprised that there was no stiffness in his body, no soreness or tension. Except for a tug of dried flesh above his ear and on the top of his head, he felt a whole man again.

When he sat up, he could see that the boy slept easily, and that the mother was not in the small room. The outside air was a sweet blessing, and he, too, found relief in the outhouse, renewed life in a vigorous scrubbing of face and hands under the flow of water from the spring. He yearned for the perfection of a swim in the sluggish river, a rolled smoke drawn slowly into his lungs. Instead he found himself squatting up against the slats of the shed wall, talking quietly to the curious paint mare, and letting the night breeze dry his face and hands.

"Jaime, you are up and feeling better?"

He stood abruptly, bumped his side on the butt end of a railing, and spun to face the woman, conscious that the paint mare had whirled through the corral and stood opposite him, head lifted, tail plumed over her back, snorting with every breath at the intruder.

"I have made a fresh pot of coffee, one that will not take the whiteness from your teeth. You would like a cup?"

There was a partial moon, a ceiling full of glistening stars, a cool sweep of air to ease the daytime heat. Jim Henry followed the woman to her house and waited outside while she poured a cup of the fresh coffee and brought it to him. They said nothing to each other but sat on the smoothly worn stumps near a flowered tree.

The coffee was bitter and strong; Jim Henry sipped gingerly, tasting the sweet strength, enjoying the feel of the tin cup at his mouth, the smell of fresh grounds, the whisper of air around him. Something of his pleasure must have been communicated to the señorita, for she sighed deeply and began to speak: "This has always been my home, Jaime. Even as a little girl I loved this land. There was an older brother, but he was lost years ago. He rode off to fight a war, and he never came back. There has been no accounting of him, but he lives with Papa still. This I know." She grew silent then, content with the gift of memory. When she spoke again, her voice was softer, sweeter.

"We named my son for him—Tomás. After his uncle. It is one of the reasons Papa has accepted the boy, that he may carry on a beloved one's name. Ah . . ."

There was more she wanted to say, but it stayed mute behind her interest in the cooling coffee. Then Josefina looked shyly through the length of her black hair at the *Tejano* who sat next to her, and she tried again.

"You have said you are from the barren land called the *despoblado*. My papa, he has talked of that place, of a man named Leaton and a man named Spencer. And how strange they are for trying to ranch such an unhappy land. Do you know of these men?''

It was easy to answer these questions, easier than getting up and moving away from her, from the quiet night and the comfort of her body near his. It would be rude not to answer after all she had told him of her life.

''I grew up on Spencer's Rancho,'' he said. ''Been working there since my parents . . . since I was eleven. Horses mostly, range stock, but got to work with some good blood, and them cattle Mr. Spencer brought up from Chihuahua. It weren't a bad life. I rode up to Fort Davis couple of times with the herds. Spencer got him a contract for feeding the army up there. That land's hard, can't change that. But there's a beauty there, a strength. . . .''

He ran out of the words he wanted. There was no way he could tell this woman about the people there; about the blue-eyed daughter who betrayed him or the pain and confusion of riding with Hap Railsford, and the awfulness of his family's death. The memories crowded him, and he shuffled his feet in the packed sand, made a move to stand up and walk away.

She stopped him by putting a hand on his, as if she felt his sorrow and could only offer words of her own to ease its pain. ''It was a *Tejano* who fathered Tomás,'' she told him. To my papa's great shame. One of your comrades who rode into our little farm while Papa was working beyond the hills. He could not hear me when I struggled, he did not see when the man knocked me down and took me, right in the front yard, near the corrals. It is to my papa's shame that he could not protect his daughter, his only child, from this horror. And it is why I was doubtful when Papa told me you would be our guard, our protection. He had to see something in you I could not. For he would not trust a *Tejano* again, that much I knew. He has sworn vengeance on all of your breed, as we did not know the man, did not know his name, and I could not remember his face—only his hands and the terrible smell of his breath, and the horrible feel of his body on mine.''

She let go then. The cup turned in her fingers, and its contents spilled on the ground, puddling in shiny black pools as the baked earth refused it entry. Jim Henry carefully pried the cup from her fingers and let it rest against his foot.

"Josefina? . . ."

He was worried, but there was nothing he could say, and for once he understood another's suffering.

She smiled at him. "It is all right now, Jaime. Sometimes I frighten myself with the memories of that day. But I have my papa, and my Tomás. And now I know I can trust you, can believe in you. Jaime, I was only thirteen years old when that man came to our home. I had only become a woman three months before. Not much more than a child, yet he used me as if I were an ancient."

He had no words left, so he sat with her, immobile, hands cupped to the cold coffee, eyes cast down, head lowered from her gaze. She would not push at him, and for this he was grateful. He had done nothing to earn her trust, except to make mistakes, yet she was telling him of her belief in him, giving him her pain. He became conscious of the cool air rushing into his mouth, the taste of the night's sweet bitterness on his lips, the soft matching breath of the woman beside him.

"Jaime?" Her voice could barely be heard over the sounds of his own body, the cicadas' rasp, the lift and fall of the unseen night animals. "Jaime, forgive me, but I am curious. You are still young, yet you do not speak of a family, but of working since you were eleven years old. Did they leave you in that land alone? How terrible for you, to be abandoned so. Did they not want you? I am sorry for the question. . . . Jaime?"

It had been an abandonment of sorts, but not by choice. Jim Henry did not want to talk of that past, but he felt he owed her something, and she had asked. "No, ma'am," he said. "They didn't leave me. They was killed. Indians, ma'am. Killed my ma and my pa, and a brother. Just six then. Name of Benny. He was a pest sometimes, but he—"

"How sad! That is terrible, to lose your family so. I have my papa and Tomás, my beloved Tomás. What I would do without them I do not know. Was there no one for you, no one at all?"

Jim Henry had never put the reality into words, and hearing himself speak them told him more about himself he did not want to know. "I got found by a man, name of Limm Tyler. He sort of took me in, him and a lady. Rosa Ignacio." He swallowed something big that filled his throat and almost drowned him. He knew now the words were the truth:

"They loved me as if I was their son. Limm, he taught me what Pa hadn't got to, horses and knives and caring for myself. And Rosa, she loved me, and that was enough. I never knew till now, but she loved me to fill my life."

Josefina nodded. "Love is special, Jaime. And sometimes we do not know of its existence until we have gone past it and it is no longer there."

Josefina Iberra could feel the tension in the man seated beside her, she could hear him draw away and tighten until she thought he would explode. What she had spoken were only simple, truthful words about love. Perhaps in his language they held a different meaning, but she had thought most carefully before she spoke his English, to be certain in her mind that the meanings were clear.

It was as if something broke inside him; his body sagged beside her, his shoulders folded forward, and his head disappeared. The long legs pushed out in front of him as if the knees no longer were a spring, and the empty cup held so long in his hand sailed out and rolled over, clattering as it hit a rock. He did not react to this strange sound but slumped deeper over the stump on which he sat.

She could not help but worry, so she put her hand to his back, felt its trembling even before she heard the sobs. "Jaime, it is all right. You—"

"I done nothing right for a long time now. Fought with my friends, didn't hate the enemy, didn't tell Limm and Rosa I loved them. Nothing right."

She knew of no other way to help him. Her hand slid down from the bone of his shoulder and gently stroked the protrusion of his ribs, went under the loosened tail of his shirt and found the tight, warm flesh. She rubbed the muscle above his buttocks, where she had lately patted ointment into cut tissue. Stroking carefully around the healing wound, she let her hand follow the contours of his frame and reached the folded skin of his belly, the joining of his thigh and hip to the gauntness of his chest. There was a sprinkling of wire hair around the indentation of his navel, and she tugged at it gently, playfully, not knowing where the knowledge came from within her, but waiting for the lift of his head, the new pleasure in his eyes.

Her mouth opened, she tasted the inrush of air over her lower lip. The stump beneath her grew hard, unyielding; she shifted her weight, stretched out her legs alongside his, pulled her skirt above her knees, and saw the glisten of her skin in the night colors.

"Jaime, there is always love. . . ."

Josefina knew only the mechanics of lovemaking, the making of sex: the insistent howling of the dogs around a bitch, the long coupling tied off together in tiredness . . . the short thrusts of the donkey on a mate, the ludicrous mounting of a bull over a bellowing cow. And she knew the painful thrust of a man. But she did not know the sweetness of a lover.

"The boy is asleep, Jaime," she murmured. "But I am not tired. And you . . . I would take you to my bed, but . . ."

It was more than she could speak, and she was ashamed of having said so much to this tall foreigner. She turned away from his face, let her hand drop from the warmth of his skin and felt a rush of tears behind her eyes. It was for Jaime now.

He had felt her hand on his belly and the immediate swelling in his groin. The ache traveled through his entire body, opened his mouth, and pounded in his head. The gentleness of that hand . . . a light touch to bring such fire . . . fueled the need in him to hold her and search out her warmth and empty himself of all his fears, all his passion, into her waiting. He bit the side of his mouth and tasted the blood; she had been most brutally taken already. This was not what the hand was seeking, yet its continued touch told him he would be welcomed by her.

He let instinct lead him, reached with one hand to turn her face to him and put his mouth gently on hers, feeling the exhale of her breath, the rise of her own passion to meet his.

They remained seated on the two stumps, joined by the touching of their lips. Then she broke away, and Jim Henry feared he had been wrong.

"Jaime, take my hand, come with me," she said softly.

He followed her to the small barn, to the scattered remains of the winter's loose hay. There was a blanket covering an old saddle. It unfolded to a length that became their bed. Josefina lay down and spread her hair behind her on the hay, loosened her blouse from her brightly colored skirt. Jim Henry stood above her and marveled at her beauty.

Then she sat up, bent her head, and offered him the chore of slipping free the white blouse. He knelt to the task, wondering at the fineness of the cotton as he gathered it in his fist, then felt the smoothness of her shoulder under his hand. He lowered his head and touched his mouth to that satin smoothness, and she flinched from the caress. Tears stung his eyes, yet he kept his mouth on her flesh and let his hands touch her freed breasts, until she settled into his arms and moved stronger into his hands.

What was inside him was beautiful, a tenderness he had never felt before. He knew her instinct was fear—of his wanting her, of her own wanting, even though it was she who had begun their joining. He eased her back until she rested on the blanket, then untied the cord of her skirt; she raised her hips, he caught the fabric in his fingers and drew it slowly down the length of her. She lay there for him, eyes averted from his face, lower lip caught in her teeth. He could see her shiver in the warm night air, and he began to unbutton his own shirt, let it fall away from his heated skin. For a moment he was blinded.

It was her hand that found the buttons at his waist and undid them and tugged him free of the woolen pants binding him. The throbbing between his legs stood immediately erect, and he felt a wave of shyness. She touched him then, and he heard a wordless sound as her hands explored the length of him, so softly, so gently, he stuttered in his throat and felt he would explode from the touch. He found the courage to open his eyes and look down at the woman kneeling in front of him.

"You are beautiful . . . so beautiful."

He knelt to her. The words had never meant so much; her loveliness was an enchantment. He watched his rough hands take her chin and bring her head around to him, to look at him. Whatever shame there had been disappeared in the shining darkness of her eyes. He let his fingers trace her mouth, then follow the line of her throat to the hard tips of her breast. There had never been flesh like this. He groaned from the luxury of touching her, and her eyes widened, her lips formed sounds he barely heard.

"You are beautiful." She mouthed his thoughts back to him and brought her hand to his belly. There was a gathering in his groin, a rush of urgency he thought would tear him apart. She smiled then, at his sweet vulnerability as he knelt above her, and she put a hand to each side of his ribs, tugged at him until he fell forward with his weight on his hips, his elbows resting on either side of her face.

He did not remember moving, but there was a sudden pressure of warmth around him, and he gasped in the new sensation. She moved under him—drawing her body away from him, then swinging it back around him—and he exploded, light blinding him in a fiery celebration.

They lay motionless together as Jim Henry fought for breath. Then she began her movements again, and this time he moved with her, against her, savoring the grasp of her body, delighting in the easy rhythm they found with each other. Soon the gentleness was not enough for either of them, and he rose above her, thrust himself hard into her wet core, and heard a groan from her lips. Instantly he stopped moving, terrified he had hurt her. But she grabbed at his shoulders and dug her nails into his back until he winced.

"Don't stop, please don't stop. Jaime!"

His name was a wail, her command what he wanted. He rode into her then, rocking them both, lifting her above the piled hay and driving himself into her as deeply as he could. Her muscles grabbed him, stroked him, milked him until he could last no longer and again exploded inside her. She climbed his back with her arms and legs, dug her feet into his thighs, and drew more from him with the long muscles clamped around him. Head back, eyes rolled, she drew from him a prolonged cry, which she joined with a scream of her own until there was nothing left within her.

He sagged onto her, head buried in the black hair framing her face, mouth wide open to grab at the air, chest heaving, belly clenching and releasing, slowing in its response. She was quiet for a moment under him, then her fingers touched him between his legs, and he jumped and heard her childish giggle. If he opened an eye, he could see the red mouth beside him, feel the air draw in and out of its fullness. He breathed her name, then again, louder . . . and sighed when she touched him along his ribs, a touch so soft, that drew so much feeling in its path, it became painful for him to bear.

"I did not know . . . that it could be like this. I did not know."

He wasn't certain then if it was his voice or hers that had spoken the words, but he knew the thought lay in his heart. A bewildering tiredness took hold of him, complete and draining, leaving him inert and heavy. Josefina shifted underneath him, and he was rolled away until they lay side by side. He could turn his head the smallest amount and see into her eyes. He could lift his fingertips an inch and feel her hip, marvel at its pliant skin, the pleasure taken from it.

Then a shred of guilt claimed his immense pleasure, and he tried to turn away from her. Josefina stopped him, not with her hands, but with the accuracy of the words she spoke. Once again he loved her.

"Jaime, we have done nothing wrong," she said. "You are beautiful, you are kind and loving. You have given me a gift, as I have given to you. Do not deny this gift by taking on a guilt that is not real."

She took his hand then and placed it on the silky mound between her legs. He marveled at the great heat coming from inside her and the slippery feel of the triangle joining at her legs. She surprised him even more by placing her own hand on his mound of hair, threading her fingers in the sticky curls and letting her hand drift down to rest on the dangling softness he had become. The ultimate intimacy frightened him, yet it was natural to touch these places after the pleasure they gave when joined together.

He knew it was the right thing to lift himself above her

and cover her mouth with a loving kiss. He could feel the rightness through his body. He brought his fingers from the hair of her mound and kissed their wetness, then rewound them in the warmth and kissed her mouth again. Her eyes widened so close to his, and he could feel the grin spread from his lips to hers until both were laughing like innocent children.

Past that, when the laughter had exhausted them, they slept wound in each other's arms. Sometime before the chill of dawn, Jim Henry roused himself enough to draw the full skirt and scratchy trousers over their bodies, and they lay comfortable under the new warmth, content with the touching and the sleeping kisses.

Jim Henry awakened first, conscious immediately of the burden Josefina carried with her wounded son. She would need sleep, so he left her there, curled in the wrinkled, unraveled blanket, covered with the folds of her brightly patched skirt.

Outside the shed, shivering in the new dawn, he was glad there were no others to see him—naked as he was born, long-legged and spiked with bits of old hay. It was a torture, but he splayed his legs and leaned under the flow of the well, splashed water over his head and back, let it trickle down between his legs. His organs drew up inside his body from the invading cold, and he laughed. He scrubbed at the tangled hair between his legs, cupped water under his arms, across his belly, over his head and neck, and again bit his tongue to keep from crying out at the indignity.

It was a glorious morning. The paint mare whinnied when she saw his shadow, the old brown gelding found the energy to kick up in a small circle. Jim Henry returned to the shed and picked up his pants and shirt from the tangled pile of discarded clothing. He placed Josefina's wrinkled blouse over her exposed feet, and she smiled in her sleep, which pleased him greatly.

He drew water in a bucket and lit a fire inside the house, watched over the boy for a moment and envied him. There was a renewed energy inside him, a burst of faith in the day ahead, the days to come, as if the woman and the night had been magic. He smoothed Tomás's black hair and could not help but smile. He let the coffee boil and watched a tin pot of cold water build to a slow warmth on the fire.

Josefina smiled at him when he presented her with these gifts, a smile he had to seal with a kiss. She returned his kiss, then got to the practicalities of the day: bathing her face and hands in the warmed water, sipping at the hot coffee. She chased him from the shed before she finished her bathing ritual, and Jim Henry did not mind.

He called to her as he stepped outside the shed that he would feed the animals, and that the boy was still asleep, but he would start their breakfast now.

CHAPTER 26

HE THOUGHT NOTHING would ever change, that he would never think on leaving. That Tomás would smile up at him from the narrow bed as he brought in the water and started up a fire, put the coffee on to boil. The routine became comfortable for them all; Jim Henry surprised himself by enjoying the domestic chores, found a simple pleasure in watching Josefina, hearing her laugh with her son or take time to plant a few flowers at the side of the jacal. She was his daily breath of air.

Sometime in the uncounted days, the neighbor returned Eduardo's flock of sheep and goats. Josefina talked a long time with the man, who looked past her at the quiet *Tejano* and scowled fiercely. When the neighbor left, he took with him the story of Antonio, and the boy, and Jim Henry's part in their lives. The man did not beg to ask questions of why the Anglo remained or what was his place in this household. Her papa's word was law in the small valley, and the *Tejano* was here at his request. So the man grinned a wide-toothed smile and tipped his hat as he rode his mule from the yard.

But as he left, after he made certain the sheep were settled in with directions to watch the growing lambs, Jesús Gurule eyed the *Tejano* and spoke to the woman, said that he would tell Concita and Imelda, and those others who would want to know, and she could begin to expect visitors. If she so wished.

"When the señor is no longer here, and the boy is well healed, you will want to see your friends. When the señor leaves . . ."

Jesús was much too polite, and too aware of Josefina's temper and her past, to ask his questions, and Jim Henry knew there were no answers that would please the man, so they agreed on a silence that was acceptable to them all. Jesús rode out on his mule, and Jim Henry watched him leave. But the unsaid words raised questions in his mind, and the look on Josefina's face told him she had her own unvoiced concerns.

He had learned one thing from the visit: this was not his home, these were not his family. This place belonged to the Iberras, the grandpapa Eduardo and his daughter, and their beloved Tomás. It was not home for a restless, long-legged *Tejano* cowherd and horse breaker. A sense of loss surfaced in Jim Henry, an ache he did not understand, a separation of heart and mind. He picked up a long stick and drew aimless circles in the hot sand, saw the paint mare raise her head, heard her inquiring whinny.

Then he stopped thinking and went back into the jacal, gathered his gear stored along a wall. The old saddle hung from a peg in the barn, where he had been sleeping. The saddle was well repaired, his pants patched and washed clean, a shirt of her papa's cut to fit him, an ancient vest of fine tanned leather ready to carry his diminished tobacco supplies and his paper of parole.

He was well rested and repaired; the head wound was healed, the daily meals had added flesh to his spare frame. He had laughed when he had to let out his belt a notch, it was a new experience for him. The paint mare had the beginnings of a hay belly, and he anticipated a good bucking out before she would take to the trail again.

The urgency with which he moved told him clearly it was time to leave. The intimacy of that one night had not continued, and neither of them had wanted it to. He had seen the relief washed in politeness when he had done nothing more than kiss Josefina lightly on the cheek that next night before heading to the barn for his sleep. It had not seemed right to expect more, and now he knew he had done the correct thing.

It was the boy and the family . . . the permanency of a world that was not Jim Henry's. As he gathered his belongings, he knew the woman watched, and even Tomás made his clumsy way to the edge of the doorway to look. The boy knew it was past time and said nothing to his idol. Jim Henry

reached down and touched the thick black hair that needed
to be cut. As the width of the small head fitted in the span of
his hand, he wanted to say something special. There was a
moment when he bit down on the need and almost left without
speaking, but he had learned some things on the trip
down La Bajada and the distance to this isolated farm.

So he bent down, let his weight sit on his heels, and
touched the child again, on the fine-boned shoulder. There
was still a bulk of cloth tied around the boy's injury, and the
long night of fever left him easily tired. But the boy would
survive, and thrive with the love of his mother and the attentions
of his grandpapa.

"Tomás, it has been a gift for me, to know you," said Jim
Henry. "Thank you. For sharing with me. For teaching me."

He spoke correctly, in the boy's tongue, and knew his
words were what he wished to say. The boy rose from his
seat on the edge of the doorway and for a moment was eye
level with the Texan. Jim Henry saw the thin face and leaned
over slightly to touch that face with a gentle kiss.

It was then that Tomás cried, wrapped his arms around
Jim Henry, and hugged him with a fierceness that pleased
them both.

"You are a tiger, Tomás. A strong and good friend. Now,
let us go and trap that wild mare I must ride, and see if I can
tame her again. It will be a sight, that we know."

The mare was not a disappointment. She shook as Jim Henry
tightened the cincha around her belly and tried to bite him
when he thrust his fingers in her mouth to open it for the bit.
He grasped the cheek of the bridle and brought her head to
his knee before he tried to place his foot in the stirrup. She
knew what was coming, and her eye showed a white ring as
she stood trembling, waiting for him to climb aboard.

The little mare was gracious enough to let him almost find
the off stirrup before leaping sideways in a quick dance that
turned into a skyward leap. She plunged forward and came
down stiff-legged, pulled the reins through his hands, and
snaked her head between her legs. Then she squatted back
on her quarters and reared again, taking several steps in the
air before spinning in a high circle and dropping to the dusty

corral floor. Jim Henry groaned with the snap of his head, then found her rhythm and goaded her into flying across the pen.

It quickly became a dance with horse and rider—no longer a contest, but a celebration of hard muscle and high spirit. Then Jim Henry drew in the reins, found the mare responding to his guidance, and let her trot once around the corral, puffing and blowing, tail flagged over her rump, head lifted into his hands.

He saw his audience and angled the mare to them. The little paint pretended to be spooked by their cheering and tried to take her head from Jim Henry. He spanked her on the neck, spoke to her, and made her take the steps. The woman had his belongings piled by the fence: an extra shirt and the army hat, already badly faded and torn along the brim by Antonio's bullet. There was also a brightly striped blanket, a gift from Josefina, and a canvas sack heavy with supplies to carry him on the journey.

Tomás's eyes were wide with awe as he reached a hand through the fence railings. "She is beautiful, Señor Jaime," he said. "Such a fine mare, such power, such strength. She will carry you to your home and then give you many fine colts who will be as strong and as proud as she. A magnificant mare, Señor Jaime."

Jim Henry grinned at the boy; he would never tell him the truth—that the little paint mare was ewe-necked and goose-rumped, that her legs were too straight behind, too crooked in front, with upright pasterns and a short shoulder. Good for a few more years, she would wear badly and end up as a meal for a prowling cat or a band of coyote.

It was a pity, for the mare had a big heart, but it was the law. And there was little Jim Henry could do to change its nature . . . unless he kept the mare in the backyard as a pet when her legs gave out. He patted her soaking neck and slipped out of the saddle. She was tired enough to stand now while he wrapped and tied the blanket-covered clothing and food in back of the high cantle. Sweat dripped down his face and hair, stinging the fresh skin of the healed wound. He eyed the height of the sun; he could make a few miles before it grew too hot, and then he and the mare would have to find some shade and wait until it was cooler. They would travel this way through the hot summer days until they came to the *despoblado* and the safe island of Spencer's Rancho.

"Jaime, you will be careful?"

It was her voice soft at his ear, her body close to him, its heat touching his elbow. He knew before he looked that there would be black eyes shining through a mist, skin flushed a gentle red, hair allowed to fall free and face from him.

"Yes, ma'am. We will be careful. Ah, Josefina, I thank you. . . ."

They had never found the words about the one night; neither of them would mention it, but it was there between them. Jim Henry felt a closeness to the woman that went way beyond the wildness of their pleasure. He could not speak it, nor could she, but the knowledge was sweet with them both.

"Josefina, it comes to me now I got to travel. You know what month it is? Don't need to know the day, or even the week, but once I hit going downriver, I need to know the time of year. Those springs depend on seasons, some stay good all year 'round, others dry up come the hot months."

He had to grin at her. Time got all tangled for him that last night of the fighting in La Glorieta Pass, and he'd never caught up with its motion. It hadn't mattered much, until now. But the woman would know, for it was tied to the farm cycles, the sheep's birthing, the slow growth of next winter's hay, the sudden spurts to the boy. It was something fixed in her life, something set he had no part in. It all mixed too quickly in Jim Henry, and he could not look at Josefina's face, could not bear the sadness in the boy.

As if she understood, Josefina put a hand on his arm, and he could feel its comforting strength.

"It is the month you Anglos call July, Jaime. Jesús told me when he brought back our herd, she said. "You have . . . we have been here for almost fifteen days. I have counted. To watch the sheep, to know the crops. It is important for me to know."

There was nothing more to be said. Jim Henry gathered the reins, found the stirrup with the tip of his boot. The mare swung into him, restless and ready to go. He settled lightly in the saddle and let her take two quick strides, then remembered and hauled her in.

"Tomás, I got something for you," he called. "Man gave it to me when I weren't much older'n you. Been with me through the war, thought you might carry it for me for a while."

It was a small carved figure of a horse, high-headed and with flagged tail, correct down to the delicacy of the hooves, the cupped muzzle, and flared nostrils. The horse Jesús had carved him many years back . . . charred slightly on the edges, smudged and oiled by the touch of his hands. The boy's mouth fell open at the perfection of the figure, and Jim Henry was well pleased.

He tilted his hat to the woman; he had a present for her, a part of his life—a knife with a fine handle carved of bone and bearing the names of his family, the names of Limm Tyler and Rosa Ignacio. He was careful to say nothing when he presented her with the gift, for he knew she would see the names and remember the knife in his hands and would know its value to him.

There was truly no value in giving a gift if the present meant nothing to the giver. Josefina slid the knife from its sheath and held it gently by the handle, turning the worked bone in her hand. Jim Henry grinned to them both; this was how he would remember Josefina Iberra.

Then he looked past her, to the endless roll of the desert that would take him south—first to Fort Bliss and then to the border town of Franklin, now called El Paso. And from there into the dried-up, rock-hard soul of the *despoblado*. Waiting for him, offering him the embrace of its raging summer heat.

"Josefina . . ." It was all there was left to say, and then he was gone, letting the little paint mare move out in a run. He welcomed the eagerness in her that took him quickly from the faces and the kindness left behind.

CHAPTER 27

S HE WAS TO be twenty-two in ten days or so, and her son was already eight years of age, more than two months past. That was how she knew the month and could tell her *Tejano*. She had been nothing but a child herself when she conceived her son, when she had been defiled by the hated Anglos who came up from their beloved Texas to take the land, and the people, by force. There had been months when she cried every night, when her papa had held her in his arms and cursed under his breath, curses she was not supposed to understand in their violence and their hatred.

At first they had not considered she would carry a child from the attack. Josefina had only just become a woman, and there was no regularity to her monthly bleeding. But it was soon evident: the swelling of her belly, the morning illness, the strange lassitude that held her. These were symptoms of the birth to come.

She loved her boy despite his birth; she basked in his growth, his bright questions and sweet nature. She had been thankful the Anglo who fathered him had not been one of the light-complected ones, with pale, colorless eyes and lank straw hair. Her child was dark, as he should be, with only streaks of red in his thick hair and a lighter cast to his brown eyes to hint at the impurity of his breeding.

She told him a lie about his birth—that she loved his papa and that his papa had loved her. That lie had come from her own father, wise to the need for love. He gave his love to his grandson without question, proud of the boy's fine bearing and good mind. The child was loved; nothing else mattered.

Josefina never thought of another man. The horror of that hot fall day stayed with her, denying her the few men who passed through her life, who sat at the door with her papa and talked with him of unimportant things. Who watched her as she did her chores and thought of her beauty and her value. These men were easily discouraged, and she had been left alone . . . except for the persistence of the hated Antonio Encinias. A man who had no farm, no family, who was rumored to be one who rode a high trail. Who lived from what he could take or from the few days of work he would do for the fall crops. As if these few days of effort gave a legitimate reason for his drifting in and out of the little isolated community.

He had fixed a notion about Josefina, taken her in his mind as the woman for him. Once, she had thrown his words back at him, and he had cut her with his answer. She would never forget.

"You, too, are an outcast, señorita," he had said. "A woman with a child and no husband, and no man. No ring, no papers, no ceremony, no death. You believe you are accepted here, that you are better than me with my twilight living. But we are both outlaws, señorita. No better than scavenger dogs living at the edge of a village, taking what few scraps we are given. Do not think you are so fine. We are alike, you and me. And you will soon learn this and be grateful I am willing to have you, you and your child and your high-headed opinion and fine airs. I will wait; you will come to me."

She had cried from the words, much later, when he was gone and her papa had taken a bottle with him to sit in the barn alone. She had cried bitterly and bitten into her lower lip. The truth Antonio spoke was part of her indignation, and she wept for her arrogance as well as her fear and her pain.

Now she stood in the dusty barnyard and watched a tall Anglo ride away. A hated *Tejano* with soft hazel eyes and streaked bronze hair; a man far removed from what she had dreamed would be her savior. The anger and the distaste had been mutual between them, products of their separate lives. Yet he had come to trust her, to talk with her and try to understand. He had touched her at her choice, taken her as a man did with a woman, and in the end she had not been afraid.

Josefina felt the heat flush her face, and she wiped her knuckles hard across her cheek. The boy must have seen some of her confusion, for he grabbed her hand and held it tight. He, too, had been affected by their *Tejano*. He, too, had learned to trust across an invisible barrier.

"Come, Tomás. We must do our chores. I would want you to bring fresh-cut grasses to the mother goat. She is having trouble nursing, and we must give her special care."

She could not bear the look in his brown eyes, and she hugged him to her, holding him so tightly that he cried. It had to be he cried because she crushed him; he would not cry for a *Tejano*.

"Tomás, he is gone. There is no need for us stand here and watch a cloud of dust until it, too, disappears. He will not be back. There is no use wondering, Tomás. Señor Jaime will not come back."

No one had to tell Josefina she was talking more to herself than to her son. But the words would impress themselves on the boy, and perhaps he would sleep more easily at night. She . . . well, she knew they would come back to her for a while, when she lay on the tossed quilt and felt her loneliness. Then, gradually, feelings would fade and disappear. He would not be back.

CHAPTER 28

HE SAW THE first signs of a town: shanties tucked under the hanging cliffs, grasses cropped too close, muddied water holes, and the inevitable trash littering the riverbank. Rusted air tights, broken harness, twisted bits and stirrups. Human waste coloring the sluggish water pools. He wrinkled his nose at the sights and smells and let the small mare pick her way down the embankment.

It would be Fort Bliss ahead of him, garrisoned by Federal troops. Jim Henry patted Colonel Canby's parole, folded in the laced pocket of the old leather vest. It was his pardon, his safe travel. But he would still be halted at gunpoint and brought in under guard; there would be harsh words about his Texas drawl, the faint scrawled words on the stained paper. And more time lost to his journey. There was a restlessness to him now, pushing him to run the mare by the half-manned fort and the dubious comforts of the surrounding town, pulling at him to make his way down the sandy hills to the bitter *despoblado*.

His trail south had crossed Indian sign, and he had felt the absence of the blue-coated soldiers from the wagon train. He felt even more the loss of Josefina and the boy Tomás. It was practical to miss the soldiers, their protection, their supplies, their night guard. But the woman held to his heart, and he could hear her voice in the long silences, and had answers for the questions the boy could no longer ask.

This was a new loneliness for Jim Henry McCraw—to miss the company of a certain person, to look for what would please them and not be able to share it with them. To see a pretty flower and have no one there to tell. The scent of a honey vine, a burst of cool air, an exposed vein of rock carrying special colors . . . He jerked on the paint mare and pushed her faster to cross the shallow river.

He lost all track of time. Water was scarce, as he knew it would be, and it was made scarcer by the constant presence of the Indians. Jim Henry remembered the hidden springs, owned by the Comanche and the Apache. Yet he could not stay to the river, for it, too, was under Indian domination, crossed and recrossed daily by unshod ponies bearing the weight of fierce riders. With the new moon he could travel at night, sometimes walking on foot to give the mare some rest. His pants slipped down his hips, and he had to punch new holes in the thin strip of leather that served as a belt. The mare dropped weight rapidly, eyes dulled by the constant moving, the lack of forage, the few sips of water he could find for her.

Yet when he came to the unnamed village below him, he still hesitated before approaching any of the buildings. He did not want to see people, to suffer their curiosity, the hunger of their questions. But the mare gave a plaintive whinny when they neared a house, and he was forced to stop and beg for water. He offered chores and chopped wood for a meal and a night's sleep for himself, a corral and a handful of dried mesquite beans for the mare—and all the water both of them could drink.

The closeness of the black-haired family, the smiling curiosity of the five children, cut into him somehow, reopening feelings he thought had been closed off in the time and miles he'd left behind him. One boy looked too much like Tomás, with a reddish tint to his hair, a sweet smile. Jim Henry tried talking with the child, but the boy was simple-minded, and his mother apologized as she held him in a gentle hug.

When Jim Henry rode out in the early morning, barely remembering his manners to say good-bye, he knew the husband would speak sharply to his wife about the rude Anglo who was too good to share their jacal and their generosity. It was easy to see the bad, take it as an insult when something was not understood. The man would be wrong about Jim Henry's rudeness; it was the memory of a good woman and her son that drove him from their home, not any sense of his own superiority.

The hard outlines of the mountains rode with him: sullen lands, barren rolls of uplifted rock and dirt that carried little life other than stubborn cactus and rough-skinned lizards. Jim Henry could not help but think of the dark beauty of the mountains that rose above Santa Fe, and he knew a sadness when they disappeared behind the harsh rim of La Bajada. The mountains around Fort Davis had some of their majesty, but he was not headed that way. The fort would be in ruins, abandoned by the Union, desecrated by the Indians and the few travelers daring to crawl through the hills.

Past the unnamed village, before the small and flourishing town of Presidio, lay the place known as Leaton's Fort. Here Jim Henry stopped to give the mare water, dismounting at the invitation of a man he did not know: one-eyed, thin, walking slowly with a cane; not much older than Jim Henry himself.

He was a survivor from the vainglorious march north under Sibley, but Jim Henry did not want to exchange words or retell tales of battle. The one-eyed man stared briefly at Jim Henry, and it was clear that he, too, was unwilling to speak of the past. Jim Henry let the mare rest in the shade of an adobe wall and even took the liberty of offering her oats from a storage bin. The one-eyed man nodded his compliance and then disappeared. Jim Henry was relived to be alone again.

Horse and rider endured another two days of slow travel before reaching Spencer's Rancho. There the river disappeared behind high cliffs, and the sand desert bunched and turned, lifted and fell, challenging the mare's careful footing. Jim Henry walked most of the way, suffering with the mare's abraded feet. His boot soles wore through, and he limped on the edge of the leather, not always successful in avoiding the multiplying cactus.

A dry camp added to his welcome home. Jim Henry had to sit up most of the night, too tired and too dry to lie down in any comfort and sleep. The mare was restless, shuffling and snorting in the darkness, stamping her feet and once whinnying as if something out in the night were calling her.

In the morning he didn't bother to bit her. His eyes scratched beneath dry lids, and he coughed incessantly. Hunger had swollen his belly, while the mare could only pick at the beans he offered her, the dry grasses he pulled. She, too, suffered from the lack of water: her droppings were hard, her urine a dull orange. Jim Henry questioned his commitment to this hard land, yet he could do little more than walk on. Leaton's Fort was as far behind him as the rancho was ahead of him, if he could still read the landmarks.

Somewhere along the way, the river leveled out into a wide, quiet flow. Jim Henry had to force the bridle on the mare and pull her back hard when she smelled the clean breath of the water. He let her carry him down the crumbling bank, holding on to her tail and the ends of the reins. But he would not let her drink her fill, nor could he kneel down and drink as he wished for fear she would pull away from him and drink herself into founder. After almost an hour of walking the mare in tight circles and then letting her drink a few more mouthfuls, she began to show signs of satiation, and Jim Henry took his turn.

He buried his face in the water, cupped the liquid, and poured it over his head and neck, drew in its coldness over clenched teeth and spat it back out, then held it in his mouth and gradually let some trickle down his throat and into his shriveled belly. Eventually he lay flat on a rock and lowered his head and chest into the river, luxuriating in the coolness, inhaling the sweet smell, drowning in the abundance. It was his first memory of the *despoblado* as a child, his first lesson in the salvation of water.

This time he rebitted the mare and checked his cincha, mounted her, and let her carry him up the bank and onto the faded trail. The water had renewed her enough to offer a token buck, and Jim Henry laughed with her good spirits. The little mare might be a no-account range scrub, but she had heart.

There was a lot behind him he needed to keep in his mind. He didn't think much of mares, for one thing; no good vaquero did. It was an insult to ride a mare, an affront to a man's pride. Yet this one had come to him when he needed

her and had carried him almost home. He could not forget
that.

Nor could he forget the woman named Josefina, and her
son, Tomás. Or the grandfather who had had faith in a nameless Anglo, a hated *Tejano*, enough faith to entrust his family
to the man. Jim Henry silently thanked Eduardo Iberra, and
the other forgotten dark-skinned men who had come and
gone in the hot adobe cell. They had had a faith, and they
shared it with him, asking little in return.

He shoved the winter army hat back on his head and looked
around him. If he hadn't gotten himself lost, the shimmering
bulk of red mud ahead was an adobe wall, the demarcation
of Spencer's Rancho. He was only an hour from its safety.

When Jim Henry rode through the slatted, iron-bound gates,
he had the mare in a dancing walk, and he sat straight up
and proud, despite the growling pains in his belly, the shimmering headache, the spots in front of his eyes. He was not
going to return as a defeated man.

There was little surprise in the near-empty corrals, the
general air of half-done work—the sagging post and broken
rails, the huts abandoned with their doors open to the yard,
their chimneys cold. Too many men had ridden from the
rancho never to return.

There was one man, hidden under the octillo ramada,
seated in a slow-moving rocking chair. He rocked back and
forth, his beat constant and unchanging even at Jim Henry's
entrance. No one else was visible in the compound of the
once-powerful rancho. Jim Henry angled the little mare toward the dark corner of the main house.

Something about the man was familiar. Jim Henry reined
in the mare, both of them grateful for the ribboned shade of
the octillo. He searched the shaded ramada carefully, alert
to the man's slow rocking. The head was rested on the high-
backed chair, the hands were set and motionless on the loose
arms. Jim Henry relaxed; those hands made no move toward
a weapon. A long rifle lay propped up against a new carved
pillar, but the figure in the moving chair made no effort to
reach out and protect itself.

Jim Henry halted the grateful mare. He pushed back his

hat and had to lick his lips three or four times to unstick his mouth. "How do, mister. Got a mind to water me and the mare, if you got no objections."

He waited a beat, curious now as the rocker slowed and then stopped. The body inclined forward, the head tilted in question. The particular movement of the head, the length of the raised hands, the set of the shoulders, excited memory in Jim Henry. He spoke again: "It sure is good to be home again. Ain't been here for a year or more. Before that god-damned battle up north." He clamped his mouth shut, bit the side of his cheek. He had no business speaking up so familiar to a man he still could not see. But the sound of his own voice, spoken in company, at the safety of Spencer's Rancho, pure unnerved him and shook loose his common sense and his tongue.

Jim Henry patted his right thigh and shifted in the saddle, wanting the man hidden in the shadows to hurry up and speak—or fight. Get it over with: he wanted to come home.

Hap had a bottle beside his chair, and he raised it in mock salute to Jim Henry, then took a deep pull. He made no effort to share with Jim Henry but slammed the bottle down and rocked back in his chair. "Well now, kid. You look beat all to hell. What happened to you up to that Mex jail? You find you like it there, or you just slow coming to know your real friends? Whatever it is, you is rough as hell now."

He gestured to the worn, slatted chair next to him. "Come on up, set a spell. Have a drink you got a mind to. Food somewheres in the house. Got to put flesh back on you if Spencer's going to hire you back on. He's gone up to El Paso, but he sticks close to the ranch. Been hiring back some of us veterans to that Sibley Brigade. Sort of like he feels sorry for us. 'Course, not too many of us come back. Not too many of us."

Even Hap shut down talking when he mentioned the war. Jim Henry drew in his first real breath of the rancho, expelled the dust, and stepped down from the mare.

Hap pulled out corn shucks and dried silk and rolled a poor smoke, then handed the makings to Jim Henry, waiting while he rolled a lumpy cigarette. One strike lit up two cigarettes and Jim Henry drew in the bitter smoke. Hap leaned in his chair and said nothing, as if he had already run out of conversation.

Jim Henry ground the poor excuse for a smoke under his heel. Hap made no move to talk to him. It was a hell of a welcome home.

Jim Henry led the tired mare to the back corral. Along the compound wall he could see the familiar adobe hut, where he guessed Limm and Rosa still lived. He couldn't know if they were alive; Hap had done nothing but talk of his own trouble.

An adobe hut built a long time ago, shared easily with the orphaned child until he grew too fancy to live with an old man and a one-time Mexican whore. The bitter words hurt when he mouthed them, a goad to the end of his long traveling. He unsaddled the paint mare and rubbed her down, scratched her ears, scrubbed at the wet marks of the cincha and saddle blanket until the little mare threw her head in objection. Jim Henry wanted desperately to be lost in the mindless chore.

Finally he turned the mare loose in an empty pen and went back to the crude leaning shed. There he hung up the salt-stained Federal hat on a high nail and removed the Navy pistol from the waistband of his woolen pants. He had no need for the pistol now; he needed only a courage he did not own.

Jim Henry closed the door to the shed and went to find Limm Tyler and Rosa Ignacio.

About the Author

William A. Luckey lives in Santa Fe, New Mexico.